Warwickshire County Council

KT-231-447

Ken 7/17			
1/8			
7/8/17			
26.8.17			
15.9.17			

This item is to be returned or renewed before the latest date above. It may be borrowed for a further period if not in demand.

To renew your books:

- **Phone the 24/7 Renewal Line 01926 499273 or**
- **Visit www.warwickshire.gov.uk/libraries**

Discover • Imagine • Learn • *with libraries*

Working for Warwickshire

Independent on Sunday on *Turning Forty*

'A funny and frank account of a hopeless romantic.'

The Times on *My Legendary Girlfriend*

Also by Mike Gayle

My Legendary Girlfriend
Mr Commitment
Turning Thirty
Dinner for Two
His 'n' Hers
Brand New Friend
Wish You Were Here
Life and Soul of the Party
The Importance of Being a Bachelor
Men at Work (Quick Read)
The Stag and Hen Weekend
Turning Forty
Seeing Other People

Non-fiction

The To-Do List

The Hope Family Calendar

MIKE GAYLE

First published in Great Britain in 2016 by Hodder & Stoughton
An Hachette UK company

First published in paperback in 2016

1

Copyright © Mike Gayle 2016

The right of Mike Gayle to be identified as the Author of the Work has been asserted by him in accordance with the Copyright, Designs and Patents Act 1988.

All rights reserved. No part of this publication may be reproduced, stored in a retrieval system, or transmitted, in any form or by any means without the prior written permission of the publisher, nor be otherwise circulated in any form of binding or cover other than that in which it is published and without a similar condition being imposed on the subsequent purchaser.

All characters in this publication are fictitious and any resemblance to real persons, living or dead is purely coincidental.

A CIP catalogue record for this title is available from the British Library.

A format ISBN 978 1 473 62689 8
B format ISBN 978 1 473 60895 5
eBook ISBN 978 1 473 60893 1

Printed and bound by Clays Ltd, St Ives plc

Hodder & Stoughton policy is to use papers that are natural, renewable and recyclable products and made from wood grown in sustainable forests. The logging and manufacturing processes are expected to conform to the environmental regulations of the country of origin.

Hodder & Stoughton Ltd
Carmelite House
50 Victoria Embankment
London EC4Y 0DZ

www.hodder.co.uk

For my Girls. Thank you for being you.

PART ONE

'He that conceals his grief finds no remedy for it.'

– *Turkish proverb*

I

If I could be around more, I would

Tom

It was late when I reached home from work. Home, just so you know, is a four-bed house in Reigate, Surrey. It was Laura who found it. I don't think the house had even properly come on to the market when she took me to see it. The owner was deceased. Having lived there all her life, the elderly lady had passed peacefully away in her sleep, apparently. She died intestate and so one of those 'heir-hunter' companies had got involved. In return for a slice of the action, they informed a middle-aged bookkeeper in Llanelli that she had just inherited an entire house from a great-aunt she'd never met. With no desire to move to the Surrey commuter belt, the bookkeeper called an estate agent on the High Street to put the property on the market, and a matter of moments after the agent had finished taking down the details in walked Laura, heavily pregnant and sick to her back teeth of renting. We went to see the place that same night and Laura fell in love with it. First thing the following morning she convinced me to make an offer for the full asking price, even though the house needed everything doing to it. It was a big gamble but it paid off in spades, leaving us living in a house that after the market picked up we couldn't have come even close to affording. But that was Laura all over: somehow everything she touched turned to gold.

Anyway, as I was saying, I'd just arrived home from work, or to be more accurate I'd come home from work via dinner with a couple of talent agents who'd spent the entire evening singing the praises of their clients, in a bid to get me to have them on one of my shows. I'm a TV producer by trade, mainly entertainment stuff, the sort of shows people love to watch on a Saturday night. In fact, when I was the subject of a profile in *Broadcast* magazine, the title for the piece was 'Mr Saturday Night'.

The house was quiet, which was to be expected. Left to their own devices the kids would stay up until their eyes fell out, but thankfully they didn't. They had Linda. And, I suppose, Linda had them too. It was an arrangement that worked well for everyone concerned. The best thing about Linda was that she was an early-to-bed type. Never stayed up much past ten o'clock if she could help it, which meant that if I timed it right, generally speaking, most nights I'd get the ground floor of the house to myself. Tonight was different, however. As I stood at the kitchen counter, bottle of red in one hand and an empty wine glass in the other, I turned around to see Linda, cocooned in her fluffy blue polka-dot dressing gown, standing in the doorway.

'Good day?'

'Long day.' I sighed and set both wine and empty glass down on the counter. 'Can't sleep?'

'I was actually waiting up for you. Have you a moment? There's something I need to talk to you about quite urgently and, well, you don't seem to have received any of the messages I've left for you lately.'

My heart sank. All I'd thought about for the entire cab ride home from the station was this next hour of my life: how I was going to pour myself a large glass of wine, put on a little music, sit on the kitchen sofa in semi-darkness and try my best to think about absolutely nothing. But now that wasn't to be. Linda had made sure of it.

We sat down to talk on the very sofa where I should have been enjoying my glass of red. I looked over at Linda. You know that thing where you look at someone and it dawns on you that they look nothing like you'd pictured them? Well, in my head Linda was a youthful sixty-six. Yes, she was grey of hair and wrinkled of skin but she'd always had a sparkle in her eye, a spring in her step and a laugh that was just the right side of filthy. The woman next to me, however, looked like she was auditioning for the role of 'old lady' in a comedy – not quite half-moon glasses and a walking stick, but not that far off either. She seemed old. Proper old. Old like if she died you'd think, 'At least she had a good innings.' Sixty-six isn't old these days. Or at least it shouldn't be. I wondered if she, like me, hadn't been sleeping very well of late. A couple of rough nights can easily add a few years on here and there. I thought briefly about offering her one of the sleeping tablets I'd picked up on my last trip to the States for work, but I could see that she was waiting for me to ask her what she wanted and so, with no little reluctance, I obliged.

'It's about the weekend after next.' Her eyes scanned my own for signs that I recognised the significance of the date in question, as though she thought it could possibly have slipped my mind. 'The girls have been talking with me about what they might like to do, and they've said that they want to go to Southwold. And well, I for one think it's a great idea. You know how much Laura loved Southwold.'

Linda was right. Laura always did love Southwold. It had been her favourite place to go to get away from it all, even before the girls came along. She'd often talked about us retiring there, so that when the girls were older and had families of their own we'd be able to take our grandchildren for long walks on the beach. Southwold was Laura's place, and the perfect setting in which to remember her. I was all for it, up to a point.

'That's a great idea. You should definitely take them. Spend what you like, they deserve a good treat.'

'So you'll be coming too?'

'Me? I'd love to, Linda, really I would, but with everything the way it is at work at the moment – two shows in production, one in pre-production and more in development than we can handle – there's no way I can take the time off. You've seen for yourself how little I've been home at the weekends.'

'I've noticed,' said Linda pointedly. 'One might almost think that you lived at the office, the amount of time you spend there. Do you really need to work quite so hard? The girls miss you terribly.'

'And I miss them too,' I replied. 'And once things calm down, I promise that you, the kids and me will take a proper break somewhere really special. I can see it now: the girls jumping in and out of the pool all day while you sunbathe in a slinky two-piece, sipping on a cocktail.'

A few years ago the gag about 'a slinky two-piece' would've had her chuckling away and making jokes of her own, but today it got nothing. Zero. In fact, it seemed to make her visibly angry.

'You think this is all a joke, don't you?'

'Far from it.'

'Those girls need you, Tom, they need you to be their father and at the moment you're just never around.'

'And I've told you I'm working, Linda. If I could be around more, I would.'

She shook her head. 'I knew you'd say that . . . which is why I had no choice but to take matters into my own hands.' She stared at me with a steely defiance. This wasn't a bluff. She'd done something sneaky, something I hadn't seen coming at all.

'What are you talking about?' A trace of urgency in my voice.

'You didn't leave me any choice.'

'What have you done?' The panic in my voice grew more pronounced.

'I called your MD this morning and demanded that he let you have the time off.'

I lost all pretence of being in control. 'You did *what*?'

'You said yourself that you'd come if you weren't working. Well here you are: he says you can have the weekend off. He said it was no problem at all. He was actually quite delightful about it.'

I was so thoroughly enraged, so utterly livid that I rose to my feet and as I did so, an equally outraged Linda did the same. We squared up to each other, all six foot of me and all five foot five inches of her, like two comically mismatched boxers.

'You had no right to do something like that!'

'And you have no right to be acting like such a selfish pig! Your daughters need that weekend, Tom. They need you to be there with them while they remember their mother. It's *their* rights I'm concerned about, not yours. They need this. And if plotting and scheming is what it takes to get you to go to Southwold with them, then that's what I'll bloody well do! I'm the only grandparent these girls have got, so believe me when I say that there isn't a damn thing in this world I wouldn't do to make them happy.'

Linda

Tom didn't talk to me again for the rest of that week. As a tactic it probably would have had more impact on me if he'd been particularly given to long chats over the dinner table but as it was, these days we barely spoke at all anyway. During the year I'd lived with him and the girls, my relationship to him had morphed into an unsettling mix of housekeeper, childminder and (chaste) wife-substitute. I cleaned the house, washed and ironed clothes and looked after his children, and in return he gave me a room of my own, paid all the bills and gave me more spending money than I knew what to do with. We weren't friends any more, at least not in the way we used to be, but we weren't enemies either. We were simply two people, side by side, miles from land with no hope of rescue, treading water in a bottomless ocean and getting more tired by the day.

It had all been so different when we first met. It was the summer of 1997 and Laura was at university in London in the final year of her photography degree. I'd just split up with Tony, my partner of the last nine months, following my discovery that his relationship with his ex-wife wasn't anywhere near as over as he'd led me to believe, and so Laura had invited me to stay with her for a couple of days. Desperate to do something for the weekend other than mourn the passing of yet another relationship, I'd leaped at the opportunity and travelled to London straight after work on the Friday evening.

The following morning I took Laura clothes shopping on Oxford Street and later, over lunch in a nice little café on Monmouth Street, she told me all about the new man in her life: Tom Hope. Tom, she told me, was twenty-five and originally from Reading but had lived in London for the past four years, working as a researcher for a TV production company. She told me he was tall and handsome and easily the kindest man she had ever met. Always the concerned mother, I asked her what his parents did for a living and crossed my fingers, hoping they might be better than the last lot – a pair of hippy types who thought nothing of offering me 'a smoke' five minutes after I'd met them for the first time. Laura told me that Tom's mum had run off with another man when he was young, and his father had died two years ago following a long battle with lung cancer. Though I knew he was a grown man and had, no doubt, long since come to terms with his situation, it was such a sad state of affairs that I couldn't help but feel sorry for the poor lad. Even grown-up children need their parents. Even young independent men like Tom need a mum.

After lunch we went back to Laura's flat in Hammersmith and met up with all her flatmates again, including her best friend Marina, who she'd known since her first day at university. The sizeable age gap between Laura's friends and me didn't stop us from cracking open a few bottles of wine and having a real hoot talking about men and the like. They all had something to say about my recent experience with Tony and, fuelled by the vino, we started cooking up all manner of plans as to how I should take revenge. Then who should call on Laura's landline but the man himself? He said he needed to talk to me, and against my better judgement I agreed to listen. Sensing that I might need some space to take the call, Laura and her flatmates took themselves off to the supermarket to get a few things in for supper.

My call with Tony was every bit as wearing as I knew it would be, but I remained resolute to the end that he and I were through. Afterwards, however, as I sat alone in Laura's flat reviewing the time I'd wasted on yet another excuse for a man, all I could think about was how unlucky I'd been in love throughout my entire life. If I hadn't known any better, I would've thought I'd been cursed. Before Tony there was Andrew (who ended our two-year relationship after falling for his secretary), before Andrew there was Christopher (who didn't so much want me, as a free babysitting service for his kids), before Christopher there was Stephen (who seemed to delight in ruining my peace of mind by blowing hot and cold on a whim) and before Stephen there was Edward (who, much like Tony, had an ex-wife who it turned out was anything but).

The list of losers went on and on, spanning more than forty years, but right at the top was the one who started the whole thing rolling – King Rat himself – Frank Smith, Laura's father: the very first man to well and truly break my heart.

Right in the middle of this painful reverie the door buzzer went, not just once or twice but five times in quick succession! I wasn't the kind of woman who enjoyed having her thoughts interrupted at the best of times, but at this particular moment I was in no mood to be trifled with and so, angrily, I made my way downstairs. I flung the front door wide open, ready to give the caller a piece of my mind, only to find a tall, kind-faced but somewhat scruffily dressed young man on the doorstep. I guessed who he was from Laura's description and the bottle of bubbly in his hands, along with the bouquet of what were clearly garage forecourt flowers, only served to confirm what I thought: this was Laura's new man.

His face bore a look of thorough confusion. 'I think there's been a mistake. I was buzzing Flat Three.'

'Yes, I'm well aware of that, my ears are still ringing.'

'So . . . you know Laura Wood, then?'

I laughed and raised an eyebrow. It was naughty of me but I just couldn't help myself. 'I should hope so.'

It took a while but finally the penny dropped. 'You're Laura's mum, aren't you?'

I nodded. 'And you must be Tom. Weren't you supposed to be working this weekend?'

'We finished early. And I completely forgot that you were stopping with her tonight. I should go.'

'Don't be daft. Laura and her friends have just popped out, you're more than welcome to come in and wait, if you like.'

You should have seen the panic in his eyes. Make small talk with his new girlfriend's mum? I think he would've sooner bitten off his arm and thrown it at me.

'No, really, I'll come back later,' he said, flustered. He thrust the bubbly and the flowers in my direction. 'Could you give Laura these for me?'

'You can give them to her yourself,' I said. 'She's right behind you.'

I should've known from the size of the grin that appeared on Laura's face the moment she saw Tom that she was in love. It was like she'd been lit up from inside and couldn't help letting her light shine out. If someone could make you that happy just by turning up unexpectedly then you were definitely on to a winner, make no mistake about it.

With her arms around his neck, Laura fixed her eyes on Tom like she was boring down into his very soul. 'I've missed you, Tom Hope.'

They kissed on the spot and probably would've carried on for some time had Tom not recalled the fact that I was still in the doorway.

'Er . . . Laura, your mum's here.'

Laura laughed. 'I know, I invited her.'

'But . . .'

'It's freaking you out a bit, isn't it?'

Tom nodded.

'No need,' she said, turning towards me. She looked so beautiful, so happy at that moment, I couldn't take my eyes off her. 'You don't bite, do you, Mum?'

'No,' I replied, and gave Tom a cheeky wink. 'At least not very hard.'

The easiness of our initial introduction seemed to set the tone for the rest of our relationship and as Tom and Laura grew closer, so did Tom and I. When Laura and I went on holiday the following year, it was me who insisted that Tom came too; when Laura's granddad died a few months later, it seemed only natural to ask Tom to do a reading at the funeral, because by that time he was practically one of the family; and when Tony refused to repay the money I'd lent him from my savings for his printing business, it was Tom who, unprompted by me, drove up to York with a few of his friends and convinced him to repay the loan, with interest.

It wasn't just the things he did either, but the way he was too. He loved to make people laugh; he worked hard and always had a plan for any situation. And as for the way he was with Laura, I honestly couldn't have wished for a more dutiful, kind and loving partner for my beautiful girl. If I'd been cursed when it came to love then, thanks to Tom, it looked a lot like Laura had been blessed beyond belief.

That said, I admit when Laura told me she was pregnant I was worried at first. After all, it hadn't been planned – they'd only been together two years and she was still only twenty-four. As a single mother I knew first-hand that raising a child wasn't going to be easy, even with the added luxury of a loving partner helping out.

'Mum, we'll be fine,' she said, as though I was making a fuss over nothing. She'd always been so sure of herself, that girl, so sure that she was indestructible. It's the quality I loved about her most because it was so unlike me.

'But what about your photography?' I asked. 'You've only just got started with your career. If you have this baby now, how will you make it work?'

'I'll do what I can,' she replied. 'And if it doesn't work out that's fine, I'll do something else. Things don't always go to plan, Mum, but do you know what? I wouldn't want it any other way. I've got a whole life ahead of me, more than enough time to chase dreams, but right now, all that matters is me, Tom, and this little bean growing inside me.'

That 'little bean' came into the world eight months later in the early hours of 2 February. They called her Evie, and she was the bonniest baby I've ever seen. You only had to catch her eye for a moment and she'd smile at you like you were her favourite person in the world. Five years later, Evie's arrival was followed by that of another little bean, at ten minutes past four in the afternoon of 3 September. They called her Lola, and I fell in love with my little Lolly on the spot.

Though Laura was still relatively young, she took to motherhood like a duck to water. She was an absolute natural and seemed to take greater pleasure in being a mum than she had in her pursuit of photography. And though there were times when I wondered whether she had taken on too much too soon, those times were few and far between. For the most part she seemed far happier and more full of life than I'd ever seen her, and everything she did for the children spoke of an inner determination to only ever give them her best.

As for me, to say that those girls transformed my life is a massive understatement. They lit up every corner of my world so that there was no longer any darkness left. I stopped worrying about whether I'd grow old without a man; I stopped grumbling about the ill-mannered primary school children I taught, their equally ill-mannered parents and the seemingly endless wave of demands that senior management placed on me. Nothing else mattered now that I was a grandmother. After a lifetime that had seen a lot of heartache, finally I had a happiness that no one could ever take from me.

2

I just can't

Tom

There was nothing remarkable about the day that Laura died. No comets warning of impending doom, no meteors crashing to earth. Nothing whatsoever to suggest that it might be anything other than just an ordinary autumnal day in October.

I awoke that morning to the sound of the alarm clock: two bursts of high-pitched, two-note beeps signalling it was six thirty. With eyes still closed, I hit the snooze button as was my habit and Laura pushed herself closer to me as was hers. And there we lay, skin to skin, warmth to warmth, hiding from the world until the alarm clock indicated once again that it was time to get up and this time it really meant it. In a few minutes Laura would be in the shower and then once she was done, I'd follow. By the time I emerged from the bathroom in a cloud of steam, Evie and Lola would be awake too, putting on school uniform and (in Evie's case) finishing off homework.

Breakfast was a big deal in the Hope household. Laura made sure of that. It was important to her that we ate together as a family as often as we could. Most evenings the girls had long since eaten tea by the time I reached home, so breakfast was it. Our time to break bread and check in with one another, and no one – not even me – was allowed to skip it.

I wasn't naturally a morning person, much preferring to say or do as little as possible before my first coffee of the day, but nonetheless I loved Laura's insistence that breakfast was sacred. It showed exactly what her priorities were: family first, everything else second. In a world where it's all too easy to lose sight of what's really important, it felt good to know that there was a captain of our ship guiding us in the right direction. When it came to our family, Laura was the top dog, boss of bosses, CEO of The Family Hope plc.

It's odd how much I can recall about that morning but it's all there: the smell of Laura's shampoo in the hallway, the Taylor Swift song playing on the radio as I entered the kitchen and the first words I was greeted with as I approached the kitchen table.

'I poured your cereal for you, Dad.'

It was Lola speaking. She was pointing to an unholy concoction of Cheerios, Coco Pops, Sugar Puffs and Raisin Wheats. Never had a solitary bowl of cereal looked quite so unappealing.

'I don't know quite what to say.'

Laura nudged me with her elbow. 'You could start with thank you,' she said pointedly. 'Lola was explaining to Evie and me that she was very concerned you weren't getting the right level of vitamins and minerals in your diet.'

'We're learning about them at school,' said Lola.

'You're studying Cheerios at school? I wouldn't mind a few lessons like that.' I waggled my eyebrows to indicate that she'd become yet another unsuspecting victim of a Dad joke, the lowest form of humour known to mankind.

'No, we're studying vitamins and minerals, Daddy,' she corrected patiently. 'Food makers put lots in our cereal so we can be healthy.'

'Well it looks disgusting,' snorted Evie in a manner that of late seemed to be her chief method of communicating. 'You wouldn't catch me eating that for a million pounds!'

'Well, you'll never know just how delicious this really is then,'

I replied, grabbing a spoon and wolfing down a mouthful of Lola's concoction. 'Delicious,' I mumbled, while trying not to visibly baulk as the sugar ravaged my taste buds. 'Just what the doctor ordered.'

Despite Laura's best intentions, breakfast rarely if ever concluded as sedately as it began. Sometimes it would be Evie who drifted off from the table, in order to reply to her friends' texts; other times it would be Lola, as she suddenly recalled the half-dozen parental consent forms abandoned at the bottom of her school bag that needed signing; and once in a while it would be me, briefly checking my email at the kitchen table only to stumble across some work-related emergency that required my full attention. However, sometime after the disintegration of breakfast but before the mass exodus from home, Laura would somehow bring us all together again for the morning briefing. Taking the family calendar off the hook on the wall next to the fridge, she would hand out the next lot of tasks and reminders. And the day we lost Laura was no different.

To Evie she said: 'You've got swimming today, sweetie, have you packed your kit yet?'

To Lola she said: 'The eggboxes that Mrs Baker wants are in the cupboard next to the sink. Could you bag them up and leave them by the door, please?'

To me she said: 'Don't forget you're picking up Evie from Mia's on your way home. And Lola's parents' evening is tomorrow so if anyone tries to book you in for a meeting after five, make sure you tell them no.'

With that, she scanned the calendar one last time, double-checking that she hadn't missed anything, before returning it to its rightful place on the wall.

Sometimes I used to joke that if there was a fire and she could only rescue three things from the house, it would go: kids first and second, and the family calendar third. Owning it, adding to it and reflecting on it seemed to bring Laura a peace that nothing else could. Because while there were things to dread about it (tax returns, dental appointments and MOTs), there was also a lot to look forward to (holidays, theatre trips and birthdays), and above all there was order. In a world where all manner of random events could occur, from home-grown terrorists blowing up buses, to train crashes caused by signalling errors, it helped us to believe that no disaster could ever overtake us, because we knew exactly what the future looked like – we could hold it in our hands.

Besides always eating breakfast together, the other golden rule of the Hope household was this: no one was ever allowed to leave home without first saying a proper goodbye. Not Evie distracted by a phone call, or Lola lost in a daydream, or me fielding a text: everybody said goodbye without exception. And as – more often than not – I was the first to leave, it was always me who got my goodbyes in first. On that day I got a big wet kiss from Lola, the offer of a forehead against which to place my lips from Evie and then finally, a big old-fashioned smooch from Laura.

'Back usual time?'

'Should be. I can't remember, are you at uni today?'

'No, but I've got a deadline looming.'

'Need me to pick up anything for dinner?'

'A nice Shiraz wouldn't go amiss.'

'Like that, is it? Not looking forward to today then?'

She leaned and pressed her lips against my cheek. 'Put it this way,' she said, 'I'll be glad when it's over.'

I was about to ask more about her university assignment when we heard the girls' raised voices from upstairs. They were both threatening each other with the ultimate sanction of 'telling Mum!' I put down my bag, ready to go upstairs and give them both a good talking-to but Laura stopped me.

'I'll deal with it,' she said. 'You're already late as it is.'

I checked my watch. Indeed, I'd have to pray to the gods of traffic just to be in with a hope of not missing my train. Before I left, I told her not to let them give her any grief, and then I kissed her again and jumped into the car without a backward glance, never once considering that this would be the last time I'd ever see her alive.

Linda

I remember, when I woke that morning, lying in bed in my little terrace in York making a mental list for the day ahead. You know the sort of thing: buy milk, find new energy provider, take old clothes to charity shop, defrost freezer. I was also planning to help out with lunch at the local homeless shelter like I usually did on a Friday, and in the afternoon I'd pencilled in a visit to the library. These were the sorts of things I filled my days with after retiring. It's strange really, I genuinely thought it was going to be just another day, another day of filling time and keeping busy. But it wasn't any other day at all. This was the day after which no day would ever be the same again.

Tom

I was in a taxi when I got the call about Laura. I was on my way to a restaurant in Marylebone for a lunch meeting with a couple of senior executives from Channel Four about a news quiz we were pitching. I answered my phone and a female voice with a pleasant Scottish burr asked me to confirm my identity, which I duly did, and then she broke the bad news.

'I'm afraid your wife, Laura, was involved in a collision on the M23. She was cut free from the wreckage of her car by the emergency services, flown by helicopter directly to St Francis Hospital and immediately taken down for surgery.'

I felt so sick that I yelled at the cabbie to pull over to the side of the road. I couldn't deal with being in moving traffic while trying to make sense of something that fundamentally didn't make any sense at all. Why would Laura have been on the M23? She hadn't mentioned doing anything with her day apart from sorting out her coursework. I racked my brains trying to think where she might have been going but drew a blank, then it dawned on me that someone somewhere had messed up. This wasn't my Laura Hope: I'd been handed a tragedy meant for some other poor sod.

'I think there's been some mistake,' I explained. 'My wife wasn't travelling anywhere today. You must have the wrong person.'

The police officer kept her cool. She went over the details again and everything tallied perfectly, even down to the fact that the vehicle involved in the accident was a red Nissan Micra like the courtesy car Laura had been given while the local garage fitted a new exhaust on her own car.

Still it wouldn't sink in. Still I refused to believe it. I put the officer on hold and dialled Laura's number, willing her to pick up. When she did, my body flooded with relief and gratitude. She was safe. The officer had got it wrong after all. My Laura was okay. And I'd never take her for granted again. Things would be different from now on. I was just glad she was safe. Then all at once, the bone-crushing realisation that it wasn't her at all at the end of the line. She told me to leave a message, she told me she'd get back to me as soon as she could.

Panic-stricken, I gave the cabbie the new destination and told him it was an emergency. I must have been convincing because he pulled away so quickly that he neglected to check his wing mirror and only narrowly avoided knocking over a cyclist. As the two men exchanged expletives I dialled Linda's number. She needed to know what had happened. She needed to know I was on my way to be with her daughter.

We were family, Linda and I, and not simply because she was my wife's mother or my children's grandmother. We were family because that was the way she'd treated me from the day we first met. We were family because in the years I'd known her I'd never once doubted that she was as devoted to me as she was to her own daughter. But mostly we were family because she cared as much for me as I did for her, which was why it broke my heart to have to tell her what had happened.

'It's Laura,' I said, speaking up so she could hear me over the noise and chatter in the local homeless shelter where she was helping out at the time, 'she's been in a car accident. I'm on my way to the hospital now. They're operating on her right now. They've promised me she's in the best hands possible. Everything's going to be okay. Laura's a fighter. Everything's going to be okay, but you have to come and be with her straight away.'

Linda

I don't think I've ever been quite so terrified as when I got that call. Tom was always as cool as a cucumber, even in a crisis. I remember once when he and I were out with the girls, we saw someone get knocked over and there was blood everywhere. You should have seen Tom, he was so calm and collected, comforting the injured woman, and directing people to call an ambulance and help out with what needed to be done. He was completely unfazed by the whole situation. Like it was an everyday occurrence. But in his call to me, though I could tell he was trying to hide it, I could hear the panic in his voice and it made me scared. It undermined all the assurances that he gave me. It made me think the worst.

I was so struck by the horror of it that I think I might actually have dropped the bowl of soup I was holding, but to be honest everything that happened between that moment and my arriving at the hospital is a blur. I know that someone must have driven me to York station. I know I must have endured a three-hour train journey desperately wishing I was already by my baby's side. I know I must have constantly checked in with Tom for updates and news of Laura's condition. And I know I must have travelled across the capital to the hospital. But truly I don't remember much of anything until seeing Tom, hunched over, head in hands, in a waiting-room chair.

'Any news?'

'Nothing yet.'

He stood up and I held on to him tightly, squeezing my eyes shut and willing myself to keep calm. It was harder than I thought and it took several attempts before I felt able to let go of him. He sat down and I took the seat next to him. 'But it must be good that we haven't heard anything, mustn't it?' I said. 'It must mean they're still busy making her better.' I felt a tear roll down my cheek and I quickly wiped it away. This wasn't the time for tears. I could save them for when she was out of danger. Right now everything had to be about her.

Tom

I could only imagine what Linda was going through. I know if it had been one of the girls lying on an operating table I'd have been an absolute wreck, even if they'd long since grown up and started families of their own. Your children are always going to be your children, that's just the way it is. No matter how old they get or what responsibilities they take on, they'll always be yours to protect. I wanted to be strong for Linda even though I was as worried about Laura as she was. I wanted her to know that I was there for her. 'She'll be fine,' I said. 'I know she will. She's strong.'

'And fit and young and healthy too,' said Linda, drying her eyes. 'I still can't believe it though. I've always hated motorways, such horrible, dangerous things. And people drive so selfishly these days, speeding and cutting each other up, it's a wonder anyone makes it to their destination safely any more.'

'According to the police, it happened not far from the end of the M23 while she was most likely heading back to Reigate. I can't think where she might have been. I did wonder if she'd been somewhere for her course but she didn't say anything to me about going anywhere today. Did she mention anything to you?'

For a fleeting moment Linda's face changed and I thought perhaps she was upset at being asked about seemingly irrelevant details, but then as I saw her tears I realised that it was far more likely to be a delayed reaction to the horrible reality of her only child being in a mangled car wreck.

I put my arm around her. 'She'll be all right,' I promised. 'They've said she's in really safe hands.'

Linda

I thanked Tom for his kindness. He'd always been such an amazing son-in-law and there was so much that I wanted to say to him at this time: things about the past and the present, things I needed to share and explain. But in my distress I couldn't find the words, and by the time I'd composed myself it was too late:

the door to the waiting room swung open and a silver-haired gentleman dressed in pale-blue hospital scrubs walked towards us. I had no doubt that he was Laura's surgeon but found it impossible to discern anything from his expression. His face was set to neutral. It could easily have been the look he wore for success as much as for failure.

'Mr Hope?'

Tom nodded. 'And this is Linda, Laura's mum.'

'I'm Steve Evans, senior consultant on the team who attended to Laura this afternoon. It's bad news, I'm afraid. We tried everything we could to save her but on this occasion it simply wasn't enough. I know they're only words but I really am very sorry for your loss.'

In an instant, time slowed down. Sounds distorted around me. I felt like I was drowning, like I'd forgotten how to take even a single breath, and I'm sure I would have stayed that way if I hadn't become aware of what Tom was going through.

Until that moment I don't think I'd ever given much thought to the idea that there might be a hierarchy to grief. You just know instinctively that the strong should always look after the weak, don't you? But what if you're both strong? What if you're both weak? What if, over time, your weaknesses and strengths ebb and flow like the tide? What if you're a mum who's just lost her only daughter? What if you're a husband who's lost the mother of his children, the only woman he's ever loved? Who looks after whom? I can't speak for others, I can only talk about what happened to me, which was this: I knew I had to comfort Tom. It broke my heart listening to him – oh, the sobs and the howls that came from him. He sounded like a wild animal caught in a trap. Any mother would put aside her grief to comfort her own flesh and blood, and while I might not have been his biological mother, biology didn't seem to matter in a moment like this.

The nursing staff on hand helped take Tom and me aside to a small room, and I tried my best to get Tom to lie back on the bed but he wouldn't be persuaded. Instead, he sat up, knees drawn to his chest, hands covering his head as though trying to protect himself from an invisible onslaught.

I don't think I'd ever seen a man quite as broken as Tom was at that moment. It was like he'd disappeared to somewhere deep within himself and all attempts to comfort him were futile. Wherever he was, whatever dark place in his heart his grief had taken him to, he was lost and alone and incapable of reaching out to the real world.

I'm not sure how long we stayed in that windowless room. Time seemed to lose all meaning. It could have been half an hour, it could easily have been a lot more but what I do remember is the sound of Tom's phone ringing. Tom didn't even react to it but I couldn't rest while its wretched racket filled the air. I fumbled through his jacket and eventually found it but as I went to switch it off I saw Evie's name on the screen, and so I answered the call.

'Dad?'

'It's not Dad, sweetie, it's Nanny.'

'Where's Dad?'

'I'm with Dad, sweetie, we'll be home soon. Where are you?'

'I'm at home with Lola and Auntie Marina. Where's Mum? I've called her phone, she's not picking up.'

'We'll explain everything soon.'

'But I want to know where Mum is.'

'And we'll explain everything soon.'

'What's going on, Nanny? Has something happened?'

I couldn't possibly tell her over the phone. I wouldn't be able to bear not being there to comfort her in person.

'Evie, sweetie, do you love me?'

'Of course I do.'

'Do you trust me?'

'Course.'

'Okay, then trust me when I say we'll be home soon.'

I put the phone down and with great difficulty got Tom to look at me. The children had lost their mother. It would be too much if they lost their father as well.

'Tom, sweetheart,' I began, 'I know you're hurting, love, of course I do, but you can't let go like this, you can't give in. Evie and Lola need you. They need you more than they've ever needed you in their lives. You have to be strong for them, Tom, you have to be strong for them and for Laura too.'

'I know I do,' he said. 'I know but I just can't, Linda. I just can't.'

3

Are we clear?

Tom

Martin Freer, MD of Pluto Productions (and according to the *Guardian*, the twelfth most powerful person in the UK media), wasn't particularly noted for being touchy-feely. I'd known Martin since he gave me my first job in TV as a runner over twenty years ago and in that time I'd seen him sack countless people on the spot, for crimes as insignificant as eating an apple in the studio or standing in his eyeline when he was trying to concentrate. I'd seen him get into fistfights with other TV executives and had lost count of the number of times he'd had to pay off former employees to stop them from suing the company. With me, however, Martin had never so much as raised his voice. He liked me and I liked him and while we weren't exactly friends, we weren't all that far off either. So the day after my run-in with Linda over the Southwold trip I was, it has to be said, fairly confident that I could convince him that Linda was off her tablets and that if anybody needed a weekend break, it was her. I couldn't have been more wrong.

'You're lucky I'm only forcing you to take the weekend off,' he barked. 'If I was following my gut I'd make you take a full-on sabbatical. It's a year since your wife died, Tom. And no matter how much you might want to, you can't just hide from it by working. Your mother-in-law might be mental, then again she might not be. To be honest, I don't much care. But though you hide it well, I know for a fact that you're a mess and have been for a long while. Turn up here on the dates you're meant to be away and I will sack you on the spot. I mean it, Tom, you might be one of the best exec producers in the business but I will not hesitate to fire you. Sure, you could walk into a new job tomorrow or even start a production company of your own, but we both know that you belong here at Pluto.'

Linda

The day after I told Tom about Southwold, Tom's boss, Mr Freer, called me up. He told me that he'd given Tom a right talking-to (his actual choice of words was a lot more colourful) and sure enough a few days later I found a note from Tom on the kitchen counter: 'Linda, after much deliberation I have decided that I will come to Southwold after all. Have booked off from one o'clock on the Friday to Monday morning. Let the kids know, Tom.' I was overcome with relief as I read that note. It felt like, I don't know, I suppose like things were coming together. That all we needed to do was make it through the anniversary and once we were on the other side, somehow things would start getting better.

On the morning of our trip it was the sound of Tom heading out for his half-day at work that woke me up. Switching on the radio, I reached for the notepad and pen on the bedside table to carry on with my to-do list, but only managed to jot down half a dozen items before there was a knock on the door and Lola came into the room, still in her pale-grey rabbit pyjamas.

'Morning, my beautiful!' I pulled back the duvet so she could get into bed next to me. 'How are you today?'

'Excited,' she said eagerly and cuddled up to me. 'I dreamt that we went swimming in the sea and all of the waves were lapping around us. Daddy kept splashing you, me and Evie and we all ganged up on him and dunked him under the water.' She looked up at me, her eyes practically sparkling, and for a moment all I could do was marvel at how much she looked like Laura when she was young. Sometimes, holding her in my arms felt like travelling back in time.

'Evie said that she's not going to go swimming in the sea because it'll be too cold,' said Lola, still gazing up at me. 'But it won't, will it, Nanny?'

'Of course not,' I replied, even though I had my doubts. This was the North Sea in October we were talking about, after all. 'And even if it is a little bit chilly we'll soon warm up with all the fun we'll be having.'

We stayed in bed chatting contentedly until there was another knock at the door. It was only quarter to seven but Evie was already dressed in her school uniform and had her bag slung over her shoulder. I smelled a rat: Evie was never up this early.

'We've got a thing on at school,' she explained quickly. She kissed me on the cheek and ruffled her sister's hair. 'I was just coming in to say goodbye.'

'And what is this "thing" at school?'

Evie shrugged. 'It's just a thing.'

'And it needs you to be in early?'

Evie nodded. 'I'm already late.'

'So where's the letter?'

'What letter?'

'The letter from school telling me that you need to be in early.'

'There wasn't one.'

'Sweetie, this is the school that sends letters out if you've so much as needed to blow your nose, they're hardly going to overlook sending one if they need you in early. So come on, tell me where you were really off to.'

Evie crossed her arms and scowled. It didn't seem to take very much to set off that temper of hers these days.

'But everybody else is going.'

'Everybody else is going where?'

'Starbucks, for breakfast.'

'And you thought I'd say no?'

'I knew you'd say no.'

I patted the bed next to me for her to come and sit down, leaned over and put an arm around her shoulders.

'What was Mum's golden rule about breakfast?'

'That we always eat it together.'

'And you want to break that?'

'How come Dad gets to?'

'Because he's working.'

'He's always working.'

'I know, sweetie,' I replied. 'I know and hopefully that will all change some day soon.'

Over breakfast I attempted to make peace with Evie, offering up one chatty conversational opener after another, but my granddaughter stubbornly refused each olive branch, preferring instead to bolt down her food in silence. Once she'd eaten, she sat glowering until I finally allowed her to leave the table and make her way to school at the usual time.

I made Lola's sandwiches while she sat at the kitchen table learning her spellings and then we headed out, chatting all the way to the school gate. I always loved these moments with Lola and on that day, given the contrast between the two sisters, they meant even more. Time was moving fast, there was nothing I could do about it. One day, whether I liked it or not, the sweet eight-year-old who loved to tell me what was going on in her head would disappear, only to be replaced with a pressure cooker of hormones like her thirteen-year-old sister. It made me want to weep, imagining Lola growing so far away from me after being so close. I needed to savour these times, or one day I'd blink and they would be gone for good.

After drop-off I stayed talking with some of the other mums in the playground. I was touched by how willing they had been to accept me as one of them, despite the difference in our ages. Many of them had been friends with Laura, and had made a special effort to include me in their little group, even inviting me along to their monthly nights out. I hadn't known what to expect the first time I'd joined them, and was quite surprised by how much some of them drank over the course of the evening. Determined to make a good impression, however, I had entered into the spirit by regaling them with tales of my own misspent youth, which had them howling with laughter.

Smiling as I recalled that first night out, I left the playground mums and went to the High Street where I picked up some bits and pieces for the weekend, before returning home to pack. While I was used to packing for the children, it was much harder with Tom joining us on the trip. It was impossible to know what he might want to wear and so, in the end, I ironed everything that was in the hamper and left the clothes on his bed, next to an open weekend bag, so he could put what he wanted inside when he returned after midday.

When three o'clock came and went without sign of Tom, I told myself not to panic and instead sent him a quick text asking if everything was all right. When four o'clock came, it became a lot harder to keep calm but I sent another and just waited. When Evie arrived home from school and I still hadn't heard from Tom, I was so worried that I called his mobile every half an hour until six o'clock. It was only when I finally rang his work number that I discovered Tom hadn't been in at all that day.

Not wanting to alarm the girls, I explained that their dad had been held up at work and would be home as soon as possible. I settled them in front of the TV with all the snacks I could lay my hands on, while I called anyone and everyone I could think of in an effort to locate Tom. I was moments away from ringing around all the major hospitals when, a little after seven, the home phone rang and I snatched up the handset, promising myself I wouldn't get angry as long as he was safe.

'Am I speaking to Ms Linda Wood of Thirty-seven Frederick Avenue?'

The voice was well-spoken, 'official'-sounding. My stomach tightened and I felt sick — whoever this was had news about Tom.

'Yes,' I replied. 'Yes, it is.'

'My name's Phillip Pellier, duty solicitor at Oak Road police station. I'm calling with regard to a Mr Thomas Hope, who I believe is your son-in-law?'

'He is. Where is he? Is he okay?'

'I can assure you he's fine, Ms Wood, although, I must inform you that he's being held in custody under the 1988 Road Traffic Act for driving while under the influence of alcohol.'

Tom

There are few things in life more sobering than sitting on a wipe-clean vinyl mattress, contemplating your own mortality to the soundtrack of a drug addict in the next cell repeatedly screaming: 'I'm gonna kill that bitch!' Thankfully, however, as this thought occurred to me my cell door creaked opened to reveal Mr Pellier, the station's duty solicitor for the evening, and Sergeant Collins, the amiable police officer who had taken me through booking. They had good news. I'd blown under thirty-five on the most recent breathalyser test, meaning after over seven hours of incarceration I was finally free to go home.

As my shoes and belongings were returned to me, I was informed that I'd been bailed to attend the local court at a date yet to be specified but that it was likely to be in the next five to eight working days. The killer blow, however, was that because

I'd pleaded guilty to my charges, I was banned from driving with immediate effect. Not only was I not even allowed to drive myself home, but the plan I'd come up with to redeem myself in Linda's eyes (taking her and the kids to Southwold first thing in the morning and paying extra to keep the cottage for another night) was well and truly screwed. And as Linda could no more drive my Range Rover than she could drive a tank, the chances of us getting away even for a night were practically non-existent. The whole weekend was ruined. Linda would never forgive me. The kids would never forgive me. And there was a distinct chance that I'd never forgive myself either.

Linda

To say I was angry with Tom would be the understatement of the year! I was livid. I couldn't believe it! How dare he let down the children like this after they had put up with his absence for so long? How dare he ruin the plans the girls had made to celebrate the life of the mother they missed so much? How dare he sully the anniversary of the death of my darling Laura by drinking and getting behind the wheel of his car? His behaviour was a blot on Laura's memory. If anyone deserved better than this, it was my beautiful, darling, perfect angel.

The longer I thought about it all, however, the more I came to realise that in a lot of ways this whole situation was my fault. I'd let Tom get away with far too much for far too long. They say, don't they, that you can kill people with kindness? Well if it's true, then I've no doubt that when it came to my son-in-law and the year that followed Laura's death, there was definitely blood on my hands.

Tom was about as broken as a man could be in the weeks after Laura's funeral. He'd taken to his bed, curtains drawn, door shut, barely communicating with any of us at all. Nothing could entice him out of his room: not the doctor suggesting that he should get fresh air; nor friends offering to take him out; nor even his own children begging him to spend time with them. It was as though he was locked in a shell of grief, alone and unreachable, and nothing anyone could say or do would break him out of it. And while my heart said to let him be, my head said that he needed to snap out of it for the sake of his children.

Of course, I understood. In those weeks, there were times when grief would hit me with the force of a boxer's right hook: Laura was gone and she was never coming back. I'd feel my legs buckle and I'd have to reach out to stop myself from falling. There were times when all I'd do was imagine the sweet relief of giving in to it. No need to try to be strong. No need to keep my lips pressed together so tightly that they bled, for fear of letting out the anguish inside. But every time I thought about giving in, I was drawn back to that moment in the hospital when I'd had to be strong for Tom and the girls even though I'd wanted to fall apart. It reminded me that my role in the family wasn't optional. I needed to be there for the children. It wasn't a choice. There are simply times in life when you pick yourself up not because you want to, but because you have to for the sake of those depending on you.

When things with Tom were still the same a month after the funeral, I knew something drastic had to be done. I had to think seriously about bringing my stay to an end. My presence in Tom's family was making things worse rather than better. I'd allowed him to give up all the responsibilities of being a parent and deprived him of his best reason to carry on living. Much as I was terrified of the prospect of being without the girls and facing a life alone without Laura, I had no choice. It was the right thing to do.

The following Monday, after dropping Lola at school, I

decided to break the news to Tom. Convinced that I would face resistance, I went over the argument in my head as I tidied away the breakfast dishes. I'd tell him that everyone in life needed a role, a place, a function, and I had taken his. I'd say that I would always be there for him and the children but that right now he needed to be a dad again. I'd tell him I would be leaving first thing in the morning and there was nothing he could do or say to change my mind.

Taking a deep breath, I knocked on Tom's bedroom door. When I didn't hear a reply, I carefully turned the handle and entered the room. Instead of the darkened room with a crumpled figure outlined under the duvet that I was used to seeing, I walked into a bright and sunny room. Even the windows were open, and a clean-shaven Tom was standing in front of the wardrobe mirror, dressed in a suit, adjusting his shirt collar.

He turned to face me, his face neutral. It was as though the past month hadn't happened. 'I was just about to come and find you. How do I look?'

I had no idea what was going on. I wondered if he was having some sort of episode. 'Very smart indeed,' I replied, even though it was obvious from the bagginess of his suit that he had lost an awful lot of weight. 'What's the occasion?'

'Work. I'm going back. I've been emailing HR and they're fine about it, so we've agreed that I should probably start with a few half days and then build up to full time.' He came and stood next to me. 'I was thinking, if you're up for it, that you should move in permanently. It must be a nightmare living out of a bag like you've been doing. I've done some research and got the numbers of a couple of removal guys who'll even pack for you if you want them to. I was thinking you'd carry on in the spare room if that's okay, but I'd be more than happy to do a swap if you want my room, and of course it goes without saying that we'll get it decorated.'

I was speechless. How could this be the same man who'd been so grief-stricken that he'd taken to his bed? The man in front of me looked and sounded like Tom but it just couldn't be. He quite clearly wasn't right yet, and was absolutely one hundred per cent in denial.

'I don't think you should be going back to work, Tom, not yet,' I said carefully, as though he were a ticking time bomb. 'It's amazing that you feel ready and I don't want to hold you back, but don't you think you ought to spend some time with the children first? They've missed you so much these past few weeks.'

'And I've missed them,' said Tom. 'I really have and honestly, Linda, once I'm back on my feet I promise you I'll be spending more than enough time with them. But this is something I have to do, and while obviously I'd love you to be the one looking after the kids, if it comes to it I'm more than happy to get outside help.'

I wasn't sure if it was a threat or a simple statement of fact. Not really knowing what his current state of mind was, it could have been either or both. The mere thought of the children being looked after by strangers after what they'd already been through was simply too much for me.

'Of course I'll stay,' I replied. 'Nothing would make me happier.'

And that was that. Later that week a small removal van brought everything I needed down from York and the week after, Tom returned to work full-time. I then became the closest thing the girls had to a parent and Tom threw himself into work, giving up any and all pretence of being a father to them. But I'd always known Tom couldn't bottle up his grief forever. I'd always known that one way or another it would all come out.

Tom

When it came to the anniversary of losing Laura, all I ever wanted to do was run and hide. I didn't want to commemorate. I didn't want to be reminded of the good times. And I certainly didn't want to be cooped up in a chocolate-box cottage on the coast with my family. All I wanted to do was forget – as if that might actually have been a possibility – all I wanted to do was hide from reality. So when I woke from a restless sleep on the morning of the Southwold trip, I made up my mind to banish all thoughts of the anniversary and concentrate instead on taking each moment as it arrived.

Instead of dwelling on the emptiness in my heart, I answered work emails as I lay in bed. Instead of addressing the ache in my soul, I got ready for the day. The only concession to my real feelings came as I looked in on each of the girls before I left for work. Evie was wrapped up in her duvet like a caterpillar in a cocoon, while Lola was sprawled like an octopus across her bed with her Disney princess duvet draped half across the floor. I wanted to kiss them both. To tell them how sorry I was for not having been there for them these past twelve months. I wanted to tell them that I would change. But I couldn't bring myself to do either, so in the end I simply blew each a silent kiss and left.

As usual I drove to Redhill station, left the Range Rover in the car park, bought a couple of newspapers at the kiosk, a coffee from a concession stand and got the 06.24 into London. On the train I skim-read the papers, drank half of my coffee and checked a few more emails. At Victoria I made my way through the crowds to the underground, got on the Tube to Holborn, and along with hundreds of fellow passengers, made my way up the escalators, through the ticket barriers and out on to the bustling street above. It was at this point, less than a few hundred metres from the Pluto Productions offices, that things went wrong. I was struck with a sort of panic and overwhelmed by the idea that something bad would happen if I went to work. For ten minutes I stood rooted, buffeted on every side by commuters, but no amount of trying to talk myself down off the ledge made a difference. Finally I turned around, retracing my steps down to the Tube, and immediately my panic subsided. Within an hour I was sitting in a virtually empty carriage returning to Redhill.

For much of that morning I sat on a bench overlooking the tennis courts in Memorial Park, thinking about Laura. I thought about the night in a Brixton bar that we first met through friends of friends, how fashionable she'd looked in her denim dungarees and bright orange T-shirt and how interesting she'd seemed as we talked. I recalled how nervous I'd felt asking for her number at the end of the night, sure that she would rebuff my request, and the relief as she'd scribbled it down. I called her the following morning and we met for lunch in Camden and spent the afternoon wandering around the market. I remembered our first kiss, a snatched moment before the doors of a southbound Northern Line train opened and how, as I'd watched the train pull away, I'd known even then that I'd finally found what I'd spent a lifetime looking for.

When it started to rain around midday I left the park and took shelter in my car. I turned on my phone and was immediately inundated by messages demanding to know my whereabouts. I didn't reply to any of them, instead I started the car and drove around aimlessly for a while before pulling into the car park of the Red Lion. My first drink was a lager with a whisky chaser, and so was my second and my third. On some level I knew it was a bad idea to drink so much so quickly but on another it seemed like the only thing that made sense.

It had been a message from Linda late in the afternoon that caused me to go back to the car. As I stood at the bar ordering myself yet another round of drinks, my phone vibrated. Feeling sufficiently at ease with the world, I'd lifted the handset to my ear and listened to the most recent of the several messages she'd left: 'Tom, this is Linda again. I can't believe how selfish you're being! I'm beside myself with worry! This isn't right! This isn't right at all! I dread to think what Laura would say if she could see you now! Please, Tom, wherever you are, whatever you're doing, just stop and think for a minute and come home.'

Everything Linda said was right. I was being selfish. I was causing undue worry. Laura would've been livid to know how I was behaving. She would've completely taken me to task for acting like such a fool. I had to make things right. I had to go home.

Leaving the pub I crossed the car park, climbed into my car and started the engine. Convinced the Range Rover was in reverse, I put my foot down a little too heavily on the accelerator sending it lurching forward into the rear of the car in front. There was such a colossal crunch that the other car's alarm instantly went off and before I could fully register what I'd done, a small crowd of passers-by had gathered and soon word of what was going on in the car park reached the patrons of the Red Lion. The next thing I knew an overweight man with some serious arm tattoos heaved himself into my line of vision. On seeing the crushed bumper of the car I'd crashed into, his face contorted in such a manner that it was all too obvious that the vehicle I'd hit belonged to him. Any hope that I'd got the wrong end of the stick evaporated as he rained down a barrage of blows on the bonnet of my car so hard that the entire vehicle shook.

It wasn't long before the police arrived. Taking control of the situation one of the officers forced Tattoo Man to wait near the patrol car parked on the road, while another rapped his knuckles on my window signalling for me to wind it down.

'I'll tell you right now how this is going to go,' said the young officer. 'You're going to open this door and step out of the car peacefully or my colleagues and I will drag you out kicking and screaming and we'll add resisting arrest to the current mess you've made for yourself. Are we clear?'

The next thing I knew I was in the back of his patrol car on my way to Oak Road police station where I was booked for drink-driving. I then had my shoes, belt and belongings removed before being locked up in a cell, where I was to remain until they considered me sober enough to be set free.

4

I'll give it a go

Linda

It was the sound of a black cab's diesel engine that alerted me to Tom's arrival. I put down the book I'd been desperately attempting to lose myself in, walked to the bay window and gently pulled back the curtains in time to see Tom paying the driver. Over the course of the evening I'd given a great deal of thought to what I'd say to Tom when I finally got to see him face-to-face. I'm normally quite a reserved person but in the circumstances, I'd given myself permission to really let rip and give him a piece of my mind: no holds barred. The fact of the matter was, I had more than enough emotional ammunition to knock him off his feet from here until doomsday, and after the way he'd behaved I was prepared to use it too. But as Tom stood framed by the open front door he looked so pathetic, so defeated, so utterly dejected that to have launched into my tirade would have felt like kicking a man when he was well and truly down.

I asked him if he was okay and he nodded dejectedly. I muttered something like, 'Good,' trying to sound for all the world like I didn't mean it, and he didn't even react. For several moments we stood staring at each other in silence until finally, when I could bear it no more, I threw my arms around him, sobbing. And while some of the tears I shed were for Tom and the mess he'd got himself in, and others simply a mixture of relief and frustration, the majority were reserved for my dear, sweet Laura who, as the antique clock in the hallway pointed out so clearly as it struck midnight, we'd officially lost exactly one year ago today.

That night I didn't sleep too well at all. My head was full of thoughts of Tom, the girls and most of all, Laura. Even when I eventually did drift off I wasn't asleep for long and awoke early, determined that the girls should have their weekend away. There was no choice but for me to set aside my fear of Tom's huge car and my terror of busy roads. Every second of the three-hour, one-hundred-and-thirty-four-mile journey scared the living daylights out of me, but the round of applause I received from the girls as we reached the cute little cottage that was to be our home for the weekend made it all worthwhile.

To begin with the weather was mild for the time of year, and during the day the girls and I visited the pier and tried our hand at crabbing. By evening, however, there was no doubting it was October as we, along with Tom, wrapped up against the cold for an alfresco fish-and-chip supper and late-night beach walk. Half an hour into our walk I came to a halt and took off the rucksack I'd been carrying. From inside it I pulled out a black bin liner from which, much to Tom's surprise, I withdrew a large firework.

'What's this?' asked Tom as the children gathered round.

'The girls and I bought it last week,' I explained.

'We want to set one off every year on this day,' said Evie.

'We think Mummy would've loved it,' added Lola. 'She used to love fireworks didn't she, Daddy?'

I handed the rocket to Tom and corralled the children back a few yards for safety while he lit the fuse. For a moment nothing happened, and then it fizzed and crackled, shooting white-hot sparks into the wet sand, and at last with a high-pitched scream it shot into the air and burst into a flurry of brightly coloured stars. As the children let out squeals of delight I glanced over at Tom, hoping to gauge his reaction, but his eyes were fixed on the sky above our heads. It was only when all traces of the firework had gone that he finally looked down and I saw the tears in his eyes.

Later that night, long after the girls had gone to bed, I went in search of Tom to see if he wanted a cup of tea and found him sitting in the darkness on a bench at the front of the house. He was looking up at the stars intently as though he genuinely believed that Laura might be one of them.

I sat down next to him. 'You'll catch your death if you stay out here all night.'

'It's not that bad,' he replied. 'Anyway, I'll be in soon.'

'Tonight was good, wasn't it? I think the girls really got something out of it, don't you?'

'I suppose you're right, although I'm not sure what my presence added.'

'You're their dad, they need you.'

'For what? It wasn't me who organised this weekend, was it? You know exactly what they need and how to give it to them.'

'And you would too, if you'd only spend more time with them. A lot of what it takes to be a good dad is just showing up and being there for them. Laura never had that and I wonder at times if I did enough to make up for her dad not being around.'

'Don't be daft,' he said, smiling at me with genuine warmth. 'She didn't miss out on anything. She always said that you were all she needed.'

'Maybe,' I replied. 'But that doesn't mean I don't still feel guilty. Children need their fathers. They just do.'

We sat in silence for a while longer and then I fished in my pocket for a business card I'd been carrying around for weeks waiting for the right moment, and pressed it into Tom's hand.

'What's this?'

'I came across it in the library a while back. I think it might be just the thing you need.'

'COPE, Bereavement Counselling Group,' said Tom, reading the card aloud by the light of his phone. 'Here to help you help yourself.'

'You must know you can't carry on like this, don't you?' I said, meeting his questioning gaze. 'You need help, Tom.'

He contemplated the card a moment longer.

'I'll give it a go,' he said.

'Thank you,' I replied. 'That's all I ask.'

Tom

Things were a lot better between Linda and me after Southwold. It was as though now I'd reached rock bottom the only way was up. So when the Tuesday of my first group-counselling meeting came around (which just so happened to be bonfire night) and she asked me if I still intended to go, I said yes, of course. That evening, against a backdrop of intermittent fireworks exploding in the sky, I made my way through the damp streets of Redhill to the Methodist Church on the High Street.

Peering through one of the small glass panels in the door leading to the main hall, I spotted a circle of a dozen or so chairs, half of which were occupied. The more I tried to imagine myself entering the room and taking a seat, the more it became clear just how much I didn't want to be here. I wanted to be at home but would have settled at the very least for anywhere other than here. I didn't want to be sat in a church hall with a bunch of strangers talking about my dead wife. I wasn't that kind of person at all. But I owed Linda big time. So if the idea of my doing this made her happy, it was the very least I could do.

'How nutty do they look?'

I turned around to see that the person addressing me was an old man in his eighties. He was wearing a blue baseball cap and a black suit jacket teamed with grey trousers that were slightly too short. His outfit gave me the impression that he'd long since given up the idea (if indeed he'd ever possessed it) of clothes being anything other than functional. If it hadn't been for the glint in his eye and the mischievous grin on his face, I'd have put good money on him being a bit loopy. As eccentric as he appeared, however, I had no doubt that he was in possession of his full quota of marbles.

Without waiting for me to reply to his question, the old man joined me at the door. 'So come on then, what are they like?'

I moved aside to let him get a better look.

He peered through the glass for a long time then stood back shaking his head. 'They *all* look like nutters and if I'm not mistaken, bedwetters too.'

It was a strange relief to hear someone speak so irreverently about the bereaved. It made a welcome change from the pained expressions and hushed tones reserved for those who had suffered loss, myself included.

'So who made you come tonight?' I asked, warming to the old man. 'I'm guessing you're not here of your own free will.'

'My granddaughter,' he replied. 'Wouldn't stop droning on about how I wasn't dealing with my Dot's passing properly! As if sitting in a room with a bunch of morons is suddenly going to make my missus come back from the dead. How about you?'

'My mother-in-law,' I replied without further explanation.

The old man shrugged in a manner that acknowledged my right to keep my business to myself, while at the same time making it clear he hadn't been all that interested anyway.

'So are you going in or what?'

It was a good question. I took a deep breath and pushed open the door. As the old man and I entered the room everyone in the circle turned to look at us. A man with small round John Lennon glasses and long, dark brown hair swept up into a ponytail smiled at us. He had the air of being someone in charge.

'Welcome, guys.' He gestured to us to sit down. 'Come on in, the more the merrier.'

Evidently the old man wasn't impressed at being addressed as a 'guy' by someone young enough to be his grandson, because he tutted under his breath so loudly that he might as well have shouted his displeasure. He and I took seats next to each other and after I'd exchanged a number of awkward smiles with the rest of the group, Ponytail checked his watch and announced that he was officially beginning the session.

'First off,' said Ponytail, 'I'd just like to say how wonderful it is to see a few new faces . . . and a few old ones too! For those who have never been before, here's what we're about in a nutshell: coping. That's what we're all here tonight to discover: how to cope; how to process some of the thoughts and feelings that might be going through our heads; how to talk to people who might not understand the way we're feeling; how to stay positive when frankly, that's the last thing we want to do. This is a completely safe space, somewhere you can say what you're feeling and thinking without fear of criticism or ridicule; it's like our motto says: "We're here to help you help yourself."' He clapped his hands as if attempting to summon some much needed energy into the room. 'Right, before we begin, why don't we introduce ourselves? Tell us your name and something about yourself that you're happy to share. I'll start: my name's Alan, I live with my partner and two little ones in a flat not a stone's throw from here, and I've been a grief counsellor here at COPE for just under four years.' He clapped again, and added, 'And that's me in a nutshell,' before looking pointedly at a mousy-looking woman next to him.

'Hello, everyone, I'm Karen, I'm a part-time piano teacher, and this is my first time at COPE. I lost my brother to bowel cancer three years ago. I just miss him so much.' One by one everyone in the circle introduced themselves and revealed a tiny snapshot of their fractured lives to Alan, until finally there was only me and the old man left to share.

'I think everyone's waiting for you to introduce yourself,' said Alan, looking at the old man encouragingly.

The old man sighed loudly as though even the thought of addressing the group was more work than he'd signed up for.

'My name's Clive Maynard,' he began. 'I served in Her Majesty's Armed Forces for ten years reaching the rank of corporal, followed by a thirty-year career in the police force reaching the rank of sergeant, and I've never had a day off work in my life. I don't like women who wear trousers, young men with their arses hanging out of their jeans and cats – I really, really hate cats.' He folded his arms in defiance. 'And that, Alan, is *me* in a nutshell.'

'That's great stuff, Clive,' said Alan, letting Clive's 'nutshell' dig wash over him. 'I feel like I got a real sense of who you are from that. Thank you.'

Alan smiled, and nodded towards me. I could feel the eyes of everyone in the room on me. In my job I was never lost for words. There wasn't a situation invented in which I'd ever felt intimidated, but at this moment I was completely at a loss. Finally, I cleared my throat and decided to say the first thing that came into my head.

'Hi, I'm Tom,' I began, 'and if I'm honest I don't want to be here. My wife died just over a year ago, and I feel like ever since then all I've done is spend every waking second of every day trying not to think about just how completely and utterly empty my life is without her.'

Linda

I was reading an old Sunday newspaper magazine I'd been meaning to catch up on, when I heard Tom arrive home from his first bereavement meeting. While I was desperate to know how it had gone, I was equally keen to respect his privacy.

'Tea?'

Tom nodded. 'That would be lovely, thanks.'

I filled the kettle. 'Is it cold out?'

'Not too bad.'

'And the bus journey?'

'Uneventful.'

I momentarily ran out of questions and so switched on the kettle in silence and took two mugs out of the cupboard – one was plain, the other emblazoned with the inscription, 'World's Best Mum'. Hoping Tom hadn't noticed, I quickly swapped it for one that said, 'Number 1 Boss' instead.

'It went well,' said Tom, as I dropped a teabag into each mug. 'I'm glad you suggested that I go.'

I could feel my face lighting up. 'So you'll be going back?'

'Absolutely.'

I couldn't help myself. I hugged him so tightly I almost squeezed the life out of him. 'I'm so glad to hear that. I've got a really good feeling about this.'

'I know you have,' replied Tom. 'Me too.'

Tom

The truth was that I felt completely and utterly drained by my first COPE meeting. How was it possible that so much grief could be contained in so few people? While neither Clive nor I said another word over the course of the hour-long meeting, we were forced to listen to a young man reveal how he coped with grief by making dinner every night for his girlfriend even though she'd been killed in a car accident; a middle-aged woman whose sister had died of leukaemia a decade earlier confessed to crying every night of those ten years; and a respectable-looking woman in her fifties admitted that from the day after she buried her soldier son, who had been killed in action in Afghanistan, she'd shoplifted clothes on a weekly basis from Marks & Spencer, none of which she ever wore.

It was hard to deny that hearing these people's stories had comforted me to a degree. Knowing that ordinary people, people who, if not exactly like me then at the very least like people I knew, were going through a kind of pain I recognised, made me feel considerably less isolated. I wasn't 'weird' because I sometimes imagined my grief like a monster from *Dr Who* lurking in the shadows. I wasn't 'odd' because in the past I'd sat, late at night on the floor of the bathroom with my back against the door, face buried in a towel that I'd sprayed with Laura's perfume just so I could smell her again. I wasn't 'strange' because I refused to cancel Laura's mobile phone contract so that I could still listen to her outgoing message whenever things got too bad. But even as the session closed and Alan began suggesting homework – 'Write a letter to your loved one' – to do for the coming week, I knew that I was never going to come back. It just wasn't for me.

Linda

A few days later I had a lovely surprise when my dearest and oldest friend Moira called all the way from Melbourne, Australia. Moira and I had known each other since teacher-training college in Manchester. We met on our first day and clicked immediately and it was through Moira's brother, Paul, that I had first met Frank, Laura's father. Moira was with me when I took my pregnancy test and found out that I was carrying Laura; it was Moira who comforted me when Frank disappeared after writing a letter telling me that he wasn't ready to be a father; and it was Moira who held my hand and mopped my brow for the eleven and a half hours that it took for me to deliver my beautiful, smiling girl into the world.

In fact, through all the twists and turns of the past forty or so years, I can say Moira had been an ever present force for good in my life and had remained so even after love took her over to the other side of the world. In spite of the distance, we always made sure to be part of each other's lives, even if it was at the end of a telephone line. I was there for her when her new husband Peter passed away from colon cancer after only ten years of marriage, just as she had been there for me when my dear Laura left us.

Anyway, Moira wanted to have a proper catch-up as we hadn't spoken for a while and so I listened to her news and told her mine and at the end of it all, like she always did, she invited me to come and stay with her and have a proper holiday, and as always I told her she should be careful making offers like that because one day I might actually take her up on it.

5

How about that son-in-law of yours?

Tom

A week after my first COPE session I had a meeting at the offices of Peters and Whitelaw, the Islington-based law firm recommended to me by my boss. The first thing Mr Whitelaw did when I sat down was look down at his notes. 'I see you admitted the charge,' he said. 'I'm confident that we can get around that *if in the sober light of day you have decided to change your plea*.'

I shifted uncomfortably in my seat and, ignoring the 'nudge and wink' tone to his voice, replied, 'Actually, I haven't.'

The solicitor nodded as if this was only a minor hindrance. He returned to his notes. 'You said in your statement that the reason you were in the pub that day was because you'd decided not to go to work. Can I ask what it is that you do?'

'I work in TV. I'm the executive producer of, amongst other things, *The Big Night Out*.'

Mr Whitelaw nodded again. 'It's not my sort of thing at all but I'm sure my wife has been known to watch it from time to time.' He looked back at his notes. 'Would you say yours is a stressful profession?'

Stressful was something of an understatement. I think the only sphere of employment that out-performed it in burning out young professionals before their time was the army. 'It has its moments,' I replied.

'And you say that on the day in question you were on your

way to work when you decided to turn around and go home. Can I ask what brought about your change of mind?'

He was looking for a mitigating factor, anything he might be able to use to get me off my charge. What he didn't know was that I wasn't prepared to use Laura's death to save my own skin. I'd made up my mind that it was time I started owning my mistakes.

'I just did,' I replied. 'That's all. Sometimes you get to work and realise that work is the last place you want to be.'

Mr Whitelaw nodded half-heartedly. He clearly knew something was amiss. 'Would you say you have a problem with substance abuse?'

'Not at all.'

'Would you say you have a problem with stress?'

'No more than the next person.'

'Okay, can you think of anything at all that might have happened on that day that led to your drinking and in turn to your driving which we might be able to use in court? I see in your statement to the police that you informed them that you needed to go home because you were supposed to be going away for the weekend. Was it for a special occasion perhaps?'

'It was something my mother-in-law arranged. I didn't have a great deal to do with it.'

Mr Whitelaw sighed wearily, put down his pen and took off his spectacles. 'Mr Hope,' he began as though addressing a schoolboy, 'you do realise that the offence you've been charged with is a very serious one, don't you? While admittedly this is your first misdemeanour, the truth of the matter is that the courts tend to take a very dim view of drink-driving and you could be looking at a custodial sentence, not to mention a three-year driving ban.' He put his spectacles back on and picked up his pen ready to write. 'Now bearing all this in mind, are you absolutely convinced that you can't think of any mitigating factors that might help your case?'

A custodial sentence? I'd barely been able to handle seven hours in a police cell let alone seven weeks. All I needed to do to make the threat go away was play the dead-wife card and it would all disappear. I could tell him how it was almost exactly a year since I'd lost Laura. How I'd been thinking about her all the time. How I'd only started drinking to stop my thoughts from overwhelming me; how I'd only got in the car because I was supposed to be taking my motherless children away for the weekend.

I swallowed hard and met Mr Whitelaw's gaze. 'I'm afraid there aren't any mitigating factors. I did what I did – it was a stupid thing to do – there's no one to blame but myself.'

Mr Whitelaw was clearly a man who didn't give in easily and in the time that remained he made it crystal clear that without anything to offer the judge in mitigation he would undoubtedly lose the case. Even with all the talk of custodial sentences, I refused to give him what he wanted – it just didn't seem right – but when I finally left his office, I felt like I'd gone twelve rounds with a boxing heavyweight.

As I made my way to the Tube through the dark, wet streets of Islington my phone buzzed. I checked the screen to see the weekly reminder I'd set the day after I returned from Southwold: 'COPE meeting 8.00 p.m.' Even if I hadn't just been informed that I might be going to prison, I doubt that I'd have changed my mind about not going. One meeting really had been more than enough for me. Of course, that left me with a dilemma: should I tell Linda that COPE wasn't for me and risk disappointing her again, or lie and sort out my problems on my own? I think I must have deliberated on the matter for all of half a second before I tapped out a message to Linda: 'Don't forget I'll be late home tonight. Have COPE meeting.' Returning my phone to my coat pocket, I caught the Tube to Victoria, hopped on the 18.05 to Redhill and spent the evening alone in a pub near the station, nursing nothing more alcoholic than a pint glass of apple juice and soda water. At nine thirty on the dot, bloated on one soft drink too many, I left the pub, took a taxi home and joined Linda in the kitchen.

'Good meeting?' she asked.

'Gruelling stuff,' I replied. 'But it was worth it.'

She put a comforting hand on my shoulder. 'You're so brave, Tom, you really are.'

'Thanks,' I replied, only too aware that I'd just sunk to an altogether new level of degeneracy. At the rate I was going, I'd be roasting kittens alive and eating them for kicks by Christmas. 'It means a lot to hear you say that.'

Linda

I couldn't begin to express how pleased I was with Tom. He really was giving his weekly COPE meetings his all and although I remained concerned about how hard he worked and how little he still saw of the children, I felt hopeful that change was just around the corner. So when his commitment to his grief-counselling meetings refused to wane even when the relatively mild October weather gave way to a particularly wintery November, I truly believed that what I was actually witnessing was my son-in-law building up the strength to turn over a new leaf in the New Year.

On the first Monday in December, I met up with the members of my local book group. I'd been with this particular daytime group for a little over eight months, having spotted their advert on the noticeboard of the library. Once I'd got to grips with the full-time running of a family home after a twenty-year break, I'd begun to feel the need for a bit of company. I'd been a member of several book groups back in York and had always found them a fun way to meet new people, so without a second thought I'd put my name down.

I didn't enjoy this group at first, mostly because Faye, who'd set it up a year earlier, constantly bullied us into reading the most dreary literary novels imaginable, always refusing to take anyone else's perfectly reasonable suggestions on board. After my third meeting, where she tried to foist the latest Booker Prize winner on us, me and a few of the other ladies staged a coup, resulting in the next book being a cosy crime thriller that disgusted Faye's literary sensibilities so much she left the group for good. These days we didn't even bother reading books at all, preferring instead to meet at the café on the High Street for a chat.

This particular morning the talk amongst the group was of their families: chiefly how disappointed they were in them, and the fact that Christmas was looming seemed to make matters worse. Margaret, a retired social worker, was broken-hearted over the grandson she never saw because her daughter-in-law was refusing her son access; Lillian, a part-time librarian, was incensed at her two daughters, both of whom were in their early forties and hadn't so much as given her a whiff of a grandchild; and Gill, a retired GP, was much troubled by her youngest son, who to date had three children with two women and had just announced he'd managed to get a third one pregnant.

'I feel terrible,' I sighed as Margaret finished telling us about another failed attempt to make contact with her grandson. 'I get to see my grandchildren every day.'

'Oh Linda, don't be silly,' replied Margaret. 'You've paid such a terrible price for that.' The other ladies around the table nodded in agreement.

'How about that son-in-law of yours?' asked Lillian. 'How's

he keeping? I saw him in The Plough the other week. Is he all better now?'

'He's fine,' I replied. 'In fact, he seems to have turned a corner lately. Why do you ask?'

'I don't know,' mused Lillian. 'He just looked troubled that's all. He was sitting in a corner on his own, nursing a pint glass of apple juice.'

I cast my mind back, trying to think when that might have been, and when I drew a blank I asked Lillian when she'd seen him.

'It was last Tuesday,' she confirmed, 'my birthday. The girls surprised me with a meal there. I don't quite know why they bothered. I'd much rather they surprised me with a grandchild: IVF, adopted, surrogated, even knocked-up by a total stranger, at this point I'd take whatever was on offer!' The table erupted with raucous laughter from everyone except me.

'I haven't spoken out of turn, have I?' asked Lillian, no doubt spying the stern look on my face.

'Of course not,' I replied. 'I was just thinking that's all. Are you sure it was last Tuesday you saw him?'

'Absolutely.'

'About what time, would you say?'

'Well, he was certainly there when we arrived at seven and I'm almost certain he was still there when we left at nine.'

My inner Miss Marple leapt into action. On the day in question I'd been in the kitchen replacing the name labels that had fallen off Evie's gym kit when Tom returned home, allegedly from his meeting. The first words out of his mouth had been about what a wonderful session he'd had and how he was really feeling positive about life.

I set down my cappuccino firmly on the table and, as one, the book group leaned in, sensing a scandal unfolding in front of their very eyes.

'He's been lying to me!'

'Who?' asked Lillian.

'My son-in-law,' I replied.

I hadn't told the book group about Tom's arrest. It hadn't seemed right somehow, but now I told them everything, starting with the crash and his promise to attend counselling, through to the fact that today was the day of his court hearing for drink-driving.

'So he's supposed to go to this group every Tuesday?'

'Every Tuesday, for the past seven weeks! He's been lying to me once a week for practically two whole months!'

'That's outrageous,' said Lillian. 'So what will you do? Confront him?'

'Shake some bloody sense into him if I get my hands on him! How could he lie to my face just like that? I must mean nothing to him!'

'I doubt that,' reassured Margaret. 'He's obviously got a problem.'

'We've all got problems, Margaret, and you don't see us lying to our loved ones, do you!'

'Have you tried getting him to talk to his GP?' asked Gill. 'They can point him in the direction of one-to-one help if that's what's needed.'

'They could point him to the moon for all the good it will do. That boy's not going to get better unless somebody makes him. And that somebody is going to be me.'

Tom

Linda was washing up at the kitchen sink when I returned from my day in court. She'd been texting me all afternoon asking about the result but I hadn't been able to bring myself to reply.

Linda dried her hands on a tea towel and turned towards me. 'How did it go?'

'A stern telling off from the judge and an eighteen-month driving ban, plus a sixteen-hundred-pound fine.'

'I thought that lawyer you had was supposed to be the best there is?'

'He is,' I replied. 'He's why I'm here talking to you and not in jail introducing myself to my cell mates.'

While Linda filled the kettle for a brew, I sorted through the post at the kitchen table. There was nothing at all of interest in there: just bills and junk mail, some of which was addressed to Laura.

'I was just wondering about how you're getting on with your COPE meetings,' called Linda from across the kitchen as I stared at an envelope addressed to Mr T. Hope and Mrs L. Hope. 'You haven't mentioned them in a while.'

'They've been going well,' I replied, tearing open the envelope and thumbing through the water bill within. I made a mental note to call the water company in the morning to get them to take Laura's name off the bill even though I knew I'd never actually do it. 'Nothing much to report.'

'And you feel like you're making progress?' She was standing next to me now, holding two steaming hot mugs of tea. She set one down in front of me.

'Slow progress but progress all the same.'

'And of course, you'll be going there tomorrow?'

'Absolutely,' I replied. 'I'm actually looking forward to it.'

Linda banged down her mug of tea on the table so hard that some of it sloshed over the sides. Rather than clear it up, however, she stared right at me, eyes blazing with anger. Her barrage of questions about my COPE meetings suddenly made sense. I'd been caught out.

'I can explain.'

'I'm sure you can!' she snapped. 'Not that I'd believe a word of it! How could you lie to me like this?' I opened my mouth to reply but Linda held up her hand. 'I don't want to hear it, Tom, I just don't!' She sat down heavily in the chair opposite, her whole face suffused with tiredness. 'I blame myself, of course. If I'd just let you and the girls get on with your lives, I know you would've risen to the challenge. I know that you'd be okay now. But I didn't, did I? I just had to go and poke my nose in where it wasn't wanted.'

I wasn't made of stone. No matter how self-involved I might be, I couldn't help but feel guilty listening to her talk that way. If it hadn't been for Linda looking after the girls I don't know what would've happened to them. Why couldn't I have just carried on going to those stupid sessions? 'You weren't sticking your nose in where it wasn't wanted, Linda. You were helping us. I don't know where we'd be right now if it wasn't for you keeping us afloat. There's no way we would have coped.'

'Well soon you're going to have no choice in the matter,' she replied. 'I've had enough, Tom, I'm leaving.'

She was bluffing. She had to be. 'You don't mean that, Linda. You're just lashing out.'

'You can think whatever you like but it won't make any difference,' she replied. 'I'm leaving first thing in the New Year, Tom, and there's not a thing you can say to stop me.'

She was being melodramatic. There was no way she'd ever leave the girls. They were her life. No, she was simply trying to get my attention.

'Look, Linda,' I began, 'we both know that would never work. What would you even do back in York? The girls are your world. You wouldn't last five minutes. But I get what you're saying though and I—'

Linda interrupted, 'I'm not going to York.'

'So where are you going then?'

'Australia,' she replied. 'My friend Moira, she's been asking me to visit her there for the longest time and today I finally agreed to go.'

I closed my eyes, sighing with relief. She wasn't talking about leaving for good. She was talking about taking a holiday. It would be difficult but if it came to it, I could probably manage to look after the girls for a few weeks while she had a break.

'Is that all this is about? A couple of weeks in Australia? You really had me going there for a minute. Look, Linda, I completely get where you're coming from on this. And you've every right to be—'

Linda shook her head. 'I'm not talking about a two-week holiday, Tom, or even twice that. I'm going to Australia for six months.'

I felt like I was going to be sick. 'Six months? That's madness! You can't leave me alone with the kids for six months. You're being selfish.'

Linda laughed. 'Selfish? Me? I suppose it takes one to know one. This has been a long time coming, Tom, a very long time indeed. But believe me when I say I'm going and just so you know, even when my trip's over there'll be no guarantees I'll be coming back.'

This was serious. I hadn't looked after the kids for as much as an hour in all the time since Laura died. There was no way I'd be able to look after them on my own. I needed to make this right with Linda and I needed that to happen now.

'Linda . . . look . . . Linda . . . I'm sorry, really I am. Obviously, you're right, I let things get out of hand but I promise I'll get them sorted. I'll go back to counselling.'

'You couldn't, even if you wanted to,' she replied. 'They had their funding cut and had to shut down at the end of last month.'

'So I'll find another one.'

'You can do what you like, Tom, but I'll still be going.'

'But you love the girls, they're your only grandchildren.'

'Of course I do. They're my world.'

'So why would you do this to them? They'll never forgive you.' It was a low blow and I was far from proud of it but these were desperate times.

'I know this has all come as a bit of a shock to you,' said Linda, staring at me with eyes filled more with pity than rage. 'But you'll get used to it. As I said, I'm not planning on going until after Christmas so you should have more than enough time to get yourself ready. You need to look after your girls, you really do, because they've already lost their mum, the last thing they need is to lose you too.'

This was a terrible situation. I could no more be a full-time carer for the kids than I could fly. Couldn't she see I was a mess? Couldn't she see that the girls needed looking after by someone who was actually up to the task? I had to make her see sense. Thankfully, the thing about me is that I thrive under pressure. There's no greater high than walking out of a pitch with a broadcaster knowing that you've absolutely nailed it. I'm good at thinking on my feet, so what I was thinking as Linda was talking was that I'd screwed up big time and Linda needed to know that I understood this, and was going to do everything I could to make up for it.

'You're absolutely right,' I said, 'I do need to be their dad again and what I said just now . . . about them never forgiving you, that was completely out of order. But I'm going to make it up to you. I've got to head back into work right now but tomorrow, you, me and the girls will go out for a meal, spend some proper time together and I'll prove to you that I really mean it: I'm going to change.'

6

It's for the best

Tom

The kids could barely believe their eyes the following day when they returned home from school to find me at home, let alone believe their ears when I announced that we were all going out for a meal.

'And you're coming with us?' asked a sceptical Evie.

'Of course I am,' I replied.

'But aren't you usually at work?' asked Lola.

'Usually,' I replied, 'but not today. Today I said, "Forget about work." I'm going to spend some proper time with you guys.'

'Where are we going?' asked Evie excitedly.

'Giraffe,' I replied, and I waited for the girls to start getting excited but instead their faces fell and they looked at Linda. I didn't understand quite what was going on. It had always been their favourite place, ever since they were small.

'Giraffe is for babies,' said Lola, clearing echoing something she'd heard Evie say.

Evie elbowed Lola sharply. 'You can't say that, it's rude.' She turned to me whilst fending off a half-hearted attack from Lola. 'That sounds great, Dad.'

Linda took me aside. 'I don't think they're quite as keen on Giraffe as they used to be,' she explained. 'I think Pizza Express is more their thing now.'

I shrugged. So what if I didn't know what the girls' favourite restaurant was any more? Right now I'd take them to the Ritz if it helped change Linda's mind about leaving the country. So Pizza Express it was. We got a table near the window, which was festooned with spray-on snow and tinsel. Fighting hard to be heard over *The Dean Martin Christmas Album* as the girls looked through the menu, I told them to choose whatever they wanted. After the waiter took our orders, the girls chatted to Linda and me about their day at school, but gradually I tuned out as the fact that I hadn't known this was their favourite place began to bother me.

It was only a small thing, of course. Nothing to make a big deal about at all. Still, I couldn't help wondering what else I didn't know about them any more. I'd long since learned that children were continually changing. I remember when Evie was younger she used to have a doll that went everywhere with her and then one day I noticed that she'd neglected to take it with her to pre-school. When I pointed this out to Laura she just laughed and told me that 'Annabel' was living on borrowed time. Sure enough, a fortnight later, I found the doll abandoned beneath a pile of books and dressing-up clothes under Evie's bed. After that, I got better at spotting when a change was coming and could predict with a fair amount of accuracy the day of a formerly favourite plaything's excommunication. But that was then. Now the changes were subtler. It was less about things and more about the girls as individuals. The way they saw themselves and the world at large. But after a year stuck inside my own head how could I even hope to know who they were, let alone anticipate who they might be in the future? Evie, after all, wasn't the ex-primary school kid who had just transferred to secondary school any more. She had spots, and a mobile phone that seemed to be her lifeline to the outside world. Were her thoughts those of a typical teenage girl? Was her head full of clothes and boys? And what about Lola? She hadn't exactly stuck in aspic either. Was it me, or did she seem a lot more introverted than she used to be? Was this just the new and more grown-up Lola, or a reaction to losing her mum? Of course, part of me wanted to know the answers to these questions, to know more about the girls and their lives, but most of me was terrified of what they might mean. Without Laura by my side I wouldn't even begin to know how to address them. I didn't have a natural parenting bone in my body. It was part of the reason why I'd left it all to Linda this past year. She was their grandmother, she loved them beyond words and represented the closest thing they had to the mother they missed so much. Me, I was just the guy left in charge when there was literally no one else to do the job. Yes, I was the girls' dad but really what did that even mean?

I tuned back into the girls' conversation and even attempted to join in a few times. I kept it light though: no politics, religion or asking them about what they wanted to be when they grew up. Instead we talked about school, friends, music, books and Christmas presents. We debated which were the best Christmas movies of all time too (*Elf* came top, followed closely by *It's a Wonderful Life*). I was actually doing really well, cracking jokes and making the girls laugh, but then towards the end of the meal, as the waiter cleared our plates and handed us dessert menus, Linda announced that she had some news to share with the girls.

'Maybe we should save it for later,' I said quickly, hoping the girls wouldn't notice. 'We're all having such a nice time.'

Linda and I engaged in a battle of glares. Mine said, 'What do you think you're doing?' while hers said, 'I don't care what you say I'm going to tell them anyway.'

The girls zeroed in on the tension.

'What's going on?' asked Evie.

'You're both being funny,' said Lola. 'I don't like it.'

'I've got some news I need to tell you girls,' said Linda,

avoiding my gaze. 'The thing is, it's all come about quite quickly but I'm afraid that I won't be here any more after the New Year.'

'I don't understand,' said Lola. 'Are you going away somewhere?'

'I'm going to Australia,' said Linda. 'You remember my friend Moira, don't you? I've told you about her lots and she met you both when you were younger. Anyway, she's lives in Australia and she's invited me to come and visit her.'

'But we're going too, aren't we, Nanny?' said Evie. 'I've always wanted to go to Australia.'

Linda placed her hand on top of Evie's. 'No, sweetie, *we're* not going to Australia, I'm going alone. And I'm afraid not just for a few weeks but for six months.'

'Six months!' gasped Evie. 'You can't go away for six months! Who'll look after us?' Linda looked at me, and Evie's eyes followed her gaze, incredulous. 'You're going to leave Dad in charge of us?'

'It's for the best,' said Linda.

It was time for me to calm the situation down. 'Nanny's not going anywhere,' I interrupted. 'She's just making a point, that's all, okay? There's nothing to worry about.'

'I'm not making any point, Tom,' said Linda, incensed. '*I am* going to Australia and *I am* going for six months!'

Lola's eyes were brimming with tears. 'But I don't want you to go, Nanny! I want you to stay here with us!'

'Dad, tell her that she can't go,' demanded Evie, her eyes raging with defiance. 'Tell her you're not well, that you can't look after us.'

The news that I was 'not well' hit me like a slap to the face. Was this how Evie had processed my absence as a father? Had she reasoned that I wasn't feckless or selfish, but ill? Whether or not that was true, it hurt hearing her say it aloud.

'I'm afraid Nanny's made up her mind, sweetheart.'

'Then don't just sit there!' snapped Evie. 'Make her change it! Make her see she has to stay!'

I looked at Linda, hoping to see someone whose resolve was on the verge of crumbling. Her face, though etched with sadness, showed no sign of surrender. This was it. Her mind was made up. She really was going. For a brief moment I thought about work, and it occurred to me that if a pitch that went well was the best feeling in the world, then one that went badly was the absolute worst. And this pitch had crashed and burned.

Linda

I can't begin to tell you how angry I was with Tom. Couldn't he see I was doing this for the best? Couldn't he see that this was hurting me far more than it was hurting him? But of course, the moment I asked myself those questions the answer that came back was a resounding no. Tom couldn't see that this was for the best. He couldn't see that he was hurting me. He couldn't even see the distress he was causing the children. All he could see was his grief. All he could feel was his terror at the prospect of no longer being able to hide.

Later that evening I knocked on the door of the living room, where Tom had been lurking ever since he'd stormed ahead of the girls and me after leaving the restaurant.

'Can I come in?' I asked tentatively, popping my head around the door.

'I think you've made it clear that you can do whatever you like,' he snapped. 'Why start asking now?'

I sat down on the sofa opposite him. He picked up the TV remote and switched it off, plunging the room into silence.

'Tom, I know you're angry with me—'

Tom laughed. 'That doesn't even begin to cover it.'

'Well that's as maybe,' I replied, trying to remain calm. 'But you know you need this, Tom. Yes, it'll be a steep learning curve, yes it'll be difficult at times but I wouldn't be leaving the girls with you if I doubted for a moment that you would rise to the challenge. You need the girls to need you, Tom. You need to be a dad again. And well, what I need is to make right the wrong I've done in not pushing you to do this sooner.'

'You've told me all this before,' sighed Tom scornfully. 'I still don't see why you need to be so extreme. You want me to take more responsibility, fine, I'll do that. Just don't go, okay, there's no need. Your point has been well and truly received.'

'But I don't think it has, Tom,' I replied. 'And I don't think it will, as long as I'm here. You've always been a wonderful father, Tom. Always. When the girls were small you used to do their night feeds, change nappies and run bath times too. I know how hard you've worked to give them a home and put food on the table. And I know that if I hadn't been standing next to you in the hospital when you got that terrible news, if you hadn't trusted that I'd love and comfort the girls as much as you would, you'd never have given into grief like you did. No matter what the pain you were feeling, you would've picked yourself up, dusted yourself off and been there for those children. And that's why I can't stay, Tom. The mistake I made that day was to let you opt out of being a parent. Now the only way to fix it, is to take away that choice altogether. Whatever happens next is up to you.'

January came around far more quickly than I'd ever imagined. It felt like one moment Tom and I were waging a cold war over my plans to leave, and Christmas had been and gone and I was standing in the hallway with two large suitcases and a travel bag at my feet.

'I still can't believe you're actually leaving,' said Evie, slipping her arm around my waist as we waited in the hallway for the taxi that would be taking me to the airport. 'Six months is ages! Anything could happen in that time.'

'It'll be over before you know it,' I said firmly. I'd promised myself I wasn't going to cry in front of the children and I was determined not to. 'Just you wait and see. You'll blink and before you know what's happened I'll be right back with you.'

'But I don't want you to go,' said Lola, pressing her head against my hip. 'If you really have to go and see your friend, couldn't we go and see her too?'

'That would be nice, wouldn't it?' I said, ruffling Lola's hair. 'And who knows, maybe next time around we can arrange it.'

The sound of a car horn brought us all to attention. The kids called upstairs to Tom that the taxi had arrived. As he came down, his every look seemed to say, 'I can't believe you're doing this to me after all I've been through,' and not for the first time I wondered if he didn't actually even hate me a little.

'I'll take your bags,' he said, without looking at me.

'Thanks,' I replied quietly, and then I told the girls to join their father in the cab while I locked up.

Alone in the house that had been my home for over a year, I allowed a small portion of the tears I'd been holding in all morning to fall and then, wiping all trace of them away, I checked my make-up in the hallway mirror and took one last look around. *This is absolutely the right thing to do. I can't back down now. I have to see this through.*

Tom

As much as I was angry with Linda for leaving, the truth was I was angrier with myself for acting like a petulant brat. Everything she'd said about me was right. In the past year I'd been so caught up in my own hurt, I'd lost sight of what was important. I'd put my faith in work to get me through this, instead of in my family. I'd thought of no one's feelings but my own. She was right. I needed to look after my daughters, I needed to be a dad again and yet, somehow the determination required for such a challenge wouldn't come. How could I take care of anyone else when I was barely able to look after myself? The sheer amount of love, care and attention they required terrified me. Linda seemed to be a natural at it, and Laura, well Laura had made the whole thing seem effortless. How could I ever do the job half as well as either of them? How could this whole situation not end up with me inadvertently ruining the lives of those two perfect children?

I was only ten when my mum left my dad to run off with some bloke she'd met, never to be seen again. Even at that tender age I knew that my dad was going to struggle to look after me. He worked long hours and couldn't so much cook as open a can and reheat its contents. For the most part I looked after myself. He always left money for food, and I knew where the chip shop was. As time passed, however, the trousers of my school uniform rose up past my ankles, the dust on the mantelpiece grew deeper, birthdays passed uncelebrated and both of us forgot how nice it felt to have someone stroke your head for no other reason than to show affection. It gradually became apparent that my mum did a lot more around the house than either of us had been fully aware of at the time. I'm not knocking my dad. He did the best job he could. But sometimes I wondered what I might have turned out like if it had been Dad who'd left rather than Mum. Would I have grown up to be kinder, more sensitive and considerate? And had it happened that way round, would I even be bothering to speculate about how things might have been? I suppose the point I'm trying to make here is that I'd seen this episode of *The Single Dad Show* before, and it seemed hopelessly optimistic to think that the script might change just because I'd had the misfortune to be cast in the starring role.

Linda

Gatwick North Terminal on the first Saturday of the New Year was heaving. There were families pushing overloaded trolleys, young couples dragging tiny suitcases behind them and smartly dressed business people chatting on their phones. I didn't want to believe that I was about to become one of them: a traveller, on my way to a destination that wasn't home. I still desperately needed to make things right with Tom. I needed for us to be friends again, family even. The girls, momentarily distracted from their heartache by the buzz and excitement of a busy airport ran off to see if they could find my check-in desk on the big display screens, giving me a small window in which to try and bring Tom round.

'Is this really how you want to leave things?'

Tom puffed out his cheeks and sighed. 'I could ask the same question of you. I can't believe you're actually going through with this ridiculous idea. You know you'll hate every moment away from the girls. Why would you put yourself through all that just to make a point?'

'I'm not making a point. I'm trying to save you from yourself.'

'I don't need saving,' spat Tom. 'I just need you not to let me down like this.'

The girls returned before I could reply. 'Your check-in desk is number sixty-seven, Nanny,' said Evie, eagerly pointing in the direction of a queue. Even without looking at him, I felt Tom's stare burning into me. 'Can I push your suitcase?'

'And I'll push the other one,' said Lola and she made a grab for its handle only to discover that it was heavier than she thought. 'Actually, I might need a little help.'

I attempted to catch Tom's eye, hoping he might be as frustrated as me at not being able to talk things through, but he was looking away, his face set hard like stone.

The children and I joined the back of the queue. Tom casually announced that he was thirsty and disappeared in the direction of a coffee concession. Much to my relief the girls chattered away, endlessly distracting me from all thoughts of Tom. It was as though they wanted to share their every last thought with me while there was still time. What meals would there be on the flight? Whereabouts on the plane was I sitting? Had I ever been on a flight this long before? What time was it now in Australia? Would I still be able to watch British TV? The girls asked so many questions that people queuing around us laughed and caught my eye, and I smiled proudly as if to say, 'Yes, they are my grandchildren, and yes, I know just how lucky I am to have them in my life.'

Another check-in desk was opened and soon I'd handed my luggage over. Armed with my boarding pass we went in search of Tom, only to find him loitering, coffee in hand, near the escalators.

'Nanny's got her boarding pass,' said Lola excitedly. 'It's what you need to get on the plane. I wish we had boarding passes too!'

'I know you do, sweetheart,' said Tom. 'Maybe one day.'

A second attempt to catch Tom's eye was as fruitless as the first. I told the children that it was time to go and we stepped on to the escalator heading up to Departures.

'It looks like I'm going to have to say my goodbyes now,' I said, kneeling down in front of Lola a little away from the first passport check. A wave of emotion that I fought hard to keep at bay crashed over me. 'I need you to tell me again the three things I've asked you to remember. Can you do that?'

Lola nodded tearfully. 'The first one is look after Daddy, the second is look after Evie and the third is to remember that you love us.'

'And that's right, isn't it?' I said as Lola's tears began to fall. 'Nanny loves you just the same whether she's right next to you or on the other side of the world.'

It was Evie's turn next.

'I miss you already,' said Evie, swapping places with her sister. The effort she was putting into not crying was heart-breaking.

'Me too,' I replied. 'But that's good because if I miss you it means that I love you lots and there's nothing bad about love, is there?'

Evie hugged me tightly. 'I don't want you to go, Nanny. Please say you'll stay.'

'I can't, sweetie, but you'll be brave for me, won't you? And remember to look after Dad and Lola too. And if you need anything at all, day or night, you can call me and talk to me. Daddy has all the numbers.'

Finally, I turned to Tom who was standing a distance apart. I told the girls to wait, and then took Tom by the hand and led him aside.

'I know you think this is the wrong thing to do,' I began. 'I know you think that I don't understand what you've been through, but I'm telling you now you're wrong on both counts. You need to be a father to these girls and you have to let these girls be daughters to you. You need each other and all I'm doing is giving you room to get on. I know you can do this, Tom, you might not think so, but I do.' I dried my eyes and looked up at him. 'I know you can do it, I know you won't let me down.' I dug into my bag, pulled out a gift-wrapped package roughly about the size of a folded newspaper and handed it to Tom.

'What this?'

It was a little joke, something I'd hoped to give him once we'd made up, but as we were still at war I wasn't at all sure he'd see the funny side. Still, whether he was amused or not he was going to need it. 'Open it and find out. You're in charge now.'

7

You're thinking about the girls, aren't you?

Tom

My first morning without Linda proved to be about as much fun as my first evening, which hadn't actually been any fun at all. The girls had barely acknowledged me on the journey back to Reigate, and the moment we reached home they disappeared into Evie's bedroom, slamming the door behind them as if it wasn't already patently clear to me that I wasn't welcome to join them. That night I microwaved two spaghetti bolognese ready meals, and left the food on a tray outside Evie's room. When I returned half an hour later, the plates were empty and on the tray there was a note in Evie's handwriting: 'We're never going to talk to you again unless we get Nanny back!' I screwed it up into a ball and stuffed it in my pocket, and after I'd tidied up the kitchen I spent the rest of the evening on the sofa repeatedly listening to the outgoing message on Laura's mobile phone until I fell asleep. When I woke the next day on the sofa, with the phone still resting on my chest, I'd hoped that the girls might have been at the very least willing to call a truce, and so I made a huge breakfast with all their favourite things like pancakes and bacon and three different types of eggs. While on the plus side they were happy to eat breakfast, on the minus side they didn't say a single word to me the whole time they were sat at the table. And later they took it upon themselves to make a point of leaving any room I entered, as if I was a bad smell they were trying to escape. In the end, rather than spend the whole day in silence, I decided it would be better for all of us if we got out of the house for a few hours, and that's how we ended up at Marina and Richard's.

Marina and Rich were Laura's oldest friends, who over the years had become good friends of mine too. Before Laura died, we spent a lot of time together as they had kids of a similar age to the girls, and although I'd done my best to avoid seeing them since the funeral (as I had with most of my friends), that hadn't stopped them from regularly inviting me and the girls round to theirs for weekend lunches.

'We're so glad you called,' said Marina as her kids and my mine raided the kitchen cupboard for biscuits.

'I'm really sorry I haven't been in touch,' I said sheepishly as the children exited the room en masse carrying fistfuls of baked goods. 'It's just that—'

'Mate, there's no need for explanations,' said Rich, handing me a small bottle of imported beer. 'This is us you're talking to. We're just glad you're here.'

As we sat chatting in their kitchen-diner I reflected on how easy and familiar this felt. So much so that I almost expected Laura, fresh from her usual nose around the house to admire their latest renovation project, to come and join us. I think we all felt Laura's absence and I think that was half the reason I'd avoided them for so long. Now that I was here, however, I was grateful that they hadn't given up on me.

After lunch, as the kids battled it out on the Xbox in the front room, the conversation among the adults turned to Linda's departure.

'So she's actually gone?' asked Richard.

'Yesterday morning,' I replied.

'And she won't be back for six months?' asked Marina. I nodded, pleased that my friends were in agreement that Linda's behaviour was completely reprehensible. 'But what is she thinking? It's only been a year since you lost poor Laura, you can't possibly be expected to work full-time *and* look after two young children.'

I hadn't been aware of it when I'd made my plans to visit Rich and Marina, but this was exactly why I was here: for sympathy. Before you're surrounded by it twenty-four-seven no one really bothers to explain quite how addictive sympathy can be. One moment you're a regular fallible human being and the next, due to some bizarre twist of fate, suddenly the normal rules of human interaction don't apply to you any more. From now on you can do no wrong.

And I have to say that I loved the sympathy. Not in a cynical or calculating way, I hasten to add. But simply because it made me feel like I wasn't losing my mind. The thing is, grief feels a lot like madness. It drives you to act in the weirdest of ways. I remember one occasion not long after I'd returned to work, I was alone in the break room and for no reason at all picked up a boiling kettle and hurled it at the wall. Hearing the commotion, at least half a dozen colleagues rushed to find out what was going on but when they saw me, not a single one of them questioned my actions directly. *He lost his wife*, their looks seemed to say as they tidied up around me, *I guess killing kitchen equipment is just a stage he has to go through.*

Anyway, after weeks of having Linda take me to task for my behaviour, being around Marina and Rich was a relief. They reminded me just when I needed it most, that actually I'd been through a trauma and therefore had the right to do what I wanted, when I wanted, without fear of culpability.

'Of course, you know that we'll help out all we can at weekends and the like,' said Marina an hour later as we said our goodbyes at the front door while the kids kicked a football down the street.

'I do,' I replied. 'And it's really appreciated.'

'What do you think you'll do?' asked Rich.

I'd had a whole month in which to rustle up a contingency plan for Linda's exit. A month in which I could have spoken to my boss about taking a sabbatical or going part-time or even simply handed in my notice and gone freelance for a while. Instead, however, I'd opted for denial. I'd metaphorically jammed my fingers in my ears and shut my eyes hoping it would all go away. Even as I'd told Rich and Marina my problems, I still found it impossible to comprehend that when I got home, Linda wouldn't actually be there waiting for us.

Now, thanks to my procrastination, I was in real trouble. Around the time Lola would need dropping off at school I had a breakfast meeting scheduled in Soho, and around the time she'd need picking up again I'd be stuck in meetings until gone seven-thirty at the earliest. And even if by some miracle I managed to get through Monday without Child Services being called, with an overnight trip to Amsterdam scheduled on Wednesday (to meet with the producers of a new light entertainment format that Pluto wanted to license), chances were I'd be up in court for child neglect before the weekend.

I looked at Rich, who was still waiting for an answer to the question he'd posed. Finally, I gave it to him.

'I'm screwed,' I said, and we both laughed as if I wasn't actually being deadly serious.

Marina kissed my cheek tenderly, 'You will take care of yourself, won't you?' I wondered how much she knew or had guessed about this past year without Laura. How I had cut myself off not just from friends but from family too. I wondered what she would've thought about my drink-driving ban. Would I have received a free pass on that too? As they waved goodbye and the girls and I pretended to walk down the road to my non-existent car, I wondered if perhaps I hadn't kept so many secrets from my friends because they would have confirmed what

Linda already knew: that even after a year without Laura I was still a mess.

The kids barely said a word to me on the way home and once we were indoors they immediately disappeared upstairs. I considered tidying up the breakfast stuff that was sitting in the sink. I further considered the question of whether they had clean uniforms and if not what I might do about it. Finally, I considered Linda, chiefly where she was, what she might be doing and why she ever thought that leaving me in charge of her granddaughters might be a good idea.

My phone buzzed. It was a text from Marina: 'Just off phone with sister. Her old nanny – who is amazing – has just had a new job fall through and I thought of you straight away. Call her asap because she'll be snapped up in no time! Big love, M xxx.'

I hadn't given any thought to nannies, au pairs or even child-minders, partly because I knew Linda would hate it but mostly because I didn't like them myself. After my mum left I spent a lot of time being looked after by a whole host of indifferent next-door neighbours and friends of friends. For the most part it was fine but it occasionally went wrong. Like when I was left with Mr and Mrs Catteridge down the road and their wild-eyed Alsatian started barking at me so savagely that I wet myself. Or when Joan, an old friend of my mum's, failed to notice me sticking nails into a live plug socket. Or when Mrs Hughes left her two sons in charge of me while she ran errands and they thought it would be a laugh to lock me in an airing cupboard while they pretended to be monsters scratching at the door.

But that was then, of course. They had stringent checks and tests for people who wanted to look after kids nowadays, and if this nanny had been good enough to take care of Freya's kids – Marina's sister was the very definition of fastidious – then she'd have references by the dozen. I called the number Marina had given me and a young woman with a Canadian accent answered.

'Hi, Brooke, my name's Tom Hope. Your old employer, Freya, was talking about you to her sister who is friends with me. She told me that you're looking for work and I just wondered if you'd be free to come around to my house for an informal interview?'

'Oh, yes,' she replied. 'In fact, I only just got off the phone with Freya. She sketched out your situation for me and I'd love to help out. When's a good time for you?'

I looked up the stairs, imagining the girls sticking pins into a fuzzy-felt effigy of me. 'How does now suit you? The truth is I need someone pretty urgently.'

Linda

In Australia it was Monday morning. Four thirty-four a.m. local time to be exact. And finally, after twenty-three long hours in the air with a short stopover in Singapore, I'd reached my destination. Back home, however, it was mid-afternoon on Sunday, easily my favourite time of the week. Having had Sunday lunch, the girls would be curled up on the sofa together watching a DVD, but instead of being there with them, I was here, on a plane, thousands of miles away.

I missed my girls. I missed them with every fibre of my being. With the exception of a couple of residential weekends and sleepovers, I hadn't been apart from either one of the girls for longer than the school day since I moved in with them. And now without them, so far away, not able to hold them, or touch them, or tell them how much I loved them, it almost felt like too much to bear. It was as though my very soul ached for them and it ached all the more not knowing how they were getting on with Tom.

Tom

I was loading the dishwasher when Brooke arrived for her interview. The doorbell rang and I'd opened the door to a young woman full of smiles and outdoorsy goodness, a veritable real-life Disney princess. As we spoke in the kitchen, I half expected the girls to pop in, their curiosity piqued, desperate to find out what I was up to, but they were nowhere to be seen.

A cursory half-hour chat with Brooke told me everything I needed to know about her suitability as a live-in nanny. Back home in Montreal her parents owned a nursery and she'd helped out there ever since she was small. She had a degree in Child Psychology from the University of Toronto and was in London having a couple of years out before she started teacher training. In her last position with Marina's sister she'd been more than happy to cook, clean, and run errands and was willing to do the same here. And when I told her that the girls' mum had died and that I tended to work quite long hours, her response was: 'That's fine, Mr Hope, really it is. I don't tend to have much of a social life anyway.'

'So what normally happens now?' I asked. 'I've never actually done this before. Do we need to shake hands, sign a contract, what?'

Brooke laughed. 'Well normally the thing to do right now would be to introduce me to the girls and leave us alone for a while to see how we get on.'

The girls. I'd all but forgotten the role they played in the proceedings. The last thing I needed was for Brooke not to take the job because they were being brats. 'Before you meet them I ought to tell you that they're sort of not talking to me,' I explained, hoping that honesty in this case would be the best policy. 'They blame me for their gran going off to Australia and so now I'm in the doghouse.'

Brooke was unfazed. 'That's fine,' she said, 'leave them to me.'

In the hallway I called up to the girls and after a long wait they appeared at the top of the stairs, staring down at me blankly.

'Look, I know you're mad at me but I need you to call a truce in this war you're waging against me, because there's someone here I need to—' I felt a tap on my shoulder and turned to see Brooke by my side.

She smiled at me and then she addressed the girls. 'Hi girls, I'm Brooke, and I'm a live-in nanny, which if you don't know is sort of like a cross between a big sister and a best friend. Basically your dad is thinking about hiring me, which would mean we'd be doing a lot of hanging out together. Now if we're going to be doing a lot of hanging out together we should probably hang out a bit now and see if we like each other. So what do you say, shall we take a bit of time to get to know each other?'

Evie tried hard to look unimpressed but her eyes gave away the fact that she was intrigued. Lola, however, didn't even try and put up a fight. She was completely and utterly wide-eyed and in love.

'I want to show you my room!' she said, bolting down towards Brooke.

'Lola, come back,' called Evie, fists clenched in annoyance at the sight of her one and only comrade breaking ranks. 'Remember what we talked about.'

'But that was about Dad,' pleaded Lola. 'Not about this lady, and anyway I want to show her my room.'

The conflict played out across Evie's face. As much as she wanted to punish me for supposedly sending her Gran away, at the same time she didn't want to miss out on an opportunity to show off to the cool new nanny.

Evie fixed her sister with a hard stare. 'Brooke won't want to see your room anyway, Lolls, it's full of baby stuff. She'll want to see my room first.'

Lola was scandalised. 'My room is not full of baby stuff!'

Brooke flashed them a hundred-watt smile, rendering them both silent. 'Come on, girls,' she said. 'I want to see both your rooms and we've got all the time in the world.'

Linda

It took me the best part of an hour to make it through Passport Control and collect my luggage – two large suitcases so heavy that I had to ask the young man standing next to me for help getting them off the carousel – and as I emerged through the doors into Arrivals I was hit by a wave of exhaustion. My body ached from head to toe and all I wanted to do was close my eyes and sleep, but the moment I saw Moira the weariness disappeared.

'It's so good to see you,' she cried, wrapping her arms around me. 'It's been far too long.'

'I can't believe I'm here,' I said, brimming over with emotion. 'It's so good to see you too.'

Moira had offered several times to come over to visit after Laura died but I'd always declined, telling her that I needed to concentrate on looking after the girls. So, for one reason and another, it had been over five years since we'd last seen each other in the flesh. Five years, yet she still looked amazing and seemed far more at peace with herself than when I'd seen her last, not long after she'd lost her husband. In some way she gave me hope for my own situation. If she could go through the sort of tough times she'd been through and come out smiling, then at the very least I could manage to survive six months away from my two little beans.

'I was thinking we'd stay local for the first few weeks,' said Moira as we emerged from the dimly lit underground car park into the muted light of a brand new day. 'Maybe do a little shopping and visit a few galleries, and then after that we could go to Sydney, and maybe spend a week or so there, and of course you can't come all this way and not see the Great Barrier Reef. Then there's a sunrise trip to Uluru, which I've done before and you'll love, and we just have to find the time to squeeze in a trip to Lizard Island – some of the beaches there are just to die for – and in between that we'll have to make a couple of visits to vineyards and sample some local wines. How does that sound?'

This was so typical of Moira. Even when we were young she'd always been so much more of a planner than I ever was.

'Honestly?' I replied. 'Right now it sounds amazing, if a touch overwhelming. I'm sure I'll get there eventually.'

'That's just the jet lag talking,' said Moira. 'Once you've got some rest in you, you'll be raring to go.'

Wondering what the girls might be up to, I instinctively checked my watch, forgetting that I'd changed to local time on the plane. I was so tired I wasn't even sure I was capable of doing the maths to work out the time difference and suddenly I felt disconnected from both my granddaughters and the world back home.

'You're thinking about the girls, aren't you?' said Moira.

I nodded. I couldn't think about anything else.

'It's only to be expected,' continued Moira. 'You've been so close to them this past year. It's bound to be a bit of a wrench leaving them behind for so long.'

'It feels more like having my heart ripped out and it's all the worse for the state Tom's in.'

'I thought you said you were sure he would rise to the challenge?'

'I wouldn't be here if I didn't think he would, it's just . . . I don't know . . . I wish we'd made our peace before I left. I hate feeling like we've got unfinished business.'

'If he's even half the man you've told me he is, he'll rise to the occasion,' said Moira. 'Mark my words, this'll be just the sort of kick up the backside he needs.'

I felt a lot better after Moira's pep talk and for the rest of the journey we chatted about the girls and how quickly they were growing up. Before long we'd arrived at Moira's place – a lovely ranch-style house on the outskirts of St Kilda – which, for the next six months, would be my new home.

My luggage unloaded, Moira gave me a guided tour of the house, concluding with the sweet little guest room with double bed that overlooked the garden, that was to be mine for the duration of my stay. We returned downstairs and Moira asked if I wanted anything to eat before I took a nap. Seeing my face, she laughed and said, 'You're not interested in either of those things are you? You just want to call the girls.'

Tom

I was at the kitchen table, wrangling with a supermarket Internet shop, when the phone rang. I answered it, half thinking it might be Marina wanting to hear how I'd got on with Brooke, unprepared for the idea that it might actually be Linda. Somehow I'd imagined her stuck in long-haul limbo, permanently on her way to her destination without actually arriving. At least that way I didn't have to face the prospect of telling her that she'd flown to the other side of the world in vain. Brooke had decided to take the job. We'd agreed terms and conditions an hour earlier, and now she was on her way back to Guildford to get her things. Linda's plan to redeem my soul through the joys of hands-on parenting had failed, and now a complete stranger would be looking after her grandchildren instead of her. It wasn't news I wanted to deliver to Linda in this or any other lifetime. Her reaction would be at the very top of the Richter scale. This could be the one thing she might never forgive me for.

'Linda . . . wow . . . I wasn't expecting to hear from you so quickly. The time really has flown. How are you?'

'Good, thanks. The flight was a bit rough on my old bones but it's to be expected when you get to my age. Anyway, how are you?'

'Oh, you know, hanging in there.'

'And the girls? Have you had a good day with them?'

'It's been okay, actually. We went to Rich and Marina's for lunch.'

'Oh, that sounds lovely! Rich and Marina are such sweet people. I'm sure you had a wonderful day. I'm guessing it must be early evening now in England, what are the girls up to?'

'Eating tea in front of the TV. They'll be over the moon to finally be able to talk to you. I'll go and—'

'Tom?'

'Yes?'

'Do you think you could wait a minute before you get them? It's just . . . well . . . I think we need to talk. I hate the way that we left things. We used to be so close, you and I, and it feels wrong that we're not like that any more. You must understand, Tom, my leaving wasn't personal, I wasn't trying to get at you, I was trying to help you. All I've ever wanted is for you to know the joy of looking after those two wonderful girls. Honestly, Tom, I know it might not feel like it now but I really do think this is going to be the making of—'

I couldn't take it any more. I had to come clean.

'Linda, listen . . . you're not going to like this but I think you ought to know, I've hired a live-in nanny to look after the girls.'

'You've done what?'

'She's moving in tonight and starts work first thing tomorrow.'

'Oh, Tom, please tell me this is a joke.'

'I'm sorry, but it isn't. She's really lovely though. Her name's Brooke, she's from Canada and her references are—'

Linda started to cry. 'I can't believe you, Tom,' she sobbed. 'How could you care so little about the girls to not even try?'

'What did you expect would happen when you left?' I snapped as the guilt I felt twisted into anger. 'That I'd give up my job, stay at home and play happy families? And what would we live on, fresh air?'

'Oh, Tom, do you really think I'm that stupid? I've seen your bank statements. I know exactly how much money you've got sitting in your current account from Laura's insurance payout and how long it's been sitting gathering dust. You're not working to put food on the table. You're working to hide from life. Even a whole year off work wouldn't make a dent in the pile of money you've got rotting away, let alone six months.'

She was right, at least about the insurance payout anyway. Written in the small print of the policy was a clause that I hadn't been aware we'd got, which said that if Laura or I died before the kids turned sixteen we'd receive a double payout. The insurance company ended up depositing a sum so large into my regular current account that almost weekly I received calls from my bank advising me to transfer it somewhere more suitable. It was meant to be a safety net, a means by which the surviving parent could forget about the worries of money while they looked after the children.

I tried to defend myself. 'It's not that straightforward, I—'

'Don't!' said Linda, her voice shaking with emotion. 'I don't want to hear it any more. This was meant to be your chance to get to know the girls again, to be their dad. But you don't care about that do you? All you care about is yourself. I can't tell you how disappointed I am, you've let me down more than I thought possible. And I think that if Laura could see the way you are now, she'd be sorry she ever laid eyes on you.'

8

All I want to do is go home to my babies

Tom

'We're making scrambled eggs,' said Lola excitedly as I entered the kitchen on the morning following my run-in with Linda. 'Do you want some?'

'I'd love some,' I replied, walking over to join her at the hob as Evie, too, greeted me with a hearty, 'Good morning.'

I'd set my alarm early so I could give Brooke a hand on her first day but had managed to sleep through it. When I finally woke in a panic, I'd knocked on the girls' bedroom doors but they were nowhere to be seen. It was only as I'd passed Brooke's door that I'd heard laughter coming from downstairs, and following it all the way to the kitchen, I'd stumbled into what I can only describe as a picture of domestic bliss: Lola standing on a stool next to Brooke, stirring a pan on the hob, while Evie busily buttered slices of toast. Both girls were dressed in their school uniforms and their hair was perfectly in place. I'd glanced at the kitchen clock to see that it was still only five to seven.

'Everything okay?'

Brooke smiled. 'Couldn't be better, could it, girls?'

'You do know what time it is, don't you?'

Brooke laughed. 'We started a bit early today,' she said, and gave Lola a playful wink. 'But it was fine, I was up and ready anyway so we thought we'd take the opportunity to make a special breakfast, didn't we?'

'And Evie didn't want to be left out so she joined us too,' added Lola.

'And what time was all this?' I asked, almost dreading the answer.

'Not far off five thirty,' said Brooke. 'But like I said, I was up anyway.'

I apologised profusely to Brooke and explained that it wouldn't happen again but she seemed genuine when she said she didn't mind the early start. As it was, it didn't seem to have done her any harm. She was as bright and bubbly as she had been when I'd first met her. I could only wonder how she'd be after a full day in charge of the house.

Thc reason I'd overslept that morning was in no small part due to the fact that I'd been up most of the night thinking about my argument with Linda. Her comments about Laura regretting ever meeting me had really got under my skin. Had she been right? Would Laura have been ashamed of me? That night I'd given myself a million reasons why the opposite was true. I told myself that Laura would've understood that I was only doing what was best for the girls in the long run. That she would sooner have wanted the girls to be looked after by a nice girl like Brooke than a father like me, still grappling with the grief that often threatened to overwhelm. That it wouldn't have mattered to her that I was paying someone to look after the girls so long as they were happy. Linda, I told myself, had got it all wrong. I wasn't the bad guy here. I was the victim. It was Linda who had put me in this situation. All I'd done was react.

It wasn't long before we sat down to breakfast and between mouthfuls of overcooked scrambled eggs (Lola had allowed herself to get a little distracted during the cooking proccss), the girls chatted relentlessly to Brooke. It was nice hearing them sound so happy and carefree. Had it just been me looking after them, I didn't doubt that the only conversation I'd have got out of them would have been that which I'd forcibly extracted. This change in them was all Brooke's doing. She was making them happy. And yet, despite the evidence of my eyes and ears, the longer I sat there, the more I began to wonder if perhaps Linda had been right after all. Maybe Laura would've hated the idea of me leaving our daughters with a stranger. Maybe it would have turned her stomach to see another woman in her own home being paid to feed the kids that she loved more than life. Perhaps I was letting her down after all.

'What's up, Dad?'

It was Evie's voice. I looked up to see that all eyes were on me.

'You were staring at your plate like a nutter,' said Evie.

'I was thinking about work,' I replied.

Evie yawned. 'Work's boring.'

'I know it is,' I replied. 'But someone's got to pay . . .' I allowed my voice to trail off before I condemned myself any further. 'Anyway . . .' I stood up and kissed each of the girls. 'That was a lovely breakfast but I think it's time for me to head out.'

Linda

I'd promised Moira that I'd sleep on it. No rash decisions until I'd had a good night's rest. But I didn't get one. I tossed and turned all night going over that conversation with Tom time and time again. The matter-of-factness in his voice when he told me how he'd hired some girl to look after *my* grandchildren made my blood boil. It was as if he didn't care! As if my leaving meant nothing to him. As if he genuinely believed the love and devotion I'd shown to those children was just another commodity to be bought and sold like a packet of cornflakes! I could've screamed when he told me what he'd done. I don't think I'd ever felt anger like it. I was shaking with rage by the end of the call. I'm not a violent person at all but if Tom had been within swinging distance when he'd told me his plans for the girls, he'd have been looking at a black eye. He'd crossed a line hiring a nanny and I wasn't sure there was a way back. What Tom had done wasn't fair on me and it certainly wasn't fair on those two motherless mites. I'd be damned if I was going to stand by and watch it all unfold unopposed. If it hadn't been for Moira I would've grabbed my suitcases and been on the first plane back to England, but as it was I promised her I'd sleep on it. Now it was morning, and I'd done all the waiting I could do. I needed to take action.

I put on my dressing gown, picked up my handbag from the chair next to the bed and as quietly as I could, so as not to wake Moira, made my way downstairs. In the semi-darkness I searched out the phone in the kitchen, dialled the number for the airline that I'd scribbled on the back of an old envelope, and waited. I was initially put through to one of those phone menu things and after much button pushing was eventually delivered to a real live person.

'I'd like to change the return date of my flight back to London please.'

The agent took me through a number of steps in preparation for the changes I wanted to make and for a moment I thought, 'Oh, here I was worrying it was going to be complicated and actually it's no problem at all,' but then she asked what day I wanted to fly.

'I'm afraid we need at least forty-eight hours minimum for a ticket change,' she said. 'If you want to be on this afternoon's flight to Heathrow you'll have to buy a new ticket altogether.'

I asked her how much it would cost and was horrified. It was as though they'd picked a four-figure number out of thin air. It was twice what I'd paid for my return ticket. I even checked to see if she'd misheard and put me down for first class instead of economy. She hadn't.

'That's daylight robbery,' I protested. 'All I want to do is go home to my babies. Isn't there anything cheaper?'

'Not for another forty-eight hours,' she replied. 'Would you like me to make the booking?'

'Yes, I would,' I said stubbornly. I was getting on that flight even if it cost me all of my savings.

She took me through the booking procedure and I began to relax. It might cost me a small fortune but soon I'd be back with my girls where I belonged. Finally she asked for my credit card details. I dug around in my bag and brought out my purse but the card wasn't in it. I tipped out the entire contents of my bag, then asked the operator to hold while I began frantically searching, trying to remember the last time that I'd seen it. I was sure I hadn't used it at all since I'd left England. It made no sense for it to be missing when the rest of my cards and money were still safe in my purse. But it wasn't where it should have been.

'I took it out of your bag last night.'

I turned around. Moira, dressed in her nightgown, was standing in the doorway, a look of steely determination on her face.

'You did what?'

'I had to. I know you'd do absolutely anything for those girls but if you go back now it'll be a mistake.'

'I can't leave them in the charge of a complete stranger.'

'But if you go back now, nothing will change. You've said yourself, Tom needs to face up to his responsibilities. If you go rushing back over there you won't be giving him the time or space to do that.'

'I can't think about any of that right now. All that matters is the girls. I should never have left them. If something happened to them, I'd never forgive myself.'

'They'll be fine. Tom's not a monster. He's not going to leave them with just anyone. I think at the very least you should give him a couple of weeks to figure things out for himself.'

'And what if he doesn't?'

'Then I'll pay for your ticket and drive you to the airport myself.'

My head felt like it was spinning. Everything Moira said made sense and yet I still had to fight the instinct to rush home with all my strength. 'I just want to do what's best for everyone.'

'Then stay here, be strong and we'll wait it out together.'

Tom

That first week with Brooke looking after the girls went by without a hitch. Most evenings I'd call from work, usually after the kids had eaten their tea, and ask how the day had been. Brooke would give me a recap of what the girls had been up to, and with my conscience appeased, I'd head out to dinner with colleagues or clients and not return home until late. Usually there would be a little note waiting for me on the kitchen counter from Brooke, telling me that the girls had gone to bed okay and informing me of any money she'd needed to spend. Depending on my mood, I'd either just scribble a smiley face on her note or jot down a few lines thanking her for her hard work. On the night of my return from my trip to Amsterdam, I wrote practically an entire side of A4 telling her what sterling work she was doing, but then thought better of it. It sounded too much like I was compensating for the fact that I hadn't seen my kids all week, and so I tossed it in the bin and scribbled a smiley face on the note she'd left, along with the words, 'Thanks so much! You really are indispensible!'

On the Friday, I failed to make it home at all. With *The Big Night Out* returning to the TV schedules on Saturday night, I got my PA to book me into a hotel just in case I was needed in the studio. No such need arose, and for the most part all I did that weekend was drink coffee and tell the team they were doing an excellent job. Still, it gave me what I suppose I wanted: a place to hide and a reason to believe that my absence from the family home was somehow for the greater good.

At the beginning of the second week of the new regime, Marina called. I was at work at the time, down at the studio watching a run-through for a new segment for *The Big Night Out*. Although I had a few notes, the piece as a whole went well, and I'd been about to call over the team and run through my ideas when my phone rang. As I prepared to speak to her, I recalled that she'd rung some days earlier and I'd neglected to get back to her. Only now did it cross my mind that perhaps my failure to return her call had more to do with wanting to keep her in the dark about how little I had to do with running my own family than it had with being too busy to make a five-minute phone call.

'Hi, Marina, you okay? Sorry about not getting back to you last week. Been rushed off my feet.'

'I can imagine. Rich and I watched the show with the kids. We thought it was amazing. Were you pleased?'

'Absolutely. We smashed last year's opener by a mile: 6.2 million viewers and a 36.8 per cent share.'

'That sounds incredible. Well done you. You must be over the moon.'

She was right, I should have been. I'd worked harder on that show than any other I'd ever been involved with over the past year, and yet even as colleagues started popping champagne corks and patting me on the back when the viewing figures came in, it was impossible to escape the emptiness of it all.

'I'm really pleased with how it went.'

Marina laughed. 'That's so like you, always underplaying your achievements. You should let me and Rich take you out to celebrate. You need to be made a fuss of.'

'Thanks,' I replied, even though I didn't agree. 'That's really kind of you.'

'Anyway, Mr Big TV exec,' said Marina. 'As much as I love hearing about how well you're doing at work, that's not the reason I'm calling. I want to hear all about how you've been getting on with Brooke. She's amazing, isn't she?'

'She's like a Canadian Snow White.'

'And do the girls like her?'

'They love her.'

'I knew they would. She's just so bouncy and full of life. Freya's kids thought she was the best thing since—'

'I think I'm going to have to let her go.' I hadn't known I was going to say those words until they'd actually left my mouth, but now that they were out there I realised I'd probably been wanting to say them from the moment I handed Brooke her own set of keys. Linda was right: I hadn't been fair to her, the girls or Laura's memory.

'What's wrong, Tom? Has something happened?'

'Yes . . . no . . . look, I'd better go but I promise I'll call you later and explain everything.'

Brooke and the girls were upstairs when I arrived home from work that evening. I could hear Lola, who was getting ready for bed, calling for help finding her pyjamas and Evie was telling Brooke about a girl getting told off in class. For a moment I thought about going up to surprise them, as they clearly hadn't heard me come in, but then I thought about the conversation I needed to have with Brooke and decided that I'd leave it a while. Instead, I went to the kitchen and poured myself a glass of water and as I did so, out of the corner of my eye, I spotted a pile of things on the kitchen counter that Brooke must have collected together as she'd been tidying. On the top was the day's mail but right at the bottom was the gift-wrapped present Linda had given me at the airport before she left. I'd all but forgotten its existence, having lost track of it from the moment I'd discarded it in the kitchen. I'd assumed it to be somewhere underneath the growing pile of unread newspapers and magazines lurking at the end of the kitchen table but I hadn't been at all sure. Now, with nothing better to do, I picked it up and ripped open the wrapping paper. Inside, was a brand new family calendar for the year ahead. I could only presume that Linda had wrapped it so carefully and presented it to me to make some sort of point about responsibility – a message I'd been determined would fall on deaf ears. I walked over to the calendar on the wall, took it down and replaced it with the new one, but rather than throwing the old one into the recycling I sat and flicked through it. It was page after page of school assemblies and sleepovers, dental appointments and birthday parties, school trips and family holidays, ballet recitals and family outings. It was a year-long register of all the moments I'd never been part of; an inventory of all the time I'd missed with my growing daughters; but most of all it was proof of just how far I'd fallen and how much I'd let my poor Laura down. The hiding from my family, the fear of responsibility, the giving in to grief: it all had to stop now. Linda was right, this year-long pity party I'd thrown for myself had to end.

I broke the news about Brooke to the girls the following evening, after coming to an arrangement with her to stay on for the few days until I'd left work, in return for an extra month's pay.

'But who'll look after us when Brooke's gone?' Lola asked.

'Me,' I replied, sitting her down on my lap. 'I'm going to look after you just like Mum used to.'

'And you'll take me to school?'

'And pick you up afterwards too.'

Evie laughed as though it was the most ridiculous proposition she'd ever heard. 'What? And you'll make dinner and help me with my homework?'

'And wash your games kit, sew missing buttons back on your school uniform and do the ironing,' I added. 'Everything Mum and Nanny used to do for you I'm going to do from now on. No childminders, cleaners, nothing.'

'But how will you do all that and go to work?' asked Evie.

'I won't,' I replied. 'I'll be here.'

'You mean you've given up your job?'

Martin had been incredible when I told him I needed time off. He would have been well within his rights to subject me to one of his legendary, temple-throbbing tirades, given that one of his biggest shows was now without an executive producer. As it was, all he said was, 'It's been a long time coming,' and offered to pay for me to go and see his Harley Street shrink, an offer I politely declined. He suggested I take a year off, starting from that afternoon; I told him I only needed half that time and wanted to see out the next two shows, just to make sure everything was going smoothly. In the end we compromised and agreed that Saturday would be my last show, and as for my return, we'd talk when Linda was back from Australia.

'I've taken what's called a sabbatical,' I explained to Evie. 'It's sort of like an unpaid holiday from work. I'll be going into the office for the rest of the week, just to make sure everyone knows what they're doing, and then as of this coming Sunday I'll be here for good.'

'But if you're not working, what will we do for money? Are we going to be poor? Will I still get my allowance?'

'We'll be more than okay for money,' I replied, barely able to conceal a smirk. 'And yes, your allowance will be safe. Right now though, the really important question isn't about money. It's about whether you guys think I can actually pull this off. So what do you think? Has Dad got what it takes to look after you both until Nanny comes back?'

The girls looked at each other and shrugged. I had my answer, or at least the closest thing I was going to get to one. They weren't sure I could do this and truth be told, neither was I. The whole thing was a gamble and the stakes didn't get any higher, but it was this or nothing. Well, I'd tried 'nothing' – I'd given up for a whole year and more in its pursuit – and that had resulted in me having a criminal record. The only real option left was to give being a dad everything I'd got and hope that, somewhere along the way, I got lucky.

Linda

I cried when Tom told me the good news. I sobbed so much I thought I'd never stop. Every time I opened my mouth to tell him how proud I was of him, how relieved I felt or even how much I regretted all the horrible things I'd said to him, all I could do was cry. But I think he knew what I was trying to say. In fact I know he did, because through his own tears he kept saying over and over again, 'I won't let her down this time, Linda, I promise I won't. Whatever it takes, I'll make Laura proud of me.'

PART TWO

'Everything depends on upbringing.'

– *Leo Tolstoy, War and Peace*

9

It's about boys

Tom

It was half past eight on my first morning of looking after the girls on my own, and I was firing on all cylinders. So far I'd emptied the drier twice, put on two loads of washing, ironed the girls' school uniforms, taken Evie's temperature to work out if she was telling the truth about being ill (she wasn't), made breakfast, helped Evie with her chemistry homework (hence the faking being ill), all before waving her off to school. After that, I'd helped Lola with a painting of Henry VIII, ironed a new school top to replace the one she'd managed to spill black paint down, and now all I needed to do was finish making Lola's sandwiches and I'd be all but done for the morning rush.

As I picked up the large bread knife to slice through a cheese, ham and Branston pickle sandwich, Lola came and stood next to me, carefully watching my every move.

'You okay?'

She nodded.

'Are you sure?'

She nodded again and watched intently as I cut the sandwich into quarters, carefully wrapped it in cling film and then placed it inside her diamante kitten lunch bag along with a tangerine, a bottle of water and two jaffa cakes.

'There, all done,' I said, zipping up the lunch bag with a satisfied flourish, and checked the clock on the front of the oven. All my morning jobs finished with time to spare. I was absolutely rocking this parenting thing.

'Dad?'

I looked down at Lola, her brow wrinkled in a disconcerting fashion. 'Yes, sweetheart?'

'Who are those sandwiches for?'

I laughed. 'You mean the cheese, ham and Branston ones that I just put in your kitten lunch bag?' She nodded, oblivious to my sarcasm. 'You, sweetie.'

'Oh,' she replied. Lola had always been mistress of the understated. 'Oh.' It was sort of her trademark way of letting me know I'd made a mistake.

'Why "Oh"?'

'Nothing.'

'Are you sure?'

She nodded. 'I know you're only trying your best, Daddy.'

Now I was absolutely certain I'd messed up somehow.

'What have I done?'

She sighed heavily. 'It's the sandwiches,' she said. 'I like them cut in triangles not squares. I can eat squares though, it's just that I like triangles.'

I unzipped the lunch bag and stared at the contents. Whenever I used to make the girls their Sunday tea time snacks, Laura would always remind me how the girls liked their sandwiches and I'd roll my eyes as if to say, 'Does it really matter?' But it did matter, at least to her it did anyway. Details were everything to her.

I fished the sandwiches out of her lunch bag, put them aside and began buttering another slice of bread.

Lola wrinkled her nose and looked at me. 'What are you doing?'

'Making you a new sandwich.'

'But you don't need to. Square taste just the same as triangles.'

'I'm not sure you're right about that,' I replied. 'Square sandwiches don't taste anywhere near as nice as triangular ones. I know this for a fact because when you're a grown-up like me, they make you eat square sandwiches all the time, only children get to eat triangular ones.'

Lola laughed. 'That's not true, Nanny used to eat the triangle ones too.'

'That was because she had a special licence from the Queen saying it was okay. That's why I don't eat them. A friend of mine at work once ate one of the triangle ones and the very next day the police took him to the Tower of London.' I smiled. 'I'll make you your triangular sandwiches, sweetie, but only so that you don't get arrested, okay?'

Once I was done making the sandwich, I double-checked it for any further potential sources of disappointment, packed it away in Lola's lunch bag and handed it to her.

'Happy?'

She nodded.

'Good,' I replied. 'Because we really have got to go.'

Given how late we already were for school, we probably should've run the whole way but the thing was I couldn't remember the last time it had been just Lola and me walking to school. Not for a long time, if at all, and it seemed wrong somehow to rush this moment rather than savour it.

'Is your favourite colour still yellow?' I asked as we sauntered hand in hand down the road as if we had all the time in the world.

'Yellow and then pink and then green,' replied Lola, pulling on the tassels of her rucksack absentmindedly. 'But yellow is definitely best.'

'And how about your favourite book? Is it still *Charlotte's Web*?'

Lola shrugged. 'I still like it lots but my favourites are the *Famous Five* books. Before Nanny left she'd just finished reading the first *Harry Potter* to me and that was really good too.'

'And what about friends? Have you got a best one?'

'I've got hundreds,' she replied. 'I'm easily the most popular girl at school.'

'That's good,' I said. I could just recall a handful of names from various birthday parties that I'd taken her to on Saturday mornings past. 'How's Lucy?'

'She's okay.'

'And . . . what was the name of your friend who really liked football?'

'Parminder.'

'That's the one.'

'She's okay too.'

'So out of all of your hundreds of friends, who are your really, really, really best friends?'

'Do you want me to list them all?'

'Not if you don't want to.'

'If you really want to know there's Amelia, Poppy, Abigail and Skye. We play skipping games every lunchtime and everyone wants to play with us.'

'And do you let them?'

She shrugged. 'Sometimes.'

Despite my concerns about being late, we arrived at school with time to spare and as I entered the playground, crowded as it was with parents and their offspring, I was struck by the knowledge that I was officially the new kid on the block. I didn't know anything about this world and I didn't know any of its inhabitants either. I was the veritable fish out of water and the only guide I had to help me was an eight-year-old girl who, even at the best of times, was never all that sure what was going on around her.

'We need to put my sandwiches away,' said Lola, pointing in the direction of a wooden locker where children were casually abandoning their lunch bags with complete disregard for their contents. She took my hand and I followed her, nodding and smiling uncomfortably along the way to parents whom I vaguely recognised. There was the trendy red-haired mum who Laura used to say gossiped madly; the tall Indian dad in the turban who lived six doors down and his three identical daughters; the new age mum with the prematurely grey hair who used to teach Laura's yoga class down at the local leisure centre. It was probably in my head – after all, I wasn't that interesting – but I couldn't help feeling that they were all registering my presence in a way that made it clear that I was something out of the ordinary, something to be noticed. Something denoting change.

'Right then,' I said as we dropped off her lunch bag, just as the morning bell rang. 'Have you got everything you need for today?'

Lola nodded and I kissed the top of her head. 'Have a good day, sweetie.'

She smiled and said, 'You too, Dad.'

As children from across the playground began filing into school, I stood watching Lola as she made her way towards her form room. Compared to the other kids in her class, she seemed so small and fragile that it took all the strength I had not to pick her up and take her back home. How could a child so small not have a mother? How could it possibly be fair that someone who didn't even know their eight times table should know the meaning of death?

Linda

It was the beginning of my third week in Australia, and Moira and I were sitting on the terrace of a posh seafood restaurant, watching the late summer sun dapple the surface of the Yarra

River. We were both wearing expensive new frocks that we'd bought that very morning at a chic designer outlet in Melbourne along with the new heels we'd bought to match from an upmarket department store. We were even wearing new jewellery too (a silver bracelet for me and gold necklace for Moira) purchased from the same store. In fact, since Tom had agreed to take responsibility for the girls, I'd made it my business to try and let my hair down, relax and enjoy myself. After all, here I was halfway around the world with no responsibilities at all, able to do what I wanted, when I wanted. So far Moira and I had shopped ourselves silly and treated ourselves to spa days where we'd been rubbed, scrubbed, bathed and polished. We'd breakfasted at sweet little cafés overlooking the sea and long-lunched at highly commended restaurants in the city. We'd spoiled ourselves rotten but the reality was, though I was trying very hard, I wasn't enjoying any of it, a fact Moira confronted me with as we ate dinner that evening.

'You're not happy are you?' Moira speared a plump, juicy prawn from her seafood paella and popped it into her mouth, all the time eyeing me with measured suspicion.

'Oh, I am,' I replied. 'It's such a lovely restaurant, just look at these views.'

'I'm not talking about the restaurant, I'm talking about being here in Oz.'

I sighed heavily. 'Am I that obvious?'

Moira smiled. 'I've known you since you were twenty, Linda, you don't have to be obvious. I'm guessing you're still finding it difficult without the grandkids?'

It felt ungrateful to admit it out loud and so I simply nodded. 'I was just thinking to myself that about now, Tom would be taking Lola to school for the first time. I just hope they get on okay.'

'It's a walk to school,' said Moira. 'How hard can it be?'

'I'm being ridiculous, aren't I?' I replied, 'It's just that I can't seem to stop missing the girls. I try really hard not to. I keep telling myself that they're with their dad and that I've got nothing to worry about, but it doesn't seem to make any difference.'

'And why would it?' asked Moira. 'Of course it's great that your son-in-law is back to being a dad again, but none of that addresses the fact that you've played a huge role in the girls' lives this past year. That's an almost impossible role to walk away from. The fact that you did is an absolute credit to you.'

'I'm not so sure about that,' I replied. 'It wasn't as though I had much of a choice, and anyway it wasn't my role to take on in the first place really. But you're right, being part of their lives this past year has meant everything to me. You know how it is, the older you get the more you feel you have to fight to find your place in the world. Back in England, I've got friends who never quite recovered from their families growing up and leaving home. It's almost as if once you've raised a family that's all you're ever going to be content doing.'

'I felt that way for a long time after Peter died,' said Moira. 'It had been Peter and me – us – against the world for such a long time, and then suddenly, overnight, it wasn't. I was back to being the version of myself I was before I met him, and the truth is I didn't know who that person was any more. I didn't know how to be by myself, and I think that's the problem you've got too. You've got to learn how to be the Linda you were before you started looking after the girls.'

'But even then I was still Laura's mum, and anything before that feels like a lifetime ago.'

'It's hard, I know,' said Moira, putting a comforting hand on my arm, 'believe me, I've been there, and at times I'm sure you'll think it's nigh on impossible, but you have to keep trying to move on, because if you don't, you could end up stuck in the past for good.'

It was late when we reached home. I joined Moira in the kitchen for a cup of tea. She looked thoughtful and I wondered for a moment whether anything was wrong.

'Are you okay?'

'Me? I'm fine. It's you I'm worried about. I so wanted you to have a wonderful time here and you seem more down than you were before you arrived.'

'I know, I'm sorry. I really am grateful. I just need to snap out of it, that's all.'

Moira shook her head. 'That's not what you need. What you need is something nice to look forward to. Like a party.'

I didn't like the sound of that at all.

'A party? What kind of party?'

'A "Welcome to Oz" party,' she replied. 'We'll get lots of food and drinks in and I'll invite all my friends and get them to bring their friends along too and you'll be the guest of honour. What do you think?'

It sounded like a terrible idea, the kind that would normally have had me running for the hills. Parties always make me feel tense, like it's my own fault if I'm not having a good time. A party held in my honour would be my worst nightmare.

'I think it's a great idea,' I replied, unwilling to let Moira down after how wonderful she'd been these past weeks. 'I think a party is just what I need.'

I went to sleep that night thinking up ways I might be able to escape having to attend. The following morning I awoke fresh from a continuous stream of party-related anxiety dreams, the most recent of which involved me taking guests' coats and handing them champagne, only to realise halfway through the evening that I was naked from the waist down.

As much as I wanted to, I didn't bother trying to go back to sleep as I was so desperate to call home and hear all about

Tom's first day of being properly in charge of the girls. I wanted to hear about every detail of it. I didn't want him to leave out a single thing. At the same time, however, I didn't want Tom thinking I was checking up on him, because I wasn't at all. This was my dilemma. A dilemma I decided to get around by calling Tom under the pretext of having something of a senior moment.

'Hello, Tom, it's me.'

'Hi, Linda, is everything okay? You weren't due to call until Friday.'

'That's right, I wasn't, was I? Silly me, I think I must still be adjusting to the time difference. I know it's been a while but I still don't know whether I'm coming or going really, half the time. Oh, well, I'm here now so I might as well make the most of it. I hope you don't mind.'

'Of course not,' said Tom. 'The kids and I have just finished tea and I'm just clearing up.'

'What did you have?'

'Partially burnt cottage pie and vegetables. I think I had the oven on a little too high. Still, it's only my first day.'

'Oh, of course it is. It completely slipped my mind. Did it go well?'

'A few teething problems but on the whole it went okay.'

'That's wonderful news, Tom, it really is. And how lucky is it that I called today of all days? I want to hear absolutely everything about your day, don't leave anything out.'

Tom

It was half an hour before Linda had finished grilling me about my day, and another half an hour before the girls were done talking to her. Before the call, I'd promised Lola that I'd read with her before bed – something I hadn't done since before

Laura died – but it was long after her bedtime now, and the last thing I wanted was to keep her up any later.

'I'm afraid we're going to have to give stories a miss tonight,' I explained as Lola climbed into bed. 'It's late and you need to get your rest.'

'Can't we even have a small one? Just a few pages, not even a whole chapter.'

I could feel my resolve crumbling.

'Have you got a book in mind that you want to read?'

'I don't mind,' she replied. 'You can choose whatever you like.'

Climbing off her bed, I knelt down in front of Lola's bookshelf and scanned the titles. Laura had been adamant that the kids should grow up with a love of the written word and when she was pregnant with Evie, it seemed like every other week she would arrive home with yet another children's classic that she'd picked up on her travels. This bookshelf was Laura at her most considered and thoughtful, books for every occasion and to suit every mood, covering everything from *The Gruffalo* to *Treasure Island*.

'How about this?' I said, plucking *The Lion the Witch and the Wardrobe* from the shelves.

'Nanny and me read it over the summer,' she replied. 'It's really good. Aslan is my favourite.'

I tried again, *Just William* by Richmal Crompton, I'd loved those books as a boy. Maybe Lola would like them too.

'It's about boys,' she said, pulling a face.

'What's wrong with boys?'

Lola rolled her eyes. 'What's right with them?'

Finally I spotted *Maltida* by Roald Dahl. Not only had it been one of Laura's all-time favourite books, but the copy on the shelf was the actual one she'd read when she was Lola's age. I'd found my winner. I showed the book to Lola.

'I really liked *The BFG*,' she said as I showed her the book. 'So this one might be good too.'

I agreed, and retracing my steps to the bed I was about to sit down when, for the first time since entering her room, I noticed something odd on her bedside table. It was a Clark's shoebox, resting on its side and the inside of it had been painted bright yellow. The remarkable thing about it, however, was that glued to the back and sides were photos of Laura, ones which I was pretty sure had once resided in the photo albums that lived on the bookshelves in the living room. In the centre of the box, propped up on a handful of cotton wool balls, was a photo of Laura with Lola and Evie. They were sitting on the sofa in the kitchen with their arms wrapped around each other. I was lost for words. When had Lola made this thing? How long had it lived on her bedside table? Had she made it on her own or had Linda helped her? And what exactly did it mean that she felt the need to make it in the first place?

Seeing me notice the box, Lola placed her hands on my face, forcibly turning my head away from it.

'Daddy, don't look!' she said, clearly worried that I was about to tell her off.

'Sweetie, you're not in trouble,' I replied, putting my arm around her. 'It's just that I've never seen it before. It's lovely. Did you make it yourself?'

Lola nodded. 'I know I should have checked before I borrowed the pictures but I really wanted to do it. I made it the night that Nanny left. I was really missing Mummy and I thought it might make me feel better.'

'And does it?'

Half biting her lip, she nodded shyly and turned the box around so that I could see it properly. 'They're all my favourite pictures of Mum.' She pointed to each one in turn. 'That was when she was at university the first time round, that one was when you and Mum got married, that one is the first picture she ever let me take with her camera, and the big one in the middle is the one we took at Christmas when Santa brought me my blue bike.' She stopped pointing and looked at me. 'Do you like it?'

'It's absolutely amazing.' Every word I spoke caught in my throat. 'I think Mummy would've liked it very much. I think she would've thought it was the best thing in the world.'

10

By all means, fire away

Tom

It was the Friday morning of my first week in charge of the girls, and as I dropped Lola off at school it occurred to me that I'd been through something of a baptism of fire. Thanks to the family calendar, so far that week I'd remembered to take Lola for her swimming lesson (but forgotten to bring her swimming kit); got her to her piano lesson but somehow managed to get hopelessly lost on the way to ballet; and spent a bewildering hour and a half listening to a talk about GCSE options at Evie's school. While the family calendar had initially seemed too resolutely twentieth-century for my tech-head tastes, it had proved itself invaluable. As well as helping me keep track of school meetings and the girls' extra-curricular activities, it had stopped me from missing countless appointments and reminded me of bills I'd needed to pay. At work I'd had a PA who'd helped me with this sort of thing, but now I just had the calendar and I couldn't imagine life without it.

Waving goodbye to Lola, I turned around and began weaving my way through the parent crush. Thanks again to the family calendar, I was on my way to a 9.15 a.m. appointment at the bank, to find a better home for the insurance money that was still sitting earning nothing in my current account, when I looked up to see a woman smiling in my direction. She was in her late thirties, had short, brown hair cut into a neat bob, and was wearing a blue jacket, jeans and tan boots. A small child's scooter dangled from her right hand. I had no idea who this woman was but she certainly seemed to think she knew me, and when she noticed me noticing her she came over and spoke to me.

'It's Tom, isn't it?' she said. 'I'm Ellie, Ellie Sallucci. I was friends with Laura. Your Evie and my Stella used to be in reception together.'

'Pleased to meet you,' I replied. Her name definitely rang a bell but I couldn't remember much that Laura had said about her, other than she was part of the group of mums that she used to see quite a bit before she went back to university.

'I've seen you in the playground all week,' she continued, 'and I've been trying to pluck up the courage to ask you if everything's okay. It's just that I know your mother-in-law used to do the school run, didn't she, and then last week and the week before it was a young blonde girl, and now you're suddenly here? I hope you don't think I'm being nosey.'

'Everything's fine,' I explained, wondering if she really was concerned about me or just on the look out for playground gossip. 'Linda's gone on holiday to Australia for a much-needed break and it's coincided with me deciding to be a stay-at-home dad for a while. We had a little bit of help to begin with but now it's just me.'

It was the truth, or at least as close an approximation of it as she was going to get in the crowded confines of the school playground.

'A full-time stay-at-home dad, you say? That's impressive. It's all I can do to get my husband to even remember our kids' names.' She laughed self-consciously and then her expression changed to one of embarrassment. I'd seen it happen a million times before: people feeling bad at making light of life in front of the man who'd lost his wife.

'I don't know what got into me,' she said. 'Of course, your situation's different. Laura was such an amazing woman. You must still miss her awfully.'

'I do,' I replied. 'I really do.'

We spoke for a little while longer, mostly about her daughter and the son whose scooter she was holding, and then the conversation seemed to come to a natural close and we parted ways. I'd only taken a few steps away from her, however, when she called out after me and I stopped and turned around.

'I was just wondering,' she began. 'I'm sure Linda's filled you in on everything you need to know about school, but if there are any gaps in your knowledge I'd be more than happy to help fill you in, if you'd like. Maybe we could go grab a coffee one day after drop-off or before pick up and I can tell you how this place really works.'

Linda

It was Saturday in Australia and finally, after three hours preparing food, two hours spent at the hairdresser's and three changes of outfit (the first one, picked by Moira, proved a little too outré for my tastes and the second, chosen by me, was rejected by Moira for being too conservative), the night of Moira's party was finally upon us. Despite my anxiety dreams and initial hesitations, now that it was here I was rather glad about it. I'd felt quite shy to begin with, especially as Moira insisted on telling her friends that the party was in my honour. Time and again I was asked what had brought me to Australia, and even if their eyes weren't glazing over listening to me jabbering on, mine certainly were, repeating a potted version of my life story over and over again. Moira's friends, however – a mix of British ex-pats and dyed-in-the-wool Aussies in their fifties and sixties – were a fun crowd to be around and their laid-back attitude to life was infectious. Eventually, with the help of a few gin and tonics, my own inhibitions gave way to the idea of letting my hair down and having fun.

It had been such a long time since I'd properly let go in a social situation, so long, in fact, that I couldn't remember the last time. So much of my life had been about responsibility and doing the right thing, whether as a daughter, a teacher, a parent or even a grandmother. Of course, I didn't resent the sacrifices I'd made in life as a young single mum or the years spent looking after my elderly parents, these were simply the things you did for love. But still, there was no doubting that they'd taken their toll over the years. When Laura was young she used to say that I needed to learn how to have fun, and my reply was always the same, 'That's why I had you, so you can teach me.' Bless her, she never did tire of encouraging me to let loose once in a while, but I was never very good at it. I think the thing is, once you get used to keeping it all buttoned up, it's difficult to get your head around the idea that you're allowed to undo your collar from time to time.

But here on the other side of the world, with a drink in my hand and no one to look after but myself, I completely forgot about my usual sense of reserve. It was quite freeing actually. I was chatting with anyone who came within a few feet of me, telling anecdotes that made people laugh out loud, singing along to the music of my youth and dancing like a demon. A few people said I was the life and soul of the party, but I'm not sure I'd go that far. That said, I'm sure if the girls had been around (Evie especially) they would've been mortified to witness me, their grandmother, acting like I hadn't a care in the world. It was like being eighteen all over again. This was my night off being boring old Linda who worried about everything. Tonight was my night to suck the marrow from life, consequences be damned.

This, I think, more than explains how at midnight I found myself with Moira outside on the deck, dancing on the patio table to the Monkees' 'I'm a Believer'. I'd always loved that song when I was young. I used to put the seven-inch on my little Dansette and bop around my bedroom to it over and over again.

Anyway, Moira and I had been outside grabbing a spot of fresh air when it had come on the stereo, and just hearing those few opening bars made me feel as light as air. I grabbed Moira's hand and said, 'Let's dance on the table!' and she laughed, thinking I wasn't serious. I decided to show her I meant business and, buoyed by one gin and tonic too many, I kicked off my shoes, stood on one of the garden chairs and clambered up on to the table. Once we were up there, Moira and I could barely stand up straight because we were laughing so hard, and soon everyone at the party joined us outside, dancing and clapping to the music. Everything would have been okay had I not got carried away joining in with the chorus. I lurched backwards, completely losing my balance, and toppled off the table. It was one of those moments when everything suddenly went into slow motion. All I could think was, 'You silly old woman! What are you doing dancing on a table at your time of life? This is going to put you in hospital!' I was almost certain that when I hit the floor it wouldn't just be a question of cuts and bruises but of broken bones. I thought about my travel insurance, and whether it would be enough to cover the treatment I'd need, and imagined myself having to be flown home with my legs and arms in casts like someone out of a *Laurel and Hardy* film. But instead of hitting the decking and breaking my bones, a pair of arms appeared as if from the ether and caught me in mid-air. When I looked up, I saw a bearded man with smiling green eyes looking back at me.

'Pleased to meet you,' he said. 'The name's Desi.'

Tom

Partway through my second week in charge of the girls, it occurred to me that perhaps it might be a good idea to take Ellie up on her offer to explain the confusing world of primary education to me. It seemed like a day didn't go by without a letter home from school, or an email in my inbox, asking me to attend or contribute in some way towards an event or task that I didn't quite understand. What, for example, was 'Woodcraft Week'? Where exactly did they expect me to get half a dozen jam jars from by the middle of next week, and what did they want them for? And should I have offered to help out on the Year 4 theatre trip to see *Charlie and the Chocolate Factory* when the truth was I could only just about look after my own children, let alone anyone else's? I needed to know the answers to these questions and more, and so at the end of that week I turned up at the school gates an hour early for pick-up, as agreed, to meet up with Ellie.

I felt distinctly odd as Ellie and I walked from the school gates to the High Street, and I wondered if she did too. I'd never been much of a one for having women as friends even when I was younger, and certainly not since I'd been married. It seemed wrong somehow to be walking along, making small talk with an attractive married woman who wasn't a work colleague or for that matter even a friend.

'Am I right in thinking you were working in TV before you decided to stay at home with your kids?'

'That's right,' I replied. 'I was exec producer for Pluto Productions.'

'Would I have seen anything you've made?'

I reeled off the names of half a dozen shows, leaving *The Big Night Out* until last. As much as I loved that show, I hated the idea that people thought it was the only thing I'd ever done.

Ellie seemed impressed. 'I've seen all of those! And you were responsible for helping to make them?'

'Actually, I came up with the original format for a couple of them.'

'That sounds so exciting. Far more exciting than the boring old work I do.'

'What is it you do?'

'I'm an accountant by trade, although at the moment I'm working three days – depending on the week – as a financial controller for a firm of solicitors in Bromley. That's why I couldn't make all those days you suggested. Nothing to do with having a diary packed with glamorous events like yours is, I'm sure.'

'Not any more,' I corrected. 'These days it's mostly swimming and music lessons and taking overdue books back to the library.'

'And do you miss work?'

This was the first time anyone had asked me this question and it took me by surprise. 'Do you know what?' I said as I reflected on the past few weeks. 'I don't think I do.'

Ellie laughed, clearly unconvinced. 'Is that you being politically correct? Or is it that it's still a novelty for you?'

'I suppose it is, to a degree,' I replied. 'Everything still feels new and I'm still getting my bearings whereas with work—'

'—the novelty was wearing off?'

'You could put it that way.'

'And how would you put it?'

'I don't know,' I considered. 'I think sometimes you just wake up and realise that there are more important things in life.'

At the café, I ordered drinks and a slice of carrot cake each while Ellie found a table. By the time I joined her, she'd brought up the school calendar on her phone. She proceeded to take me through everything on it, from the annual decorate-an-egg competition ('It always seems to come out of nowhere and it's always a complete pain in the arse.'), through to the school fair ('You'll be able to get away with a bought cake because you're a man, but even if you do happen to be a good baker keep it to yourself, otherwise you'll get roped in for everything and I do mean *everything*.'). There was so much I didn't know. So much I hadn't even known I *needed* to know. Not for the first time in the past few weeks, I wondered how Laura kept on top of all she did without going crazy.

Ellie concluded her guided tour of the school year and I thanked her. 'I'd never have known what to look out for in a million years.'

'I didn't either, to begin with,' she said. 'It's one of the things people forget to tell you when your kids start school: just how much you have to be on top of everything. Sometimes it feels like a full-time job. Sometimes it actually is!'

With the school stuff out of the way, to kill time Ellie told me about herself. She was originally from Buckinghamshire, by way of Gloucester, and had moved to London at nineteen to go to university, where she met her husband Marco. They'd married three years after she graduated, and moved to Reigate not long after the birth of their daughter. She told me Marco worked long hours during the week and at the weekend tended to be too tired to spend time with the family, but she said it in such a resigned manner that I couldn't help thinking that he sounded like a bit of a loser, until it occurred to me that up to a couple of weeks ago I'd been just like him.

It was after three when we left the café. And although I'd enjoyed our time together I was glad that it was coming to a close. As much as Ellie was easy-going and chatty, I found it hard to get my head around spending time like this with another man's wife. I'm not sure I'd have liked Laura becoming friends with some lonely single dad any more than Laura would've liked me hanging out with the scores of young, pretty female graduates that came through Pluto Productions' trainee scheme. It might seem boring to some people, but I was a great believer in keeping things as straightforward as possible, if only because nine times out of ten doing anything else ends up making life distinctly more complicated.

We were only a few hundred yards from the school gates when Ellie broke off from the school gossip she'd been telling me and out of nowhere, without the slightest preamble, asked me if I'd started dating yet. The moment she saw the reaction on my face (which to be honest was more bemusement than offence) she apologised wildly.

'I'm such an idiot! Please ignore me.'

'It's fine, really it is.'

'Of course it isn't fine. It's none of my business. I don't know what I was thinking.'

'You were making conversation and to be honest it's a fair question. More than anything, I'm disappointed by how dull my answer is, which is: no, I'm not seeing anyone.'

'Well, of course not, it's still early days.'

'It's not that, exactly.'

'So what is it?' She covered her mouth quickly, her face the very picture of embarrassment. 'I'm doing it again! What's wrong with me? It's like I've got a nosey version of Tourettes – asking people I barely know questions about their personal lives. You must regret ever speaking to me.'

'I wouldn't go that far . . . seriously, it's fine to ask questions, in fact it's a bit of a relief to be around someone not treating me like I'm made of glass. The truth is I haven't started dating, simply because I can't see the point. I hit the jackpot with Laura, the chances of me finding someone who matches up to her is minimal.'

Ellie didn't reply and for a moment I thought that she might not have heard me, but then she stopped and looked at me.

'Would you mind if I said something?'

'By all means, fire away.'

'Are you absolutely sure though? I feel like I've already

opened my big mouth a little too much this afternoon as it is.'

'Believe me you're fine.'

She smiled, seemingly reassured, and tucked a stray strand of hair behind her ear. 'My mum died a few years ago and it really knocked me for six. She was such a strong woman, such a force for good in my life that the thought of never seeing her again really threw me. For months afterwards I'd tell the children stories about her and how wonderful she was and kept it up for nearly a year and a half, until one day my sister sat me down and told me that I needed to stop making out like Mum was a saint. She then reeled off half a dozen instances off the top of her head when Mum had been anything but. Now, of course, I'm not saying that Laura was anything like my mother. What I am saying, however, is that when you lose someone you love, there's a natural tendency to only ever remember the best things about them. If you make Laura out to be a saint then no one will ever be able to come close to her, but if you remember that she was human just like you then, well, maybe one day you might actually find someone you like enough to give it a try.'

I didn't give too much credence to Ellie's women's-mag psychology at the time because, well, one: I was in the middle of the street on my way to pick up Lola; two: I could see that she meant well, even if she was wrong; and three: I'd learned a long time ago from working in TV that life is a lot easier if you just pretend to agree with people, even if you don't. And so rather than embarrass her by telling her that she was talking nonsense, that I wasn't making Laura out to be a saint because she was dead, but because she'd never been anything other than a perfect wife and mother, I told her that she'd made a good point and that it was definitely food for thought.

I didn't think about Ellie again until she texted me later that evening. She said in her text that she'd enjoyed our time together and hoped we could do it again soon. I was about to tap out a reply to her when Lola came into the kitchen, crying because Evie had been teasing her, and so by the time Ellie crossed my mind again, the evening had disappeared and I was lying in bed ready to drift off to sleep.

Was I guilty of beatifying my dead wife to the extent that no mere mortal could compare to her? Had I jettisoned all memory of her imperfections and made her into something that she had never been? Was I falsifying recollections and editing the past as a way of coping with the present? All these questions and more played on my mind as I lay there, forcing me to trawl through the past from our early beginnings through to my last memories of her alive. And yes, we'd had issues in the past but they were things to do with worries about careers, fears about the future, concerns about the kids and doubts about which direction our life should take, and their existence alone didn't negate the fact that Laura was, and continued to be, everything I ever wanted.

I wasn't misremembering anything. I tried hard to recall her at her worst, to give her memory some perspective, but there was a reason that our lovers' quarrels, late-night tiffs, and arguments over whose turn it was to feed the baby barely featured in my memory: *scale*. The arguments of the past were drops of rain in a vast ocean, mere grains of sand on a beach a mile wide compared to the overwhelming impression of having loved and been loved. In the end, there was so much good in what we had that the bad didn't even register any more.

11

How's that family of yours?

Tom

It was sleeting hard and I could barely see as I emerged from Snappy Snaps on the High Street, clutching the set of prints I'd had made for Lola's school project. Despite having known about the project 'My Life So Far' for a week, she'd only informed me about its existence that morning over breakfast and now we had less than twenty-four hours to complete it. Given the time constraints, we'd reasoned that the more illustrations it contained, the easier it would be for us to get it done, and so as she'd brushed her teeth upstairs, I'd rummaged through the albums on the bookshelf in the living room for photos I thought might fit the brief. It hadn't been an easy task, raking through a past that contrasted so starkly with the present, and several times I found myself lingering on photos of Laura for just a few moments too long, wishing for all the world that she was back with us, but eventually I selected four photos I thought would do the trick: Laura holding Lola for the first time, minutes after she was born; Lola age three at a friend's princess party, not giving a damn that she's the only child who has ignored the dress code and come as Spiderman; Lola beaming proudly next to Evie by the front door on her first day at school; and then finally, Lola on the morning of her last birthday, in her bedroom surrounded by presents (a photo that must have been taken by Linda as, if I remember correctly, I'd long since gone to work by then). The last thing Lola had said to me when I dropped her off at school before heading to the High Street was, 'Don't forget the photos,' little knowing that there was absolutely zero chance of me forgetting the ones I held in my hand or those in the albums on the bookshelf at home.

Huddled underneath my umbrella, numerous memories popped up in my mind. They were snapshots really, much like their inspiration, brief moments from my past with Laura: lying on sunloungers on a beautifully white sandy beach on our honeymoon in the Seychelles; the day we brought Percy, our old cat, home from the rescue centre; a pregnant Laura painting Evie's bedroom three weeks before her due date . . . a car horn . . . a car horn . . . a car horn.

Snapping out of my reverie, I gave the car horn my full attention. It was coming from a tiny bright yellow Honda that was crawling at a snail's pace alongside me, backing up traffic all the way down the High Street. I bent down to get a look inside the car, expecting the driver to be a friend, work colleague or even a parent from Lola's school, so I was more than a little baffled when it turned out to be the old man from my one and only group-counselling session at COPE. I'd have recognised him anywhere. Old men wearing baseball caps have a tendency to stick in the mind.

Oblivious to the abuse being directed at him by the drivers he was blocking, he wound down his passenger window. 'I thought it was you, lad. I spotted you coming out of that shop up the road. It's Tom, isn't it? I never forget a face – that's the ex-copper in me coming out there! Anyway, long time no see, son! How you doing?'

I tried to recall his name. Keith? Carl? Clive. That was it. Clive. 'I'm fine, Clive, thanks for asking. How about you?'

'Can't complain, and no one would bloody listen if I did anyway! Fancy a lift? I'm not in any sort of rush so it wouldn't be a bother.'

As much as I hated the sleet, I wasn't sure I was in the right frame of mind for a stroll down memory lane with a total stranger who was prepared to stop traffic in order to pass the time of day. I decided to politely decline.

'It's a very kind offer but no thanks, I'm fine.'

Clive tutted under his breath in much the same manner he'd done at our first COPE meeting: *loudly*. 'Look, just get in and stop making a song and dance about it, all right? It's a lift up the road not a bloody marriage proposal!'

Quite how Clive managed to turn an offer of a lift into a test of my own masculinity is anyone's guess but that was exactly what he did, and it succeeded. Trying my best to avoid eye contact with the drivers he was blocking, I quickly got into the car and he pulled away.

'So how have you been keeping?' he asked as we headed down the High Street. 'How's that family of yours?'

'Growing all the time,' I replied. 'And how about you . . . it's your granddaughter you live with, isn't it? How's she?'

'Still bossing me about like I'm a child.' He shook his head in disappointment. 'Did you ever go back to that counselling thing at the church? You should've heard the fuss my granddaughter kicked up when I told her I wasn't going again!' He gave me a wink. 'I dug my heels right in though, in fact I even brought you into it. I told her it wasn't just me who thought it was a pile of steaming horse whatsit, I said my mate Tommy thought so too!'

'My mother-in-law made my life hell too,' I said, and I sighed thinking how if I'd only kept it up things would be so different now. 'I don't know, looking back, maybe it wasn't that bad after all. Maybe we should've given it another go.'

Clive was incredulous. 'You're joking, aren't you? It was a travesty from beginning to end. A bunch of bedwetting lightweights yapping on about their feelings? It wasn't for the likes of me and you, Tommy boy, it was everything that I can't stand about the modern world wrapped up in a handy sixty-minute *session.* We never had *sessions* in my day! Do you know what we had instead? The Luftwaffe trying to blow the living daylights out of our country! Sessions! I ask you! Whatever happened to people putting things on and folk just going along? Now everything's a bleedin' *session*! You've got "OAP sessions" at the doctors; "readers' sessions" at the library; and "meet and greet sessions" at the community centre! I'll tell you what, the day someone invites me along to a "Slap some sense into the useless toerags in charge session" I'll be first in the queue!'

For what remained of the journey, Clive railed against dustbin collections, 'posh knobs at the BBC and their leftwing propaganda' and bank interest rates. And while he was often vitriolic ('If it was up to me I'd sack every last one of the people in the top jobs at the council and replace them with monkeys.'), he was never boring, ('Did I ever tell you about the time back in the late sixties when I saw a UFO? No? Well it's too long a story for now but suffice it to say I was never the same afterwards.').

'You know what, Tom,' said Clive when we finally reached my house. 'I've really enjoyed talking to you. Most weeks I go up to the day centre near me for an hour or two just to see what's going on and there's not one of them is as good a conversationalist as you. I think we should meet for lunch sometime and do this again, what do you reckon?'

If I'd learned anything about Clive in the two occasions I'd met him, it was that there was little point in saying no to him. Even if I attempted to decline his offer, he'd simply browbeat me into meeting with him regardless. And anyway, I wasn't sure I actually wanted to decline his offer. In a world where so few people spoke their mind, he was a breath of fresh air and truth be told, I'd rather enjoyed my short time with him.

'I'd like that a lot,' I said, jotting down my number on the back of an old supermarket receipt. 'Give me a call when you're free.'

Linda

Moira and I had just returned home from a week away visiting her friends Isla and Peter in Sydney. Although we'd had a wonderful time seeing the city's famous landmarks and eating out until we were fit to burst, I was glad to be back in the relative calm of Melbourne and was looking forward to little other than drinking cups of tea and catching up on my reading. Life, however, had other plans that were made known to me when Moira screamed at the top of her lungs for me to come quickly.

I burst into the kitchen expecting to find her grappling with burglars but instead she was holding the phone and grinning like an idiot. 'What's wrong?' I asked.

'I was just listening to my messages and there's one for you!'

'From Tom and the girls?'

'Do you really think I'd make that big of a deal if it was them?' said Moira frowning. 'They've only got to sneeze and you're on the phone making sure they're all right. This is something actually exciting!'

I was losing patience. 'So tell me who it was then!'

'I'll give you a clue,' teased Moira, and she adopted a posh voice. 'It's a gentleman caller enquiring about your availability next week for an outing to the botanical gardens . . . Desi's asking you out on a date!'

'You're pulling my leg.'

'I'm doing no such thing!' Moira offered me the phone. 'Have a listen yourself if you don't believe me.'

I listened to the message. It was exactly as Moira described. 'Well,' I said, handing the phone back to her, 'that's a turn up for the books.'

Given the untold injuries Desi had saved me from after I'd fallen off the table on the night of Moira's party, I'd felt obliged to spend much of the rest of that night talking to my rescuer. Thankfully it was quite an effortless obligation to fulfil because as well as having a knack for catching tipsy dancing women, he was also incredibly easy to talk to. Within the space of half an hour I knew everything about him. He was divorced with no kids; his biggest regret in life was that he and his ex-wife had never started a family; he'd become friends with Moira and her husband after doing some work on their house; and he was retired from the building trade but still kept his hand in with the occasional project for friends and family.

Desi had seemed like a kind and gentle man, the sort of man that, had I met him at a similar sort of party in England and he'd called me up afterwards for a date, I almost certainly would've said yes to. But this wasn't England, it was Australia, and I was far too old to even contemplate a holiday romance, let alone conduct one. Anyway, I'd come to Melbourne to make my life less complicated, not more, and a romantic entanglement would almost definitely make it the latter.

'I can completely and utterly vouch for Desi if you're worried about his character,' said Moira, eyeing me suspiciously. 'He's an absolute sweetie and was a real rock for me after Peter died. You really won't find a better guy.'

'Which makes it even worse,' I replied. 'I admit he was rather handsome, and we did get on really well that night, but I'm only here for a while and the last thing I want to do is lead him on.'

Moira made it clear that this was not the response she'd been hoping for. 'I love you to bits, Linda, you know I do, but sometimes I really do think you've got a screw loose. The man's not asking to marry you, he just wants to take you out for the day. Where's the harm in that?'

'But letting yourself be taken out for the day is how relationships begin, isn't it? And I don't want a relationship, at least not now.'

With a barely restrained sigh, Moira rested the phone on the kitchen counter. 'I bet the Linda who was dancing on the table at my party would go on a date with him.'

'I bet she would too, which is why I'm grateful she's decided to retire to the country and take up needlepoint.'

'But I liked her, she was fun. I want to see more of her. She was up for anything. Not like you, you boring old fart!' We both started chuckling and Moira handed me the phone. 'Go on,' she encouraged. 'Live a little, carpe diem and all that! After all, when you really think about it, what's the worst that could happen?'

Tom

Without coming close to breaking into a sweat I could have thought of at least a dozen places that I'd sooner have lunch than the café at the Reigate branch of Morrisons. 'It's there or nowhere,' Clive had insisted when we'd spoken on the phone. 'They make a decent brew, the girls behind the counter know me and always put the crispiest bits of bacon in my bap, and best of all they don't have bloody music blaring out all over the place. How anyone can digest their food properly with the top bloody forty being blasted in their ears is anyone's guess.'

Entering the café, I spotted Clive straight away. He was dressed smartly in a checked shirt, jacket and tie, only this time no baseball cap. He was lost in the pages of the *Daily Mail* and it wasn't until I was practically standing over him that he looked up, startled.

'Tom, you bugger! How long have you been lurking there? Have a seat and take the weight off and I'll get us sorted.'

'I'll get this,' I said. 'My treat.'

'You'll do no such bloody thing,' he said sternly. 'I invited *you* to lunch not the other way around. The day I can't get a friend a bacon butty and cup of tea will be the day I give up and let them cart me off to one of those bloody old people's homes. Now sit down, stop making a fuss and tell me how you like your bacon.'

It occurred to me as I sat down that I didn't have particularly strong opinions on bacon. I quite liked it but I wasn't too fussed about its appearance or texture. I ate it however it came. But from the little I'd learned about Clive so far I was pretty sure that such a position was untenable, and so I bluffed.

'I'll take it crispy, with tomato ketchup, on the side, not in the bap.'

Clive nodded appreciatively. 'Good choice, Tommy boy,' he said. 'The last thing in the world you want is a damp bap.'

I really enjoyed my lunch with Clive. His bluntness frequently made me laugh out loud and I lost count of the number of times it crossed my mind that with the right format I could probably make him a TV star. With his no-nonsense attitude and his 'calling a spade a spade' interviewing style I was sure I could find a cable station, or even one of the majors, that would love the idea of putting the world's most belligerent man on TV.

'It's pea-brained ideas like that which are the reason I've ripped up my TV licence,' said Clive when I jokingly told him my idea to make him a star. 'It's like that show on ITV with the four women in the too-tight dresses. It's a bloody travesty! All they do is cackle away every time one of them opens their mouth. Honestly, these days they'll put any bloody rubbish on the television and think we'll watch it. Alan Whicker must be turning in his grave!'

We carried on like this – me making small talk only for Clive to find some way to get angry about it – for a good half hour by which time I think even he was exhausted. I was about to suggest that I get him another mug of tea (the only thing I could imagine he wouldn't complain about) when I caught sight of a stern-faced young woman wearing a black leather jacket and jeans, purposefully striding towards our table. She had dark-brown hair, partially hidden by a cream woolly hat, and a face that was incredibly pretty even when it was scowling, as it was right now.

Ignoring me, she addressed Clive. 'What's going on?' she demanded. 'You told me this morning you were meeting a friend for lunch.'

'And what does it bloody look like I'm doing?' replied Clive. 'Knitting hats for the homeless?'

'So who's this guy?' she asked in a voice loud enough to demand the attention of every single diner in the café. 'He's not exactly one of your mates from the bowling club, is he?' She glared in my direction. 'What's your game, mate? Are you some sort of con merchant? Do you get your kicks targeting vulnerable old men for their pensions?'

'Vulnerable old man'? Had this woman ever met Clive before? In the course of my TV-making career I'd met hardened criminals who were more vulnerable than Clive. 'I think there's been some sort of mistake,' I explained. 'I'm not after anything.' I held out my hand and she pointedly ignored it. 'I'm Tom. I met Clive at the tail end of last year at a grief-counselling thing at the Methodist Church.' I looked at Clive and grinned. 'Apart from me, he was the only normal person there.'

A look of horror gradually spread over the young woman's face. She turned to Clive, glaring as if he were to blame. 'Why didn't you just tell me who you were meeting?'

'Because the last time I checked it was none of your bloody business!' he replied. 'I mean, what are you even doing here? Spying on me?'

'I came to borrow your keys,' she sighed. 'Reached home after my meeting in London only to find that I'd forgotten to take them with me again.'

'How many times have I told you that you need a system?' scolded Clive. 'A place for everything and everything in its place.' He fished a set of keys from his pocket and handed them to her. 'Problem sorted.' He turned to me, his face the very picture of disenchantment. 'I'm so sorry about all this, Tom. You must think I've got some right idiots for family.' He glared in the woman's direction. 'Anyway, for what it's worth this here is my granddaughter, Fran.'

I held out my hand again and this time she shook it. 'Lovely to meet you, Fran, I'm Tom Hope.'

'Nice to meet you, Tom,' she replied, looking like she wanted the earth to open up and swallow her whole. 'I know this is going to sound pathetic given that I've pretty much accused you of being a criminal and chewed you out in front of a café full of strangers, but I am so, so, so sorry. And be assured that I will never live this down.'

'You were just looking out for your granddad, which is the way it should be,' I replied. 'I'll tell you what, why don't you take a seat and join us.'

'I couldn't. I've already ruined your lunch. I don't want to make things worse.'

'I insist,' I replied. 'Now, how does tea and a bacon butty sound?'

'Honestly,' said Fran reluctantly, 'it sounds amazing. I completely forgot to have breakfast this morning.'

'She never listens to a bloody word I say,' fumed Clive. 'How many times have I told you breakfast is the most important meal of the day. It sets you up properly. If Churchill had been the type to go without breakfast we'd all be talking German and goose-stepping around Marks & Spencer.'

Fran and I exchanged smiles, albeit the stifled variety. Clearly there were times when even she found Clive as entertaining as I happened to.

'Right then,' I said, 'one tea and bacon bap coming right up.'

'Are you sure?' she asked.

'It would be my pleasure,' I replied.

On my return, Fran told me all about herself. She was twenty-nine, born and bred in Middlesbrough and Clive's second eldest granddaughter. Her profession was graphic design and up until a few years ago she'd been living and working in and around the north-west, but following the death of her gran she'd moved in with Clive to keep him company. Now she worked a few days a week at a small ad agency in Clerkenwell, and the rest of the time undertook freelance commissions and occasionally worked on her own illustrations, which she sold via her website.

'I know it's a pretty crass question,' I said. 'But would I have seen your stuff anywhere?'

'Depends,' said Fran. 'Are you an avid reader of *Mind and Spirit* magazine – the number-one read for spiritually connected modern women? I've had three pieces in there in the last six months.'

'I think my subscription must have run out,' I joked, 'but I'll make sure to renew first thing tomorrow if you've got more stuff going in.'

It was a little after half two by the time we all decided to go our separate ways. Standing outside the entrance to the supermarket, Clive and I said our goodbyes and I was about to go when Fran took me to one side.

'I just wanted to say how sorry I am for before,' she said. 'It must have been so embarrassing having me going on at you like that. If it's any consolation I know for a fact that Granddad will take great pleasure in telling the whole family about this.'

'Really, it was fine,' I replied. 'I work – sorry worked – in TV, and I can assure you I've had a lot worse.'

'That's really kind of you to say, especially given everything you've been through.' She looked down at the floor. She and Clive had obviously taken the opportunity to talk about me when I'd gone to the loo earlier. 'I really am sorry for your loss.'

'That's very kind of you to say,' I replied, grateful that I'd long since stopped finding such pat phrases irritating. There's only so long you can get annoyed at people for just trying to be nice.

There was an awkward pause as we both stood looking at each other blankly. Finally I said, 'Anyway, it was really nice to meet you.'

'You too,' she replied. 'And next time I promise not to bite your head off.'

12

Dot, this is Tom

Tom

Of all the things I'd been dreading since Linda left for Australia, the celebration for Evie's birthday was right at the top of the list. We'd been in negotiations about it pretty much since Linda left, with me pushing for a pizza and bowling party and her pushing back with equal determination that pizza and bowling parties were for little kids. Now that she was fourteen, what she wanted was a house party to which she could invite all her friends.

I'd read enough 'Home trashed after teen party goes viral' newspaper reports to know that unchaperoned teenage parties were to be avoided at all costs, which was why I was pushing the pizza and bowling so hard. While I wasn't about to let my house end up as a lead item on the ten o'clock news, Evie equally wasn't about to give up without a fight, and she used everything in her arsenal, from emotional blackmail ('If you loved me you'd let me have a party'), to downright belligerence ('If I can't have a party then I don't want anything') to try change my mind. Finally, with only a few days to go before the big day, the situation escalated considerably when I completely lost it with her one evening over tea after she told me that not letting her have a party was tantamount to child abuse.

I got up from the table with such force that I knocked over Lola's glass of water in the process. 'That's it! I don't want to hear another word about this! And nothing you do or say is going to change that!'

'But that's not fair!'

'How exactly is me offering to pay for half your school to have pizza and go bowling not fair?' I was over the other side of the room by now, angrily scraping the contents of my half-eaten dinner into the bin. 'If you seriously think it is, young lady, then I'd like to know your thoughts on global poverty and countries where girls your age are physically prevented from going to school!'

I was pretty sure I'd lost the argument the moment I allowed my temper to boil over, and the fact that I'd used the phrase 'young lady' only made matters worse. Laura would never have handled the situation like this in a million years. She was the absolute queen of conflict resolution, both with the kids and with me too. She just had a way about her where no matter how angry or annoyed you were at the beginning, you always ended up in a place where you felt you'd been listened to and understood, even if you didn't get the result you'd been hoping for.

Evie stormed out of the kitchen in tears, slamming the door behind her, leaving Lola and me alone. We exchanged sheepish looks. Mine said, 'Sorry about that,' and hers said, 'Even I could see you handled that badly, Dad, and I'm only eight.'

Wiping my hands on a tea towel, I made my way upstairs and knocked on Evie's door. After waiting long enough for it to be clear that she wasn't going to invite me in, I entered the room.

She was lying on her bed, face down, sobbing.

'I think I owe you an apology.'

She turned over, eyes with daggers at the ready.

'What for? Ruining my life?'

I had to bite my lip. An accusation of ruining the life of a teenager surely had to be right at the top of the parental bingo chart of 'Things your kids will say to you once they hit puberty'.

'I just want to say sorry for losing it like that. It was wrong of me and I'm sorry, okay? Look, why don't we compromise?'

She sat up immediately. 'Compromise how?'

'Well, put it this way: I still don't think you're old enough to have a party without proper supervision, but how about throwing one where I stay around?'

'Where would you be?'

'In the front room.'

'And where would Lola be?'

'With me, watching TV.'

'And you wouldn't come out at all?'

'Oh yes, believe me I'll be coming out, and you won't know when either.'

'But Dad, you'll ruin the party if you do that.'

'Well it's that or nothing. Take it or leave it.'

She considered the deal on the table for all of half a second. 'I'll take it,' she said gleefully.

'I have other conditions too,' I added quickly. 'First: maximum number of friends, twenty. Second: no advertising it on social media. Third: if I so much as suspect that anyone has or might have had alcohol I will make it my mission to make your life and those of everyone attending a living nightmare.' I held out my hand. 'Deal?'

Evie was practically beaming with delight. 'Deal,' she said, shaking my hand. 'I promise, Dad, you won't regret this.'

Linda

I was in the middle of debating with Moira whether I needed to go to the loo or not (thanks to my nervousness I'd been twice in the past half-hour alone) when the doorbell rang and I practically leapt out of my skin.

'Do you think it's him?'

'Who else would it be? The tooth fairy?' replied Moira, with more than a hint of exasperation in her voice. She left the kitchen and answered the door, and moments later returned with Desi. He was wearing a cream linen jacket and jeans, both of which looked like they were brand new, and what hair he'd got had been neatly trimmed. He looked a lot like an overgrown schoolboy on his first day at school. But it was nice to see him so smart. It felt like such a long time since anyone had felt the need to impress me.

I went over to say hello and he kissed my cheek. His neck smelt of freshly doused aftershave, sandalwood with a touch of lemon oil: clean and fresh.

'You look lovely by the way,' he said, and I thanked him and told him that I wasn't wearing anything special even though it was the fifth outfit I'd tried on.

He handed me a small bouquet containing red and white carnations. 'Moira said these were your favourite.'

'They're beautiful,' I replied. 'I know a lot of people think they're too ordinary but they always make me feel quite jolly when I see them.'

I carried them to the sink and was about to run the tap so I could leave them there, when Moira took them from me. 'You two get off and I'll sort these out,' she said, placing the bouquet on the counter and ushering us out the door. 'Have a lovely day and don't come back 'til late. That's an order!'

From the moment I got into Desi's car (a very sleek executive-looking thing with cream leather seats), he made me feel at ease. He confessed how nervous he'd been all morning and I told him about my own butterflies, and we both laughed at how ridiculous we were being. 'Let's pretend we're old work friends having a day out,' I suggested. 'That way we won't feel quite so on edge.'

Desi laughed but agreed all the same. 'Work mates it is,' he replied. 'But I think we ought to be the kind who tease each other from time to time.'

On the journey over, we both admitted to not knowing very much about plants at all.

'I've never been much of a gardener besides putting a few bulbs in pots in November in preparation for spring.'

'I love to see a nice garden but having spent my working life doing up houses six days out of seven, the last thing I wanted to do on my only day off was gardening.'

'Why don't we just enjoy what we see today and make a note of anything we like the look of? Who knows, it might inspire us!'

We visited the tropical glasshouse and Tacoma pavilion, strolled around the fragrant herb garden and explored the lower Yarra River habitat, and while for the most part we talked about the plants and the flowers, every now and again I'd ask Desi the odd personal question or he'd ask me, but it never went very deep at all. I think mostly we were happy just being in each other's company.

It was after three by the time we decided to leave, having had lunch sitting on the grass overlooking the beautiful ornamental lake at the heart of the gardens. As we walked to Desi's car, he asked if I was ready to go home and before I really knew what I was saying, I said, 'Not really, if that's okay with you.'

'You're not bored?'

'Why, do I look like I am? I shall have to get a better face if I do.'

'It's just . . . I don't know . . . I really wanted today to go well, that's all.'

'And it has,' I replied, and then as bold as you like I took his hand, and leaving the car where it was, we went for a walk around the city. We started off by taking in the greenery of Melbourne Park and Fitzroy Gardens, then went on to admire the architecture of Parliament House and St Patrick's Cathedral. We didn't push ourselves too hard, and felt no guilt at all about stopping for the occasional ice cream or coffee along the way and, having grown more comfortable with each other over the course of the day, we talked a lot more about our lives. Desi told me more about his ex-wife and his divorce; I told him all about Laura's father and my trials as a single mother, and even touched on losing Laura. It felt good to share my story with him. It felt like we were becoming friends.

'You've really been in the wars, haven't you?' he said as we stood gazing up at the spires of St Patrick's. They were so tall, I felt positively dizzy looking up at them.

'I think we both have,' I replied.

We went for something to eat after that, a little Italian restaurant that we both liked the look of. I had linguini with clams and Desi had lamb shank with rosemary potatoes, and we ordered a bottle of rosé to go with the meal. It was sweet and light and tasted like pop, and we were both as surprised as each other to find the bottle empty at the end of the meal.

We took a taxi back to Moira's and Desi walked me to the front door.

'I had a wonderful day,' I said as I searched in my bag for my keys. 'I'd love to do it again if you're free sometime.'

Desi didn't say anything for a while. I could see he was wrestling with something he wanted to say, but then he sighed as if he'd made up his mind not to speak. I wondered if he, like me, felt as though we'd made a connection, that this had been what he'd been struggling to say, and then he took me in his arms and planted a kiss right on my lips, which caught me completely off guard. But then I kissed him right back, which I think surprised him equally as much.

Tom

Despite numerous impromptu pop-ins conducted by me throughout the course of the evening, the worst behaviour I came across at Evie's party was a group of boys I caught filming each other competitively gargling lemonade in the kitchen. Mostly, Evie's guests were well behaved if a little too engaged with their phones, and apart from the lemonade gargling the only other thing of note that occurred came about an hour before the end, when I noticed that Evie and a couple of her closest friends had disappeared. Before I could even think of interrogating her guests about their whereabouts, Evie emerged from the downstairs loo flanked by her friends, each of whom had an arm around her. One look at Evie's face told me she'd been crying.

'I was dancing and banged my knee on the edge of the sideboard,' she explained quickly.

I asked if she wanted me to take a look at it but she declined. 'Honest, Dad, I'm fine. I just want to get back to the party.'

It was obvious that there was more to the story than that. My top guess was that she'd fallen out with one of the other girls at the party, because now they were teenagers it seemed like there wasn't a day went by without someone not talking to someone else. Well aware that if I tried to get involved I'd only make matters worse, I told her I'd be in the front room if she needed me and reluctantly retreated there with Lola.

Even with my presence at the party, it was hailed by Evie's guests as a success, with some asking as they left if there would be one next year. Although I promised to give the idea some thought, my every instinct told me that having got away with it once, I'd be wise not to push my luck. Even so, over the February half-term holiday that followed, I found it hard not to feel distinctly pleased with myself for having successfully hosted my first teenage party without recourse to the police. It was a win, one to tuck under my belt in the time that remained until Linda's return; a sign that maybe, just maybe I wasn't as completely hopeless at this being a full-time dad thing as I had initially thought.

I dined out on my 'Evie's birthday victory' story for as long as people would let me, which turned out to be not very long at all. Everyone had bigger things going on in their lives: Ellie and her husband still weren't getting along, Rich and Marina's youngest had broken her wrist in a playground accident and Linda, well Linda just seemed distracted. Though she was still devoted to the kids and was more than happy to dispense pearls of wisdom with regard to childrearing,when it came to general conversation about what she was actually doing in Australia her mind seemed elsewhere.

A few days after the girls returned to school following half-term, Clive proposed meeting up, and having spent the whole of the previous day getting on top of the washing, I told him that today was as good as any, to which he replied, 'Good, because I think it's about time I introduced you to my Dot.'

I had to make sure I'd heard right. 'You want to do what?'

'You heard me.'

'Well I'm not sure I did, actually. Because for a moment there I thought you were saying that you wanted me to meet Dot, as in your wife, as in, "Hi, I'm Tom, lovely to meet you," kind of thing.'

'That's exactly what I do mean,' said Clive. 'I've told her all about you and I think it's about time that you met her in person.'

I still wasn't getting it. 'In person?'

'How did you ever get to be some big-shot TV person when you haven't got the brains you were born with? I'm talking about taking you to see her at the cemetery, not summoning up her spirit on a Ouija board. Whatever's the matter with you? Actually don't answer that or we'll be here all bloody day! I'll pick you up in half an hour and make sure you're ready. If there's one thing my Dot never could stand it's tardiness.'

There were numerous reasons why I wasn't relishing Clive's offer of an introduction to his wife. For a start I doubted my ability to pull off the pantomime of making small talk with a dead woman, but the ultimate reason, of course, was that I hadn't set foot in a cemetery since Laura's funeral, and I wasn't keen to start now.

'What's wrong with your face?' Clive asked half an hour later as I climbed into his bright yellow Honda. 'You're not sick are you?'

'I'm fine it's just . . .'

'What?'

'I haven't been to a cemetery since . . . you know . . . I lost Laura.'

'And?'

'And, well I'm not sure it's the best thing for me.'

'Think it'll dredge up some bad memories, do you?'

I nodded, relieved that he understood. 'Yeah, something like that.'

'Cobblers,' said Clive and without another word he started up the car.

As it turned out, Clive was right. There were no flashbacks to the day of Laura's funeral or sudden outbursts of emotion. In fact I didn't feel much of anything as we pulled up in the car park and made our way along the gravel path to Clive's wife's burial plot, or even as we finally came to a halt in front of a white granite headstone and I read the inscription: 'In Loving memory of Dorothy "Dot" Maynard. Wife, Mother, Grandmother. To live in the hearts of those we love is never to die.' Touching words, made all the more guilt-inducing by virtue of the fact that I'd never seen Laura's headstone, or had any idea what was written on it. It was one of the many things Linda had dealt with when I had been unable to do so and from which I'd been hiding ever since.

Clive cleared his throat and addressed the headstone. 'Dot, this is Tom, the friend of mine I've been telling you about. I thought you might like to meet him because he lost his wife too. He's got his faults . . .' He paused and looked at me pointedly. '. . . but he's a good sort and I'm sure you two will get along well.'

While the lightness of voice seemed to say, 'Of course I'm joking, I know she can't really hear me,' the lost look that appeared in his eyes as he spoke seemed to convey an altogether different message. Either way, I was in a difficult position. Having lost my dad years before I lost Laura, I'd long since reached the conclusion that when you are dead you're dead and that was all there was to it. For me to have taken part in Clive's pretence would have been patronising in the extreme but on the other hand, to have condemned him with silence in order to make some point about the necessity of living in the 'real world' seemed too cruel to contemplate. So, patronising it was.

I cleared my throat and crouched down next to the headstone, my voice barely registering above a whisper. 'Hello, Dot, I'm Tom.'

Clive shook his head and tutted his disapproval. Presumably there was a right and wrong way of addressing the dead and I'd already managed to get one strike against me. 'You'll have to speak a bloody sight louder than that if you want her to hear you. Even with her hearing aid in she'd have needed you to speak up.'

I tried again, this time louder. 'Hello, Dot, I'm Tom.' This time Clive nodded approvingly, so I continued. 'I've sort of been keeping an eye on your Clive for you, you know keeping him out of trouble, although I suspect he's told you it's the other way around. He's told me a lot about you and . . .' My voice trailed off. I couldn't do it any more. 'No offence,' I said, feeling like a terrible friend. 'But all this just isn't me.'

'To be honest,' said Clive, resting the weight of his right hand on my shoulder in a supportive fashion, 'I don't think she was all that much interested in what you had to say anyway.'

We stayed in the cemetery for nearly an hour, during which time Clive chatted constantly to Dot while he tidied up around the already immaculate grave, wiping down the headstone with a cloth and some spray he'd brought along for the purpose. He brushed away stray leaves, straightened the numerous flowers arranged around the base of the headstone and even trimmed the grass immediately surrounding the plot with a pair of scissors. As he worked, he chatted to Dot about council-tax rebates, family news, gas bills and even how the makers of their favourite fruitcake had changed the recipe, an act that Clive described in all seriousness as 'a right bloody travesty', as though she was standing right next to him. By the end of the hour I think it was safe to say that if Dot really was listening from the 'other side', there genuinely wasn't anything she didn't know about the little corner of the world she'd left behind.

Afterwards, Clive drove us back to his house and I stayed for a cup of tea before announcing that I needed to head off to collect Lola from school. I'd barely reached the hallway, however, when the front door opened and in came Fran.

I'd scarcely thought about Fran since we'd met at Morrisons and yet the moment I saw her again I felt a curious lightness of spirit as though someone had just told a joke and I was still caught up in laughter.

'Oh, right . . . Tom, I didn't know you were visiting Granddad today.' Strangely, she sounded a lot less happy to see me than I would have hoped, but then I heard a male voice behind her ask, 'Who is it?' and suddenly everything fell into place as a tall, studiously scruffy man lumbered into view. He had long shaggy hair and the sort of eyes that I was pretty sure most women would describe as piercing. In his hands he was holding two bulky weekend bags.

'I should make the introductions, shouldn't I?' said Fran. 'Johnny, this is Tom, my Granddad's friend that I was telling you about, and Tom, this is Johnny, my boyfriend.'

Following my encounter with Fran's boyfriend I'd felt distinctly odd, as though I'd forgotten or lost something important, and it was only as I reached Lola's school as the bell rang for the end of day that I'd realised what I was feeling was none other than plain old-fashioned disappointment, a fact made all the more difficult because until that moment it hadn't occurred to me that I actually had anything to be disappointed about.

Although I refused to address it – I couldn't imagine any good would come of doing that – the feeling stayed with me as I peeled potatoes and carrots for the stew I was making for tea, and continued as I emptied a load from the drier and shoved another pile of wet washing into the machine, and it was still there as I collected the laundry basket from where it lived in the store cupboard under the stairs and toured the girls' bedrooms on the hunt for dirty clothes, while Lola watched TV downstairs. In Evie's room I gathered together T-shirts, socks and pyjamas and as I reached across the bed for a pair of abandoned tights I noticed something poking out from underneath her pillow.

I pulled it out and examined it. It was a pink patterned notepad covered in stickers. At first I assumed it was some kind of homework book and was about to tidy it away when out of curiosity I flicked it open, to discover that what I had in my hands was Evie's very own personal journal.

I sat down on the edge of the bed and weighed up my options: I could slip it back where I'd found it and leave the room or I could open it and read it. In retrospect, I suspect if I hadn't felt so odd about Fran, I might have listened to my conscience and left it well alone but as it was, I still felt distinctly disjointed and reasoned that reading Evie's rave review of her birthday party might cheer me up.

As I flicked through the book, trying to find the entry I was looking for, I started to regret my decision. This book, after all, contained my daughter's private thoughts and feelings, and while none of it was anything you wouldn't expect from the pen of a teenage girl (lists of pop bands, pages of doodles, poems and a number of startlingly good self-portraits) none of this was ever intended for my eyes. I was about to close the book and return it to its hiding place when I happened across the last entry, dated on the night of her birthday party, and it truly broke my heart. In large letters that took up the whole page, Evie had written in her own inimitable scrawl: 'WHY AM I SO UGLY THAT NO BOYS LIKE ME?'

On the upside, Evie's words put paid to any disenchantment I felt about Fran. In fact, they pretty much obliterated all thoughts of anything that wasn't related to my little baby girl.

13

Why are you being weird?

Tom

It was an odd feeling, the change from not knowing a secret about someone to knowing everything about it, even more so when that 'someone' was my own teenage daughter. From the moment Evie arrived home from school, dropping her school bag in the middle of the hallway like I'd told her a million times not to, through to the moment she pecked me on the cheek and told me she was going to bed, I couldn't take my eyes off her. Every yawn, sigh, frown and gaze seemed imbued with meaning. While she appeared to be like any other teenage girl – sarcastic, self-centred, awkward, argumentative, with the occasional flash of awe-inspiring kindness – there was no escaping the truth: the young girl who'd done her Spanish homework at the kitchen table was the very same one who'd written in that journal, and as such needed my help.

I left it a good hour after Evie had gone to bed to make the call to Linda, partly because of the time difference (Australia was only just waking up) and partly because I wanted to make sure that Evie was asleep in case she came downstairs and overheard me asking her grandmother for advice. I'd briefly considered talking it over with Marina or even Ellie, as neutral third parties, but felt that this was one to keep in the family. I was, after all, on the dodgiest of ground: attempting to do the right thing about information I'd come across in the wrong way. And while I didn't doubt that it was a good thing I had seen what was written in her journal, I was aware that Evie (should she ever find out) might have a different take on the situation.

Since her arrival in Australia, Linda had gradually weaned herself off daily calls to the girls and was now down to one a week on a Friday night (UK time) along with an occasional prearranged Skype call, and so I knew that calling out of the blue on a Wednesday morning (Australian time) would set off her every alarm bell. With this in mind when Moira picked up the phone, my first words were to tell Linda not to panic, not that it did any good of course.

'Tom, why are you telling Moira to tell me not to panic? What is it that you don't want me to panic about?' The concern in her voice was writ so large she might as well have been speaking in capital letters.

'Everything's fine. I just need some advice that's all . . . about how to handle something with Evie.'

'What about her? I knew it, I knew something was wrong.'

'There's nothing wrong. It's just, I think she might be having some sort of body issues and I'm not quite sure what to do about it.'

'Body issues?' she repeated, sounding the words out as if they were a foreign tongue. 'What kind of *body issues*?'

I explained the situation, but even as I spoke I wasn't sure whether I was making a big deal out of nothing or should've been speed-dialling a child psychologist.

'She seems fine in herself,' I concluded, 'and of course I can't tell her I know what she's written . . . and I get that she might not have been feeling great about herself one day and then was fine the next, but . . . but . . . what if there's more to it? I've got no kind of reference point about what to do here. I've got nothing at all.'

'Of course you have,' said Linda with a sharpness that took me by surprise. 'You're a father, aren't you? So you should do what any good father would do if one of his children was upset. You give her a big hug and tell her how much you love her and then carry on doing it for the rest of her life.' She sighed and all the venom seemed to disappear. 'All girls go through phases like this, Tom, I'm sure even Laura did, it's all part of growing up.'

As comforting as Linda's words were, I still wasn't convinced. Before reading the journal I'd thought that I'd been handling things pretty well, but now that I knew Evie was suffering I felt out of my depth, and without Laura by my side to calm me down I was terrified of what this might turn into. 'But what if it isn't just a phase, Linda? What if this is the beginning of something worse? What if she's already starving herself or cutting herself or any of those weird things teenage girls do? What if it's to do with missing Laura? What if right now all she wants is to have her mum back and here she is saddled with me?'

Linda reprimanded me straight away. 'Don't you dare say that, Tom Hope! Evie hasn't been "saddled" with you any more than she's been "saddled" with me.'

'Hasn't she?' I replied. 'Come on, Linda, surely even you can see it's not me she needs right now. Laura always knew the right thing to say and how to say it, and I don't even know where to begin. As the next best thing I'm asking . . . in fact I'm begging . . . please, just talk to Evie for me?'

'No,' said Linda forcefully, 'she needs you, not me. Mums don't always get things right with their daughters just because they're the same sex, any more than dads always get things right with their sons. Don't you get it, Tom? You're Evie's father and you love her more than life itself and that's all the frame of reference you need to make things right for her. No bells, whistles or secret handshakes: all you need to do is just be you.'

Linda

I stayed on the line with Tom for a good half hour and he seemed a lot calmer as we said our goodbyes.

'So you're going to be okay?'

'I'll be fine. You're right, I just need to reassure her, that's all.'

'That's right, be a listening ear. That's all she needs. It's a tough time for girls of that age – their hormones are everywhere – lots of cuddles and kisses and I promise you, she'll be as right as rain.'

For a moment after I put down the phone I thought I was going to be fine. I felt calm, sure I'd given Tom good advice, and didn't doubt for a moment that he'd do his best for Evie. But then Moira appeared next to me asking how everyone was and I started to cry, and before I knew it I couldn't stop. I just missed my two little beans so much, and it hurt not to be with them.

The funny thing was, if someone had approached me before I took Tom's call and asked me on a scale of one to ten how happy I was, without blinking an eye I would've told them I was a ten. I couldn't remember a time when I'd been so happy – at least certainly not since losing my lovely Laura – and it was all thanks to Desi. He truly was a wonderful man.

Since our kiss over a fortnight ago, we'd seen each other nearly every day, either for a walk along the beach at St Kilda or for a day out, like the one we took to Point Cook Coastal Park. Sometimes we'd have dinner afterwards and other times we'd just have a coffee and a slice of cake. Desi would make me laugh with his daft jokes, make me feel as though I was the only thing that mattered in the world and when we kissed, I felt young again. I didn't know if it was the sunshine, or being on holiday, but I felt a lightness and contentment I hadn't felt in years. I decided not to over-think it or worry about where it all might be leading but just to go with it. Perhaps the Australian laid-back attitude to life was rubbing off on me.

So my tears felt even more incongruous, in the light of my recent mood, and it took a good cup of tea before I felt able to tell Moira about what had happened back home, but once I started talking she listened to everything I had to say without interruption.

'I just feel like I want to go home,' I said. 'I hate thinking of Evie like that.'

'And if you go home now you'll undo all the good work you've done with Tom. Is that what you want?'

'No, of course not.'

'Then let him get on with it. He'll never learn anything if you keep running back every time he encounters something difficult. I know it's tough but he'll thank you for it one day, I promise.' Moira rubbed my arm affectionately. 'Now, you're meeting Desi today, aren't you?'

'We're going for coffee at that nice place on the High Street, you know, Veronica's. He's got a dentist's appointment beforehand so I said I'd meet him there, then maybe we'd go for a drive along the coast.'

Moira laughed. 'A day out with a hot bloke who's had his teeth fixed! If that isn't something to look forward to, I don't know what is.'

It was a little before eleven as I walked into Veronica's. I bought myself an iced tea and took it to a table in the window overlooking the street. I picked up an abandoned copy of the *Herald Sun* but lost interest somewhere around the business pages and by way of Evie and her issue, ended up spending quite some time thinking about Laura.

I'd told Tom that I was sure Laura had had similar issues to Evie growing up, and although thankfully it was nothing like you hear about these days, she'd had her moments. Laura's problem had been that she was insecure, always comparing herself to others and feeling like she wasn't good enough. It didn't help that she did really well in her eleven-plus exam and ended up going to grammar school. I often thought that if she'd have gone to the local comprehensive as I'd wanted her to, she would've felt better about herself, less angst-ridden. As it was, she ended up surrounded by all sorts of high-achievers for whom everything seemed easy. I only became aware there was an issue when the school told me she'd fainted in class one day (this was when she was about fifteen) and she confessed to not having eaten for the best part of a day and a half. I took her to see the doctor the same day and he told me that eating disorders were quite a common thing amongst girls of her age and that I shouldn't worry as they often grow out of it, but I did worry and made her promise that she would never start that silly business. Thankfully, as far as I know, she never did. But even as an adult she'd always seemed so determined to prove herself, to be perfect.

My phone buzzed, breaking my reverie. It was Desi, telling me that he was all done with his dentist and would be with me soon. I considered getting another iced tea but the café had begun to fill up and I didn't want to lose my table, so I decided to wait until Desi arrived and passed the time instead with a spot of people watching.

Despite the milder temperatures now that autumn was settling in, it was such a beautiful day that there were plenty of people out on the street to observe. Some walked purposefully while others strolled along as though they had all the time in the world. Across the road, the shop next door to the hardware store was being refurbished and I could see workmen in overalls pointing up at the ceiling and then referring to the plans in their hands. After a while some of the workmen came and stood outside the café in the shade for a cigarette break, while the others carried on working.

My attention was drawn away from the window by the sound of crockery crashing to the floor. One of the young waitresses must have overloaded her tray because when I turned there were shards of glass and broken cups and saucers littered across the floor. I sat and watched as a clean-up operation began, and soon everything was back to normal, so I returned my gaze to outside.

Across the road at the hardware store, a man emerged from the exit and immediately caught my attention. He was tall and grey-haired and carrying what appeared to be two large cans of paint, which he loaded into the back of a white pickup truck parked directly outside the store. He was wearing jeans and a checked shirt with the sleeves rolled up and so I imagined that he was some sort of painter and decorator perhaps, getting some materials he needed for a job. As he loaded two more paint tins on to the truck I was struck by the idea that he seemed familiar. Was he a friend of Moira's or perhaps someone off the TV? Maybe I'd just seen him out and about when I'd been with Desi? No matter how hard I tried I simply couldn't place him but then as he began reversing out of his parking space, I saw his face in profile and knew exactly who he was. I leapt to my feet and ran to the entrance of the café but it was too late. His truck was already halfway down the road and even if I'd been forty years younger I wouldn't have had a hope of catching him up.

I was rooted to the spot long after the truck disappeared from view, my mind reeling. I'd never thought I'd see that face again, certainly not here, not now. I was brought back to my senses by a couple trying to squeeze past me; I apologised for blocking their way and with a heart still racing, returned to my table.

I sat staring into space until Desi arrived and it must have been obvious how shaken I was, because the first words out his mouth were: 'What's wrong, Linda? You look like you've seen a ghost.'

Tom

If, as a teenager, someone had told me that one day I would become one of the world's foremost lay experts in the self-esteem of pubescent girls, I would've thought them insane and continued leering at my 1989 Kylie Minogue calendar. And yet, two days after my panicked call to Linda, this was me, clued up beyond belief.

I started my journey towards understanding the mind of a teenage girl by working my way through countless newspapers and academic journal articles online about the subject, and the experience left me feeling confused and more than a little guilty. As a lifelong fan of the female form, I'd done my fair share of objectifying women's bodies and so by default I was part of the problem, which was confusing because I'd rather hoped to be part of the solution. I wanted my kid to be fine with how she looked but the more I saw the world through her eyes, the more I began to understand how difficult this could be. With my new understanding, it seemed a day didn't go by when I wasn't confronted with images of lithe, hopelessly attractive women wearing next to nothing, irrespective of whether they were advertising yoghurt, underwear or cars. Regardless of the sales pitch, the message was always the same: women's bodies were public property and it was hard not to conclude that the world truly was a creepy place in which to be a fourteen-year-old girl.

Feminist discussions aside, my reading uncovered numerous pearls of wisdom to help teens with body-image issues including:

1. Talk to your teen about her self-image
2. Create an environment where your teen can open up to you
3. Encourage your teen on the journey that is womanhood.

My main issue with the advice above wasn't that it was obvious, patronising and more than a bit 'out there', no my problem was that virtually all of the advice I'd come across was aimed at women talking to their daughters, as though it had never occurred to the authors that there were fathers like me out there raising girls on their own.

I couldn't talk positively about the shape of my own female body because I didn't have one. I couldn't create an environment where 'my teen' would feel comfortable talking about her body issues, because I was almost certain a place in which Evie could talk about 'her body' with me didn't exist. In the end I decided that what I needed to do was find a way to encourage the growth of her self-esteem without letting her know that I thought she had issues in the first place.

To begin with, I thought the answer might lie in leaving my copy of *Everything Your Teen Needs To Know* lying around for Evie to discover for herself but during the hour and a half that it sat on the kitchen table, the only person to pick it up was Lola, whom I'd found wide-eyed and startled with her nose buried deep in its pages. A few days later, I came up with a different line of attack while Lola was upstairs having a bath and Evie was at the kitchen table working on a geography project.

Me (casually)**:** You look really pretty today.

Evie: Thanks.

Me: Not that you don't look really pretty every day, of course.

Evie: Thanks.

Me: But today you look especially pretty.

Evie (glaring): You're being weird, Dad. Why are you being weird?

That night I lay in bed wondering what to do, when I was struck by an idea that was the closest thing to a moment of genius I'd ever experienced. The following morning over breakfast I told Evie my plan.

'I'm going to give you two hundred pounds to spend on clothes, and on Saturday I'm going to take you and your friends to Bluewater shopping centre so you can spend it.'

Evie spat out her cornflakes. 'What?'

'I can give you the money now if you want,' I said, reaching for my wallet.

She held up her hand. 'I . . . I don't understand. It's not my birthday any more.'

'I was looking in your wardrobe, and it occurred to me that you might need some more clothes.'

'I can't believe it,' said Evie, still in shock. 'Can I call my friends now and make sure they're free for Saturday?'

'Of course you can,' I said, basking in her excitement. 'I just want you to be happy.'

That weekend I booked a cab to take Evie and her friends, along with Lola and myself, to the mecca of consumerism that is Bluewater shopping centre. She and her friends went one way while Lola and I went the other, with an agreement that we would meet up in three hours. In the time that we had, Lola and I managed to pick up some tops, a couple of pairs of tights and a few bits of school uniform, but this was nothing compared to the haul that Evie was loaded down with when we met up at the end of the day. I could see that she was worried that I might think she'd gone over the top but when all I did was offer to take her and her mates for a meal, she couldn't have looked more relieved and if the truth be told, I doubt that I could've either.

Faced with the problem of my daughter's low self-esteem and my own lack of oestrogen, I'd circumnavigated the female self-help industry with its constant mantra of the need for 'talking' and 'sharing' and cut to the heart of the matter by deducing the plain obvious: nothing quite gives your self-esteem a shot in the arm like spending a bucket-load of cash on things that might make you feel good. And as I watched Evie and her friends practically skipping to Nando's, I concluded that I hadn't just thought outside the box, I'd well and truly unfolded it and turned it into an origami swan. A fact confirmed when I allowed myself to check her journal one last time. The first entry on the page after the weekend read: 'Can't wait for school disco on Friday!!! New clothes! New make-up! I'm gonna absolutely kill it!!!!!!!'

On the night of the school disco, it was all I could do to get Evie to stop by the kitchen table for five minutes to shovel down some pasta before disappearing back upstairs to carry on with her preparations. I hadn't a clue what she was doing up there, for all I knew she could've been dyeing her hair purple or bathing in ass's milk. What I did know, however, was that she was happy and excited, and judging from the thud of music and laughter emanating from her room, all the more so since her friend Kuldip had arrived.

I was watching TV with Lola when the doorbell rang, signalling the arrival of Evie's lift to the disco. I waited, fully expecting Evie to come thundering down the stairs to answer, but when the doorbell rang again I realised that chances were she hadn't heard it over the din coming from her room.

I opened the door to Evie's friend Anya's mum, who looked a little harassed.

'I've left Anya in the car and I'm parked on double yellows. Are they ready?'

I turned to call Evie, only to see her and her friend coming down the stairs, and stopped dead in my tracks. Whilst Kuldip was sporting a fairly standard teenage outfit of shorts, tights and sparkly jumper, Evie was wearing clothes I could only assume she'd bought during her shopping trip. Clothes which, had I been present at the time she bought them, I definitely would've vetoed. Clothes which could be summed up in a single word: inappropriate.

It didn't take a genius to work out that this moment was quite possibly the single most important of my career as a father to date. My daughter, dressed in a short, tight-fitting glittery purple dress and black platform sandals was experimenting with her identity, trying to figure out who she was and what she wanted to be like. If I criticised her outfit, I ran the risk of undoing all of my good work and scarring her for life. On the other hand, if I gave it my blessing and she went to the disco as she was, I didn't doubt that she would spend the entire night fending off the amorous advances of every single boy in her year, the thought of which made me shudder.

I tried my best to think what Laura would've done in this situation. I was pretty sure that one thing she wouldn't have done was lose her cool, so I opted to keep mine. Another thing that occurred to me was that she wouldn't have embarrassed Evie in public, so I waited until Kuldip followed Anya's mum to the car before I took her to one side. Finally, I concluded that much as Laura loved it when the kids expressed themselves, there would be no way on earth that she would've let one of her daughters leave the house in that dress and in those heels. I knew exactly what I had to do.

'You look really pretty, sweetheart.'

Even with her eyes fixed to the floor, I could tell Evie was petrified. 'Thanks, Dad, it's some of the things I bought on Saturday. I think they look great.'

I was about to respond when Lola emerged from the living room, took one look at Evie and drew a comically sharp intake of breath. 'Wow, Daddy, look what Evie's done to her face! She looks just like a clown!'

Evie scowled, 'No one asked you, you freak!'

Fearing an outbreak of World War Three, I bustled Lola back into the living room and closed the door. A car horn sounded. Anya's mum was getting anxious. I needed to make a decision.

'Have you got money?'

Evie nodded.

'And your phone?'

She nodded again and sighed, 'Can I go now?'

I kissed the top of her head. 'Okay then, have a nice time.'

As I watched her teeter down the front path, I tried to put my finger on why I hadn't followed through with my plan to do what Laura would've done. I had a number of competing theories covering everything from acute fear to total spinelessness, but it was only as the car pulled away with Evie and her friends inside that it dawned on me that it wasn't enough just to do what Laura would've done any more. These were uncharted waters. Evie wasn't just a young girl, she was a young girl without a mum. I wasn't just a dad, I was a husband without a wife, and somehow it didn't seem appropriate to keep referring to the old way of doing things. If I was going to be the girls' dad, if I was going to be the one they came to with their troubles, if I was going to be a potential model on which they based their understanding of men, then I was going to have to find my own way and not just pass myself off as a counterfeit Laura. I was going to have to do things my way and suffer the consequences.

14

Yes, Mr Hope?

Tom

All was quiet on the home front for the next few days. Having banned myself from reading any further entries in Evie's journal, there was no choice but to rely on what I could observe. She seemed infinitely less bad-tempered with Lola, she moaned less (about life, school, homework, everything) than usual and even began undertaking a number of extra afterschool activities. Lola continued being Lola: a quiet and thoughtful little girl who seemed to be as happy with a book in her hand as she was slumped in front of the TV. Things were going well for me too: a quick scan of that week's page of the family calendar revealed that I'd been for coffee with Ellie again, a bracing walk in the park with Clive and had managed to catch up with Rich and Marina too. And it was due once again to the family calendar that when Lola had a school trip to the Roman Museum the following week I remembered to pick her up later than usual.

However, the coach arrived much later than advertised and was met with a ripple of mildly sarcastic applause from the waiting parents. Whisking Lola off the coach, I checked the time and, as it was nearly half past four, made a unilateral decision to postpone my plans for a healthy homemade tea and replace them instead with a fish-and-chip supper we could pick up on the way home.

Lola seemed quieter than usual but I put this down to the fact that she was probably tired from the journey. Rather than pushing her for details, I told her about my own day and halfway through a jokey story about a dog I'd seen that looked like a sheep, Lola interrupted me.

'Dad,' she said, pointing across the road, 'what's Evie doing over there with that boy?'

Over the road, a couple of teenagers in school uniform were kissing on a bench near the bus stop. The girl was sitting on the boy's lap with her face turned away from us. Admittedly (from the back at least) she did resemble Evie, but I knew it couldn't be her because a) she didn't have a boyfriend and b) she had texted me less than ten minutes earlier telling me that she was still at school rehearsing some sort of play that her form was involved with.

'That's not Evie, sweetie,' I replied. 'It looks like her but it's not.'

Lola scrunched her face crossly. She hated being corrected when she was convinced she was right. 'Yes, it is Evie, Daddy, I can even see her bag.'

Okay, so the girl's bag certainly looked like Evie's: it was the same style and pattern but that wasn't anywhere near enough evidence for me to conclude that the girl was Evie.

'It's definitely not her, sweetie,' I told Lola, 'and just to prove it's not, I'll call her right now.' I dialled Evie's number and as it rang the girl on the bench stopped kissing her boyfriend and reached inside her blazer pocket for her phone. She checked the screen and returned it to her pocket at the exact moment that my call went through to Evie's voicemail.

As I stared at the kissing couple, it occurred to me that one of two things had to be at play here: either I was witnessing a series of uncanny coincidences or my fourteen-year-old daughter was indeed across the road with her face attached to a boy I'd never seen before. The mystery quickly resolved itself the moment the boy noticed himself being observed by Lola and me. He whispered something in the girl's ear and in response she tilted her head to get a better look at us. The expression of unadulterated horror on her face said it all: Evie was one hundred per cent in the biggest trouble of her entire life.

Linda

I was alone in the house, having rejected Moira's very kind offer to join her and some friends for a morning of shopping followed by lunch. Instead, I was sitting at the kitchen counter still in my dressing gown, staring at the blinking cursor on the Google homepage of Moira's laptop. For probably the hundredth time over the past few weeks I typed the name 'Frank Smith' into the search bar followed by the word 'Melbourne' and clicked 'search'. It was ridiculous really. If, as they say, the definition of insanity is doing the same thing over and over again and expecting different results, then my actions that morning proved beyond any doubt that I'd almost certainly lost the plot.

'I think I saw Frank,' I'd said to Moira three weeks earlier as I arrived home from my café date with Desi.

Moira had put down the mug of tea in her hand, frowning. 'Frank who? I don't know any—' She stopped suddenly. 'You don't mean *your* Frank do you?'

'Believe me, Moira, I know exactly how completely mad and utterly implausible this sounds, but yes, that's precisely what I'm saying: I think I saw Frank. He was loading paint into the back of a white pickup truck parked outside the hardware store opposite Veronica's.'

'You mean Baxter's Hardware?'

'I only caught a glimpse of his face and, well I know it's been over forty years but I'm convinced it was him. It sounds like madness, doesn't it? And to make matters worse, Desi arrived just as I saw him and I didn't want him thinking I was mad so I just pretended I was fine, but I don't think I did a terribly good job of it. I was all over the place. Every time he spoke to me, I either didn't reply or got so flustered that I forgot what I was saying. He must think I've gone completely gaga.'

'Well, let's just put Desi to one side for a moment and concentrate on the matter at hand: how likely is it really that the man you saw was Frank? I mean, what would Frank be doing in Australia, let alone shopping for paint in the middle of the day at a hardware store less than twenty minutes away from here.'

'You don't have to tell me that it doesn't make any sense. I don't remember him ever expressing any sort of desire to live in Australia, let alone leave teaching to become a handyman. But then again, when we were in our twenties who would have thought you'd be living in Oz either?'

'But really, Linda, sweetheart, wouldn't that be too much of a coincidence? Isn't it a lot more likely that your brain is playing tricks on you? You're still missing Laura, maybe you've even been thinking about how different things might've been if Frank hadn't left you all those years ago, and your subconscious has put both those ideas together and suddenly people from your past are springing up out of nowhere.'

'That's exactly what I've been trying to tell myself the whole way home but the idea won't shift. I even told Desi that I needed to run some errands after our lunch so I could go to the hardware store by myself.'

'And what did you learn?'

'I asked the young man behind the counter if he remembered serving a tall, white-haired gentleman an hour and a half earlier and he just looked at me like I was mad and explained that he'd only just come on shift and didn't have a clue what I was talking about. I would've pressed him further but there was a long queue of people waiting to be served and I just felt so ridiculous that I left and came straight here.'

'And what would you have done if it had been him?'

'I've no idea.'

'Exactly,' said Moira. 'So maybe you should just try to forget about it. The odds are that it wasn't him and even if it was, the likelihood of you ever finding him again are minuscule.'

'I used my phone to check the Internet; there are six hundred and eighty-five Frank Smiths in Melbourne alone, not including the best part of fifteen hundred F. Smiths registered with just an initial.'

'So no matter what you do it'll be like looking for a needle in a haystack,' said Moira, putting an arm around me. 'Linda, I know this has upset you, and if I thought there was any substance to it then you know I'd be right there with you, but I really think this is just one of those things you have to forget and chalk down to your mind playing tricks on you.'

No matter how hard I tried, I couldn't let go of the idea that the man I'd seen was Frank. So much so that over the next fortnight I used every conceivable excuse I could think of to walk past Baxter's Hardware. Under the guise of wanting to get fitter I told Moira I was taking afternoon power walks, when in truth I was simply walking up and down past Baxter's. Veronica's suddenly became my favourite place to have lunch with Desi (we ate or drank there at least a dozen times) and overnight I went from having no interest at all in Moira's laptop to being on it constantly – allegedly researching family holiday ideas for when I got back to England, when in reality I was trying to work out which, if any, of the Melbourne 'Frank Smiths' I'd found on the Internet was the Frank who'd left me nearly forty years ago. I became so obsessed that I even began turning down Moira's kind offers to take me out for the day, just so that I could stay home and search the web, which was how I came to be sitting at the kitchen counter looking through the results for 'Frank Smith' plus 'Melbourne'.

I was about to give up and take a shower when I decided to have one last go. In the past I'd tried all manner of word combinations along with 'Frank Smith' in the hope of finding something I could work with. But as my fingers hovered over the keyboard it occurred to me that the one combination I hadn't tried was 'Frank Smith' plus 'Melbourne' plus 'Baxter's Hardware'.

The first hit that came up on the screen was a newspaper report from four years earlier. It was an article about a charity event thrown by Baxter's Hardware in aid of a local children's hospital. The name of the proprietor, 'Mr Frank Smith' was mentioned several times but it was only when I examined the accompanying photo that I realised it was really him. After all these years, after so much heartache, after travelling thousands of miles to the other side of the world in a bid to save my son-in-law, I'd stumbled across the one skeleton from my past that I'd never expected to see again: Laura's father.

Tom

It was almost three weeks to the day after I caught Evie with her new boyfriend. I was packing away a supermarket delivery, while dreaming up new and inventive ways in which to make my eldest daughter's life a misery, when the doorbell rang. Leaving the tub of ice cream I'd been holding on the counter, I answered the door to find Fran on my doorstep.

With one thing and another, I hadn't given Fran much thought but now she was standing right in front of me, she was all I could think about.

It felt odd being attracted to a woman who wasn't my wife, and even odder knowing that the feeling wasn't mutual. I felt like I'd been flung back to my early teens when it had seemed like my entire reason for being was to torture myself by falling in love with some new and unattainable girl.

'I only dropped by to give you this,' said Fran, rejecting my invitation to come in for a cup of tea and reaching into her bag to take out a book.

I recognised the jacket even before she handed it to me. It was *On Grief* by C. S. Lewis, the sixth copy of the book I'd received from well-meaning friends since losing Laura. I'd still yet to read a single page of it. Somehow there never seemed to be a good time to settle down and read about the very thing I was spending my whole life trying to avoid.

'Oh, I've heard of this,' I said, accepting it from her. 'Is it good?'

'I've never read it,' said Fran. 'Granddad's been going on for days that he wanted to lend it to you but I think he was too shy to just drop round with it.'

'Did he find it helpful?'

'Put it this way,' said Fran, 'two days after my mum gave it to him he was using it as a coaster for his morning brew.' Fran laughed and tucked a stray strand of hair behind her ear. 'Anyway, enough about Granddad, how are you?'

I told her I was fine and then, for reasons I can't quite explain, I corrected myself.

'Actually I'm having girl trouble.'

'As in "girlfriend trouble"?'

I shook my head, wishing desperately that I hadn't tried to sound so clever. 'I mean "girl trouble" as in I've recently discovered that my fourteen-year-old daughter has been lying to me because she's gone and bagged herself a boyfriend.'

I told Fran all about the situation with Evie, how due to my intervention to help her self-esteem I'd indirectly helped her seduce Oliver, the boy in her class who had rejected her at her party only to very much change his mind the moment she turned up to the school disco dressed like a pole dancer, and how now because of the almighty row we had she once again wasn't talking to me.

'Girls can be such a nightmare at that age,' sympathised Fran. 'Just hearing that story makes me want to give my dad a hug and beg his forgiveness. You have my full condolences.'

'And they're much appreciated. Any tips on what I should do?'

Fran laughed. 'I'm the last person you should take advice from about raising kids. I can't even look at a pot plant without killing it. Is the problem the lying or the boyfriend? Or both.'

'The lying,' I replied, 'but if I'm honest the boyfriend thing bothers me just as much. I think she's much too young.'

'All dads think their daughters are too young to date. I think mine's still trying to get his head around it and I'm twenty-nine.'

'So you think I'm being too strict?'

She shook her head. 'I think you're looking out for her best interests.'

'So what should I do then?'

Fran sighed. 'Are you sure there's no one else you can ask? I'd feel terrible if I told you the wrong thing.'

'Well, I've decided not to tell my mother-in-law or any of my friends – partly because I want them to think I can deal with this myself, but mostly because it was my clueless efforts that helped Evie bag a boyfriend in the first place, so no, there is no one else to ask. You're it.'

Fran laughed. 'No pressure there then.' She sat down on the step and considered the question and I sat down too. I felt good sitting down next to her like this, almost as if we were old friends.

'I think you've got two choices,' she said eventually. 'Tell her no boyfriends and run the risk that she'll do it anyway or tell her you trust her to make her own decisions and hope she makes the right ones.'

I didn't like the sound of those choices at all. 'Surely there's got to be a third way?'

Fran shrugged. 'Well . . . you could do what the parents of one of my friends did when they found themselves in a similar situation . . . and invite the boyfriend over for dinner.'

'Do what?'

Fran laughed. 'I promise, it's nowhere near as bad as it sounds. It's one meal but it could sort all your problems. The thing is girls love to rebel so if you invite him round and are really nice to him it will show her that you're taking her feelings seriously, and take all the mystique out of Mr Bad Boy Oliver. Before you know it, she'll have dumped him for being boring and you won't have to worry about what she's up to any more.'

It was good advice, certainly a lot better than anything I had in mind. 'You're pretty good at this, aren't you?'

Fran smiled. 'If only I was this good at sorting out my own love life.'

'Everything okay?' I tried not to sound too hopeful, even though I had everything crossed that she'd dumped her boyfriend and was in need of a shoulder to cry on.

'It's fine,' said Fran. 'Or put it this way, it's nothing I can't handle. Just more of the same, really.'

I made Fran the offer of a drink again in the hope of finding out more but she stood up and told me she was heading off to work. I waved her goodbye and was about to close the door when she called out to me.

'Tom?'

'Yeah.'

'I know I don't really know you or your kids but for what it's worth I think your girls are lucky to have you as a dad.' She smiled and for a moment I thought she was going to say more, but then she looked at her watch and muttered that her boss would go mental if she was late again. She managed to get about halfway down the path before something occurred to me and I called after her.

'Fran?'

'Yeah?'

'What happened with your friend whose parents invited her boyfriend round for dinner? Did he lose his mystique so that she dumped him afterwards?'

Fran laughed. 'Not exactly, they ended up going out together for the rest of school and now they've got three kids and live in a four-bed house in Halifax. On the plus side, though, they do seem really happy.'

Despite the twist in the tale of Fran's story I did indeed get Evie to invite Oliver round for tea and a few days later he turned up at the house. He didn't look much like a rebel at all. He looked like a tall, spotty, hopelessly skinny teenage boy.

'Dad,' said Evie. 'This is Oliver.'

We shook hands. His were remarkably cold and clammy and made me want to wash my hands immediately. 'Nice to meet you, Oliver.'

'Nice to meet you too, Mr Hope.'

I tried my best to make small talk with the boy but every time I asked a question Evie glared at me as though I was being unduly harsh, so much so that in the end I gave up and suggested that they watch TV until dinner was ready, an idea they leaped at without any need for encouragement.

It was after six by the time we all finally sat down at the table. They helped themselves to food and began eating but no one said a word. After a while, the sound of five people politely chewing mouthfuls of pasta and beef sauce became so deafening that I couldn't stand it any longer.

'So Oliver—'

'Yes, Mr Hope?'

'Evie was telling me you're on the school chess team.'

'I am. The school didn't have a team at all, so I asked my form tutor Mr Laramie if we could make one and he said that he'd help us.'

I nodded. 'Impressive. You must be really excited. Have you played any matches yet?'

'Six.'

'How many did you win?'

'None.'

'None at all?'

Evie glared at me from across the table. 'Dad, stop it, you're embarrassing him!'

Oliver frowned at Evie as though they were an old married couple. 'He's not, he's just making conversation.' He turned his attention back to me. 'I don't mind not winning because my dad always says that the only way to improve your skills is to play people who are better than you so I think I must have learned quite a lot!'

He forced a polite laugh, as though impressed by his own sense of humour, but it was obviously a joke his dad had made in the past, which Oliver had reproduced for my benefit.

'Well, hopefully you'll get a win sometime.'

'Thank you, Mr Hope, I'll try. Do you like chess at all?'

'Not really, rugby was more my thing. Played for the school and the county. Do you play any sport?'

'I played football for a while when I was in primary school but I was never good enough to make the team.'

'It's not always about being good, you know. You can play sport to enjoy it.'

'I was terrible at it and I pretty much hated every second.'

Lola put down her fork and gave Oliver a hard stare. 'So why did you play it?'

Oliver shrugged. 'Because it seemed to make my dad really happy.'

Once dinner was over, without prompting Oliver helped to clear the table, which massively impressed me given that I usually had to shout several times at the girls before they'd even acknowledge I was talking, let alone asking for help around the home. He continued to impress me when Lola got out her maths homework and asked me for help, only for Oliver to offer his services instead.

'It's all right, Oliver,' I intervened. 'I'll sort her out in a minute once I've finished clearing up in the kitchen. You get off and watch TV with Evie if you like.'

'I'd actually really like to help her if that's okay. I quite like little kids. I think it's because I'm the youngest and my older brother and sister think I'm dumb. At least little kids think you're smart.'

Oliver stayed for another hour and a half before he announced that he had to go. I offered to pay for a taxi to take him home but he politely declined and explained that he'd ridden his bike over and would be fine going home. Then he said his goodbyes and Evie walked him to the door.

She was gone a good ten minutes and it took all the strength I had to resist speeding up their goodbye by making an appearance in the hallway, but finally I heard the door close and Evie came and joined me in the kitchen.

'So what did you think?'

'Of Oliver?'

'Dad!'

'I thought he was nice.'

'And?'

'And what?'

'Am I allowed to carry on seeing him?'

I shrugged. This was the million-dollar question. 'If I'm honest I think you're too young to have a boyfriend.'

'Mum was my age when she had her first boyfriend.'

'No she wasn't.'

'She was. She told me. His name was Andy and was a year older than her. She only went out with him for a couple of weeks but then she ditched him because he was really boring.' Something about the story gave me pause to think. 'I'm right, aren't I?' said Evie, studying my face.

'I'll tell you what,' I replied. 'Why don't we find out for sure?'

Upstairs in my bedroom I rummaged through the bottom of the wardrobe for a while, before finally pulling out an old shoebox and bringing it over to Evie, who was lying on the bed. She lifted off the lid. The box was filled with photographs from Laura's youth: family holidays, Christmases and birthdays. It took a while but eventually I found the picture I was looking for: a fourteen-year-old, spiral-permed Laura standing next to a tall red-haired boy wearing tight jeans and an even tighter T-shirt. I handed it to Evie.

'Is that the boy?'

'I think so.'

'Don't let it go to your head, Dad, but he's nowhere near as good-looking as you. What was Mum thinking?'

'She was fourteen, I don't think she was thinking anything.'

'We do think you know,' protested Evie. 'It's not all about hormones. We think about lots of things!'

I wondered if this was all that was in store for me now that my kids were getting older, a constant desire to keep them close, coupled with the knowledge that part of my job was to let them go.

'Fine, you can carry on seeing him if you want but no more lying, okay?'

Evie nodded. 'Never again.'

'And your school work can't suffer either.'

'I promise.'

'And I'll want to know where you are at all times.'

'But I can still see him?'

I nodded and she threw her arms around my neck in delight. It was official. My little girl had her very own boyfriend.

15

The weird kid

Tom

Given everything I'd had to deal with over the past few weeks, you'd think I was due a respite from any major crises. Sadly, however, life doesn't evenly space out one big parenting moment from another. Sometimes it lobs a bunch of them at you at once and you just have to do the best you can. So it was, that days after reluctantly sanctioning Evie's decision to start dating, I checked the family calendar and made the horrible discovery that Mother's Day was little more than a week away.

I had no memory whatsoever of the previous year's Mother's Day – the girls' first without Laura. Given the state I was in, I can only assume that either Linda didn't involve me in what she had planned or more likely, I'd been invited and had fobbed her off with some excuse or other. But that was then and this was now, and as much as I might have wanted to, I couldn't just wish the day away. Steeling myself as best I could, I called a family meeting so that together we could decide how best to celebrate the day.

'I think we should visit Mum's grave like we did last year with Nanny,' said Evie. 'It was really peaceful and the flowers we left for her were really nice.'

I looked over at Lola. 'And what about you, sweetie?'

She shrugged. 'I don't mind.'

This didn't seem like a Lola response at all. Normally if I asked her for an idea she'd give me half a dozen, straight off the top of her head without breaking into a sweat.

Rumour had it there was a bug going round school and kids were dropping like flies. 'You're not ill or anything, are you? You don't seem like yourself.'

'I'm okay.'

'Are you sure?'

She nodded. 'I'm sure.'

'What about you, Dad?' asked Evie. 'What do you want to do?'

In spite of my cemetery visit with Clive to see Dot, the idea of visiting Laura for the first time since the funeral still terrified me to the core.

'I think going to visit Mum is a lovely idea,' I said. 'We could take her some of her favourite flowers, couldn't we?'

'White roses,' said Evie. 'Those were her favourite, weren't they?'

I nodded, recalling a fractured image from the day of the funeral: Linda placing a bouquet of white roses on the lid of Laura's coffin as it was lowered into the ground.

'So a visit to the cemetery with her favourite flowers it is, then,' I said, and the girls nodded in agreement, and then one by one they left the table.

After our discussion I sensed an odd mood around the house, as though the girls were aware that this whole Mother's Day visit was a big thing for me and were deliberately playing it down for my benefit. Lola, especially, seemed not to want to talk about it, even though when I picked her up from school on Friday virtually every child in the playground was clutching some sort of handmade Mother's Day card. When I asked her where hers was, she told me that it was in her bag and refused to show it to me even when I asked to see it.

On the Sunday morning, we all woke early and after a bacon-and-egg breakfast went our separate ways to get dressed. I didn't say anything to the girls about what they should wear – I sort of assumed they'd just wear their regular clothes – but when I came downstairs in jeans and a jumper I found them both sitting at the kitchen table wearing their prettiest dresses. Excusing myself, I headed back upstairs and changed into a suit and tie, and only then did I call for a taxi to take us to the cemetery.

The journey was short, less than ten minutes in total, but it was more than long enough for me to work myself up into something approaching a panic attack: my heart was thumping double-time in my chest, I had tunnel vision, and every sound I heard seemed as though it was being filtered through a tin can. My every instinct was to tell the driver to turn around and go home, but I couldn't. The girls needed this, they needed me to be here with them, and so I shut my eyes firmly, swallowed down my anxiety and waited for the storm to pass.

'Dad,' said one of the girls, my head still so foggy it was impossible to pick out which. 'Dad, we're here.'

I opened my eyes. The cab had come to a halt in the cemetery car park and the driver was looking at me expectantly, but the tunnel vision, the heart-racing and the weird hearing thing had gone. I was safe.

'Sorry about that, I must have fallen asleep.' I paid the driver and we all got out of the car.

Evie put an arm around my waist. 'Are you okay, Dad? You seem a bit spaced out.'

Deep breath, exhale and repeat. 'I'm fine, sweetie, let's go.'

Flashes of the day of Laura's funeral came back to me as we walked: the stillness in the air; the sound of the gravel crunching beneath my shoes; the shape of the treeline ahead of us: all memories I'd thought forgotten but had never lost at all.

With a sureness of foot that I lacked, Evie, clutching the flowers to her chest, led the way while Lola and I followed close behind. I had no idea where we were going. Some parts of the journey seemed familiar, others not at all. Finally, we came to a halt in front of a grave marked by a black marble headstone inscribed with gold lettering:

Laura Elizabeth Hope
Wife, mother, daughter, friend
4th August 1974 – 26th October 2012

I reread it several times. Concise, eloquent and true. In summing up the breadth and depth of Laura, Linda had achieved the impossible; and I was about to say something to that effect when I felt Lola tug on my hand.

'Look, Dad,' she said, pointing to the ground. 'Someone's already left some flowers.'

At the base of the headstone was a small bouquet of white roses that seemed relatively fresh. I tried to think who might have laid them there without my knowledge. Marina? Possibly, although I'm sure she would have told me. Perhaps some of the mums from Lola's school? But then surely Ellie would have mentioned it? It seemed odd that someone should have left the flowers, and even more odd that they'd been left when it wasn't close to her birthday or the anniversary of us losing her. I wondered if an absent-minded mourner had made a mistake, and so I plucked the attached card from the flowers and read it: 'To Laura, with love, R.'

Whoever had left the bouquet had cared enough about Laura to bring flowers, and as I returned the card to the bouquet it was hard not to feel even guiltier than I did already: Laura was my wife and visiting her grave was supposed to be my job. It was a poor show on my part, a very poor show indeed. Clive would've been horrified.

'They must be from one of mum's friends,' I explained.

'What do we do now?' asked Lola.

Evie handed the flowers to Lola. 'I think you should put them down, Lolls, because I did it last year.'

Lola took the flowers and laid them neatly in front of the headstone, and then reaching into her bag, withdrew the card that she'd made at school and placed it next them. On the front of the card was a brightly painted daffodil under which Lola had written in her best handwriting, 'Happy Mother's Day'. She stood and took my hand again. No one said a word.

'I think we need to say something,' said Evie after a while. 'At least that's what Nanny did when we came last year.'

The girls looked at me, their eyes full of expectation. I was the adult here. The one who was supposed to know the rules. They needed me to say something but my mind was blank.

'I don't know what to say.'

Evie squeezed my hand. 'Just say whatever comes into your head.'

I thought hard but there was nothing. At least nothing that made any sense. But I couldn't let them down. I'd done enough of that to last a lifetime.

'Laura, it's us,' I said, 'we've come to wish you a Happy Mother's Day and to let you know that we still really miss you . . . and we won't ever stop.'

Linda

I was in the kitchen, finishing a mug of tea before heading out for a walk along the beach with Moira, when the doorbell rang. Moira called from the hallway that she would answer it and when she returned, Desi was with her.

'Long time no see,' he said and he gave me a hug that was awkward for both of us. 'Did you have a good time on your travels?'

My face flushed. I'd hated lying to him. He deserved so much better.

'About that . . .' I replied as Moira slipped out of the room leaving us alone. 'The truth is . . .'

Desi smiled. 'You didn't go anywhere?'

I nodded. 'How did you know I was lying?'

'To be honest, Linda, I'd sort of guessed. I knew from the way you were avoiding me that something was up. What's this all about? Have I done something wrong?'

'It wasn't you, really it wasn't. I've just had a lot on my mind lately and I was feeling a bit overwhelmed.'

'Problems with your son-in-law?'

'No,' I replied. 'Something a bit more complicated than that.'

Desi and I had barely spoken since the day that I saw Frank, over a month ago. As much as I was sure he would've understood had I told him what was going on, I was so focused on finding Frank that I didn't have space for Desi in my head. Every time he'd called to ask me out for the day I'd made up excuses, until finally I lied and told him that Moira and I had booked a two-week sightseeing tour and that I'd call him on my return. It wasn't very nice of me but I simply didn't have the energy to deal with him as well as Frank.

'Things haven't been right between us since the day when I was late to meet you at Veronica's,' said Desi as we sat down at the kitchen table, holding two steaming mugs of tea. 'I know something happened that day, I just don't know what.'

'It was the day I saw Frank.'

Desi raised an eyebrow. 'And Frank is who exactly?'

'An old boyfriend of mine,' I replied. 'And the last time I saw him was nearly forty years ago when he walked out on me when I was pregnant with Laura.'

It was five days after my twenty-fifth birthday when I found out that I was pregnant. I hadn't felt right for a couple of days and I made myself an appointment at the doctor's. One of the first questions he'd asked me was whether I could be pregnant and I told him it was impossible because I was on the pill. He asked me lots of questions, listened to my heart, checked my breathing and told me to call back in a few days to find out the results. I barely slept until my next appointment when he broke the news that I was, in fact, pregnant.

Although I had told Moira straight away it took me a week before I plucked up the courage to tell Frank. We'd been together for the best part of eight months and while in a lot of ways it was still very much early days for our relationship, we were undoubtedly very much in love or at least I was with him. Frank was all I thought about day and night and I genuinely believed we had a future together.

The first words out of his mouth after I'd told him I was pregnant were, 'Are you keeping it?' I knew it wasn't exactly great timing – after all, we'd only just got our careers going, and money would be tight – but it hadn't once crossed my mind not to have the baby. The truth was, I'd already fallen head-over-heels in love with this tiny life inside me and while I hadn't set out to be a mother so soon, now that I was, there was no going back.

But Frank had other ideas. He thought we were too young to start a family, and pleaded with me to reconsider. When I refused, he stood up and left without another word and I never saw him again. I went around to his digs and was told he had moved out without leaving a forwarding address.

About a week later, I received a letter from him postmarked Bedford. In it he accused me of trying to trap him by getting pregnant deliberately. He said that while he did have feelings for me, he was certain he didn't want to be a father. He finished his letter by telling me I shouldn't try to find him but that he would do his best to stay in touch. He signed off by wishing me 'all future happiness', but really he needn't have bothered because by the time I'd reached that point in the letter, I'd made up my mind that I didn't need him or his good wishes. My baby and I would be fine on our own.

And we were. Laura and I were the happiest little unit ever. We didn't need or miss Frank. In fact, I doubt that I would've given him a second thought apart from the odd passing 'what if?' had it not been for losing Laura. It changed everything. Since her funeral I'd been thinking about him off and on, wondering where he was, what he was doing and how he might react to the news that the daughter he'd never met had died. And so the discovery that Frank was not just here in Australia but owned a hardware store less than half a mile away from Moira's house knocked me for six. Now that I knew where he was (or at least how to find him) I had a huge decision to make: should I tell him about Laura? Did he even deserve the right to grieve the loss of the wonderful human being that she was, when his only contribution to her life began and ended with her conception?

I needed advice, but the only person I'd felt able to ask so far was Moira and she was firmly of the opinion that I didn't owe Frank a damn thing. I'd thought about telling Tom in the hope that he might be able to shed some light on the situation. A couple of times I nearly did, but stopped myself at the last moment, reasoning that he already had enough on his plate. The most natural person to ask, of course, was Desi. Not only could he offer me an impartial view, but also there was something so wise, kind and patient about him that I didn't doubt his ability to get to the heart of the matter.

I looked at Desi sipping his tea and suddenly blurted out: 'What do you think I should do?'

Tom

It was a school night during the first week of April, and Lola was upstairs in her room. I was at the table reading a newspaper when Evie came into the kitchen. She sat down opposite me, picked up a pencil and began idly tapping it on the table as if trying to make her mind up about something. Whatever the problem was, she now had my attention.

'What's up?'

'Nothing.'

'Are you sure?'

'Well, it's not nothing exactly.'

'So what is it then?'

She shrugged. 'I want to tell you but I'm not sure how you'll take it.'

My stomach knotted several times over. I was far too young to be a grandfather. 'You can tell me anything.' My mouth was so dry I could barely get the words out. 'Of course you can.'

She glanced over her shoulder towards the kitchen door as if making sure the coast was clear. 'It's about Lolls.'

A huge sigh of relief. 'What about her?'

'I heard something about her yesterday that I think you ought to know.'

I put the newspaper down on the table between us.

'Go on.'

'Oliver's cousin Freddy is in the year above Lola, and he told Oliver that Lola's the weird kid.'

'The what?'

'The weird kid.'

'The weird kid?'

'You know,' said Evie, waggling her eyebrows up and down like a wide-eyed lunatic. '*The weird kid*. Every school's got one: you know, like the kid who puts gross stuff in their mouth just to make you laugh; the kid who completely loses it at a teacher just because they've been told off for talking; the kid who has a dead fly collection in their pencil case and thinks it's normal. The weird kid.'

'I know what a weird kid is,' I replied, recalling Adam Masterson from my secondary school, who was known colloquially as 'the kid who refuses to wear shoes'. 'But are you actually saying Lola's the weird kid at her school? What weird stuff does she do exactly?'

'Well for starters, she's got no friends.'

'That can't be right. The first day I took her in to school she reeled off a long list of them to me.'

'Well, that's the thing,' said Evie, 'she did have friends but then they all stopped wanting to play with her.'

'Why? What's she done?'

'This is the worst bit,' said Evie. 'Apparently she marches around the edge of the playground on her own, head back, arms straight like she's in the army or something, and whenever anyone asks her what she's doing, she tells them she's talking to Mum. And they all know Mum's dead, Dad, they know, so basically at school she's the weird kid who talks to her dead mum and no one wants to be around her.'

'I thought you knew,' said Ellie the following morning when I brought the subject up with her. 'I honestly would've said something if I thought you didn't.'

'I didn't have a clue.'

'And what's Lola said about it all.'

'I haven't brought it up with her. I just can't. Why do kids have to be so mean?'

'I think it's just part of the territory. Have you thought about giving her a bit of a helping hand.'

'How?'

'Arranging a play date for her or something. You know how it is, once one of the kids in her class finds out she's okay to play with, the rest will follow.'

The next morning I took Ellie's advice and floated the idea of a play date amongst some of the parents in Lola's class. I was met with excuses galore. The responses varied from 'We'd love to but we're all booked up at the moment' to 'We're not really doing play dates right now but thanks for asking'. In spite of all the rejections, I continued lobbying until finally two mums agreed to check their calendars and get back to me. This sounded a lot like I was being fobbed off but short of any other inspiration, I decided to take it as a glimmer of hope.

On my way home that morning I berated myself for not having seen this coming a long time ago. The clues had been there for a while – the appearance of her little shoebox shrine, the way she had become so much more self-contained – and I'd made things worse by accepting her behaviour as normal, instead of seeing it for what it was: a little girl desperately missing her mum.

I wanted to do something, anything I could, to solve the problem, but after my own experience of grief counselling I wasn't sure that packing Lola off to some child psychologist would be the right thing to do; a position which Clive wholeheartedly supported when I told him about the situation over lunch at Morrisons' café that afternoon.

'A headshrinker's the last thing she needs,' he said, adding extra tomato ketchup to his bacon bap. 'Bunch of quacks the lot of them.'

'So what's the alternative? I can't sit by and do nothing, can I? She's obviously missing her mum.'

'Which is why it's no one's bloody business what she does in the playground,' said Clive. 'So she talks to her mum, big bloody deal! I talk to my Dot, are you going send me to the shrink too? Poor mite, if anyone needs their heads seeing to it's those little swine teasing her, but then what do I know? It's not like I've been on this bloody planet the best part of eighty years is it?'

I was about to respond when my phone rang. Clive rolled his eyes in disgust but I took the call anyway in case it was from school, only instead it turned out to be Hayley Anderson, mother of Scarlett, the newest girl in Lola's class. Her family had just moved to Reigate from Bristol and Hayley wanted to take up my offer of a play date with Lola. 'Scarlett really misses all of her friends at her old school,' she explained, 'and I think this will help her a lot.'

Lola was mystified when I explained on our walk home from school that Scarlett was coming over for a play date.

'She's coming to our house?'

'After school on Friday.'

'Why?'

'Well, we were talking about how difficult it is for kids to settle in to a new school and so I thought I'd invite her for tea. That's okay, isn't it?'

Lola shrugged. 'You do know that I don't actually know her, don't you . . . ?'

'I know but—'

'. . . actually that I've never even spoken to her . . .'

'—that will all change once—'

'. . . and that last week I saw her being mean to Lottie Hannibal.'

'—she's been round.'

'Okay,' she said uncertainly, and then without missing a beat she started telling me the plot to the DVD they had watched during wet playtime that afternoon.

When Friday came around, not only did Scarlett's mum stay for tea, but Evie's boyfriend, Oliver, did too and he hadn't even been invited. He just appeared with Evie on her return from school and set a place for himself at the table, and halfway through the meal there was a surreal moment when I found myself looking around the seated diners in bewilderment as Scarlett's mum chatted to Oliver about the best way to teach long division, Evie fielded question after question from Scarlett about the pros and cons of secondary school, while Lola, indifferent to everything happening around her, loaded up her plate with yet another slice of pizza.

After tea, Lola and Scarlett headed up to Lola's room to play. Evie and Oliver wandered off as well, leaving me to make small talk with Scarlett's mum until just after six, when she announced that they really had to go.

As Lola and I stood waving goodbye to Scarlett, I was pretty sure that their budding friendship would be lucky to survive a week, let alone a lifetime, but even if it only lasted a day I hoped it would be enough for the kids in Lola's class to realise that perhaps Lola wasn't quite so odd after all. That's all I wanted really: for the kids to give Lola a chance.

In an attempt to be subtle, I left it until bedtime before probing Lola on how the play date had gone, but as soon as I walked into Lola's room I felt like something wasn't quite right. She was sitting on the edge of her bed in her pyjamas, appearing to read a book, but as I looked around the room I could feel her eyes on me the entire time. At first I could see nothing amiss, but then I noticed the shoebox shrine poking out from her Disney princess bin in the corner of the room. I could see from the look of worry on Lola's face that the shrine hadn't ended up there by accident. For some reason yet to be made clear she wanted to get rid of it. I fished it out of the bin and sat down on the bed next to Lola.

'Are you angry?'

'No, of course I'm not. I'm just wondering why it's in the bin.'

'I can't tell you.'

'Of course you can.'

'No, I can't.'

'Why not?'

'Because.'

'Because what?'

'I just don't want it any more.'

'That's fine, I just want to know why, that's all.'

'Can't I just not want it?'

'You can do what you like, sweetie, it's your thing, but I still want to know why though.'

She drew a deep breath and sighed. 'The other children laugh at me at school because I talk to Mum in the playground.'

'I know they do, sweetie. It's not fair, is it?'

For a moment she seemed surprised that I knew, but then she shrugged as though it didn't matter any more. 'Scarlett asked me why I didn't have a mum any more and I told her it was because she'd died, and then she asked me about the shrine and I said it was there so I don't forget my mum, and she said it was silly because it was only a shoebox, and I told her she was right, and then I put it in the bin.' She looked up at me, her eyes brimming with tears. 'I don't want a shoebox any more, Dad, I just want a mum.'

16

Now you're being cynical

Tom

Marina poured the last of the fruit juice from the jug into a glass and handed it to me as the children rushed out of the house into the garden, followed by Rich pretending to be a monster.

'And you're sure that's exactly what she said?'

'Word for word.'

'She said she wanted "a mum" and not "*her* mum"?'

'I know, it's a weird thing to say, isn't it?'

Marina shrugged. 'Maybe not.'

'How do you mean?'

'Well there are two things going on here, aren't there?' said Marina, setting down her glass on the coffee table in front of us. 'It's obvious that on one level she's still really missing Laura terribly, which is completely understandable. But on another, more basic level I think she might be missing all the things she would be getting from a mother figure if one were around. The things that she was getting from Linda before she left: the cuddles, the chats, you know the sort of thing.'

'But I've tried to give her all of those things.'

'I know you have,' said Marina. 'You're an absolutely amazing dad, and don't you ever forget it. What I'm saying, though, is that it's just different, isn't it? Surely you of all people must know that?'

She was right of course. I did know. I knew what it was like to be raised by a lone father after my mum left. Not that my dad didn't try hard to compensate with homemade birthday cakes and making a big fuss over me at Christmas, but without Mum it just wasn't the same, it felt like an imitation in both act and emotion, an attempt to recreate the past from the leftovers of the present, and it fooled no one. Was that how Lola felt? Did Evie feel like that too? The idea that they might cut me to the quick.

'So you're saying she needs a woman in her life?'

'I'm saying that she's probably sick and tired of being the only kid in the class without a mum. You know what kids are like at that age, none of them want to be different. None of them want to stand out. She wants a mum because all of the other kids have mums, and she doesn't know how else to be.'

'So what do you think I should do? Hire another nanny and go back to work?'

Marina shook her head. 'You don't want to know what I think.'

'Because?'

'Because you didn't like it the last time I brought it up.'

She was referring to a conversation a few weeks earlier when she had told me that when I was ready to start dating she had lots of single friends who would love to meet me. I'd shot the idea down straight away, saying something along the lines of, 'I'll let you know when I'm ready to start crowdsourcing my love life,' and we never spoke about it again.

'So this time around, you're saying I should start dating again just to find the girls a mum? I'm sure any woman would love that: "What was it that first drew you to me? My eyes, my smile or my sparkling personality?" "Actually, it was the fact that you were a dab hand at doing all the stuff with my kids that I'm hopeless at."'

'Now you're being cynical,' said Marina.

'I'm not being cynical; I'm being a realist. No woman worth her salt is going to come within a million miles of me if they think all I want to do is audition a mother for my kids!'

'That might be the case,' said Marina, 'but then again it might not. I guess we'll never know unless, you know, you actually put yourself out there.'

'It's like I told you before, I'm not ready.'

Marina sighed heavily. 'With the best will in the world, Tom, I don't even think you'd know what ready looked like if it stared you in the face. All Lola's saying is that she accepts the fact that her mum isn't coming back, that she misses Linda and wishes she had someone to play a similar role in her life. And the only way that's going to happen is if you make it happen. It's that "A journey of a thousand miles . . ." thing, isn't it? You know how much I miss Laura, I really do, all I'm saying is maybe it's time you finally took that first step.'

'And let me guess, you've got someone in mind?'

Marina smiled sheepishly. 'Funny you should say, but a really good friend of mine has just moved back to the UK after eight years in New Zealand. Her name's Kerry, she's a paediatric nurse, really pretty and whip-smart too. And while I'm not saying that she's going to be the next mother of your kids, what I am saying is that she's a lot of fun and I think you could probably do with some of that in your life, don't you? Give me the nod when you're ready and I'll make the call.'

That night I read with Lola and afterwards we sat chatting about nothing in particular, before I finally kissed her goodnight. I was halfway out of the room when I stopped and turned around.

'Lolls?'

'Yeah?'

'You know your shrine?'

'Yeah.'

'I just want you to know that it's on the bedside table in my room and any time you want it, you can just go and get it, okay?'

'But I don't want it.'

'I know you don't now, sweetie, I'm just saying that if you do change your mind I've got it, okay?'

'Okay.'

There was a long pause.

'Lo?'

'Yeah.'

'You know that Mum loved you very much, don't you?'

'Yeah.'

'And if there was anything in the world that she could have done to still be here with you, you know she would've done it?'

'What like?'

Not quite the question I'd been expecting. 'I don't know really.'

'Then what did you mean?'

'I don't know really . . . I just want you to know that Mum didn't want to go, she didn't have a choice in the matter. If it had been up to her she would have been with you forever.'

Evie was at the kitchen table doing her French homework when I came into the room. For a brief moment she looked up from the page of her textbook and as our eyes met, I felt like she'd read my mind. It was all I could do not to justify myself to her for what I was about to do. Thankfully the urge passed, and as she returned to her homework, I picked up my phone from the kitchen counter and texted Marina from the hallway: 'It's just me. I've been thinking that maybe you were right after all. If the offer still stands please make the call.'

Linda

I was back at Veronica's café with Moira, watching the entrance to Baxter's hardware store, only this time I knew exactly when Frank would be arriving, and this time I would finally talk to him.

'How are you feeling?' asked Moira.

'Terrified. How about you?'

'Angry,' replied Moira. 'I mean it, Linda, if he says a single thing out of line I promise you I won't hold back.'

'Believe me,' I replied, 'if he does anything like that I won't want you to.'

It was Desi who had helped me make up my mind to seek out Frank and tell him about Laura. On the day I told him all about Frank, I'd asked him whether he thought I ought to make contact, fully expecting him to agree with Moira, but his answer surprised me. 'The only person who'll hurt if you don't tell him is you,' he said. 'You'll feel bad that you haven't done right by Laura and he won't feel a thing. But if you do tell him, then you'll know for a fact that you've done what needed to be done, because at the end of the day it's not about Frank at all, but doing right by your little girl.'

He was right of course: this wasn't about my relationship with Frank, the idea that he had some sort of inalienable right to know about Laura, or even a latent desire to make him feel guilty about the amazing life that he had missed out on, it was about a mother doing right by her only daughter, no more and no less. I was telling him because in a way I couldn't quite pinpoint, it felt like what she would have wanted.

After talking to Desi, I'd called the hardware store, told them I was an old school friend of Frank's and asked when he would be in next, because I wanted to surprise him. The person I spoke to told me that Frank was semi-retired and only came in every now and again for meetings with the store manager or to help out with home deliveries, and so they weren't sure when he would next be in. I called again the following week, and this time I was told that he'd left a message only that morning to say that he would be in after two the following afternoon. Straight away, I knew my moment had arrived.

My first call after getting the news was to Desi, who reassured me again that I was doing the right thing, and the second was to Tom and the girls because I missed them more than ever. It was good talking to them, even though I sensed that there was something not quite right there. Lola seemed quieter than usual, Evie was in a hurry as she was on her way out with friends and Tom just seemed distracted. I pressed all of them, trying to find out what was wrong, but they all told me in their own way that they were fine. Still, talking to them was just the thing I needed. It bolstered my spirits and made me feel that no matter what happened when I met Frank, somehow I'd be okay.

It was quarter past two when I saw Frank's white pickup truck pull up in front of the hardware store, and before we'd even left the café my heart was pounding, I was practically shaking with fear. The plan that Moira and I had hatched on the way over was straightforward to say the least: I would go into the store alone and ask a member of staff to call the owner to the front desk. The moment Frank arrived, I would be polite but firm and tell him that I had some news I'd like to tell him privately. Hopefully he'd take me to some quiet back room where I'd tell him what he needed to know, and then once I was done I'd get up and go and never see him again.

The first flaw in the plan was the fact that instead of being hidden away in a back office somewhere, Frank was actually behind the till, which was right next to the entrance, talking to one of his employees and so the moment I walked in he looked up, assuming I was just another customer in need of a welcome to the store. I don't think I've ever seen anyone quite as gobsmacked in my life. He recognised me instantly and for a good few moments all he did was stand there with his mouth open, gaping at me like a wet fish.

'Linda? Linda Wood? Bloody hell! Is it really you?'

'Yes, it is, Frank,' I replied unsteadily, 'it's me.'

'I can't believe it! Linda Wood! It really is you!' He started coming towards me from behind the till. 'What are you doing here in Melbourne? Was it an accident or did you know I'd be here? I've got to tell you this has really blown my—' He stopped and looked over my shoulder as two young men walked in through the entrance.

'Everything okay, Dad?' asked the taller of the two.

I studied the young man who had just spoken. He had the same long nose as Frank but his face was rounder. The second young man, on the other hand, couldn't have looked more like a young Frank if he tried. All these years I'd wondered how Frank's life had turned out and now in the space a few seconds I'd found out. After walking out on me when I was at my most vulnerable, after walking away from his own flesh and blood, Frank had taken himself off to another country and started a family of his own. This hadn't been part of my plan at all.

'I've got to go,' I said.

'But you've only just arrived,' protested Frank. He looked across at his sons. 'Boys, this is Linda, an old friend of mine from teacher-training college in England. She literally just walked in off the street and said hello.' He looked back to me. 'Please, Linda, stay, I'll cancel everything I've got going on here and catch up properly.'

'Really I can't,' I replied. My head felt all funny. I couldn't string a single coherent thought together. 'I have to go.'

'At least give me a number where I can contact you,' he said. 'Are you local? Do you live here? Are you just over for a visit?' He wiped his brow with the back of his hand. 'I still can't believe it's you, right here in my little store!' He called over to the employee behind the till to bring him a pen and paper and handed both to me. I was so flustered I scribbled down Moira's number without thinking, and shoving the pen and paper into his hands I ran out of the store.

Tom

When it came to the kids I was used to being invisible. I was familiar with them trying to walk through, rather than past, me while on their way about their business; I was used to Lola's 'selective' deafness whenever I called her to help around the house; and I'd long since grown accustomed to the kids entering a room where I was watching TV and switching channels as though I didn't exist. In fact, I was so used to being invisible that when they did notice me – as they did on Easter Monday, as I was preparing to go round to Rich and Marina's to meet Kerry – I actually found it quite disconcerting.

Lola was at the kitchen table with nineteen-year-old Lucy, the eldest daughter of our next-door-but-one neighbours and the only person to have made it on to Linda's approved list of emergency babysitters. Busy making a card for the Easter Bunny to thank him for all of the chocolate eggs she'd received the previous day, but the moment I came into the kitchen she got up from the table and shot across the room to take a closer look at me.

'Why are you all dressed up?'

I wasn't dressed up at all. I was wearing a blue jacket, black T-shirt and jeans: the very definition of 'smart-casual', which had been exactly the look I'd been going for.

'Firstly, I'm not all dressed up, Lo, these are just Daddy's regular clothes and secondly I told you last night I'm going to Rich and Marina's'

Evie, who had been engrossed in her maths homework, came over to join her sister. 'I remember you saying you were going out but I don't remember you saying anything about Rich and Marina's or about getting dressed up. You never get dressed up. You look like a man in an advert getting ready for the weekend.'

Oliver, who over the past few weeks had become something

of a permanent fixture at our house, joined Evie in staring at me. 'She's right, Mr H, you're definitely looking well buff.' He sniffed the air. 'And you smell great too.'

The babysitter who was now the only person in the room not haranguing me tried to cajole Oliver and the girls into leaving me alone.

'Come on, chaps, why don't you leave your dad in peace and join me in a game of cards? Surely he's not that interesting?'

'Something's going on, I know it,' said Evie. 'You're not going to Rich and Marina's at all, you've got a job interview and you're going back to work, aren't you?'

'But if you go back to work who will pick me up from school?' asked Lola, scandalised. 'I don't want to go to after-school club!'

As I looked from daughter to daughter I wondered why nothing was ever simple, why today of all days they couldn't have just ignored me as usual.

'I'm not going to an interview,' I explained, 'and I'm not going back to work, and Lola, you won't have to worry about going to afterschool club. I really am going to Rich and Marina's to talk about a bunch of boring adult stuff. You can believe me or you can spend the whole night speculating, it's up to you but really I've got to go.'

This wasn't a date. This was one of the stipulations I'd insisted upon when Marina called to arrange the details after I'd agreed to meet her friend Kerry. It was simply two people who didn't know each other eating home-cooked food at the same table as the friends they had in common. There was nothing romantic about it. Not the slightest hint. It wasn't even to be considered a precursor to a date. Kerry should arrive with no expectations of the evening at all. As far as she was concerned I was simply there to make up the numbers.

Kerry was tall but not too tall, and fashionable without being too fashionable. She had shoulder-length auburn hair and a pretty face, and was wearing a patterned top paired with a long green skirt and tan boots. Under the right circumstances (which these certainly weren't) I was pretty sure I'd have found her attractive.

'So Marina was telling me you're a paediatric nurse,' I said to Kerry when Rich left the room in order to help Marina in the kitchen. 'That must be really rewarding.'

'It is,' she replied, 'very, although if I'm honest it's heart-breaking in equal amounts. And Marina said you're in television. That must be exciting.'

'I was in TV but I'm not any more. I'm a stay-at-home dad to two girls – one eight-year-old and one fourteen-year-old – at the moment, which is far more hair-raising than TV ever was.'

'Have you got pictures?'

I showed her the most recent ones on my phone, taken when we'd gone bowling the weekend before last.

'They're gorgeous,' she said. 'You must be so proud of them.'

'I am,' I replied. 'I really am.'

There was a semi-awkward silence while we both geared up with our second round of questions. I'd planned to ask her about her time in New Zealand but before I could come up with a question, she hit me with one of her own.

'So how long is it since your wife passed away?'

'It was a year ago last October.'

'I can't imagine what that must feel like. That must be so tough for you and the girls too.'

'It is, but we're getting by as best we can.' Feeling self-conscious I took a sip from my glass and offered up another question, just as she did the same.

'No,' she apologised. 'You go first.'

'It was nothing,' I replied. 'I was just going to ask what brought you to back to the UK.'

'I split up with my partner. We were together a long time and it really knocked my confidence. It took me two years to get my act together, by which time I realised that the one thing I really wanted to do was to come home, and so I quit my job and did just that.'

'Any regrets?'

'Only that I wished I'd done it sooner. I wasted too much time mourning someone who wasn't worthy of the tears I was shedding.' She shrugged. 'Better late than never, eh?'

Dinner was a fish recipe that Marina had apparently been dying to make for months. It was as delicious as it was complicated, and between my enjoyment of the food and the wine that went with it I finally began to relax. I think it must have been the same for Kerry because suddenly the conversation really started to flow. As well as learning all about her life in New Zealand, I learned that Kerry had spent part of her twenties working in a hospital Botswana, and that she was an expert diver and had, on a recent visit to the Philippines, swum around the wreck of a World War Two Japanese warship. She was talented too. Aside from the diving, she could play the piano and speak fluent French and Italian. At one point I told her that she sounded an awful lot like Superwoman and this became a sort of running joke for the evening: 'Oh, Kerry, would you mind scanning the fridge for the clotted cream with your X-ray vision?' and 'Is it a bird? Is it a plane? No, it's Kerry pouring me another glass of Merlot.'

The following morning Evie took Lola along to the children's art club she'd been helping out at all Easter, leaving me free to meet Clive for breakfast at Morrisons. When I told Clive about my 'not a date' date with Kerry, I half expected him to reprimand me as a traitor to the cause but oddly he couldn't have been more gentle with me.

'Being alone isn't for everyone,' he sighed. 'Who knows, maybe if I'd been younger and had a young family like you I'd be thinking that way too. And just because you don't want to be alone doesn't mean that you've stopped loving Laura. All it means is that you've finally accepted that life goes on.'

'It doesn't matter anyway,' I replied. 'I don't think we'll see each other again. She was nice enough but there was no spark.'

'What was she?' chuckled Clive. 'A bloody electricity pylon? What are you on about?'

'I mean that we got on well enough but that was about it.'

'Ugly was she?'

'Actually she was really pretty.'

'Bit dim then?'

'She's a nurse and she can speak two languages so I think not.'

'So what's wrong with her then?'

'Like I said, there was no spark. We got on fine, but that was about it.'

'It's a wonder you ever found anyone to marry you with your "sparks" and your nonsense,' said Clive. 'Do you think I'd have ever got my Dot if I'd waited around for sparks? We only got together because friends of ours were courting and they both wanted someone to talk to. We couldn't have been more indifferent towards each other if we tried. Sparks or whatever you want to call them don't just happen, they're made.'

Clive's words of wisdom stuck with me for the rest of the day. Maybe he had a point after all? Just because there had been sparks between Laura and me when we first met didn't necessarily mean that there had to be sparks with Kerry too. In fact, maybe it was better if there weren't any to begin with, because at least then we would be able to get to know each other properly and not have our judgement clouded by all the usual bells and whistles of the first flushes of love.

'Tom, lovely to hear from you,' said Marina when I called her later that day. 'So you got home okay?'

'Yes, no problem,' I replied. 'I'm just ringing to say thanks for yesterday, the food was amazing.'

'I'm not sure I'd bother with that pudding again. All that faffing around for a glorified trifle, no thanks. Anyway, I'm glad you enjoyed it.'

There was a long pause.

'And did, er, Kerry have a good time too?'

'Yeah, I think so, she was here until quite late anyway chatting over old times.'

I felt like a school kid asking a girl in my class if her friend likes me. 'And did she mention me at all?'

'Oh, right, I thought you weren't thinking of this whole thing as a date.'

'I wasn't, but something someone said to me today made me change my mind. So Kerry . . . did she say anything about me?'

'She said she thought you were a really lovely guy . . .'

'But?'

'The thing is, Tom, with one thing and another she's actually quite busy at the moment.'

'That's exactly the kind of thing people say when they're blowing you off.'

'But there was nothing to "blow off" in the first place, was there? You said yourself it wasn't a date.'

Now I was intrigued. It was one thing for me to decide that it wasn't a date but it was completely another for her to do the same. 'So come on then, Marina, what was so wrong with me that your friend could make up her mind after one single meeting that she didn't want to see me again?'

Marina signalled her surrender with the heaviest of sighs. 'She said there was absolutely nothing wrong with you per se, okay? Her exact words were, "He's a lovely guy but there was just no spark."'

PART THREE

'None loves the messenger who brings bad news.'

– ***Sophocles, Antigone***

17

This ain't my first rodeo

Tom

With my foray into the world of 'not dating' permanently on hold I decided to focus my energies on the children, paying special attention to Lola, who particularly needed a win. Although she had yet to show evidence of having made any new friends, she stubbornly refused to let it get her down and day after day put on a brave face and marched into school without complaint. Truly, she was my absolute hero. So when it was announced that there had been a mistake on the spring newsletter and that Year Three's forthcoming Victorian day was actually an Egyptian day, I immediately saw an opportunity to give Lola the boost she deserved.

According to Ellie, of all the events in the school calendar, History Days were to be feared the most. Each one required parents to send their child to school dressed in the costume of the era being studied; and to encourage friendly competition, there were class prizes as well an overall prize for the best costume in the year. Given the (at best) patchy results of my past attempts at fixing problems in my children's lives, I probably should've known better than to latch on to the idea of winning the prize for best costume as a way of restoring Lola's popularity among her peers, but when I asked her what she wanted to be for Egyptian Day and she said, 'The prettiest Egyptian princess ever,' I couldn't help myself. 'Well that's what you're going to be,' I informed her in front of Evie and Oliver over tea that evening. 'I'm going to make you the best Egyptian princess costume your school has ever seen.'

The following morning I woke up in a cold sweat as I recalled the rash nature of my promise. I could barely sew a button on, let alone make an Egyptian princess costume from scratch. A quick early morning search on the Internet, however, revealed that there was a whole industry devoted to History Day costumes, and for the small sum of twenty-eight pounds plus postage and packaging I could have a good one with me by the end of the week. With this in mind, I sounded Lola out on how she might feel about an off-the-peg number on our walk to school.

'But Mrs Barclay said it's more fun if your costume's homemade.'

'I think that was probably more of a suggestion, don't you? What if someone's mum or dad isn't very good at costume-making. It wouldn't be very fair if they couldn't get one from a shop, would it?'

She considered the question carefully. 'No, it wouldn't.'

'So you'd be fine with one from a shop then?'

Lola shook her head. 'But I thought you were talking about other mums and dads?'

'I was.'

'Good, because I think I'd much prefer a homemade one. Mum always used to make me homemade costumes and they were always the best.'

If Lola hadn't mentioned Laura I most likely would've come clean about my lack of ability when it came to needle-work, but this was the most positive thing she'd said about Laura since she got rid of the shrine. If my making a costume could help to keep Laura's memory alive for her, keep up the tradition started by her mum, then I had no choice: I had to get sewing.

Much to my surprise a quick Google of the topic, 'How to make historical costumes for kids', revealed that far from being a niche activity, it was more like a small industry with rafts of websites, blogs and YouTube channels dedicated to the subject. There was information on how to make everything from 'Stone Age man' costumes, using fun fur and a blanket, to authentic 'Abraham Lincoln beards', using only black ink, cotton wool and an empty cereal packet.

Narrowing down my search to 'Egyptian princess costumes', I eventually discovered a blog featuring a dress I thought Lola would like and which, more importantly, was straightforward enough that I was reasonably sure I could make it without too much trouble. I made a note of all the things I needed for the project and the next day, after dropping Lola at school, I set off trying to find them. Though it took a good four hours and involved trips to several different shops in the Reigate area, by mid-afternoon I had everything I needed: white thread, a glue gun, gold spray-paint, several yards of white fabric, gold trimming, eyeliner, and a pair of Size 2 gold sandals. Such was my optimism for the project that even as I unpacked my haul, my overly active imagination was already preparing the speech for my induction into *Best Dads in the World* Hall of Fame, along with fellow inductees Brad Pitt, David Beckham and Barak Obama. After all, how hard could it be? I had the pattern, the material and the time, now all I had to do was put everything together.

Linda

Moira and I were sitting in the kitchen finishing off our lunch when Frank called again for the sixth time in the past fortnight: 'Hi, Linda, or whoever's getting these messages. I'm so sorry to call again, it's just that I was given this number as a means of contact by Linda Wood – Wood is her maiden name so it might've changed – she's an English teacher – possibly retired – formerly of Wetherby in Yorkshire. I've left a number of messages for her and she doesn't seem to have received them. If you are Linda, or know where she can be contacted, please could you let me know as a matter of some urgency.'

Moira sighed. 'It doesn't look like he's going to give up, you know. You've piqued his curiosity.'

'I wish I hadn't,' I replied. 'I truly wish I'd never set foot in that stupid store of his.'

Had it been naïve of me to hope that Frank might actually have been a man of his word? That when he left me – a woman he professed to love – carrying his unborn child all those years ago, due to a desire not to be 'tied down', he might actually have stuck to the beliefs he'd expressed and never started a family? In all the many years since he left me, I'd never once pictured Frank with a family of his own. I'd imagined him married to someone prettier and more glamorous than me, of course – he had, after all, been one of the most handsome and intelligent men I'd ever met – and I'd imagined him the eternal bachelor, breaking women's hearts the moment they got too close to him – he was certainly selfish enough to do that. But a father of two young men who could only have been a decade or so younger, at best, than the daughter he'd never met? I'd never have entertained the possibility for a moment unless I'd seen it with my own eyes.

That was why I was ignoring Frank's calls. Any doubt in my mind that he might be worthy of being considered something more than a sperm donor to my dear Laura evaporated the moment I saw those two young men. Moira's only comment to me after I'd rushed out of Frank's store and told her everything that had happened was a simple: 'I knew he wouldn't have changed – that sort never do,' and Desi, meanwhile, just gave me a hug and said, 'Maybe it's better this way after all,' and so

I made up my mind not to think about him, a task easier said than done, especially when he wouldn't stop leaving messages.

'Why didn't you just make up a number?' chided Moira, clearing away the dishes from lunch.

'I told you,' I replied, 'I panicked. He kept insisting that I leave a number and everyone was staring, what else could I do?' I glanced over at the answerphone. How long would he keep this up for?

'I've a good mind to get one of those air horns you hear at Aussie rules football matches,' said Moira, 'then next time he calls . . . wham!' She mimed blasting the air horn at the telephone. 'Hopefully, his hearing will be good enough to at least give him a couple of nights of tinnitus.'

I leaned on the kitchen counter and rubbed my eyes. This was all getting out of control. 'I don't know . . .'

'You're not going soft, are you?'

I opened my eyes to see Moira glaring at me. 'Not soft exactly . . . I just don't know how long I can carry this on for. I'm supposed to be here in Melbourne relaxing and having a good time with you, and it seems to me that all I've really done these past few weeks is either think about Frank, or try my very best not to think about Frank. Last night he nearly ruined my dinner with Desi too. There was poor Desi telling me some tale from his past, and he just stopped in the middle of it and accused me of not listening, and it was true! I hadn't heard a word. I'd actually been thinking about how angry I was with Frank. Of course, Desi and I managed to straighten things out eventually – he really is the most patient man in the world – but surely even he's got a breaking point. I suppose I can't help thinking that, at the very least, if I met up with Frank he'd stop bothering us and I could stop thinking about him. Talking to him wouldn't mean I've forgiven him. It could just mean I want him out of my life once and for all.'

'You're serious about this, aren't you?'

I nodded. 'It's got to be done.'

'And there's nothing I can do to talk you out of it?'

It really was lovely how protective Moira was of me, to know that there was someone in the world who was so resolutely on my side. 'It's very sweet of you to ask,' I replied, 'but this is something that I just have to do. When Laura was young I always used to tell her that you can't run away from your problems forever, and I think maybe it's time that I took some of my own advice, starting right now with Frank.'

Tom

It was an hour after Lola's bedtime on the night before Egyptian Day and she was standing on the kitchen table yawning as she modelled the costume I'd created for her.

'What do you think?' I asked Evie.

She put her hand on her hip as if channelling her inner Coco Chanel, while casting her most critical eyes across my handiwork. 'She looks like a tramp in a pillowcase!' she pronounced. 'Everyone will laugh at her,' and then just in case I hadn't got the message she added: 'Please, Dad, don't make her wear it.'

It seemed that while I excelled at producing TV shows, putting up shelves and recalling the lyrics to songs from the eighties, my talents didn't extend to following step-by-step instructions for costume designs delivered in a mid-western drawl by American stay-at-home moms. Evie was right. My efforts at making Lola look like a princess had made her look precisely like a tramp adorned in bed linen. There was nothing even remotely right about it. There were gaps where the seams had come apart, all the gold trimmings were askew, there was glue everywhere and even the sandals I'd bought were a size too small.

Lola, ever the trooper, was a lot kinder in her appraisal of my tailoring skills than her sister. 'It doesn't look like a pillowcase at all Daddy, I think it's nice.'

'That's really sweet, Lo,' I said, helping her off the table. 'But I think this is the point at which we'll have to admit defeat.'

Her bottom lip trembled through her every word as tears sprang to her eyes. 'But Mrs Barclay said everybody has to wear a costume . . . I don't want to be the only person in the class without one!'

I couldn't bear it. I gave her a hug and told her everything would be okay. 'Don't worry, sweetie,' I assured her. 'Leave it with me. Dad will sort it out.'

'But how?'

'She's got a point, Dad,' said Evie unhelpfully. 'How exactly is that going to happen? You know magic elves aren't really a thing, don't you?'

The clock on the wall behind Evie's head said quarter past nine. Every shop in Reigate was closed and it was far too late to order anything from the Internet. I needed a miracle.

'Never you mind how,' I said, ushering them both up to bed. 'Rest assured: Dad will get it done.'

My first port of call was my phone. Working in TV I was sure I must know enough people who might know costume designers, and I'd only need one of those to be free and up for it to save the day, but after a solid half-hour of calls without a single lead, I knew I had to start thinking laterally, which was how I came across Fran's business card that she'd given me on our first meeting. Obviously it was a bit of a gamble, after all just because she was creative in one field it didn't necessarily mean that she would be creative in another, but even if she didn't know anything about costume or dress design, there was a good chance she might at least know someone who, for the right financial incentive, would help me out. I tapped out a quick text – 'Need a massive favour. Sort of urgent, are you free to talk?' – and less than a minute later my phone rang.

'Tom, what's up? Is everything okay?'

'In a word: no. I know this might be a long shot and probably massively sexist but are you, or do you know anyone at all, who is good at sewing and free right now to help me out?'

'You need someone to sew? As in like clothes and stuff?'

'Well, to be precise I mean an Egyptian princess costume.'

My ear filled suddenly with the sound of Fran's laughter. I'd clearly amused her. 'What kind of trouble have you got yourself into?'

'Let's just say that I completely over-extended myself on a promise to my youngest daughter and now I'm paying for it big time; I need a costume by morning. Do you know anyone who might be able to help at all?'

'It's your lucky day, Tom Hope. As it turns out, I've actually been known to dabble with the old needle and thread in my time. Have you got all the stuff?'

'Chances are I've probably got way too much.'

'Right then,' said Fran. 'It's sounding a lot like we've got a long night ahead of us. Get the kettle on and I'll be there as soon as I can.'

It was just after eleven when Fran arrived at the house. She was wearing a big winter coat and had a large plastic carry-case in each hand, while at her feet was a sewing machine in a box. She looked different from when I'd seen her last. Her hair was shorter and I think perhaps she might have changed her make-up too, because for some reason that I wasn't quite sure of I couldn't seem to stop looking at her eyes. It was like they were drawing me into them against my will.

'Are you okay? You looked a bit spaced out for a moment.'

'Days spent on the Internet going cross-eyed looking at patterns for Egyptian princess costumes will do that to a man,'

I replied, making light of it. 'If I have to do it any more I think I'll end up with a permanent thousand-yard stare.'

She laughed, allowing me to breathe a sigh of relief while I helped her in with her things.

'Have you brought enough with you?'

Fran laughed. 'Actually, there's more,' and she made me follow her down the front path to her car. She opened up the boot to reveal three rolls of material, another two carry-cases and several large supermarket 'bags for life' filled with what she referred to as 'stuff'.

'So when you said that you'd been known to "dabble" with a needle you were being ironic,' I said, piling up the last of her things on the kitchen table.

'Put it this way . . .' said Fran picking up Lola's costume and holding it up in the air as she quickly assessed it, '. . . this ain't my first rodeo.'

Fran, I discovered, not only had an A-level in textiles but won her sixth form college's textile prize for excellence two years running. 'For a while all my teachers thought I was going to be the next Vivienne Westwood,' explained Fran, setting up her sewing machine on the kitchen table. 'Then I did a textiles summer school and all the fashion people on it were so up themselves it really put me off, so I went for fine art instead. I don't regret it though. The fashion world always seems a bit too full-on for me.'

Once all of Fran's equipment was set up, I took her over to my laptop and showed her some of the designs I'd been following. She hated them all and, taking the laptop from me, began surfing for alternatives.

'If you want Lola to win the top prize then this is what you want.' She turned the laptop around and pointed at the screen to a photo of an Egyptian princess costume that looked like something you might see in a film.

'Lola would absolutely love it,' I replied, 'but we'd never get that made for the morning.'

Fran smiled. 'Sounds like a challenge to me. Get the tea on and I'll work my magic.'

Aside from tea making, I did what I could to help Fran as she cut out a completely new pattern and began piecing it together. It became very clear very quickly, however, that my efforts to help were actually doing little other than holding her back, so she put me permanently in charge of keeping the tea flowing, with the occasional spot of fetching and carrying. It was amazing watching her work, seeing all the different bits of material gradually take shape and begin to resemble the image on the laptop. Finally, after many, many cups of tea, a little after two thirty, Fran attached the last gold ribbon to the collar of Lola's costume, stood up with a flourish and said: 'And that is how you make an Egyptian costume in less than four hours!'

She held it up for me to see. Not only had she made the dress with a train that attached to some jewel-encrusted bracelets, but she'd also made a collar, headband and belt, and spray-painted an old broom handle for Lola to use as a golden staff. In a word, it was stunning. The best costume prize was easily in the bag. I would owe her for life.

'This is going to blow Lola's mind. I don't know how to thank you. Whatever you want – my credit card, house, kidneys – you name it and it's yours.'

Fran laughed. 'Consider it payback for the day we met. I still get cold sweats whenever I think about that. You must have thought I was a right nutter.'

'Actually, I thought it was really sweet that you were looking out for your granddad like that. Not that he needs looking out for, of course, but it was nice all the same.'

I asked her if she wanted another tea or something stronger and she laughed and told me that if she drank another thing she'd burst, and so we began collecting her things and taking them to the car. On the first run, her arms full of carrier bags and carry-cases, she stopped as she passed by the living-room door, her attention seemingly caught by something within.

'That's so beautiful,' she said. I walked over and stood next to her in the doorway to see that she was talking about the oversized framed photographic print on the wall next to the fireplace. It was a black-and-white image of a line of trees set on a hilltop but taken in such a way that they almost seemed like an army marching to war. It was one of the first pictures Laura had taken after starting her new course the year before she died.

'It's one of Laura's,' I explained.

'She was obviously very talented.'

'She was,' I replied. 'That's why I encouraged her to go back to university after Lola started school. She wouldn't hear of it at first but once she started the course, it was like she'd rediscovered a part of herself she'd forgotten about.'

It was after three as we finished packing away Fran's things into the back of her car. The entire street was soundless, the night sky clear except for a few stray wisps of cloud over the moon. One might even have called it a beautiful night had it not been absolutely freezing cold.

'You should go in,' said Fran, buttoning up her coat. 'You'll catch your death if you stay out here any longer.'

'It's actually not that bad,' I lied, stifling a shiver. 'Anyway, I just want to say there's not many people who'd come out this late at night on a sewing suicide-mission. I really do owe you.'

'Really, it was nothing,' said Fran. 'Anyway you've been so amazing with Granddad, it was the least I could do. He's been a changed man since he started hanging out with you.'

'I doubt it. I don't imagine your granddad changes for anyone unless he wants to, he's the original immovable force.'

'You might think that but I know what I've seen. He just seems so much more positive about life these days. Has he told you about his plans for his birthday?'

The past few times I'd seen Clive he'd been insistent that the only thing he wanted for his forthcoming eightieth birthday was for me and the girls to join him and Fran for a picnic in Hyde Park. Apparently it was something of a family tradition.

'He and Nan used to do it all the time when she was alive,' said Fran, 'but then he stopped after she died and said he didn't want to do it any more. Then you come into his life and suddenly it's the only thing he can think about. You are coming, aren't you?'

'Wouldn't miss it for the world,' I replied. 'And for what it's worth it's not just been a one-way street, Clive's helped me too.'

'He'll be pleased to hear that,' said Fran. 'He worries about you, you know.'

'Clive worry about me? I don't think so.'

'He wouldn't admit it if you asked him but he's said as much to me. He thinks you're still struggling with . . . well, you know. He says you're too young to give up on life like he's done. I think his exact words were: "There's still some fight left in that lad yet."'

As we both laughed I made the mistake of looking into Fran's eyes again, just as I'd done when she arrived. There was something about her that was so warm, funny and charming; and I felt so completely in her debt after everything she'd done for me; and the moment – standing in the street in the small hours illuminated from above by the light of a nearly full moon – it all seemed like the perfect accompaniment to the kind of first kiss that you end up telling your grandchildren about when you're old and grey. As I looked into her eyes I got a sense that she must have felt what I was feeling too, not least because she seemed to be looking into my eyes as deeply as I was looking into hers. I really wanted to kiss her. I knew that kissing her would make me happier than I'd felt in a long time. And I didn't doubt for a moment that kissing her would be everything that I wanted it to be. But at the same time, I couldn't escape the fact that she had a boyfriend. And that kissing her would almost certainly cause problems with her relationship. Ultimately I couldn't help thinking it would be something she would regret, but even as I reached that conclusion I was already snaking an arm around her waist and pulling her to me for a kiss to which she responded as enthusiastically as I'd hoped. All too soon, however, it was over, and it only took one look into her eyes to see that it wasn't going to happen again. Without saying a single word she pressed her lips against my cheek, climbed into her car and drove away.

18

So are we related to him?

Tom

The following morning I was woken by the sound of screaming coming from the kitchen. Half asleep, I raced downstairs with Evie close behind, to discover that the screaming had turned to laughter that sounded a lot like it belonged to Lola. As we came into the kitchen we found Lola holding her Egyptian princess costume high up in the air. She turned around and looked at me guiltily.

'I woke up early and couldn't get back to sleep and so I came down to take a tiny peak at the costume, and Daddy, it's so beautiful, is it really mine?'

'Why don't you try it on and find out?' I replied.

She slipped off her pyjamas and pulled the costume on over her head, while I helped her with her collar and her cloak. She gave us a twirl. It looked perfect.

'I've got to say, Dad, this is pretty impressive stuff,' said Evie. 'But even I can see there's no way you did this on your own. So how did you do it?'

'I had a bit of help.'

'Who from?'

I tapped the side of my nose in an annoying fashion. 'Let's just say you were wrong about the elves.'

Evie shrugged. 'It doesn't matter anyway,' she said, smiling as Lola raced upstairs to take a look at herself in the full-length mirror on the landing. 'However you did it, Pop, it's definitely a "dad win".' She kissed my cheek. 'Well done, Dad, you aced it.'

My 'dad win' continued paying dividends for the rest of the morning rush. Every now and again throughout breakfast Lola would stop, a spoonful of Shreddies halfway to her lips, and thank me again for her costume. On our walk to school we passed Pharaohs, Cleopatras, Tutankhamens, mummies, and even a number of pyramids, and without exception they all stopped Lola to admire her costume. I don't think I'd ever seen her look so proud.

'Dad,' she whispered into my ear as we stood in the playground that morning waiting for the bell, 'everyone thinks I'm awesome.'

'That's because you are, sweetie,' I replied, making sure not to look at her – the last thing she needed was for me to ruin the day with dad tears. 'You always have been, it's just taken the other kids a while to realise it.'

After the start of school I stayed chatting with some of the parents from Lola's class for a while, who all wanted to know where I'd got the costume, and when I finally managed to extricate myself from them, I was then cornered by Ellie.

'Word on the street is that Lola's a shoe-in for best costume.'

'I wouldn't like to say. I'm just happy she's happy.'

'So how did you do it in the end?'

'I had help. A friend came round last night and did the lot. She was amazing.'

'A family friend was it?'

'Sort of, she – Fran – is a relative of a friend of mine.'

Ellie laughed. 'For a moment there I thought you'd found yourself a girlfriend.'

It was such a supremely odd thing to say that for a moment I didn't say anything at all, and thankfully I think Ellie must have realised because she looked at her watch and said, 'Anyway, I'm glad you got it sorted. I've got to dash but I'd love for us to go for coffee again soon, how about later in the week?'

If she hadn't been acting so strangely I probably would've agreed but as it was, I told her that I'd have to get back to her.

'Of course,' she said with a thin smile. 'I'd better get off but hopefully I'll see you soon.'

Heading home, I could only wonder at Ellie's 'girlfriend' comment. Was it out of some sort of misplaced sense of loyalty to Laura? Whatever the reason, it had felt like she'd stepped over a line somehow, and I think we'd both felt uncomfortable about it.

I was still thinking about Ellie as I reached my front gate to see Fran standing on my doorstep.

'I was beginning to think that maybe you'd gone out for the day.'

'Sorry,' I replied. 'Lola's costume was such a hit that I could barely escape the playground. If you ever want to swap your day job for making kids' costumes you'll make a fortune.'

Fran laughed. 'So it fitted okay? I spent half the night worrying that I hadn't done a proper fitting. I nearly called first thing this morning to say I was popping round to make sure everything was okay.'

'You could've done. I wouldn't have minded.'

'I know,' she replied, looking down at the floor, 'but I thought it probably best not to.'

It was obvious that she was talking about last night, but what was less apparent was exactly how she felt about our kiss. Was she filled with regret or was she, like me, hopeful that it might happen again? The longer I stared at her, the more I came to realise that it had to be regret she was feeling. It had to be. She'd been with her boyfriend for years and had only known me a matter of a few weeks. I didn't know which one of us I felt most sorry for: me for being so deluded as to think that I was actually in with a chance, or Fran for having the unenviable task of attempting to let me down gently.

'I know what you're going to say,' I said quickly in a bid to spare her the awkwardness that lay ahead, 'and first and foremost I'd like to apologise. It was an amazing thing you did for me last night and I should never have allowed myself to get carried away with the moment like that.'

Fran laughed, which hadn't been the reaction I'd been expecting at all. 'And here I was thinking I was the one who got carried away.' She smiled. 'I wasn't up all night just worrying about Lola's costume, I was worrying about the fact that I'd taken advantage of you too. That's why I got out of there so quickly. After we, you know, all I could think was that I was dragging you into all my drama.'

'You mean the boyfriend?'

'If you can call him that.'

'What would you call him then?'

Fran wrinkled her nose and considered the question. 'A bad utility,' she said finally.

She'd lost me completely. 'I have no idea what you're talking about.'

Fran sighed and sat down on the doorstep, and because it felt weird to be the only one standing I did the same.

'It's like this,' she began, 'you know how the papers are always saying you should change banks, energy providers and your Internet and cable people every few years to get the best deal? And you know how you never take that advice because it will be the biggest ball-ache to sort out? Well, that's pretty much me and Johnny: he's basically an overcharging, underperforming utility company and I'm the mug who doesn't switch because it would take more mental energy to do than I think I've got.'

'So where does that leave us?' It seemed like a good question to ask at the time, but once it was out there I wished I could've taken it back. It sounded a little too definite, like she had to make a choice between me – the guy she'd known for five minutes – and Johnny, the guy she'd been with for years.

'I think it's probably for the best if we're just friends,' said Fran.

'Oh right,' I replied, unable to hide my disappointment. 'I was sort of hoping you were about to tell me you were going to start shopping around for a better deal. As it happens I've heard there're some pretty good ones on the market.'

'Pretty good doesn't even begin to cover it,' said Fran, casually letting her hand drop down in such a way that her fingertips came to rest on mine. 'There's one deal I've heard about that you'd literally have to be mad to pass over.'

'So why not go for it?'

'That's the million-dollar question,' said Fran. 'And I'm afraid I don't have the answer.'

As much as I liked her, there didn't seem to be much point in putting up any further resistance that was only going to embarrass us both even more, and yet I just couldn't give up quite yet.

'And you're absolutely sure?'

Fran nodded. 'You have no idea how much I wish I could be saying that I wasn't, but I think at least for now I am. I'm so sorry, Tom, I really am.'

'It's probably all for the best,' I replied. 'You know what these deals are like. They always look great until you look at the small print.' I held out my hand. 'Friends?'

'I wouldn't have it any other way,' she replied. She stood up, wrapped her arms tightly around me and then looked up: 'So I'll see you next week for Granddad's birthday then?'

'Of course,' I replied, curiously feeling both elated and deflated at the same time. 'Like I said, I wouldn't miss it for the world.'

Linda

There are moments in life so significant that there's a surreal, dreamlike quality about them. Giving birth to Laura was definitely one of them. It seemed preposterous after nine months of planning and expectation that I could actually hold her in my hands, look into her eyes and feel the warmth of her skin. It was all too unreal. Sitting across the table from Frank in the café where I'd seen him for the first time in forty years was definitely another one of those moments. I fully expected to wake up at any minute in a cold sweat.

'I can't believe this is really happening,' said Frank as if reading my mind. 'Just look at the state of me.' He lifted his hands and indeed they were shaking. 'I'm an absolute wreck. I tell you I literally couldn't believe it when you walked into the store that day, Linda. The moment I laid eyes on you I knew it was you, but I kept telling myself that it just couldn't be. It made so little sense that you might be here in my store that for a moment I was convinced I was having a stroke and that you were some sort delusion. And then you disappeared so quickly. If it wasn't for the fact that I'd got your number in my hand and that the boys had seen you with their own eyes, I'm not sure I would've believed it myself. I can't tell you how pleased I am that you agreed to see me, Linda, really I am. I've done a lot of things I've regretted in my life, things that to this day I'm still utterly ashamed of, but by far the worst is how I treated you back then. Nobody deserved to be treated like that and certainly not you.'

As I sat listening to Frank, all traces of his English heritage wiped clean from his voice and replaced with an Australian inflection, it occurred to me that I'd waited a lifetime for that apology but now it had arrived, I felt nothing. Absolutely nothing at all. He might as well have been reciting nursery rhymes for all the difference it made.

'That's very decent of you to say, Frank, but it wasn't an apology that I came here for today.'

'Oh, right, yes, of course. I expect you've got a lot that you want to say to me. Forty years' worth at least.'

Spurred by indignation, I felt my right eyebrow rise as though independent of my will. The sheer arrogance of the man made me livid. 'If you think you were that important to me that I've got forty years' worth of complaints to make you can bloody well carry on thinking. I didn't waste a single minute of my life wishing you'd come back, Frank Smith. You weren't worth the brain power or the tears.'

'I didn't mean it like that,' he said quickly. 'I just mean . . . I don't know what I mean . . . maybe I should just shut up and listen.'

'You'd like that, wouldn't you?' I could feel myself getting angry. 'You'd like that, sitting across the table from me listening to me rant on about what a despicable man you were to treat me like you did all those years ago, and then what? You just get up and walk away, feeling bad about yourself for a day or two before things go back to normal?'

'I don't know what you want me to say, Linda.'

'Well, you wouldn't, would you? At least not when you started a family of your own after telling me that you didn't want one! How old is that eldest lad of yours? Thirty? Thirty-one?'

Frank swallowed hard, as the guilt rose up into his gaze. 'Thirty-six.'

'Thirty-six?' My blood was boiling over. 'He's thirty-six? So, let me get this right: two, three years after you left me pregnant, you went off and started a family with someone else? Precisely what kind of man are you?'

'I know how it sounds, Linda, believe me I do, but it wasn't like that at all. I was young and stupid when we were together, and when you told me you were pregnant I just saw my whole life mapped out and it terrified me so much I just had to go.'

'And how do you think I felt? Didn't you ever think I might be terrified? Didn't you think I might've felt like running away too? Or did you think you were the only one with hopes and ambitions?'

'I don't know what I thought, really I don't. All I knew was that I had to get away.'

'To?'

'St Albans initially – I had family there – and then to London.'

'And then you met someone else?'

Frank nodded. 'She was a teacher too, in a school in Kilburn. Her father was an Aussie and she had dual nationality so when after a year together she said that she was moving to Melbourne, I made the decision to go too.'

'And you're still together?'

'We divorced fifteen years back – the marriage was never really up to much – she's remarried now, lives in Wallington not far from my youngest—'

'She died'

I'd been wondering all morning how I might tell Frank about Laura but I never once imagined I'd be so abrupt. The expression on his face was one of confusion. Quite rightly he needed clarification.

'I don't quite follow. Who died?'

'Our daughter,' I replied. 'The one you abandoned, the one I raised all alone, she died . . . in a car crash. Her name was Laura Elizabeth Wood. She was born at 2.32 p.m. on the fourth of August 1974 at St Margaret's Hospital, and weighed six pounds and eight ounces. The first time I looked into her eyes they were brimful of light and love, and they remained that way as she grew up to be a beautiful, passionate, kind and loving young woman. She was thirty-nine when she died, a mother to two girls – they're fourteen and eight now, the most beautiful little girls in the world, who neither want or need *you* in their life – so yes, to answer your question again, the daughter we made together died, and I have no idea why but I thought you ought to know.'

Tom

It was the second Saturday in May, the morning of Clive's birthday, and the kids and I were standing at his front gate having something of a debate.

'So are we related to him?' asked Lola.

'No,' I replied. 'He's just a friend of mine.'

'But you said it was his eightieth birthday?'

'It is.'

'So you're friends with an eighty-year-old man?'

I could see where this was going and tried to head them off at the pass. 'I'm friends with lots of people,' I replied. 'I don't think about age when it comes to friends.'

'Maybe you should,' said Evie, 'because eighty is like a million years old. Did he fight in the war?'

'He was just a little boy during the war, so no.'

'And you say he's got a granddaughter?' asked Lola.

'Her name's Fran.'

'Is she our age?'

'No, she's older.'

'So she's your age?'

'Not exactly.'

'And she's the lady who made my Egyptian costume?'

'Yes, she is.'

'I won the best costume in the year for that costume.'

'I know you did, sweetie, you did really well, now can we just stop with all the questions and go and meet my friends?'

Walking up the path to Clive's front door it occurred to me that even at their nit-picking worst, the kids couldn't take the edge off my good mood. It wasn't just that, since winning the costume competition over a week ago, Lola had had not just one friend round for tea but two; and it wasn't just that I'd managed to get Clive a half-decent birthday present of dinner in central London (no bacon butties allowed), followed by tickets to be in the audience for a filming of the BBC's *Question Time* (the thought of some poor unsuspecting politician walking into a studio not knowing that Clive was in the audience was too irresistible to pass up); and it wasn't even the fact that one morning the previous week I'd gone to change Lola's bed clothes only to discover that her shoebox shrine to Laura was back in pride of place on her bedside table; but it was the fact that after a whole week I was finally getting to see Fran.

In a classic move that could be described at best as foolish and at worst downright hopeless, I'd come to the surprising conclusion that while I wasn't in love with Fran (even I could see that might be a little too full-on) I was something close. I liked everything about her: the way she pushed her bottom lip out while trying to cool down an overly hot cup of tea; that her life seemed terminally disorganised; the way she saw the world; the fact that she made me laugh. And while I knew not-quite-falling in love with Fran was never going to end well, there was no denying that it felt good. All the more so because, until I met her, I'd never imagined I might ever feel that way again.

Clive opened the door wearing a cream short-sleeved shirt and navy trousers that made him look like an off-duty policeman. He welcomed us all into the house and made a great show of ignoring anything I had to say, instead giving the girls his best 'great granddad' performance. He pulled silly faces and made constant jokes at my expense that were all the more funny because they were true, all of which the girls found hysterical. By the time we'd reached the living room, he'd got his wallet out and was in the process of handing them a crisp ten-pound note each, with the command that they should blow the lot on sweets. It was time for me to step in.

'It's very kind of Clive,' I explained. 'But you can't keep the money.'

'They bloody well can!' said Clive. 'It's my money!'

Lola was as entertained as she was scandalised by the spectacle of an adult swearing in her presence. Evie, meanwhile, simply flashed me a look as if to say: 'Who is this guy?'

Ignoring me, Clive turned to the girls and asked them if I'd always been this boring and they both agreed that I had.

'He wouldn't even let me bring my boyfriend along!' complained Evie.

'Only because he wasn't invited,' I replied.

'That's outrageous,' said Clive. 'Why don't you call him up and ask him to come along?'

As Evie called Oliver, Fran arrived back at the house with shopping for the picnic. 'I would've been here earlier,' she said as I helped her with the bags, 'but apparently M&S pork pies aren't good enough for Granddad. They have to be the ones from the same butcher where he gets his meat.' She looked like she had a lot more to say about Clive's food-related diktats, but then she noticed the girls.

'I'm so sorry, girls,' she said, 'there's me going on about shopping and I haven't even said hello.'

'You're the lady who made my Egyptian princess costume,' said Lola. 'It was amazing and it won first prize.' She reached into her pink rucksack on the floor and handed Fran a card. 'This is for you,' she said. 'Evie and I made it to say thank you.'

On the front was a drawing of Lola wearing the costume, and out of her mouth was a speech bubble saying: 'I am the best in the world.' Inside it said: 'Dear Fran, thanks for making me the best in the world, love Lola.'

'It's beautiful,' said Fran, 'and I can tell you've definitely got an artist's eye from all the detail on the dress. I'm going to treasure it forever.'

'Right then,' said Clive, clapping his hands together. 'We can't stand about here all day! Let's get going, we've got an eightieth birthday to celebrate.'

It was after midday as we finally settled ourselves down in front of a patch of shaded grass overlooking the Serpentine. While Fran laid out the picnic blankets, Clive insisted on paying for deckchairs for us all, even though I knew that there was little chance of the kids sitting in them for more than five minutes. Soon there was food spread across the blankets, and plates being handed out, and then Oliver arrived with several bags of food his mum had made him bring along.

As the kids helped themselves to fistfuls of crisps, and Clive took his first bite of pork pie while Fran searched in the bags we'd brought along for cutlery, I wondered what we looked like to the constant stream of tourists passing by. Did they assume we were a family? A husband and wife, children and a doting grandparent? I was surprised how good it felt that they might see us this way, that instead of being incomplete, we were, even if only through the eyes of strangers, whole once more.

Like most picnics, the time it took to consume the food bore little resemblance to the effort it had taken to prepare and carry it to its destination. As I helped pack away the leftovers, Clive announced that he was getting ice creams for everyone, refusing any offers of assistance. One of the kids spotted a fish in the lake and they all ran off to get a better view; and so Fran and I found ourselves finally alone.

For a few moments we carried on packing away, and then out of nowhere Fran put down the large tub of potato salad she'd been holding.

'I think you ought to know that I took your advice.'

'About what?'

Fran smiled. 'Changing utilities. It wasn't easy, but it was definitely for the best in the long run, especially now I've found a better deal.' Her eyes scanned my face as though trying to read my mind, and then gently, very gently, we kissed.

'And about bloody time too.'

We both turned to see Clive standing over us. 'I thought you were getting ice creams,' said Fran blushing.

'That's what I thought until I found out how much they wanted for the bloody things! For that price I could buy my own van and set myself up as his competition.'

Fran reached into her bag. 'Here,' she said, handing him a twenty-pound note. 'My treat, it is your birthday after all.'

'All right,' said Clive. 'As you were, I know when I'm not wanted. Just make sure you get that potato salad back in the cool bag before it's too late.'

We waited until he was out of sight before we both burst out laughing.

'Am I right in thinking your granddad just gave us his blessing?' I asked.

'Put it this way,' said Fran. 'If he'd had any objections right now, you'd be wearing that potato salad, not packing it away.'

19

My wedding dress

Tom

I was in the kitchen, unloading the contents of a dozen or so carrier bags from a Sainsbury's delivery, when I got a text from Fran. She was up in Middlesbrough for a few days visiting her parents. The text said: 'Miss you. Hope everything's good with you xxx.' I tapped out a quick response: 'Everything's okay but it'd be a lot better if you were here. Speak to you later xxx.'

It had been a long time since I'd been this happy. So long, in fact, that I'd forgotten that it was even possible to sustain the feeling. In the fortnight we'd been together, we'd been on eight official dates and one unofficial one (we bumped into each other in Morrisons and decided to ditch the supermarket shopping and spend the day together) and each one had proved better than the last. She was so bright and optimistic – the antithesis of the person I'd felt myself becoming since losing Laura – that it began to rub off on me, and even though I'd decided that it was far too early to tell the kids about us, they noticed the change in me overnight. 'Do you know you keep smiling for no reason?' Evie asked me one evening when she caught me secretly thinking about Fran. 'You look like an idiot.' Lola's observation of me was far more kind-hearted. On the way to school one day she just looked up at me and apropos of nothing in particular said, 'You feel jolly, Dad.' And the funny thing was, I actually did.

At the same time, however, I felt a lot of guilt. Being with Fran raised all manner of questions to which I didn't have any ready answers. Did my being with her mean I was officially over losing Laura? Or that after a year and a half I was simply tired of being alone? And putting aside whether I was over losing Laura, was a year and a half enough time before meeting someone new? Then, of course, there were the questions about where this thing with Fran was going. Was it casual or more serious? And if it was serious did that mean I could envision the day when she moved in with the girls and me? And if she did move in with us, what would she be to the kids? As I said: too many questions and not enough answers but as long as I didn't think about either, I was happy.

With the shopping put away, I was about to turn my attention to tidying the kids' rooms when I noticed I'd forgotten to turn the page of the family calendar now that it was June. The next week looked fine: there was a new shed being delivered on Tuesday, Evie had an art exhibition at school the day after, and Lola was having tea at her new friend Tamsin's house the day after that; but when I checked the weeks ahead to see what was coming up, I noticed something odd on the bottom right hand corner of one of the pages. Scribbled in red ink on the 4th of July in Linda's handwriting was a note: 'Nanny back from Oz!!! Break out the bunting!!!' It was underlined several times, as though there might actually have been a chance that I would forget the date of my mother-in-law's return, which was odd because that was exactly what I'd done.

Six months had seemed like a lifetime when she'd first left, and yet here I was a month away from her return and I was still standing. Back when she'd first left I couldn't even make Lola a packed lunch without making a hash of it, but now looking after the girls came as naturally to me as making TV programmes used to. This was how far I'd come: I was the official purchaser of girls' underwear and sanitary products; I was head drier of eyes in a home that had seen more tears than most; I was the principal mender of school uniforms, the lead signatory in the signing of school planners, the prime returner of overdue library books, the top provider of sandwiches and snacks, and the commander-in-chief of homework help. Somehow in the past five months, I'd not only become a dad again but added mum and grandparent to my CV too. If I hadn't experienced it first-hand I would never have believed it possible, and it wouldn't have been possible at all if it hadn't been for Linda.

Returning the family calendar to the wall, it occurred to me that I wanted to do something for Linda's arrival that would make her proud, something that would show her beyond any doubt that I'd changed and was no longer the man that she'd had to force to take care of his own family. I wanted to do something to show her that I'd come to terms with the past and wouldn't let my grief rule over me any more. Then I remembered the list, and I knew exactly what it was I needed to do.

Linda

It's strange how grief works. I'd read somewhere that it's best to imagine it like waves on the shore. When you first lose someone you love, the waves hit hard and fast as though you're in the middle of a storm – and I'm guessing that it was this stage that Tom had been stuck in for so long – but then over time the gap between one wave and another grows large enough for moments of peace to outweigh moments of loss. I'd convinced myself that those first brutal waves had finished with me, but as I'd left a tearful and shell-shocked Frank and returned to Moira's, I came to realise quite how wrong I'd been.

As I closed Moira's front door behind me, I fell to the floor sobbing as though the heart I'd once thought healed was breaking all over again. Moira rushed to my aid, begging me to tell her what had happened, but all I could do was cry and howl through my pain. And in the midst of all the tears, the rage, the overwhelming fear of loss I felt, I was faced with the stark revelation that the peace I'd experienced this past year or so hadn't been true peace at all. By throwing myself into looking after my granddaughters, running the home and trying to keep Tom afloat, I'd been hiding from my grief, refusing to face the reality of the loss I felt. Now the terrible reality of that loss had finally caught up with me, and there was nowhere to run or hide and nothing to do except succumb to its force. It was as though I'd been thrown back to that terrible moment in the hospital watching it unfold in slow motion: the approach of Laura's consultant, the look of empathy in his eyes as he broke the news to Tom and me, and the sensation of drowning that had come over me. Only this time, rather than resurfacing for the sake of Tom, I felt myself plummet to the very depths below as it dawned on me, as if for the first time, that I'd never kiss my sweet Laura's face, touch her skin or hear her voice again. I'd never get to tell her how much I loved her, or hear her say those words to me in return. I'd never hear her laugh, or be able to comfort her in times of sadness. I'd never get to share with her the stories of my past, or hear those of her present or future. She was gone forever, and I hadn't even said goodbye.

I don't recall a great deal for a while after that, but Moira tells me I was inconsolable for days. Hiding in my room, curtains drawn, overwhelmed with grief, I hid from the world, refusing to take calls even from the girls back home. Every time I tried to rally, another wave of grief would crash over me, followed by another and another. I felt lost and alone, unable to help myself or anyone else, and if it hadn't been for Moira and Desi keeping me fed and taking it in turns to sit with me day and night, I don't know what I would've done.

It was a long while before I finally felt able to leave the house, and at Desi's suggestion we went for a walk along the shoreline. It felt good to be outside again, breathing fresh air and feeling the sand between my toes.

Hand in hand we walked along the beach in silence, watching children running in and out of the sea, groups of friends lounging in the sun and couples like us having a leisurely stroll. After some time, we naturally came to a halt and stood for a while looking out to sea.

I turned to face Desi, wondering what I'd done to have someone so wonderful in my life. 'You really have been amazing,' I said. 'You'll never know how grateful I am to you and Moira for everything you've done this past week.'

'It was nothing you wouldn't have done for me a million times over, if the shoe had been on the other foot.'

'Perhaps,' I replied, 'but still, I want you to know how grateful I am.'

He raised an eyebrow jauntily. 'Does that mean you're in my debt? Because if it does then, as it happens, I might have a small request I'd like to make of you.'

'Which is what?'

'I want you to come away with me for a few days. I've got a mate in the building trade who owes me, and he's said that he'll lend me his beach house on Hamilton Island. I've been before and Linda, I have to tell you it's one of the most beautiful places on earth.'

'It sounds wonderful,' I replied, even as I mentally compiled a long list of reasons why I couldn't go. 'But I'm not really sure I want to go anywhere right now.'

'Which is exactly the reason that you should come with me,' said Desi. 'You think you've got an unlimited store of "get up and go" in you, as though you're some sort of robot, but you haven't, Linda, you just haven't. You're human just like everybody else and if this past week has proved anything it's this: you can't go your whole life meeting other people's needs and not your own. Sometimes you have to let yourself be looked after.'

Tom

The list (as I referred to it) didn't exist in reality. It was simply a mental inventory of Laura-related tasks that Linda had passed on to me and which I had ignored. These were tasks that Linda had insisted only I could deal with, things too personal to be left for anyone else, or too complicated for her to tackle. Some jobs were small, like clearing bathroom cupboards of make-up and toiletries, and others were more challenging, like clearing out the wardrobe of her clothes, but none had been of interest to me while I'd been busy hiding from life.

Now, however, things were different. Now I was back to being the man I'd been before disaster struck. That week I advertised Laura's car for sale, removed her name from all our utility bills (no more letters addressed to Mr and Mrs Hope), deactivated her Facebook account, shredded her credit-card statements, boxed up her exam certificates, cancelled her passport and magazine subscriptions, closed her bank accounts, emptied the drawers of her dressing table, filled a bin bag with make-up and toiletries from the bathroom cupboard, and now all that was left for me to do was the hardest task of all: empty Laura's side of our shared wardrobe.

I'd always loved the way Laura dressed, from the white shirt and grey trousers she'd worn on the night we first kissed, through to the dress she had made for of our wedding. She seemed to have a gift for choosing clothing that just looked right on her every single time. Maybe that was the reason why it had never seemed like a good time to get rid of her clothes, because they were such a fundamental part of her character. Then again, maybe it was also because I didn't want to be faced with the daily reminder of Laura's absence represented by a three-quarters empty wardrobe.

Determined not to labour the task, I unfurled the roll of bin bags I'd brought upstairs with me. This wasn't going to be a walk down memory lane or a last fond goodbye. It was simply an exercise in moving forward. I'd take the clothes off their hangers, pack them away in the bin bag at my feet and repeat until the process was complete. At least that was the plan.

The first few items – a couple of old work blouses, a few jumpers and cardigans – went into the bag without a struggle, but then I reached for a white top with tiny silver strands shot through it and I had to stop. This had always been one of Lola's favourites, the top she used to call 'Mum's sparkly'. Whenever Laura wore it, even if it was the middle of March, Lola would sing Christmas carols. I couldn't possibly get rid of that, could I? And what about Evie? Even without looking particularly hard I could see at least a dozen scarves and tops that she'd have been thrilled to own.

For a moment I considered waiting until the kids arrived home from school, so they could choose what they wanted to keep for themselves. Knowing them as I did, however, it wasn't difficult to foresee a scenario where they'd want to save everything. And when virtually every skirt, blouse, scarf, coat, jacket and jumper so easily conjured up memories of their much-missed mum, who could blame them?

After much deliberation, I limited what I'd keep to the sparkly cardigan and a multi-coloured scarf for Lola; and a black military-style jacket and camel cashmere cardigan for Evie. If one day it turned out that they had a problem with me for so casually disposing of their mother's wardrobe then so be it, but for now, as far as I was concerned at least, this was the right decision for us all.

I'd all but filled up the last of my roll of bin liners when it occurred to me that I ought to check the top shelf of the wardrobe. In amongst the numerous hats, and carrier bags full of clothes that she no longer wore but hadn't wanted to throw away, was a large transparent plastic zip-up bag which I recognised immediately: it was Laura's wedding dress. Fighting my every instinct to take one last look, I squeezed it into the bin bag and tied the handles tightly, as though I feared it might possess the power to escape of its own accord. I grabbed a few more bin bags from downstairs, cleared the top shelf of the wardrobe of the last remnants of Laura's clothes, and then called a cab to take me to the nearest charity shop.

That night I could barely sleep for tossing and turning, and when I awoke I had no doubt about the source of my restless night. First thing after school drop-off I returned to the charity shop to get Laura's wedding dress back.

'You want your what?'

'My wedding dress,' I repeated to the elderly lady behind the counter of Oxfam. 'I brought it in yesterday with about seven or eight bags of clothes.'

She looked perplexed. 'I'm afraid I don't know anything about a wedding dress.' She rang a bell on the counter and after a few moments the store manager, who I'd given my donation to the day before, emerged from the rear office. 'This gentleman is apparently after a wedding dress.'

'I remember you,' said the manager. 'You had lots of bin bags, didn't you? The only problem is I didn't do the sorting yesterday and we had quite a number of volunteers, so any amount of your items could've been tagged and ended up on the shop floor. Was it important?'

'Very,' I replied. 'Would you mind checking in the back to see if it's there?'

'Of course,' she replied. 'Won't be a minute.'

That 'minute' turned out to be ten, during which time I not only went through every item of clothing in the shop twice in case it had been put out by accident, but also endured the agony of thinking that I might never see her dress again. The dress she wore on the day I promised to love her forever, never once considering just how short our forever might be.

Finally the store manager called out from the stockroom that she'd found it, the bag with it in had been hidden by another filled with curtains. As she handed the dress over to me still in its zip-up bag, I clutched it to my chest.

'How much will it be?'

'It's all yours,' she replied. 'I couldn't believe how much you brought in yesterday, and such high quality too.'

I plucked two twenty-pound notes from my wallet and left them on the counter. It was safe. The dress was safe. Everything was okay. It was a hard lesson well learned: some things I was clearly ready to leave behind, but there were others I needed to hang on to for just a little longer.

A few days later I finally sold Laura's car. A man in his late fifties came round to the house with his much younger son and took it for a test run. I explained that it had been sitting on the drive for well over a year, but after a bit of tinkering under the bonnet they got it started and took it for a quick spin. Unlike the wedding dress, when the younger of the two men drove off in the car that had once been Laura's I felt little emotion. It was just taking care of business, the last item ticked off my list.

Keen to stay on top of things, I decided to bank the cheque straight away but I'd barely reached the High Street when I heard someone call my name, and I turned to see a smartly dressed woman waving in my direction. I recognised her immediately. It was Gill, one of Laura's old university friends. The last time I'd seen her had been at the funeral. She looked older than I remembered, and for a moment it made me think about

Laura. She would've been forty-one next birthday: had she lived, perhaps like so many women of her age, she would've been worrying about the grey in her hair and spending a small fortune on creams and potions in a bid to maintain the youthfulness of her skin. Instead, she was forever thirty-nine, a youthful snapshot permanently protected from the vagaries of ageing. For a brief moment as I stared at Gill I was filled with emptiness for all the versions of Laura I'd never see, all the versions I'd never get to touch or hold.

My conversation with Gill was much like all the other conversations I'd had with Laura's old friends whenever I'd bumped into them. They'd ask me how I was and I'd tell them I was fine; they'd ask after the girls and I'd give them a potted précis of Evie and Lola's educational achievements, and show them photos of the girls from my phone; they'd marvel at how much the girls had grown and how much they looked like Laura; and then they'd hug me tightly and make me promise to arrange a day when they could come and see them and in return I'd say, 'That sounds like a great idea, I'll arrange something soon,' knowing full well that I'd do nothing of the sort. It was a kind of dance, 'The Polite Widower's Waltz', offering me all the benefits of appearing to be close to the people who'd loved Laura, with none of the disadvantages of actually following it up. In all the time I'd been doing this dance I'd never once put a single foot wrong, but as Gill hugged me and made me promise to arrange a day when she could come and see the girls, I realised that even though Linda had never told me to do it, keeping in touch with all of Laura's friends was part of my list too. I owed it to her to get her friends together. I owed it to them to give them a reason to celebrate. All this time, all of these friends of Laura had been mourning her loss alone and all their efforts to connect with her through me and the kids had been rejected. I'd pushed them away because I couldn't see anyone's pain but my own. It had to stop.

'How about next Saturday?'

Gill seemed almost as surprised as I was to hear such a definite date. 'Are you sure it's not too much bother?'

'Not at all,' I replied, warming to the idea. 'In fact why don't we make it a proper party with food and drink and dancing, and we'll invite everyone who knew Laura to come along. What do you think?'

She seemed as thoroughly excited by the idea as me, and I was convinced it was the right thing to do. As Gill and I parted, having agreed arrangements for the party, my phone pinged with a message from Fran: 'Just back from visiting the folks. Fancy meeting for a coffee in 10? xxx.' I tapped out a quick reply. 'Sounds great. See you in Café Roma. Xxx.' It didn't occur to me until I was halfway to my destination just what an awkward position I'd put myself in. There was no way around it: at some point during the next hour, I was going to have to tell my new girlfriend that I was planning to throw a party for my wife.

20

Like I'm Oliver's girlfriend

Tom

In the weeks since Fran and I had been together, we hadn't exactly done a great deal of talking about Laura. Obviously she knew the basic story of what had happened and I'd given her a rough outline of what I called 'my year of opting out', but mostly we stuck to the sort of topics new couples usually talk about: careers, school, parents, hopes and dreams etc. It wasn't as though I was being deliberately evasive. If she'd asked to hear more about Laura I would gladly have obliged, but the fact was she hadn't, just as I hadn't asked about her ex.

Fran threw her arms around my neck and pulled me into a long, deep kiss that paid no heed at all to our location – a busy high street café – or who might be watching. It was a kiss completely devoid of all sense of self-consciousness; as a relatively private sort of person I wasn't particularly big on public displays of affection, but in the moment I didn't give my natural reticence a second thought. Being with Fran made me feel freer and lighter somehow, and I didn't want to jeopardise what we had, which was why I knew I had to get the news about the party into the open as soon as I could. Even though it was still early days, I didn't want to risk losing her over some petty misunderstanding. I needed her to know that this was something I had to do, that ultimately would be good for us too. But as she told me about her time away and how much she'd missed me, I couldn't help wondering if this news might convince her that what we had was too complicated to make work.

'I've got something to tell you.'

Fran sat back in her chair. 'Sounds ominous.'

'While you've been away, I've been doing a lot of thinking and—'

She leaned forward, her face flush with anxiety. 'Are you trying to tell me you're having second thoughts about us?'

I held her hand across the table. 'No, of course not! I'm not saying that at all.'

'So what are you saying then?'

'I've agreed to throw a party at my house this Saturday.'

'And?'

'Well . . . the thing is, it's in honour of Laura . . .'

Fran blinked several times but it was hard to tell what it meant. 'Oh . . . right,' she said finally. 'What sort of party will it be?'

'Maybe party's the wrong word,' I replied. 'It's probably going to be more of a gathering if anything. It's just that while you were away, it dawned on me that it was time for me to sort out a lot of stuff I've been putting off since she died.'

'Like what?'

'Clearing out her things, selling her car, that sort of thing.'

Fran bit her lip and squeezed my hand. 'Oh, Tom, that must have been so difficult for you. You should've told me, I could've come and helped you or at least given some moral support.'

'That's nice of you to say but I think it would've been weird, don't you?'

Fran nodded. 'Still, I just hate that you went through all that alone.'

'It was fine . . . at least it was in the end. I did everything I needed to do and then well, just before you called, I bumped into one of Laura's friends who I hadn't seen since the funeral and she asked after the kids, as all of Laura's friends usually do and I just thought—'

'Let's get everybody round.'

'Is that mad?'

Fran shook her head. 'Of course not, it makes perfect sense. It's hard for everyone when you lose someone, especially when they were young. Getting all the people she cared about together for an afternoon sounds like the perfect plan. So how will it work? They all come to yours, see the kids, eat some food and remember Laura?'

I nodded. 'I just think it'll be good for Evie and Lola, for our friends and for me too. And of course, you're invited.'

Fran smiled. 'That's really sweet, Tom, but it's hardly the place to be debuting the new girlfriend is it?'

I couldn't help but laugh. 'So you're my girlfriend are you? Does that make me your boyfriend?'

Her face flushed with embarrassment. 'You know what I mean. I just don't think it's my place to be there. But that doesn't mean that I don't think it's the right thing for you to do, because it is, okay?' She squeezed my hand again. 'I know it's early days and all but I really care about you, Tom. I care about everything that happens to you. I know we're not in an easy situation, I know we've got hurdles to overcome but I believe in us, I really do. And I want you to know that when it comes to me you haven't got anything to worry about.'

'In that case,' I replied with a grin, 'I'm officially promoting you to the position of "girlfriend" and inviting you round for tea tonight, after which even though it's still early days I'm going to tell the kids all about us.'

Linda

When Desi described the place we were staying in on Hamilton Island as a beach house, I'd imagined that it might be a little bungalow. I couldn't have been more wrong. It was a ten-bedroom house that was all gleaming glass and architecturally designed sharp edges, with its own private pool and grounds. It was like something out of a glossy magazine, the sort of place where proper Hollywood film stars might be spotted 'vacationing' with their families in the pages of *Hello*. And yet here I was, born and bred in Wetherby, staring up at what was going to be my home for the next seven nights. I felt like I was in a dream.

The interior was just as impressive as the exterior; everything from the polished-stone kitchen counter to the marble flooring was top of the range and must have cost thousands.

'Just who is this friend of yours?' I asked as I opened a fridge to find that it was fully stocked with food and drink. 'He must be some sort of millionaire.'

'Actually,' said Desi, 'to be precise he's a multimillionaire.'

'Wow,' I replied. 'That's impressive.'

'Not really,' shrugged Desi. 'Basically he just got lucky and ended up with more money than he knows what to do with.'

Desi showed me around the rest of the ground floor of the house – taking in, amongst other things, a cinema room, a snooker and billiards room with its own bar, and a library – before we headed upstairs to the bedrooms.

This had been the moment I'd been dreading most of the trip. Call me old-fashioned, but as much as I was attracted to Desi and loved being with him, I wasn't at all sure that I was ready for us to share a room, and I'd come prepared with all manner of excuses to get myself out of this sort of situation. I needn't have worried, however, because he was the perfect gentleman.

'I thought you might like this one,' he said, opening the door to a bedroom that had floor-to-ceiling windows taking in views across the bay.

'It's amazing,' I replied. 'But where will you be?'

'Next door,' said Desi. 'The view's not quite as nice as yours but it's not exactly a concrete tower block either.' He lifted up my suitcase and laid it flat on the rack next to the wardrobe and then excused himself. 'I'll leave you to settle in and when you're done, come and find me downstairs and we'll go for a walk.'

With one thing and another it took me half an hour before I was ready to take the walk Desi had suggested, but once we'd started down the path and I caught sight of the beach and the ocean beyond, I stopped clean in my tracks. I think Desi might have actually been underselling it a little when he called the island one of the most beautiful places on earth. I'd never seen a more stunning view. It had everything you could want from a beach paradise: soft white sand, coconut-laden palm trees, a lagoon with crystal clear waters, and the lush greenery of the hills in the distance. And while Desi kept apologising for the lack of warmth (apparently the best time of year to visit the island was in December) for me, having just left a cold and rainy Melbourne, it was absolutely perfect.

Following an amazing afternoon in which we did little other than sit, side by side, on the sand chatting and staring out to sea, we returned to the house and while Desi dozed on the sofa in the living room, I cooked pasta with prawns in a chilli sauce, which we ate outside on the veranda next to the pool, accompanied by a chilled bottle of chardonnay. Afterwards Desi cleared the plates and dishes away, and then we put on a few more clothes as it started to get a bit chilly, before grabbing another bottle of wine and some glasses and taking a second walk down to the beach to watch the setting sun turn the water from blue to orange.

As night descended we ended up huddled together for warmth, talking until late. Desi told me about his dad, a violent alcoholic, and how he and his mum had run away from the family home when he was nine. He told me about the brother that he no longer saw because of a family dispute and the pain he felt each time the presents he'd bought for his nephews and nieces were returned unopened. He spoke about how much he regretted not trying harder to make his marriage work and his fear that he'd made it all too easy for his wife to walk away. Then finally, he told me that the days since he'd happened to be passing a garden table only to have a woman fall straight into his arms had been some of the happiest of his life.

It was late by the time we returned to the house. I helped Desi lock up the ground floor before we made our way upstairs. As we reached my room Desi wished me a goodnight, but as he tried to leave my side I reached out and grabbed his hand, pulling him towards me, and kissed him. I don't think I'd ever wanted anyone like I did him at that moment. I knew without a shadow of a doubt that I needed him to spend the night with me.

'Are you sure?' he asked.

'I've never been more sure of anything in my life,' I replied, and then without another word I gently pulled him into my room and closed the door behind us.

Tom

Laura's 'gathering' was actually looking a lot more like a party, thanks in no small part to the huge number of people who had turned up to celebrate her life. With Gill, Rich and Marina's help I'd contacted every one of Laura's friends and asked them to spread the word. At such short notice I'd only expected perhaps half a dozen or so to turn up, but within an hour of the first guests arriving, the living room was bursting at the seams and within half an hour of that, so was the rest of the house. There were friends present from every period of Laura's life. Friends who she'd made on her first day at nursery through to those she'd met as her own daughters started school. Every guest had arrived weighed down with food and drink, so much so that there wasn't a single surface in the kitchen that wasn't covered.

As for the kids, even though I hadn't seen either of them for a good hour, I didn't doubt that they were having the time of their lives, given their status as guests of honour. All Laura's friends wanted to do was meet Evie and Lola and hug the life out of them; and the constant comments about their similarity to their mother in both looks and temperament made their chests swell with pride. This was their day, as well as their mother's, and it was a day that I couldn't imagine them ever forgetting.

Excusing myself from a conversation with one of Laura's old school friends, who had come all the way down from Edinburgh just to share the day with us, I went to go and look for the girls but only managed to take a few steps before they came running towards me.

'Did you know that Mum once got a bit tipsy in a nightclub one New Year's Eve, took her top off and danced on the bar in just her bra?' said Evie gleefully.

'And did you know Mum got a *Blue Peter* badge for collecting the most milk-bottle tops in her school?' added Lola eagerly. 'Do you think we've still got it?'

'And apparently when Mum was a student she nearly got arrested for marching against student loans,' said Evie. 'And on top of that, when she was at school she used to do a really good impression of the headmaster to make her friends laugh, but then one day he overheard her and made her do the impression right in front of him.'

The delight in their eyes as they brought these stories to my attention told me everything I needed to know about whether or not this had been the right thing to do. In the space of a few hours their mum had gone from being a two-dimensional saint, who they could only ever think about in terms of loss, to a living, breathing, laughing, dancing, life-affirming, three-dimensional human being. Lola seemed to delight especially in the idea that her mum had made people laugh and after Evie told the headmaster impression story, she whispered in my ear: 'Dad, when I grow up, I'm going to be just like Mum.'

Without warning, the kids turned and abandoned me to my own devices. I reached for my phone to text Fran and tell her how the party was going, but as I did so it buzzed and I saw a message from her: 'Hope it's all going well! Granddad's trying to teach me gin rummy. Not doing v. well! See you in the morning xxx.' I tapped out a reply: 'House is heaving! Kids having whale of a time. Miss you loads, see you in the morning.'

It had been an odd moment for all of us: when I'd told Evie and Lola about Fran and me. We'd been sitting at the kitchen table, tucking into bowls of Eton Mess – the meringues for which I'd made from scratch – and the girls had been joking about, dipping their fingers in the cream and pretending to flick it into each other's faces, when I put down my spoon and told them I had something to say.

'You remember Fran, don't you?'

The girls nodded. 'She's the lady who made my Egyptian costume,' said Lola, 'and Mr Clive's her granddad.'

'That's right,' I replied. 'And, well, you know that Fran and I are friends, don't you?' The girls nodded. 'Well, over the past few weeks we've become a bit more than that, and even though it's early days and everything, I just wanted you to know.'

Lola's brow furrowed. 'I don't understand. Are you saying you're not friends any more.'

Evie elbowed her sister. 'No, doofus,' she said, 'he's saying the opposite. He's saying Fran is his girlfriend. Like I'm Oliver's girlfriend.'

Lola's penetrating gaze hit me with the force of a cannonball. It wasn't angry or accusatory so much as curious. 'So you're saying you and Fran are like Evie and Oliver?'

'No,' I replied, horrified by the comparison and then I corrected myself, 'Well . . . actually, yes, but it's different because we're grown-ups. Anyway, the reason I'm telling you this is because I don't want you to worry, okay? Nothing's going to change. All it means is that I like her, and I'll want to spend time with her just like I spend time with you guys.' There was a long pause, in which the girls just stared at me, their faces devoid of emotion. 'So, now it's out there, if you have any questions, fire away.'

The girls exchanged secretive glances and then Lola raised her hand. 'I've got one.'

'Yes?'

'But it's not a question.'

'Okay.'

'I just want to say that I like her, Daddy. I think she's nice.'

'And I do too,' said Evie. 'I think she makes you happy.'

And that was that, one of the hardest conversations I thought I'd ever have to have with the kids was over, done, just like that.

The girls asked if they could finish their pudding in front of the TV and I said yes, and so they got up leaving me, a sweaty mess, sitting across the table from two empty chairs.

Despite Laura's party being officially from two until six, it only really began to wind down after eight and I spent much of the next hour thanking our guests for making the effort and wishing them a safe journey home. I lost count of the number of times Laura's friends asked if I would consider making the party an annual event.

By ten, Lola was fast asleep on the sofa while Evie sat glued to the TV, struggling to keep her own eyes open, while I waved off the last of the stragglers, but as I returned to the kitchen to start the clear-up process I found that there was still one party-goer left.

I hadn't spoken to Ellie much during the course of the party, mainly because there were so many other people I needed to talk to, so the chain of events which had occurred that had led to Ellie ending up semi-slumped on the kitchen table, a large glass of red by her side and clearly the worse for wear, was a mystery to me. I immediately sensed trouble – things hadn't been particularly good between us ever since Lola's History Day. Twice in the past week she'd either ignored me altogether or offered me little other than a brusque hello, but when I sent out a round of texts about Laura's party she'd been among the first to reply.

Desperate to get her out of my kitchen and into a cab, I decided to be polite but firm.

'Oh, hi, Ellie, I didn't realise anyone was still here. I'll call you a taxi, shall I?'

She lifted her head up and stared in my direction. 'What time is it? Is it late?'

'Late enough,' I replied. 'I was just saying that it's probably a good idea if I call you a cab.'

'What for? Nobody cares where I am. I could stay out all night and it wouldn't matter.'

Despite my better judgement, I sat down next to her.

'I'm sure that's not true.'

'Isn't it? Marco's left me. He's taken up with some whore he met on one of his boys' weekends.'

'I'm sorry to hear that.'

She rested her head down on the table again. I felt bad for her, I really did, and if she'd been sober I'm sure I would've stayed chatting with her for as long as she wanted. But everything about this situation felt wrong.

'Listen, why don't I make you a coffee?'

She didn't say anything and so I left the table, filled the kettle and flicked on the switch before escaping to the hallway to call a cab for her. When the female radio-controller told me it would be ten minutes, I told her I'd pay double if it was closer to five.

After whisking the girls upstairs to bed, I returned to the kitchen. The kettle had long since boiled and so I flicked it on again, made coffee and put a cup in front of Ellie. Although she was now sitting upright, she barely glanced at it.

'I was just thinking about Laura.'

Her words caught me completely be surprise.

'Oh, right.'

'She was so pretty, wasn't she?'

It was a seemingly innocent question but it felt like a trap.

'Yes, yes, she was.'

She turned her head towards me slightly.

'You know I saw you the other day with that girl.'

I felt myself tense.

'What girl?'

'You were in the café on the High Street. Pretty little thing she was too. You've done well. And she seemed very pleased to see you.'

Ellie must have been in the café on the day that I was there with Fran. 'Oh, right, yes, that probably was me.'

'With Laura's new replacement.'

She seemed to be spoiling for a fight but I had no idea why. I stood up. 'Let's start getting our things together, shall we?'

'So now you want to get rid of me too, is that how it is?'

'I've called a taxi, it's probably here now, maybe we should go and see.'

I helped her up out of her chair and she leaned unsteadily on the table, gathering her things.

'You weren't fair, Tom. You led me on.'

So that was what this was all about? She thought there was something between us. I don't know where she'd got that idea from but I didn't have the mental energy to deal with any of it. I just wanted her out of the house.

'I'm genuinely sorry you feel that way, Ellie, I really am. But you have to go now.' I managed to get her into the hallway before she started to become agitated.

'What's wrong with you men?' she slurred angrily. 'Why can't you ever just be satisfied with what you've got? Marco says he loves her! Can you believe it? He says he actually loves her!' She started to sob and I instinctively put an arm around her but rather than making things better, it seemed to make things worse. She sobbed even harder, pulling herself into me and then she started trying to kiss me.

'You need to go,' I said, pushing her away.

'Oh, Tom, don't be like that,' she slurred. 'Whatever you've got going with that girl from the café isn't real, at least not like we are. I've been watching you all afternoon, the way you are with your kids, the way you hold yourself. We'd be such an amazing team, don't you think? You're so incredible, Tom, you really are. Laura must have been out of her mind to have cheated on you. If I'd been yours you would never have had to worry about me straying.'

Any trace of sympathy I had for Ellie vanished in an instant. 'You're talking rubbish,' I said, bustling her towards the front door. 'And what's worse it's insulting rubbish. I think it's best that you leave right now.'

Ellie seemed genuinely startled by the strength of my reaction, and in her drunken state I could see her trying to work me out, until finally she said. 'You didn't know, did you?'

'Because there's nothing to know,' I replied. 'So just get out of my house.'

Ellie laughed, resisting my attempts to herd her out of the door. 'She never told you, did she, about the affair? She told me she was going to tell you. I'd just assumed that she had.'

'You're drunk,' I replied, flinging open the door, 'and you need to leave now, and I don't want to see or speak to you ever again, do you understand?' I pushed her outside and slammed the door shut quickly, not caring whether the taxi was there or not.

'Well it's true, I am drunk!' yelled Ellie so loudly from the other side of the door that I thought she might wake the girls. 'But that doesn't make me a liar!'

21

It has to be today

Tom

I couldn't sleep. Ellie's awful lies about Laura had my mind racing. Why would she have made up such a thing? To get back at me just because I'd rejected her advances? Laura would never have cheated on me. She loved me too much to do something like that. She loved us – our family – too much to even consider it. Not that this sort of thing didn't happen to other people, of course. People left their partners for new lovers all the time. Dissatisfied by the current circumstances they allowed their head to be turned, thinking the new person would be the answer to everything. But Laura wasn't like that. She was happy. She loved our life. She loved being back at university and making plans for our future. She loved our family. We were her world.

I should've known better than to let someone like Ellie into my life. I'd met people like her before – eternal victims always on the lookout for their own personal saviour – I should have seen the warning signs right from the start. Her stealthy approach in the playground acting as though she was doing me a favour; the innocent coffee dates leading to revelations about marriage troubles and lack of understanding between husband and wife. I should have told her there and then that I didn't want anything to do with her. I should have kept my distance. If I'd had my wits about me, she would never have been able to fill me with her poison.

And yet . . . there had been something about the look on her face when she'd told me, the surprise registering in her eyes as though she truly believed she was telling me something I already knew. Granted she was drunk, more than a little emotional and – given her comments about Fran – absolutely not to be trusted but even so, her reaction didn't quite add up. Her attempts at painting me as a victim just like her made no sense. I was the widower, not the cuckold, the man without a wife, raising two young daughters on his own, not a victim of betrayal.

Resigned to a night without sleep, I threw back the sheets on the bed, got dressed and went downstairs. At first I tidied up for a while, but I didn't manage to do much more than clear a small section of the kitchen counter, before I abandoned the clean-up altogether and instead began rummaging through the drawers of the sideboard near the sofa. It was only after I'd virtually emptied their contents across the kitchen table that I finally found what I was looking for: the family calendar for the year we lost Laura.

I knew we still had it because a few weeks after our first Christmas without Laura, Linda informed me that she'd bought a new one and made a big point of telling me that she'd put the old one away in the drawer in case I wanted it as a keepsake. At the time I hadn't given it a second thought because the idea of a keepsake seemed ludicrous when all I wanted to do was forget, and so it had languished untouched in the drawer until now.

With the old family calendar in my hand, I flipped it open to the month Laura died and studied every word she'd inscribed on its pages. There was nothing out of the ordinary during that October, just the usual kids' play dates, appointments and university course-work deadlines. Nothing at all to indicate that Laura had been about to break some terrible news to me. Yet despite the lack of evidence of anything untoward, I couldn't stop myself searching. Gradually memories came back to me that individually didn't amount to anything of substance, but collectively left me feeling uneasy. For instance, there was a date Laura had marked down for a PTA meeting that stuck in my mind because it was the same as the day I'd heard I'd had a new show commissioned. I'd rung Laura to tell her the good news and had been surprised when the call had gone straight through to her voicemail. Five minutes later, however, she'd called me back blaming poor reception, even though we never usually had a problem receiving calls on our mobiles at home. On another date a week earlier she'd written a reminder for a dental appointment for the girls, which had never happened because it was the same day she'd gone to Brighton to meet up with an old school friend and her car had broken down on the motorway. She'd had to call Marina to pick up Lola from school and have the car towed to the garage. The funny thing was that I couldn't remember who the friend was she'd met with, or even recall her talking about the Brighton friend again. I flicked further back through the pages to August, to the dates marked down for the ten-day holiday we'd had in St Ives. As I did so, I recalled how attached she'd been to her phone the whole time we were there. At the time she'd told me it was because a friend from her university course was going through a rough patch in her marriage, but in spite of this it wasn't like her to be so distracted, especially while we were away with the girls.

Separately none of these things amounted to anything close to evidence of wrongdoing, and even collectively they didn't add up to much. Yet the unrest Ellie had stirred up in me refused to abate. I felt like the dates I was looking at were trying to tell me something, but I just couldn't work out what. Then I thought about all of the other things that didn't make sense: like the reason she'd been on the motorway on the day of her crash and the flowers left on her grave by the friend who signed their name 'R'. Then out of nowhere, a thought struck me: on the day of the crash I recalled Linda telling me how she hadn't spoken to Laura for over a week, which even at the time had seemed odd. Why would a mother and daughter who were so close they usually called each other every day not speak for a whole week without good reason? It just didn't seem right. My every instinct was to call Linda but I knew I couldn't go to her with my suspicions. I needed hard evidence. That's when I remembered Laura's phone.

Linda

Desi and I were in bed laughing. And we weren't just having a giggle either, but were eyes closed, tears streaming, out of breath and doubled over in pain belly-laughing, the kind you want to stop but just can't seem to regain control to do so. I can't remember exactly what had led to our hilarity – the reason we were laughing wasn't important – but it was another sign of how carefree and happy I had become.

These few days away with Desi had been absolutely wonderful. After revisiting the pain of Laura's loss, I'd imagined that I might never be happy again, and yet here I was with a permanent smile on my face, and it was all thanks to him. Desi made me feel like a completely new person, seeing life through fresh eyes. He made me feel like I didn't have to be sad any more, and believe that true happiness wasn't forever beyond my grasp. I had never met such a gentle, caring, loving, funny man and I had no qualms about telling him so.

'Do you really feel that way?'

'Why would I say it if I didn't mean it?'

Desi laughed. 'People say things they don't mean all the time.'

'Well I'm not one of them. Of course I mean it. I mean every word.' I brushed my hand against his chin, enjoying the sensation of his beard grazing the skin of my fingertips. 'I've never met anyone like you in my life.'

'And I've never met anyone like you either, which is why I want to ask you if you'll think about staying.'

'Here on the island?'

'No, in Melbourne with me. You could move into my place and let me show you the rest of what Australia has to offer. Maybe after that we could go travelling, and see all the places neither of us have seen and do all the things we've always wanted to do.'

'That sounds amazing, Desi, really it does but I have the girls to think about.'

'But you said yourself that your son-in-law is doing a great job with them.'

'And he is.'

'So are you planning on moving back in with them and picking up where you left off?'

'I'm not saying that.'

'So then you'll move back to York and just live for the school holidays?'

'Desi, please, it's not that easy. The girls are the last piece of Laura I've got, I need them in my life.'

'Of course you do, they're your flesh and blood,' said Desi. 'But you need to have a life too, one that you can invite them into, one where you aren't just waiting for the moments when you can join theirs.'

Slipping on his dressing gown Desi left the room, refusing to heed my call to stay. So much of what he had said was right but I couldn't imagine for a moment living thousands of miles away from them. It simply didn't bear thinking about.

I grabbed my robe and followed after him. I needed to make him see that my choice wasn't about not caring about him, so much as being there for those who needed me.

I was halfway down the stairs when for the first time during our stay I heard the phone ring, and as I reached the ground floor Desi came towards me with it in his hand.

'It's for you.'

'Is it Moira? Is she okay?'

'It's not Moira,' said Desi, 'it's your son-in-law. Apparently he's tried your mobile a few times but couldn't get through, so he called Moira and got this number.' He covered the phone with his hand. 'I don't want to worry you, but he doesn't seem right at all. He sounds quite agitated.'

I looked at the clock on the wall by the fridge. It was a little before five in the afternoon here, making it four in the morning UK time. My heart pounded. Why would he possibly be calling at that time? It could only be bad news.

'Tom, it's me, Linda. What's wrong?'

'Nothing's wrong,' said Tom. 'Everything's hunky-dory.'

'Are the girls okay?'

'They're fast asleep.'

'So why are you up? It's after four in the morning there, isn't it? What's gone on?'

'Funnily enough, Linda, that's what I'm calling to ask you.'

He was being so odd it really was worrying me. 'Stop it, Tom, just tell me what the problem is and we'll sort it out.'

'Is that so?' he snapped, his voice sharp and mean. 'Well, why don't we begin with you dropping the innocent act.'

'I don't understand, Tom? You think I'm not telling you the truth about something?'

'I know you're not,' said Tom. 'All this time, all this pain, and you knew, didn't you? And yet you didn't have the guts to tell me.'

'Tell you what? You're not making any sense. I can't explain anything unless you tell me what it is you're talking about!'

'What else could I be talking about, Linda? I'm talking about Laura cheating on me!'

I sat down heavily on the bottom step, wondering how he'd learned the truth. Had he found out on his own or had someone told him? It hardly mattered now that the cat was out of the bag. He was never going to forgive me for this, not that I was even convinced I was deserving of his forgiveness. Besides the girls, I was the closest thing he had to family and I'd let him down in the worst way possible. I should never have kept it from him. I should have told him when I had the chance. 'I'm so sorry, Tom, really, I am,' I said as tear after tear rolled down my face. 'I honestly thought I was only doing what was best for you in the long run.'

Tom

It was Laura's phone that changed everything. Bounding up the stairs two at a time, oblivious to whether I might wake my sleeping children, I headed straight to Laura's bedside table and took out her mobile phone, the only item left in the drawer I'd recently cleared out. I'd planned to hold on to it for a while longer because it contained pictures of the family and texts that I knew I wanted to keep, things I could copy from the memory at some point in the future. Grabbing my own charger, I plugged in the phone that had been dead for nearly a year and waited, half hoping, and half praying for a spark of life. Within a minute it was gaining charge and after another I was staring down at Laura's screensaver: an autumnal snap of me and the girls taken in Gatton Park the year before she died. She always used to say it was her favourite photo of us all: the one that never failed to lift her spirits even on the hardest of days.

I tapped in her password (Evie and Lola's birthdays combined) and went straight to her texts, but after ten minutes I hadn't found a single piece of incriminating evidence. If there had been messages between Laura and her supposed lover she'd been smart enough to delete them, so then I switched to her phone log and one number, stored simply as 'R', kept cropping up. No matter how hard I tried to convince myself, I knew it was no coincidence. The calls from 'R' started three months before Laura's death and continued right up until the day she died. I felt sick and angry, all I wanted in the world was to be wrong. If anyone could've convinced me that I'd jumped to the wrong conclusion it was Linda. I would have believed anything she'd told me. All that changed, however, the moment I came across Linda's final text to Laura, sent the day of her return to York following her visit to us for Lola's birthday: 'Hi Sweetie, just wanted to let you know I'm thinking of you. I know it will be tough but the sooner you do it, the sooner we can all put this wretched mess behind us, love always, Mum xxx.'

Linda

It was true. I had known about Laura's affair all along. The last time I saw Laura we spent the afternoon running errands in preparation for Lola's seventh birthday party. Loaded down with shopping bags full of food and last-minute presents, we'd stopped for a drink at a nearby café before picking Lola up from school. I'd barely lifted my herbal tea to my lips when without warning Laura, with tears in her eyes, said that she had something she needed to tell me.

'Darling, what's wrong?'

She looked down at the table. 'Mum, I've been having an affair.'

Laura hadn't gone into the details. All she said was that she'd met a man on her course at university and that there had been an immediate attraction, which she had tried and failed to resist.

She told me that it had been going on for some time but the guilt was destroying her, and she wanted to end it as soon as possible and try and make things right with Tom. Finally she told me she was sorry for letting me down. I told her she could never let me down, even if she tried, because as her mum that's what I was supposed to say, but in truth I was the last person she should've worried about letting down. I think the person she'd disappointed most was herself.

I blamed myself of course: mothers always do, and single mothers especially. This had happened because she didn't have a father. This had happened because I hadn't done a good enough job of raising her. This had happened because I'd been too hard on her; or I'd been too easy on her; because I hadn't been more involved in her life; or because I should've let her be more independent.

On the day I left to go back to York, she drove me to the station and as I got out of the car, having barely said more than a handful of words to her for the entire journey, I just came out and asked why she would do such a thing to poor Tom, when all he'd ever been was a wonderful husband to her.

'I don't know, Mum,' she replied. 'I wish I did but I just don't know.'

Laura swore me to secrecy about the affair, which put me in the most terrible position. I loved Tom. To me he was family. I didn't want to keep secrets from him but what choice did I have? She promised she would take care of it on her own. She didn't need my help. She would get it done in her own time and then tell him everything. But then the crash happened and everything changed, and I went from being an innocent onlooker to the keeper of my daughter's final secret. I had to stand by and watch Tom's heart breaking, knowing full well that he didn't know the whole truth. Was it any wonder I'd been so devoted to doing what I could to making his life easier? Why

I'd been so patient with him for so long and put up with so much of his bad behaviour? It was guilt, plain and simple, it had to be. I'd known the truth about Laura but hadn't had the strength of character to share it with him.

Tom

I wasn't thinking about consequences as I dialled 'R's number on Laura's phone. Having ended the call with Linda, I wasn't thinking about much of anything. Instead, I was running purely on instinct and my instinct was telling me to dial Laura's lover's number even though it was five o' clock on a Sunday morning. The first few times, it rang for a while then went through to voicemail but on the fifth attempt the same man's voice as on the outgoing message – deep, with just a hint of an American accent – came on the line.

'Who is this?' he demanded, sounding angry and a little frightened.

I imagined his confusion at receiving a call in the early hours from a woman he'd thought long dead. 'You don't know me,' I replied, 'but I believe you knew my wife, Laura Hope.'

A moment's hesitation at the other end of the line and then: 'Of course, yes, I knew Laura,' he said. 'She was a student of mine.'

'You were her lecturer?' I felt sick. So this was the ugly truth: Laura had fallen for someone she'd met on a course I'd encouraged her to do.

'For a while, yes, I was. What can I do for you? You do know how early it is, don't—'

I felt myself fill with rage as he tried to bluff me. 'Don't, okay? Just don't. I know everything that happened, so spare me the lies, okay? We need to talk and we need to do it today.'

There was a long silence and then his voice returned, lower than before and heavy with defeat. 'Today's impossible. How about tomorrow evening?'

'No. It has to be today.'

Another long silence. 'If you can come to Brighton I should be able to meet you first thing. I normally take a run down to the beach on Sunday mornings. I could meet you there, say around eight. There's a beachfront café called The View, it's between the two piers. I could meet you out front.'

'I'll be there,' I replied, and then I ended the call and woke the girls telling them I had an emergency to tend to at my old workplace and that I was going to drop them off with Rich and Marina. Evie didn't even bother to hide the fact that she didn't believe me, and questioned me at every point, while Lola, still half asleep, looked on with an air of disinterest as though she was still in the middle of a dream. Rich and Marina had questions too, not least why I was calling them in the early hours of a Sunday morning. I told them that I wouldn't ask them to help me out if it wasn't important, and while they were obviously alarmed by the urgency in my voice, they agreed to have the girls, leaving me free to return home, grab my car keys and drive to Brighton.

The journey was uneventful, a fact for which I was grateful given that I'd broken the conditions of my driving ban by getting behind the wheel of my car. If the police ever had stopped me I was sure that I'd have been looking at a custodial sentence, but as I walked out of the deserted car park and followed signs towards the beachfront, fear of prosecution didn't even come close to ranking in the top ten of my current concerns.

After a five-minute walk I crossed a main road and found myself facing the sea with only a pebble beach between the water and me. Following the instructions I'd been given, I continued along the promenade until I came to the café in question. Sure enough, as it came into view, I saw a figure clad in black and yellow lycra running gear standing outside, next to one of the tables.

'You must be Tom,' said the man. 'I'm Rob.' He held out his hand for me to shake but my only response was to register his wedding ring.

He was in his late forties but tall and lean, with greying hair and a neat beard. He looked good for his age and accomplished too, like he was illustrating an article in a weekend supplement about the upside of life after forty.

The café wasn't open yet, but we sat down at an aluminium bistro-style table regardless.

'So you're married?'

'I am now but I wasn't when I met Laura.'

'And that would make a difference to who exactly?'

'To no one, I was . . . it doesn't matter. How long have you known?'

'Since about four o'clock this morning.'

He shifted uncomfortably in his seat. 'You must be feeling pretty raw right now. For what it's worth, I'm sorry you had to find out at all. I can only imagine how difficult this is for you.'

'You're right,' I replied. 'You can only imagine.'

We fell silent for a moment as a couple of early morning joggers came past. Finally, he turned and looked at me again.

'So what is it exactly that you want from me?'

'I want to know.'

'About the affair?'

'About everything.'

They had met during the first week of Laura's return to university part-time, the year before she died. Rob, a New Yorker, had made the UK his home after securing a lecturing job in London. He'd liked Laura from the moment he'd met her but the relationship had been purely above-board until they started working more closely together on her final-year project at the beginning of the new autumn term. They kissed for the first time one evening following a drink after his lecture, and slept together for the first time three days later at a hotel in central London. They both knew it was wrong – Rob had a live-in girlfriend who he'd been with for nearly five years – but couldn't help themselves.

After a month and a half of snatched moments, Laura tried to end things. Apparently it was all too much for her: she hated betraying me; she felt like she was putting everything she held dear in jeopardy. Ravaged by guilt, she'd wanted things to be over between them, and on the day she died she'd driven to Brighton to see Rob and break the news to him in person. He'd begged her to reconsider. He told her that he loved her and wanted to be with her forever. He told her that he would end things with his girlfriend if it would make any difference at all. Apparently she told him it had been the biggest mistake of her life and that as soon as she reached home, she was going to tell me everything and beg my forgiveness, but she never made it back. 'I tried everything in my power to make her change her mind,' Rob said. 'But nothing I did worked. It was you she wanted in the end. You, and only you. I didn't stand a chance.'

22

It's family, isn't it?

Tom

In the car on my way back to Reigate, I went over every second of my encounter with Laura's lover a million times. The one thing that consistently surprised me was how calm I'd remained whilst in his company. Not once during Rob's confession had I felt like lashing out at him. Even when he spoke about the pain he'd felt on hearing of Laura's crash on the evening news. Even when he'd blamed himself for being the reason she'd undertaken the journey to Brighton that would ultimately end with her losing her life. I'd barely flinched as I listened to him tell me how, after Laura's death, overcome with grief, he'd made the decision to tell his girlfriend he was leaving her only for her to reveal she was six weeks pregnant. Even when he spoke of having no choice but to stay with his girlfriend because he wasn't 'that kind of guy', I didn't bat an eyelid. When he confessed to leaving a fresh bouquet of Laura's favourite flowers by her grave every month for the past year and a half, almost as if his pain was equal to mine, I didn't flinch. It was as though there was nothing he could do or say that could provoke me to anger, and I imagined that I must be so broken that I couldn't feel any emotion at all any more. But at the end of our time together, as I watched him jog away to return to the partner and child who knew nothing of Laura's existence, it occurred to me that I wasn't angry with Rob because he wasn't the person who had betrayed my trust. He was nothing to me, just as I'm sure I was nothing to him. He was simply an extra, a body in the crowd; the real story wasn't about him, it was about Laura, and every iota of anger I possessed was for her alone. How was I supposed to love Laura after what she'd done? How was I to make sense of the time I'd spent mourning her absence without feeling like a fool? I felt nothing but fury towards her now, a feeling that had nowhere to go and no way of expressing itself. Every muscle, every sinew seemed to course uncontrollably with a rage I couldn't control. I'd never imagined myself capable of feeling this way about another human being, least of all someone I'd professed to love more than life itself. Maybe it was love's fault, maybe it was Laura's, but regardless of where the blame lay it couldn't be contained any longer. I was damned if I was going to let Laura continue to occupy the home she hadn't loved enough to be faithful. Today was going to be the day I would get rid of her for good.

It was this same anger that flooded my body from head to toe the moment I returned home from Brighton. I'd never felt rage like it, and it had to have an outlet. Spying the black-and-white framed print of Laura and me standing outside the church on the day of our wedding, I threw it to the floor with such force that the glass shattered into a thousand tiny shards. Walking over the broken glass, I continued into the kitchen and grabbed a roll of bin liners from the cupboard under the sink, tore one off, and began dumping into it anything and everything that reminded me of Laura. Striding from room to room, I disposed of books and CDs, tore down family photos, gathered together all the carefully curated keepsakes of holidays past and dumped the lot into the bag. Such was the rage I felt that I even threw away the framed print that Fran had so admired. Along with it went the photo of Laura that lived on Evie's bedside table and even Lola's shoebox shrine. A better man than me would have never done something so cruel to his own children. He would have found a way to keep them out of the mess of their parents' marriage, so that they might remain forever innocent. But if I ever had been a better man, I certainly wasn't any more. All that mattered to me was excising Laura from my life. All that mattered was that she was gone for good.

Linda

It was late on Monday evening, and after what can only be described as one of the most tumultuous days of my life, Desi and I were in the lobby of our holiday home, suitcases packed, waiting for the taxi that would take us to Hamilton Island airport for our flight to Melbourne.

I sighed and looked at Desi. 'I can't believe we got to spend so little time here.'

'All the more reason for us to come back some day.'

I touched his arm gently. I felt terrible that after he'd gone to all the effort of taking me away to this idyllic place, I was the one responsible for making us leave. 'You do understand why I have to go, don't you?'

'Of course I do. It's family, isn't it?'

'So why do I feel like you're angry?'

He turned to me and smiled. 'I'm not angry with you, of course I'm not. You're only doing what you think is right. I'm just disappointed that's all. This was supposed to be your time and I wanted to be the one to make you happy.'

'And you did. Really you did. Things just got in the way, that's all. It wasn't your fault or mine or even Tom's: I think at the end of the day it was a simple case of bad timing.'

A car horn sounded. Our taxi had arrived, bringing an end to our time on the island. While the driver loaded our luggage into the boot, Desi and I went to the upstairs deck and, wrapped in each other's arms, took one last look across the bay.

'You know I'll never be able to thank you for everything you've done for me while I've been here. You really have been amazing. I don't know what I would've done without you.'

Desi laughed. 'I dread to think.'

'You know what I mean though, you've been so kind and patient with me. I wish there was some way I could repay you.'

'Well for starters you could stay.'

I smiled softly. 'You know I can't do that.'

'Fine, then I'll come to England, if you like.'

'You'd do that?'

'In a heartbeat.'

'So you'd leave all of your friends and family just for me?'

'Look, Linda, we're both too long in the tooth to mess around. If we were twenty years younger then maybe it wouldn't matter so much, but you and I both know that we like each other so why pretend? I'm telling you now, all you've got to do is say the word and I'll be on the plane with you.'

I could see in Desi's eyes that he meant every word. He really would give up his whole life just to be with me. What did it say about me that I didn't want to do the same? I really was very fond of him, and couldn't imagine meeting anyone like him ever again, but I could no more ask him to come to England than I could stay in Australia indefinitely.

'You know I'd love to be saying yes, don't you? I'd love for this to be our big happy ending, but we've only known each other a short while and this is simply too big a decision to rush.'

'So that's it, then? You leave and I never see you again?'

'Of course not, we'll always be friends.'

'That sounds a lot like a brush off to me, second prize in a quiz show, you've been a great contestant but here's where we say goodbye.'

'That's one way of looking at it, I suppose.'

'And what other could there be?'

'Well here's one for starters and it's this: that you, Desmond Reginald Banks, have changed the life of a complete and utter old fool who fell off a table while dancing when she was drunk beyond all recognition. Before I met you, I didn't think there were any proper heroes left in the world, but you saved me, Desi, you absolutely saved me, and I will never ever forget that.'

Tom

On the school run on Monday morning Lola wasn't speaking to me, and to be honest I wasn't much in the mood to be spoken to. It had been an awful weekend, made all the worse by the girls' reactions to my pathetic attempt to remove their mother from our home. Evie had been distraught when she saw the devastation I'd wreaked and had fiercely demanded to know why I'd done such a thing. Lola's reaction in some ways was worse, her bewildered silence and the searching looks she gave me hurt more than any words. I could so easily have told them everything. Uttered a few sentences to justify my actions. But even at my most enraged I still wasn't capable of shattering their illusions about their mother, when those illusions were all they had left of her. So I told them that I was just too sad to have any reminders of Mum in the house any more. Even if they did believe my lie, they hated my decision. Evie begged me to put things back the way they were and when I refused, she grabbed her sister's hand and together they hid away in Evie's bedroom, refusing to come out no matter how hard I pleaded.

Arriving at school, Lola couldn't wait to get away from me, wresting her hand from my grip and running into her classroom as soon as the bell went, without a backward glance or her usual kiss goodbye. If she was trying to hurt me then she'd succeeded. If she was trying to send me a message about how much I'd hurt her then I'd received it loud and clear. Until that moment I don't think I'd realised how much I relied on my little girl's hugs and kisses to get me through the day, and as I stood watching through the window as she put away her book bag and water bottle it was all I could do not to break down.

As I tried to leave the playground, every parent who had been at Laura's party stopped to tell me what an amazing time they'd had and what a perfect way it had been to celebrate her memory. It was impossible to know how to respond. I was still choked up at the way Lola and I had parted, and now I was being congratulated for something which I deeply regretted doing. Had they, like Ellie, known about Laura's affair? Was I an object of their sympathy or derision? Even if Laura hadn't told them, there was every chance that after a year and a half Ellie had. Was that the reason so many had turned up to the party? To witness first-hand the spectacle of a man so lost in grief that he couldn't see what a fool his wife had been making of him even from the grave? Aware that if I hung around any longer I'd be in danger of giving voice to my suspicions, I excused myself from the throng of well-wishers and headed home, only to find, as had happened twice before under happier circumstances, that Fran was waiting on my doorstep.

I hadn't seen Fran since before the party, when she and I had made plans to have Sunday lunch together. When she'd called to confirm the arrangements I'd fobbed her off with an excuse about Lola not feeling well, and with my world falling apart I hadn't responded to any of her later calls or texts, yet they kept coming. Little messages asking after Lola, small reminders of how much she cared for me. Prior to finding out about Laura these missives would have been the highlights of my day, but now each only served to remind me how hard and embittered I'd become. They no longer moved me, no longer made me smile. And by the time Monday came around, all they did was convince me that she and I were over for good.

From the look in her eyes to the way that she stood, shoulders hunched over, there was a sadness about her, which told me that she knew something was up.

'You look surprised to see me.'

'Do I? I don't mean to.' I tried to hug her but she was stiff and cold. She knew all right. I invited her into the house and made her a cup of tea. She asked after Lola and her fabricated illness. I told her she was much better, and Fran simply shrugged and sat down at the kitchen table in silence.

'I know something's going on, Tom,' she said, after I'd set her mug of tea on the table and sat down in the chair opposite. 'I don't know what it is but I'd appreciate it if you'd just come out with it, instead of being an idiot about it. I had enough of that sort of thing with Johnny. Just tell me what it is so I can make up my mind about what I need to do.'

'About what?'

She lifted her gaze briefly to meet mine. 'Us,' she replied. 'Tell me what's going on so I can make my mind up about us.'

Suddenly I didn't want to tell her. I couldn't imagine what might be gained from the exercise, other than forcing us out of our honeymoon period into the harsh, bright, unforgiving light of reality. Maybe if I just kept my mouth shut, maybe if we didn't try and talk things through, we'd be okay somehow.

'Believe me, you don't want to know,' I said, keeping my gaze fixed to a pile of unopened bills on the table. 'To be honest, *I* don't want to know either. I wish Saturday had never happened.'

I looked up briefly. Fran was carefully studying my face. 'Did you, you know . . . do something . . . something with someone at the party?'

She thought I'd met someone else. 'No, no of course not.'

'So then what happened? What's made you like this?'

I took a deep breath and I told her everything.

'I'm so sorry, Tom,' she said. 'That's so horrible. You must be devastated.'

'I'm . . . I'm . . . I don't know what I am to be honest. Sometimes I feel like her cheating taints every good memory I have of her; sometimes I feel angry that she lied to me for so long; but mostly I feel stupid, just plain old naïve. All this time I've been mourning her loss, only to discover that she didn't give a damn about me.'

Fran squeezed my arm tightly, an act of reassurance and comfort. 'But maybe it was just like the guy in Brighton said, she'd made her decision and she'd chosen you. She just didn't get the chance to tell you, that's all.'

'And that's supposed to make me happy?'

'No, of course it's not, I'm not saying that, all I'm saying is—'

I looked over at Fran, my heart breaking a thousand different ways. She didn't deserve this but it was going to happen anyway. 'I don't think I can do this any more, Fran, it's not you, please believe me when I say it's not you. It's everything that's happened. I just can't.'

Fran reached across the table and grabbed on to my hand, as tears began rolling down her cheeks.

'Tom, you don't mean that. You're hurt, you're angry and you're lashing out. But there's no need to destroy what we've got.'

'That's just it, what Laura's done to me is colouring my every thought and I don't want to look at you through that filter of bitterness.'

Through her tears she begged me to reconsider, reassuring me that we could get over this somehow. As much as I wanted to believe her, I couldn't. As hard as I tried to imagine a moment beyond this one, the vision wouldn't come. The only thing I could see was the nightmare I was living through.

Life pretty much went down the toilet after that. And it wasn't just because I was constantly in a foul mood after breaking up with Fran, or that the girls still refused to talk to me, or that Clive was winding me up by calling every five minutes to find out when we were meeting up next, or that I was still angry with Linda for the role she'd played in Laura's betrayal, or even that I was beginning to feel genuine hatred towards Laura for what she was putting me through. It was all of it. Everything. The whole damned lot. It was too much. I felt like it was all squashing me down, trying to crush me and there was nothing I could do to stop it. And then on the following Friday, almost a week after my discovery about Laura, I reached my limit and the wheels came off the whole thing and we ground to a halt.

I was in the kitchen making tea for the kids when Evie came home from school in floods of tears. I called after her to find out what was going on but she ignored me and rushed up the stairs to her bedroom, slamming the door behind her. It took half an hour of coaxing for her to tell me that Oliver had dumped her by text. I put my arms around her and told her not to cry. These things happened, I assured her, but it wasn't the end of the world, there would be other boys, better boys, boys who wouldn't be quite so self-centred. As words of comfort went they weren't exactly Oprah-worthy but they were the best I could offer, given my current take on the world of love. Evie, though, didn't hold back in letting me know just how far off the mark she considered them.

'You don't understand,' she'd sobbed. 'I loved him, he was everything to me!'

In retrospect I should've known better than to use this of all moments to make a point, but the words seemed to come out of my lips before I'd even registered that I was actually speaking them.

'You weren't in love, Evie, you just thought you were because you think love's this big thing that makes a difference to the world.' My voice was cold and world-weary, the exact representation of how I felt inside. 'You'll know when you're in love because it'll hurt a lot harder and a lot deeper than what you're feeling now. And when you do feel that pain, you really will know the difference.'

Evie's eyes widened. 'How can you say that?'

She had a point. 'Fine, I'm wrong you were right. No one in the history of the world has ever been as much in love with anyone as you were with Oliver!'

She might have been fourteen, but even Evie could spot playground sarcasm when she heard it. With her beautiful brown eyes brimming over with tears she told me that she hated me. 'I wish you'd died and not Mum! I want Mum back! Why couldn't it have been you and not her?'

I was well aware that there were some teenagers who often said hurtful things to their parents, but Evie had never been one of them. Even at her worst she'd always been aware that there was a line she shouldn't cross and yet now, here she was on the other side of it. She'd meant every word. She really did wish it had been me in that crash and not her mum and I wasn't sure that an explanation about Laura's affair would have made the slightest difference. Much as I'd tried to expunge Laura from their lives, the one place I'd never be able to touch were the girls' hearts where Laura would always rein supreme. It was an irony I couldn't overlook: even dead, Laura was still the better parent.

Evie stared at me half terrified, half defiant while her sister stood in the hallway watching everything unfold. None of us knew how to come back from this moment. This was where the script ended and we all had to improvise.

My phone rang, and had it been any other moment I'd probably have ignored it but as it was, I was glad of the distraction even if, as the screen indicated, the person at the end of the line was Fran.

'Tom, it's me,' she said. Her voiced sounded strange, strangled almost. 'It's Granddad. He had a severe stroke during the night. The doctors tried everything they could to save him but it wasn't enough.'

It felt unreal. Clive couldn't be dead. He was built to go on forever. Slowly, very slowly, the fury that had been propelling me forwards these past few days dissolved and in its place were sorrow and disbelief. These were feelings with which I was all too familiar. It was losing Laura all over again; it was the day my mum left; the day Dad died; the day I'd found out my marriage had been a sham. It was all too much.

Seeing the shock on my face, the girls rushed to me flinging their arms around me and reassuring me how much they loved me. I tried to speak, to tell them what had happened, to tell them that I loved them more than life itself; that somehow, some way, everything would be okay, but the words wouldn't come, and for a moment all I could think was, This is it, here we go again, this is where I lose myself for good. Then I heard Linda's voice in my head. She was saying the same words she'd said to me that day in the hospital, telling me to be strong for the girls, to be strong for Laura. I had a choice: give in or get up, but it really isn't a choice when you've lived through the worst option. I held the kids so tightly that they could barely breathe, I told them everything would be okay; then I called a taxi to take us all to Fran.

23

But that doesn't help me, does it?

Tom

'Are you sure that's everything you want?' asked Fran.

Fran's mum nodded, although her eyes betrayed a lack of confidence in her decision. 'If you think of anything else just add it to the trolley. I can't imagine anyone will have much of an appetite but you never know, do you?' She hugged Fran tightly. 'You will be careful, won't you?'

'Of course, I will.'

'You'll keep her safe won't you, Tom?'

'Of course I will, Mary,' I replied. 'I'll look after her.'

It had been three days since Clive had passed away: nowhere near enough time for Fran or any of her family to have fully come to terms with their loss but more than enough time for Fran's parents and various uncles and aunts who were staying at the house to have eaten every last scrap of food, which was why Fran and I were heading out to the supermarket.

'Any time I leave the house, Mum just imagines the worst,' explained Fran, as we got into her car and she started the engine. 'I know she means well but it's going to drive me nuts if she carries on like this.'

'I know,' I said, 'but don't be too hard on her. I doubt that she can help it. Grief sends your thinking into all kinds of weird places. It makes you come up with all sorts of strange rules.'

Fran touched my hand gently. 'I'm being a bitch, you're right, I should just give Mum a break, she's just lost her dad, she can be any way she likes.'

I knew what she meant. Each person had their own way of dealing with loss, and not everybody who got hit by grief had to take it to an extreme. Not everyone had to be me.

'She'll be fine. She just needs a bit of time.'

For the rest of the journey we sat in silence, and I used the opportunity to review my past few days with Fran. Whether comforting her at the hospital or being with her as she put a brave face on for her family, it had been odd being so close to grief and yet being fully aware that it wasn't mine for the taking, much like an alcoholic left in charge of an off-licence, the emotions at play were so familiar to me that it was hard not to over-connect with what Fran and her family were going through. Yes, Clive had been a good friend over these past few months, but he had been father to Fran's mum and grandfather to Fran for a lifetime and they grieved for him in a way I never could. Still, I missed that old man far more than I ever would have imagined and I knew that life would never quite be the same without his guiding hand in my life.

Fran and I didn't spend long shopping. It was pretty much a smash-and-grab exercise but then as we finished loading the car, I could see that she was reluctant to go home straight away. I suggested that we grab a drink and Fran agreed, and we were halfway to the café at Morrisons before it dawned on either of us what we were doing.

I proposed that we go somewhere else but she shook her head. 'I hate the idea of hiding from him just to save a few tears,' she said, taking my hand. 'I don't ever want to be scared of remembering Granddad, especially now that memories are all I have.'

We joined the queue and when it came to our turn, bold as you like Fran ordered two bacon baps and two mugs of tea, her stoicism intact even when one of the women behind the counter recognised her and asked after Clive and she had no choice but to break the bad news.

'I'm so sorry to hear that,' said the woman behind the counter. 'He was an absolute gentleman and my all-time favourite customer.' She shook her head and tutted. 'He always used to say we made the best food in town. He will be sorely missed by all of us.'

As we ate I told Fran about the first time I met Clive, and we talked about how odd it was that it had been she who had picked him up from the counselling session that night. Two strangers yet to meet, completely unaware what lay in store for us in the future. It should've been the perfect lead up to a conversation about us, my opportunity to tell her how sorry I was for having made a mess of things, and to reveal my desire to give us another go but just as I was about to speak, my phone pinged from inside my jacket. I read the text message half a dozen times before its meaning finally sunk in.

'It's from Linda.'

'Is everything okay?'

'She's coming home.'

'But I thought you said she's not back for another fortnight?'

'She must have changed her flight,' I replied. 'She's coming home. She'll be here on Saturday.'

Linda

Mid-afternoon. Melbourne Airport. Moira had gone to get coffee for us, leaving me alone in the queue waiting to check in for my return flight to Gatwick. I was going home, back to my girls. I couldn't wait until I could hold them in my arms.

Desi had agreed that it would be best if he didn't come to the airport; instead I'd spent my final night in Melbourne at his home. He made dinner and even though he wasn't much of a cook, somehow every mouthful of the meal was delicious. That night we went to bed and as I dozed in his arms, trying to fight sleep so that I might capture our final moments together, I felt his hold around my waist relax as he drifted off to sleep. I'd never felt so safe, so secure as I did that night in his arms and if it had been up to me, I would have stayed there forever. But I had no choice. Tom and the girls needed me. It was time for me to go home.

Desi understood that I needed to make things right with Tom, but what he couldn't comprehend was why I wouldn't commit to a future together. Time and again he reassured me that he'd be happy to come to England, and time and again I put him off with ill-prepared excuses: it was too much too soon; we were putting too much pressure on ourselves; shouldn't we at least try being friends. Desi wasn't convinced, and neither was I. All I knew for sure was that I was scared: of where it all might lead; about the sacrifices that might have to be made; of the demands of being in love. Most of all, I was scared of change. A life with Desi, whether in Australia or at home, was just too much of an unknown quantity for me to gamble everything I had. I wasn't a young girl any more and I was too old to believe in fairy tales. And while I might not have got my happy ending, what I did have was a damned sight more than most people got. I had the girls and, if Tom would ever forgive me, a place to call home too.

After breakfast, Desi took me for a drive along the Great Ocean Road with its breathtaking scenery. We stopped for lunch at a beautiful little café overlooking a bay, and as we prepared to leave, he told me that he loved me. I didn't say it back though – it would've been too hard, even though I felt it in my very bones. Instead, I took his hand and squeezed it tightly as we walked back to the car for the drive home.

It was late in the afternoon when Moira arrived to pick me up, the boot of her car already loaded with my suitcases. She stayed for a quick cup of tea and we all made an effort to keep the conversation light and airy, but when it came time to say goodbye I couldn't help myself, I just broke down. The thought that I might not see Desi again, or hold him again, it was all too much. Wrapping me in his arms, he whispered in my ear, 'You've got to be strong,' and it was like the words themselves took over, lifting my spirits and keeping me upright. I kissed and held him one last time and promised to call him when I reached England.

At the airport, I checked in and then Moira and I found a bench and sat down to enjoy our coffees. As we waited for our drinks to cool, Moira asked me about my plans.

'You mean about Tom?'

'I was actually thinking more about you and where you're going to live,' said Moira, 'but now you mention it, I suppose him too. I can't imagine what he must be going through.'

'I wouldn't wish it on my worst enemy. He sounded so lost when I last spoke to him. That's why I've been texting. I just can't bring myself to talk to him without being there face to face. I feel like I've let him down.'

'You did no such thing, you were in an impossible position.'

'But I don't think he'll see it that way. He thinks I betrayed him, and I can't blame him really. I just hope he can find a way to work through it all that doesn't end with him losing sight of what's really important.'

'And what about where you're going to live?'

'I just don't know. There's too much up in the air to say for sure. I suppose I'll just have to wait and see.'

We talked for a good hour about my situation and about how we'd miss each other. It had been such a comfort having Moira so close and even though my stay hadn't been quite as I'd expected, I'd relished the opportunity to see my old friend again.

'You've been amazing,' I told her as my flight was announced over the Tannoy. 'A true friend. I can't begin to thank you for everything you've done for me since I've been here.' My voice caught with emotion. 'I want you to promise that you'll come and visit and let me spoil you.'

Moira smiled, her eyes brimming with tears as she laughed, 'Don't you worry,' she said, 'I've already booked my flight.'

Tom

Saturday morning. Two hours before Linda's plane was due to land. The girls were beside themselves with excitement at the prospect of Linda coming home.

'Will she have a funny accent?' asked Lola as we got into the back of a taxi.

'Don't be daft,' said Evie, putting on her seat belt. 'She's only been gone a few months. You need to be away ages before you get an accent, don't you, Dad?' Lightning quick, her eyes flicked in my direction to check the veracity of her statement before her sister sensed any doubt.

'You've spoken to her a billion times on the phone,' I replied in a tone that I hoped revealed that I thought they were both as daft as each other. 'You know for a fact that she hasn't got an accent.'

As the girls teased each other for missing the obvious, the driver pulled away, double-checking our destination with me as he did so.

'Gatwick, is it?'

'That's the one.'

'You're not going away, I take it.'

He was talking about our lack of luggage. 'Picking up the girls' grandmother, my mother-in-law.'

The driver cackled loudly and I knew exactly what was coming next. 'So, it's the old dragon we're picking up is it? I hope she's less of a misery than mine. Honestly, if looks could kill, mine would be a mass murderer.'

He glanced in my direction, cheesy grin set to full power, craving a hint of recognition like a bad stand-up comedian.

'Thing is,' he continued, 'I haven't spoken to my mother-in-law in months. We haven't fallen out, mind, I just don't like to interrupt her!'

He laughed again, and I could feel him willing me to respond in kind but he'd read me all wrong. Though I still had my issues with Linda, none of them were to do with her being the clichéd interfering battleaxe. And in the light of Clive's death, even those issues I once had didn't seem quite so important.

'Mine's nothing like that.'

His expression was one of genuine surprise. 'You're having a laugh, aren't you? They're all as bad as each other!'

'Well,' I replied, 'I suppose I just got lucky.'

Linda

The rush of excitement I felt as the wheels of the plane made contact with the tarmac at Gatwick was exhilarating. After nearly a day of being dislocated from time and place, of sitting and thinking, of eating and loo runs, of bad movies and even worse meals, I had arrived at my destination. This was it. I was here. I was finally going to see my girls, and the moment I took possession of my suitcase – having endured the queues at Passport Control – I all but broke into a run. Now there was nothing between me and my girls except the distance I needed to cover in order to take them in my arms.

Emerging through the electronic doors into the arrivals hall, I scanned the crowds lined up behind the barrier. There were cab drivers holding up signs for business people, whole hosts of families waiting for their loved ones and separated lovers waiting to be reunited with their hearts' desires but there was no sign of Tom and the girls. No matter how hard I looked, they were nowhere to be seen and as much as I knew that there were a million and one logical reasons why they might have been delayed, I began to panic imagining the worst. As families and friends hugged all around me, I reached for my phone and switched it on, willing the screen to light up and display its welcome message so that I could call them. With every moment that passed the disasters I imagined became increasingly vivid.

Finally my phone buzzed: I had voicemail. As I pressed it to my ear something caught my eye and my heart leapt. It was Evie and Lola and the small commotion that was following them as they ran full-pelt towards me. I didn't care that they'd nearly knocked me off my feet, I was too busy being grateful that they were both in my arms again. I wanted to hold them, touch them, breathe them in and shower them with kisses.

I briefly held them at arms' length so that I might gaze into their faces, barely able to believe how much they'd changed in so little time. They were both so much taller than I remembered; Lola's face had grown leaner; Evie's hair was that much longer and her skin was enduring the rigours of her journey into the teenage years. But they were both as beautiful as ever, a living, breathing tribute to their mother.

'We're so sorry we're late,' gasped Lola, still breathless with excitement. 'There was a lot of traffic and we got stuck in it.'

Evie hugged me tightly. 'It's so good to have you back home, Nanny.'

'It's good to be home, I—' I stopped as Tom came into view. He looked taller somehow and far healthier than I remembered him being – I wasn't sure but he actually might have put a little weight on to that skinny frame of his – but up close I could see that the sadness in his eyes remained just the same, in fact I wondered if it hadn't become even more intense.

There was so much that I wanted to say to him about Laura, the children and everything I'd learned these past few months, but for now I just reached out and hugged him tightly while the girls clung on to my side, and in the middle of this huddle, I breathed deeply as my heart sang inside my chest. 'This is where I belong.'

Tom

I'd done a lot of thinking about how this moment would go. Part of me thought that perhaps I'd be filled with anger, another that I'd be suffused with joy; what I hadn't expected, however, was to feel both emotions at the same time and with such force. I'd missed her. I really had. But I felt a real resentment towards her too, and it took all the strength I had not to let it play out in my body language. It wasn't the time or the place for this conversation. For now I had to be grateful that she was home safely.

Linda

The girls and I didn't stop talking all the way home. They wanted to know everything about my time away: what I'd seen, where I'd been, who I'd met. Of course I gave them the edited version – the one in which their grandmother hadn't fallen head-over-heels in love with a handsome and rugged builder and met with the grandfather they'd never known – and, aside from the odd yawn here and there, for the most part they seemed entertained by the rather beige tales I had to tell. One day I would tell them the truth about my time in Australia, if only to see first-hand the disbelief on their faces, but for now I was content to be their sweet, innocent and tame-as-the-day-is-long Nanny.

Tom

The moment we reached home the girls excitedly ushered Linda upstairs on the pretext of showing her their rooms, but I was sure there was more to it than that. On the way over to the airport they'd asked me several times if they were allowed to tell her about everything that had happened since she'd left. I told them they could tell her whatever they liked, knowing full well that they would anyway. On the journey home from the airport, the girls hadn't said a word about Clive or Fran or the day I went crazy and dumped all of Laura's stuff, so I could only guess that they were saving it up until I was out of earshot.

Linda

The girls talked my ears off for a good hour before they sloped off downstairs to watch TV. Seizing the opportunity, I grabbed a quick shower and washed my hair and afterwards lay down on the bed in the spare room for a fifteen-minute nap. I don't know how long I was asleep for but it wasn't fifteen minutes. When I opened my eyes it was dark outside and all the street lamps were on. Throwing on some clothes I came downstairs and found Tom in the kitchen, loading the washing machine.

'Oh, Tom,' I chided, feeling somewhat guilty as he tossed dirty clothes into the drum. 'Have you been working all this time while I've been sleeping. You're putting me to shame.'

He smiled, his familiar big grin. 'You're jet-lagged not lazy, Linda. Do you want a tea?'

He flicked the kettle on, set the programme for the washing machine and then got out the tea and some mugs.

'I was so sorry to hear your bad news,' I said, as he opened the fridge door and took out the milk.

Unsmiling he said, 'You'll have to be more specific.'

'I mean about your friend . . . Clive. I didn't quite follow everything they told me. Was he a friend from work?'

Tom shook his head. 'I met him at the grief-counselling group you sent me to. He didn't like it either and we sort of bonded over that.'

'The children said he was quite elderly.'

'He'd just turned eighty but he was sharp as a knife. I know it sounds odd, but we were friends, good friends.'

Tom allowed me to give him a hug but even so I could sense resistance. 'When's the funeral?'

'Monday, but I probably won't go.'

I didn't need to ask why not. It was written all over his face. He'd no doubt had his fill of funerals. 'Well, if you change your mind I'm more than happy to do school drop-off or pick-up that day. It's the least I can do.'

'Thanks, I'll bear it in mind.'

The kettle came to the boil and, refusing my offers of help, Tom made the tea and brought it over to me at the table. It was impossible to gauge his mood. Was he tired? Was he angry? Was he beyond feeling anything at all?

'The girls have grown so much while I've been away,' I said, hoping that he might brighten if we changed topics. 'Lola especially, I can't believe how tall she is.'

'It feels like I only have to blink and the new school trousers that were covering her shoes are suddenly halfway up her calves.'

'And Evie,' I said. 'I've got a feeling that she's set to be so much taller than—' I stopped and looked at Tom, waiting for his reaction.

'It's fine,' he said. 'You can say her name.'

I put down my mug and looked at him. 'I'm so sorry for the way you found out about Laura. I really am. And I know you must still be angry with me but please, please know that I honestly never meant to hurt you. I was as shocked as you when she told me, and I just assumed that it would be one of those things you'd sort out between yourselves in your own time. And then when she died, well, what could I do? You were so lost, so broken, I would never have dreamed of adding to your pain. I thought if you never knew, it could never hurt you, but it did and for that I'm truly sorry.'

He met my gaze. 'I just keep going over it all in my head. What did I do wrong? Why wasn't she happy?'

It was the million-dollar question, the very same question in one way or another I'd spent a lifetime asking myself about Frank.

'I don't think she was unhappy with you, I don't think that for a moment. She loved you and she loved the kids: you were her world. If anything, I think she was unhappy with herself. She was always such a perfectionist, always wanting everything to be just so, and I think because of me and her father she felt like that all the more when it came to her family. I think she worked so hard to make the perfect family, and along the way she lost sight of who she was and what she wanted. I think that was part of the reason she did what she did. But it only served to remind her of what she already knew deep down, that you and the children were everything she needed. And she was horrified that she'd put that in danger for even a second.'

'That's all very well,' said Tom. 'But that doesn't help me, does it? I still feel betrayed, I still feel let down. And I can't see how I'll ever make peace with it.'

'But you have to, for the girls' sake.' I lowered my voice, partly out of fear that they might overhear but mostly out of shame for what I was about to say next: 'They told me how you removed all of Laura's photos.' I tried my best not to sound accusatory but it was hard to tell if it worked.

'It's like every memory I have of her is tainted now,' said Tom, refusing to look at me. 'All I had left were memories of the good times and to find out that those memories weren't real, that they weren't true, it's made a mockery of everything. I feel like I didn't know her at all.'

'I know it's hard, Tom, really I do, but I do so worry about the impact this will have on Evie and Lola.'

'Don't worry,' he said as a hard edge came into his voice, 'she's still Saint Laura meek and mild and as far as they're concerned, that's the way she'll stay.'

'But they know something's wrong. They've all but told me that already.'

He shrugged. 'So what do you want me to do, Linda? Pretend I'm not feeling what I'm feeling? Pretend it didn't happen?'

The memory of my meeting with Frank popped unbidden into my head for a second. 'Of course not,' I replied. 'You've every right to feel betrayed but you can't let it take over your life, you can't let it poison you. You can't let it define you, or colour the way you look at the world forever more. I know it's easier said than done but I think there comes a point where you have to say enough's enough and move on.'

24

Let's go for a walk

Tom

It was early on the morning of Clive's funeral but rather than being plagued by thoughts of the fragility of life, I was occupied with making sure that Evie got to school on time and with everything she needed.

'So you've got your hockey stick?'

'It's by the front door.'

'And the worksheets with your maths homework on?'

She nodded again, only this time rolled her eyes too. 'In my maths folder.'

'And how about the money for your geography field trip?'

She immediately stopped looking quite so smug and began frantically searching through her blazer and school bag. 'I put it in the zip pocket of my blazer and now it isn't there.'

I let her search for a good minute before I dug deep into my trouser pocket and pulled out the envelope. 'It was on the kitchen table where you left it after I specifically asked you to put it somewhere safe.'

Looking suitably remorseful as she took the envelope from my outstretched hand, she mumbled an apology before grabbing her bag, throwing a kiss in my general direction and heading out of the door. From the doorstep Lola and I watched until she disappeared out of sight. As we returned inside, Linda, fully dressed for the day, came down the stairs.

'Has Evie gone already?' she asked. 'I wanted to say goodbye.'

'I think she was in a bit of a rush,' I explained. 'How are you? Ready for the school run?'

Linda had kindly agreed to take Lola to school – her first time since her return – her first time since leaving me in charge. We moved into the kitchen and while Lola finished off some colouring on her science project at the kitchen table, I took down the family calendar and showed Linda everything she might need to know for the day ahead.

'Lola's sandwiches are in the fridge along with her fruit,' I began, 'and they've moved the lunchbox store to the other side of the playground, just in case you wonder where they've put it; she needs her swimming kit today, which I've left by the front door along with a signed permission slip for her school trip next week and some cardboard boxes and other stuff that her teacher wanted for junk modelling; she's got a Super Spell some time this week so if you've got time on the way to school she needs testing on her spellings; the list is in her book bag; and she's also got a maths test today. We practised her nine times table last night and she was perfect but if you could check her on that too, if you find a minute, that would be great and—' I stopped talking, mainly because Linda had a huge grin on her face.

'What's wrong?'

'It's just . . . you know . . . all this. It's a bit of a shock to the system to see you like this first-hand. You're so organised . . . I don't know, it's like . . . well, I'm just so impressed. You've come a long way, Tom, you really have.'

I had mixed feelings as I waved Linda and Lola off to school. I felt as though I was watching a film or a play of someone else's life, rather than my own, and for a long while after they left, I found myself wondering how things might be in the future. Would I return to work? Would I hand over the reigns to Linda for the running of my family? Or was there a compromise to be struck that would allow us both to play a role in raising the girls without making one or other of us feel redundant?

It was a text from Fran that brought me to my senses – a reply to one I'd sent an hour earlier assuring her that everything would be okay. It wasn't a long text by any means, just a simple 'Thank you' followed by three kisses, but it was enough to send me running up the stairs to my bedroom to finally try on the one and only black suit that I owned, the suit that Linda had bought for me to wear to Laura's funeral, the suit I'd hoped I'd never have to wear again.

In the midst of the organisation for Laura's funeral, Linda had found the time to go through my wardrobe, take measurements from all of my suits and head off to Covent Garden, purchasing half a dozen suits for me to try on at home. She'd then arranged for a seamstress to visit the house and adjust the hem of the trousers using my other suits as a guide. On the day of the funeral I'd woken to find the suit hanging from the door of the wardrobe next to a brand new shirt, tie and belt.

Back in the present I opened the wardrobe, took out the suit, shirt and tie and lay them on the bed and then, slipping off the T-shirt and jogging bottoms that I'd put on after my shower that morning, I began to get dressed. Once I was ready I took a look at myself in the wardrobe mirror, fully expecting to be transported back in time to a year and a half ago. But when I stared at my reflection there wasn't a single shred of recognition in my eyes. I wasn't transported back in time, I was very much stuck in the here and now. This was a new day, a new experience, a journey into the unknown and I could only hope that by the end of it, I'd still be standing.

Linda

It was a little after eleven thirty as I returned home from dropping off Lola at school. On the way I'd bumped into some of the ladies from the book group and they were so pleased to see me that they practically carted me off to join them all for coffee, and although I protested, it was lovely to know that I'd been missed. They wanted to know all about my trip, but the question they most wanted an answer to was whether I was coming back for good. 'It's all a bit in the air at the moment,' I told them, but the looks of sympathy they shot in my direction, as though I was an old nag being put out to pasture, made it clear to me that they were determined to read between the lines even if there wasn't any writing there to see.

Alone in the house, I tried to make myself useful and tidied up the breakfast things, hung out a load of washing, put a second load on and then went around the bedrooms looking for clothes to make up a third load. Essentially I was keeping myself busy in a desperate attempt not to think about Desi. I missed him, I really did. I missed everything about him, from his deep, resonating laugh to the gentle way he would sometimes touch my face as we lay in each other's arms. I missed the way he would look at me first thing in the morning – as if I was the most beautiful thing he'd ever seen – and the questions he would ask that made me think differently about human nature and the world around me. Most of all, however, I simply missed his presence, the space that he had filled in my life.

We'd spoken several times in the week since my return – little chats here and there updating each other with news about our lives – but each exchange seemed to make things worse rather than better, to make the heartache stronger rather than diminish it, to make me miss him more, not less. It was only a matter of time before it all got too much and one of us said that it couldn't carry on. My money was on Desi: he'd already put up with far more than most men would, and while I hated the torture of being away from him, the truth of the matter was even the ache of missing him was better than nothing at all.

With the phone in my hand I sat down to call him, hoping I might catch him at home, but I'd barely finished dialling his number when I hung up, and after rooting around in my handbag made an entirely different call.

'Hello?'

'Frank, it's me.'

I hadn't seen or spoken to Frank since that day in the café, so quite what made me think about him there and then was anyone's guess. I wasn't even sure what, if anything, I wanted to say to him, other than perhaps to find some way to properly draw a line underneath this chapter of our lives. It needed underlining, or at the very least some form of punctuation or sign, to show that things had been dealt with properly.

'Linda?' He sounded half asleep. Had he been dozing? It was after nine thirty in the evening there. 'I've been hoping you'd call again . . . especially after . . . well, you know . . . I'm so glad you've called though. Do you want to meet up again? I can meet you anywhere you like.'

'I can't, I'm back in England.'

'Already? Oh, I sort of got the impression you were here for a while.'

'A family situation came up unexpectedly and I had to come home. Couldn't be avoided, I'm afraid.'

'Nothing too bad, I hope?'

'Nothing that won't sort itself out with time.'

'And how are the family?' He was talking about the girls, his granddaughters. 'Are they okay? I bet they've missed you.'

'They did, yes,' I replied, 'but not as much as I missed them.' There was a long pause, a mutual silence as we each wondered what the other was thinking. Finally I spoke. 'Listen Frank, obviously I'd have to talk to Tom about it . . . but . . . I don't know . . . I suppose what I'm trying to say is . . .'

'What?'

'. . . I'm trying to say that if you wanted to . . . or felt the need to . . . I wouldn't necessarily stand in your way if you wanted to have some sort of relationship with the girls.'

Finally it was out there. It wasn't as though I'd been debating the pros and cons of it. I think it probably came out of a desire for peace. There had been so much upset over the past few weeks, so much needless pain that I felt like we all needed a fresh start, Frank included. After all, how could I expect Tom to forgive Laura and not be prepared to do the same with Frank?

Another long silence but this one was different. It felt like the sound of a late-middle-aged man reviewing a life lived in regret. It lasted so long I began to wonder if he was still on the line.

'Frank? Are you still there?'

'Linda.' There was tenderness in his voice when he said my name, the kind I hadn't heard in over forty years. It took me back to the last time he told me that he loved me, a long lost Sunday afternoon lying in each other's arms and hidden from the world. 'Linda, I'm speechless . . . really I am . . . I don't think there's ever been a kinder act made to someone so obviously undeserving. It only serves to remind me of what a truly remarkable woman you really are and what an idiot I was for giving you up . . . but I can't be part of their lives, not after what I did, after how I behaved. I don't deserve that kind of joy after not being a father to their mother. The girls are your reward for everything you did for Laura, and they're yours alone, but if they ever need anything, if *you* ever need anything – anything at all – don't hesitate to get in touch, and I promise I'll do everything I can to help.'

After the call, I wasn't at all sure what I should do. I felt drained and tired and wanted nothing other than to crawl under the sheets, close my eyes and forget about the world, but instead I picked up the phone again, searched out Desi's number and dialled, determined to fix our situation one way or another for good.

Tom

Clive's funeral was over and somehow I'd survived. Clutching Fran's hand throughout the service, there had been much about the day that brought back memories of Laura's funeral – memories I'd thought long forgotten – but there was much that was different too, most notably the atmosphere of the gathering, which seemed to speak of a timely passing rather than a tragedy, of a long life well lived, rather than a young life taken far too soon.

It was impossible not to feel a sense of pride as countless children, grandchildren, friends, neighbours and former work colleagues lined up at the chapel to give their eulogies. As grumpy and curmudgeonly as Clive had been, somehow, much as he had done with me, he'd still managed to positively touch so many lives. A smartly dressed elderly lady revealed how, after her husband died, Clive, refusing all offers of recompense, looked after her garden on a weekly basis until his knees started to play up; one former colleague of Clive's in the police force told the story of how he'd been stabbed breaking up a fight in a pub and it had been Clive's bravery and quick thinking that had saved his life; one of Clive's great-granddaughters, a girl not much older than Lola, told of the afternoon that her great-grandpa spent catching frogs in a local park with her; and one of Fran's cousins told a story about how on the day she failed to get into her chosen university, Clive had arrived on her doorstep with a huge bunch of flowers and took her out for a posh meal to help cheer her up. By the time the service came to a close, it was impossible not to feel uplifted rather than cast down, to feel that you'd celebrated a life rather than mourned the passing of one.

Outside in the fresh air, Fran put her arms around me. 'Thank you for coming, I know it must have been difficult for you.'

'I'm just glad it's over,' I replied. 'Anyway, how about you, how are you holding up?'

Fran smiled. 'I've had better days. Still, it was a nice service, wasn't it? All those people saying all those nice things about Granddad, it was incredible. I think I cried the whole way through. Of course I'm sure Granddad would've hated it. He always got embarrassed if anyone said anything nice about him to his face. This would've been his worst nightmare.'

Two women interrupted the conversation and introduced themselves as friends of one of Fran's aunts, and began talking about the service. As close as Fran and I were, I couldn't help but feel like an interloper, but when I tried to give her a bit of space she held my hand even tighter, and once the conversation was over, whispered into my ear: 'Let's go for a walk.'

It was a beautiful June day, the very definition of T-shirt weather. The kind of day best spent in a park lying on your back next to the girl of your dreams, doing nothing more challenging than staring at the sky and thinking about how lucky you are. We walked along the yew-lined path that led towards where Fran's grandmother was laid to rest. We were so quiet that we didn't even disturb the frantic foraging of a pair of blackbirds.

'With everything that's been going on, I feel as though I haven't seen much of you lately,' said Fran. 'How have you been? How's everything now your mother-in-law's back?'

'The kids love having her back. She's already unpacked and back in her old room. It's like she's never been away.'

'So will that mean you'll go back to work?'

'I haven't really thought about it. I suppose I could, but to be honest I think I'd miss the kids too much to go back to the crazy hours I used to work.'

'So you'd both be home full-time? Won't that be a bit tricky?'

'Maybe to begin with but I'm sure we'll work something out.'

'And what about the situation with Laura?'

My feelings about Laura had been all over the place of late, to the extent that I didn't know what I felt about her any more.

'I can't say anything's changed really. I'm still finding it difficult to accept that Linda knew about it all along. And as much as I know that Laura regretted the affair, I still can't bring myself to forgive her. The worst thing is that I feel like I'm the bad guy in all this.'

'Why would you think something like that?'

'Because Laura's not here to defend herself.'

'You've every right to feel hurt.'

'It doesn't feel like it. At times it seems that, though it was Laura's mess, somehow it's my responsibility to clear it up.' I stopped, suddenly aware of the inappropriateness of my outburst. 'I'm sorry. You don't need to hear this, today of all days.'

'I just want you to be okay,' she said. 'I hate that you feel this way.'

'I'm fine, really. Anyway, what have I got to complain about? I still have you, don't I?'

I scanned her face for a reaction. I was all too aware that the answer to my question was nowhere near as straightforward as I might have hoped. Before Clive died we'd split up, seemingly for good, but since then we'd drifted into no man's land, neither one thing nor the other. But I knew what I wanted now. And it was Fran, at least if she'd have me.

We stopped for a moment and she pressed her lips softly against mine but it was impossible to tell what it meant. And because she didn't speak, I didn't either and so we continued walking together, hand in hand, in silence. For now, it seemed this was the closest thing to an answer I was going to get.

We came to a halt next to Dot's headstone. I bent down and removed a weather-beaten scratch card and some ash leaves that had come to rest on her plot, the plot that she would soon be sharing with her husband.

'You don't have to do that,' said Fran. 'I'll come up tomorrow and sort it out.'

'It's fine,' I replied. I looked around for a bin but couldn't find one so I stuffed the litter and leaves into my jacket pocket. 'I know your granddad would have hated it being like this.'

Fran smiled. 'It would've driven him mad.'

'He must have really loved your nan to have been so devoted.'

'He used to say that she was his best friend.'

'And what did she call him?'

'Her knight in shining armour.'

We stood for a while in silence, listening to the sound of the wind in the trees around us. A smartly dressed man carrying a bouquet of flowers under his arm came towards us along the path. He acknowledged us with a brief nod of the head and continued on his way. Fran squeezed my hand and when I looked down at her face, she had tears rolling down her cheeks.

'I still really miss my gran,' she said, wiping her eyes. 'I miss her every day and now I've got to miss Granddad too. It's all too much.'

I put my arm around her and we sat on a bench overlooking the cemetery. Lost in our own thoughts, neither of us spoke for a while, but then Fran sat up straight, dried her eyes and looked at me.

'I've been thinking,' she said. 'About you . . . me . . . us, and I want you to know that I've really loved every second I've spent with you. You've made me so happy these past months, I don't think you'll ever understand what a difference you've made to me.'

'But?'

Fran smiled. 'There's always something else, isn't there? Nothing's ever straightforward, is it? I just feel like I need to get away for a while.'

My stomach tightened. This was it. I'd messed everything up. 'You're leaving? This is because of me, isn't it?'

Fran shook her head. 'I just need a break, that's all,' she replied. 'Granddad always told me that I should see a bit of the world if I got the opportunity and now seems as good a time as any. No matter how hard I tried he'd never take any rent money off me, so I've managed to save quite a bit.

'I'm off the week after next. First stop Thailand and after that, who knows? I only booked the flight last night.'

I couldn't believe what I was hearing. 'Don't you think you're being a bit rash? Why not wait a while and make sure this is what you want?'

'I know this all sounds a lot like running away, even more so because I'm twenty-nine and not nineteen, but this *is* what I really want. I feel like if I don't stop and take stock now, I'll spend the rest of my life chasing my own tail. Please say you understand, Tom. This isn't about you, it's about me.'

The sad thing was, I understood completely. She needed time to herself, time to get her head around losing Clive. Time to work out what she really wanted from life. I cared about her too much to stand in her way.

'Of course I understand,' I replied. 'You've got to do what you've got to do. But where does that leave us?'

'I don't know,' she said, taking my hand in hers. 'I really like you, Tom, and I so wanted to make this work but it wouldn't be fair to ask you to wait for me.'

'But isn't that my decision?'

'Of course it is but . . .'

'Then I'll see you when you get back.'

'But I have no idea when that will be. What if I'm away for a year or more? We've only been together a few weeks. Surely you can see it's too much pressure to put on something so fragile?'

Of course I could. I wasn't so deluded that I couldn't see the problems we faced, it was more that I didn't care. I wanted Fran. I wanted to give this thing between us a chance, not give up before we'd even left the starting blocks.

'But you know as well as I do how good we are together. Why would you want to walk away from that?'

'I don't, you must know that.' She began to cry. 'This isn't about you, Tom, or even about us. It's about where we are right now. We've both got so much to sort out, so much thinking to do. Another time, another place and this could have been so different, we could have been so happy. But I guess it just wasn't meant to be.'

She was right. It was all about timing and ours was way off. Had Clive not died, had I not found out the truth about Laura, things could've been so different. But we couldn't turn back time, no matter how much we might have wanted to. All we could do was be grateful for what we had, because what we had was something special.

I pulled her towards me and wrapped her in my arms. 'I hate it,' I said. 'I hate it but you're right. And hey, we'll always have Morrisons.'

Fran laughed, wiping her eyes with the back of her hand. 'You'll never let me live that down, will you?'

'You practically bit my head off.'

'I thought you were a bad guy.'

'And now?'

'I know for a fact that you're one of the best.'

She leaned in towards me, eyes closed, for what I knew would be our last kiss but before our lips met, her phone buzzed and the moment was gone.

'That'll be my mum wondering where I am,' she said, resting her head against my chest. 'I'd better go.'

There were several dozen of Clive's mourners lingering outside the chapel as Fran and I returned from our walk, and I was introduced to at least half of them. When anyone asked Fran if I was her boyfriend, she delighted in replying, 'No, he's my knight in shining armour.' After about half an hour people began to drift away, until only one car was left to take her back to the house where all the family and friends were gathering.

'I'd better go,' she said. 'Are you sure you won't come?'

I nodded. 'You need to be with your family,' I replied. 'I'll call you tonight though and make sure you're okay.'

Finally we kissed the long slow kiss that would be our farewell, and it took everything I had not to beg her to change her mind.

Still holding my hands, she looked up at me. 'I want to say something but I'm not sure how you'll take it.'

'This is me you're talking to,' I replied. 'You can say whatever you want.'

'Even if it's about Laura?'

'Yes, even that.'

'I don't know if you know this but it was Alzheimer's that Gran died of,' she began. 'She was sixty-nine when she was diagnosed and got progressively worse with each year. By the end, her short-term memory had all but gone and she'd taken to wandering out of the house in just a nightgown. Sometimes she could even be aggressive, kicking and biting. It was a nightmare.'

'Poor Clive, I can't believe that he went through all that and never once said a word to me.'

'He didn't like talking about it. He didn't want a lot of people to know – he didn't even really want us to know. The point I'm trying to make though is this: Granddad refused to let those last few years of Gran's life define their marriage, and I don't think you should let Laura's one mistake define yours either. You said yourself that you were happy for the longest time. While I can't claim to know everything about you, I don't imagine for a moment that if she'd come home that day and confessed everything, you would have thrown out all the good years without a second thought. That just isn't you. I think what Granddad worked out is something that so many of us still have to learn: sometimes love is more of a decision than it is a feeling. Sometimes you just have to choose to remember the good times and forget the rest.'

25
Every word

Tom

Walking home in the sunshine of the late afternoon, I felt curiously both drained and elated as I went over the events of the past few weeks, trying to make sense of them. Clive's death, Laura's affair and the intensity of my feelings for Fran only a year and a half after Laura's death, what did it all mean? How was I supposed to make sense of anything, when life always seemed to be coming at me from every direction? Had I posed such questions to Clive, he no doubt would've told me that I was thinking too much and should 'just bloody get on with it!' But that was Clive all over, wasn't it? His ability to hone in on the things that mattered and push all else aside, just as he had done with his wife's Alzheimer's, just as he had with everything in life. Maybe I was becoming more like that too, now, with all my talk that Fran's being away was nothing more than mere 'detail'. The old me would've seen the situation as too problematic but the new me, at least in this situation, seemed able to focus on what mattered most.

As I crossed the busy road at the bottom of the hill, I thought about the parallel Fran had drawn between her gran's Alzheimer's and Laura's affair. Should one bad thing be allowed to define a whole marriage? Granted, in Laura's case the bad thing was by design not accident, but still the question remained the same. Clive's way of seeing the world rested quite simply on the ranking of priorities: important things first, everything else second. And so when it came to his beloved Dot, his feelings for her came first and the effect that her hideous disease had wreaked on their marriage didn't even get a look in. And as much as Clive had made it look easy, I could see now that it was anything but. It must have taken courage to make a decision like that and stick with it, especially when no one would've blamed him for playing the victim. Instead he chose love over self-pity, to ignore the worst and remember the best.

My sweat-drenched shirt was clinging to my back as I turned into the road home, and as I walked, it slowly dawned on me what sort of advice Clive would've given me about Laura had he still been alive. He would have told me that I had to make a choice, that I couldn't just wait around to feel better, that she'd made a mistake but I could choose to leave it behind and move on. As I reached the house, I paused to take in the view of the home Laura and I had made together. This was where we'd raised our family, where we'd celebrated anniversaries, birthdays and Christmases. It was here that we'd shared our happiest moments and our saddest too; it was here that we came when we wanted to feel safe and secure. It wasn't just bricks and mortar. It was a monument to everything we stood for. It was the Hope family HQ. It was our home.

Inside the house, I called out to Linda but there was no reply. In the kitchen I spotted a note on the table: 'Gone to pick up a few things from the High Street, then straight on to school pick-up. Fish fingers and chips for tea, if that's okay by you, love, Linda. PS. Hope this afternoon went as well as can be expected. PPS. Might take Lola for a hot chocolate and a chat after school. Shouldn't be too late xxx.' The note made me smile, it told me everything I needed to know, not just about Linda but about family: it wasn't just about the big things of life but the small things too; it was about looking out for each other, providing for each other, keeping each other safe; and as I slipped her note into my pocket, I imagined that it must have been a moment exactly like this that had made Laura finally see just how much she truly stood to lose.

I opened my laptop and launched its photo-management software. The screen filled with thumbnail photos from the past: our entire digital life, and one of the few things that in my rage I had omitted to erase. I flicked through the photos, selecting my favourites: Laura on her eighteenth birthday, scanned from an old photo; Laura in a hospital bed holding Evie for the first time; Laura and Lola in the hotel swimming pool in Crete waving to the camera. Browsing through the images made me think about Laura in a different way, for the first time in a long while. All these snapshots, all these bits of Laura's life came together to build up a more complete picture of a complex person, and just as no single image could ever hope to capture everything about a person, I should never have allowed one single action to do the same.

Connecting the colour printer to my laptop, I printed out all the images I could, far more than I needed for my project. As the printer churned out facsimiles of these treasured moments, I went around the house in search of anything that might help me in my endeavour to recreate Lola's shoebox shrine.

I was still sticking, cutting and fixing at the kitchen table when Linda returned with not only Lola in her charge but Evie too, and as they gathered around no one spoke, not even Lola.

Linda

I was speechless, literally speechless. All day I'd been worried about how Tom might be after the funeral. I'd imagined it would dredge up all manner of terrible memories of the day we buried Laura, memories that would be all the more difficult to cope with given everything he knew about her now. I'd even primed Lola that her father might be upset when we saw him and that she should be extra kind, yet when we arrived home there he was in the kitchen, printing out pictures of Laura in what I could only assume was a bid to replace the shoebox shrine that Lola had told me all about. No words could capture the quiet eloquence of his actions. In some miraculous way he'd managed to come to terms with what Laura had done, somehow he'd found a way to forgive her. I never would have thought that an old shoebox covered in photos of the daughter, mother, wife and friend who had been the centre of our world could have saved the day, but it had. It reminded us that though Laura was gone, she would never be forgotten, and though she was flawed, her legacy of love remained unchanged.

Tom

As I stuck down the final photograph of Laura and leaned back in my chair, I became suddenly aware of the fact that still no one was speaking. I began to wonder if I'd done the right thing after all. What I'd wanted was, in some small way, to undo the damage of the past few weeks. I knew it was merely symbolic, a poor effort to show my daughters how sorry I was for how I'd behaved, but as I sat staring at the shoebox, I wondered if they had understood my motivations at all or would simply think I'd lost the plot.

'Wow, Dad,' said Lola, reaching over to smooth down the corner of one of the pictures. 'It's even better than mine was.'

'I think yours was better,' I replied. 'But I hope this will do for now.' I put an arm around each of the girls. 'I think I owe you both an apology.'

Lola turned and looked at me. 'What for?'

'I don't think I've behaved very well over these past few weeks. I just want you to know I'm sorry.'

'We know you are, Dad,' said Evie mischievously, 'but just so you know you're still grounded for the next two weeks.'

Linda smiled. 'The thing is, girls, we all make mistakes, even grown-ups, even old people like me. I suppose that's how we learn. Now give your dad a big hug and a kiss, and you can both come and help get tea ready.'

Linda

After the girls had gone to bed I watched TV late into the evening, then got up to find Tom in the kitchen. He sat at the table, tapping away on his laptop. I walked over to him and sat down.

'You must be shattered. Why don't you get to bed?'

'I'm okay, really. Anyway, I'm nearly done. What do you think?' He turned the screen around so I could see. On it was a holiday booking website, open on a picture of a chocolate-box-type cottage.

'It's lovely. What's it for?'

'Us,' he replied, 'well, you, me and the kids, for this summer. According to the blurb, it's only minutes from the beach. The kids will love it, don't you think?'

'I think they'll have an amazing time.' Alerted by the tension in my voice, he looked up at me. I hadn't planned to break my news until later in the week but now that the moment was here, it looked like there was no avoiding it.

'Sounds a bit ominous. Are you planning to be somewhere else this summer?'

I nodded. I felt awful. Even though he had more than proved himself capable of looking after himself and the girls, I felt as if I was abandoning him all over again. 'I only made up my mind today but, yes, I won't be here this summer . . . I'm planning to be in Australia.'

'You're going back? But you've only just come home.'

'I know, and believe me I feel terrible. I know you were counting on me being here for you and the girls but the thing is, I've met someone. His name is Desmond, but everyone calls him Desi, and he's a friend of Moira's and well . . . I think . . . well, actually I'm sure . . . we're in love.' Even as the words were forming in my head they seemed vaguely ridiculous, and now that they were out in the world they sounded patently foolish. I was talking like one of those women I sometimes read about in magazines who, after a fortnight's holiday in Turkey, abandon their family to move in with a waiter half their age. My plans sounded ill thought-out, short-sighted. It was a wonder Tom could keep a straight face and yet I meant every word. I looked at him, trying to gauge his reaction. 'What do you think?'

He came over to me and put a comforting arm around my shoulder. 'I think that's the best news I've had all day.'

'Really? You don't mind?'

'Of course not. I won't say I'm not surprised because . . . well, for you at least, it's pretty out there. But if anyone deserves to be happy, Linda, it's you.'

I felt myself welling up. 'Do you mean that?'

Tom laughed and gave me a huge hug. 'Every word.'

'But what would you do about work? I've no idea how long I'll be away. Didn't you say you've only got six months off?'

'Don't you worry, I'll sort something out. I've been thinking about only going back part-time anyway. Right now, my priority has to be the girls. Everything else can wait.' Tom grinned, and gave me another squeeze. 'Laura always said you were a bit of a dark horse when it came to men, but I never expected this. You have to tell me how it happened.'

And so that's what I did. I told him about the party, how Desi caught me as I fell off a table, and about Frank too, how I'd bumped into him in the most unlikely of places and how, when we got to talking, he'd apologised for the mess he'd made of our lives.

Tom smiled and shook his head in disbelief. 'So that was some trip then?'

'You could say that,' I replied. 'I can't wait for when you and the girls meet Desi, you'll love him, you really will. He's funny, kind and thoughtful. Actually in some ways he reminds me of you. You'll love him.'

Tom nodded. 'I'm sure I will,' he replied, and then his expression changed and I knew straight away that he had some news of his own to share.

Tom

While I was well aware that the kids wouldn't have been able to resist telling Linda about Fran, I think it spoke volumes about the awkwardness of the situation that she hadn't asked me about her directly. But even though Fran and I had split up, I still felt the need to explain myself. There was no easy way to tell the mother of my dead wife that I'd fallen in love with someone else, and now that Fran had left, it would be easier for both of us if I didn't say anything at all. But the truth was, I still had feelings for Fran, feelings that wouldn't just disappear overnight, and even after all that we'd spoken about, I still secretly held out hopes that somehow she and I might get together. So, because of this and because it seemed wrong to hold back the truth when Linda had shared so much with me, I told her everything.

I don't think she meant to cry. In fact she was trying her very best to stop herself, and when that didn't work she kept apologising, assuring me that she wanted me to be happy. In the end I put my arm around her and told her not to say anything until she was ready, and then we just sat, her head resting on my shoulder until she calmed down.

Finally she sat up and dried her eyes. 'You must think me an old fool the way I'm behaving.'

'I think you know me better than that.'

'I really do want you to be happy—'

'But it's complicated.'

'I still miss Laura so much.'

I thought about everything that had happened since I'd found out about Laura's affair. It had made me question the whole of our lives together, shaken the foundation of all I'd taken for granted, and made me wonder who exactly I'd been mourning. I'd been through just about every emotion there was, from love to hate and back again, but even now if I could wish for anything in the world it would be for her still to be with me.

I looked at Linda. 'And I do too.'

'But you have to move on, don't you? You can't stay stuck in the past. What do you think you'll do about Fran?'

'There's nothing to do. She needs to clear her head and I don't want to stand in her way.'

'But what about when she comes back?'

'I don't even know if she's ever coming back, let alone when.'

'But aren't you going to tell her how you feel?'

'She knows. For now, all I can do is hope. But whatever happens in the future, nothing will change between you and me. This will always be your home, and we will always be your family.'

Linda shook her head resignedly. 'But things change don't they?' she said quietly. 'Maybe not now, maybe not even a year from now, but at some point in the future you'll meet someone who'll tick all the right boxes and she's not going to want me hanging around, is she?'

Once again I put my arm around her shoulder. 'Look, Linda, aside from the girls, you're all the family I've got. I never really knew my mum, and my dad's been gone for a long time. You opened your heart to me from the first day we met and you've got me through the worst time of my life. I want you to be part of our lives no matter what. I love you, Linda, and I don't know what I'd do without you.'

Turning towards me, Linda gave me a hug. 'I really do hope you work things out with Fran.'

'And I hope that things work out for you and Desi too,' I replied.

She took my hand in hers. 'We've been too sad for too long but I've got a good feeling about this next chapter of our lives, a really good feeling.'

I was about to reply when I caught sight of the family calendar in its usual place by the fridge. It struck me that no matter how meticulously we plan, none of us truly knows what the future has in store, good or bad. But regardless, we keep on buying them, filling them with hopes, dreams and the busyness of life, trusting, always trusting that somehow things will go our way.

I squeezed Linda's hand. 'I've got a good feeling too,' I replied. 'I think everything's going to be okay.' And I wasn't just telling her what she wanted to hear. I wasn't just trying to fob her off with some woolly notion to make her feel better. I really did feel positive about the future. And even though that feeling was based on nothing more substantial than the wish for a better day, it was all the substance we needed. The past was the past, but the future could be anything we wanted it to be, so long as we never gave up on hope.

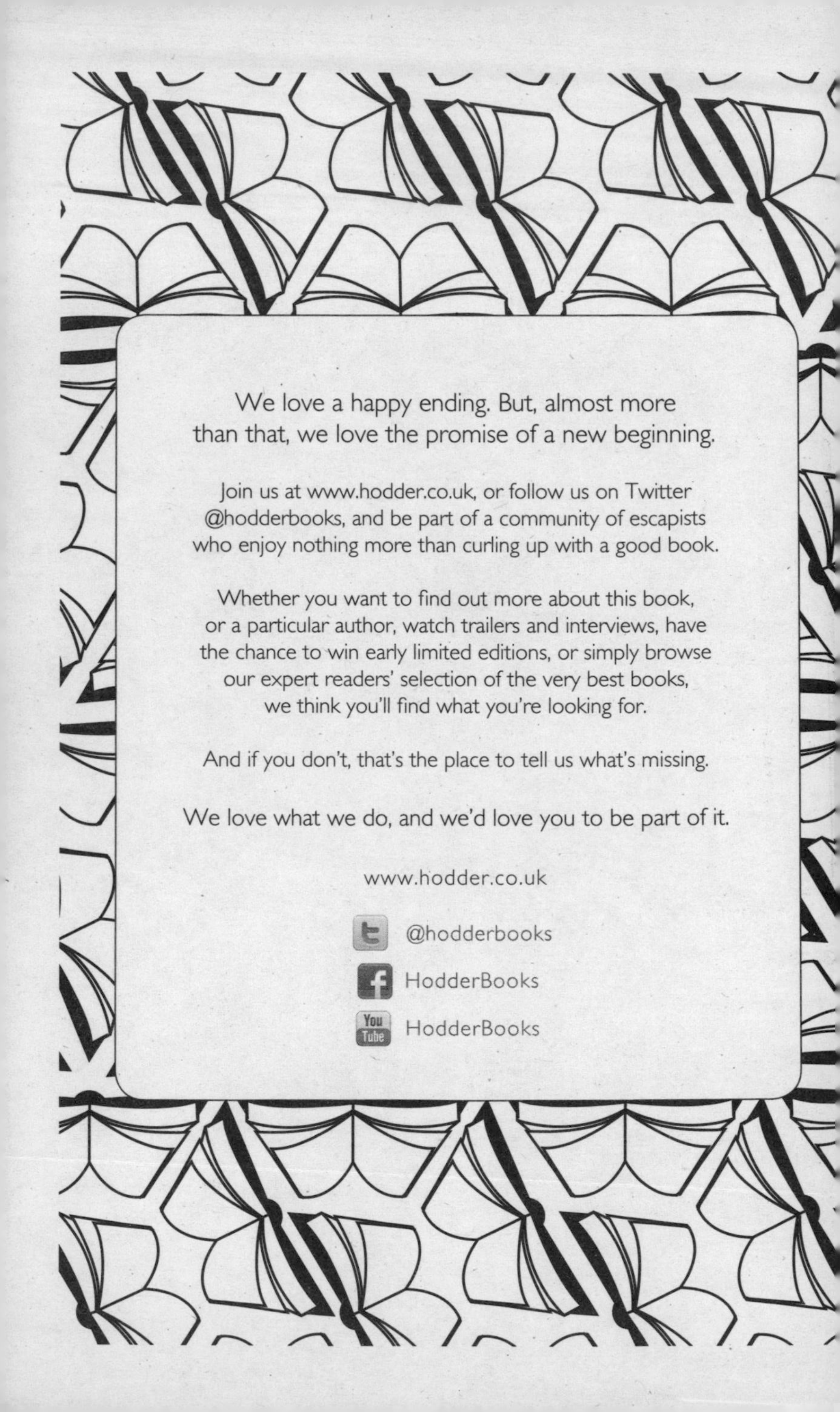

We love a happy ending. But, almost more than that, we love the promise of a new beginning.

Join us at www.hodder.co.uk, or follow us on Twitter @hodderbooks, and be part of a community of escapists who enjoy nothing more than curling up with a good book.

Whether you want to find out more about this book, or a particular author, watch trailers and interviews, have the chance to win early limited editions, or simply browse our expert readers' selection of the very best books, we think you'll find what you're looking for.

And if you don't, that's the place to tell us what's missing.

We love what we do, and we'd love you to be part of it.

www.hodder.co.uk

@hodderbooks

HodderBooks

HodderBooks